THE BEAUTY OF DIGGING DEEP

By

Rebecca Moll

To Sister Michelle —
To Love, Peace, & Hope —

Rebecca Moll
December 2015

This book is dedicated to the American immigrant, past, present and future. To those I hold familial bonds and to those only bonds of humanity, I applaud your determination, desire, and dreams for a better way of life.

For my husband, my one true love, for whom I see beauty, for whom I dig deep.

Table of Contents

PROLOGUE
Year 2017

The room was filled beyond capacity. Overhead fans in high ceilings did little to add comfort. Three hours into the auction, Sotheby's most ardent clientele posturing, the evening's event for tickets only, the room was silent, except for the auctioneer, his monotone litany a slow narcotic, punctuated by the slam of a gavel, the win of a bid.

In the back of the room, a tall, young woman, dressed for travel, hiking boots and shorts, white t-shirt and backpack, her long curly hair pulled back in a ponytail just moments before entering, stood quietly next to an extremely tall and large man, a wealthy, famous novelist, inheritor of Jackson timber fortune, his body threatening to break free of the fine clothing that confined. Dark sunglasses and a firm jaw made no promises and not once did he raise his paddle.

The last item, the reason the tickets sold out and the house was packed, was up for bid.

The auctioneer began the description, "An unknown treasure, a sleepy town in Michigan, a legacy of Americana ingenuity and brass. Made of the finest Jackson timber, late 19th century cherry, this drop-leaf desk is the work of artisan craftsmanship. With delicate carvings and scenic landscapes, it holds an heirloom history that would sell novels in the thousands. Murder, intrigue and religion engrained in the very wood, it defines the term covet and yet by itself it pales. A partner, a small and delicate gold key, encrusted with rare Irish Diamonds and fine American Emeralds, the merging of the Old Country with New Frontiers, marries the pair for an opening bid of two million."

Thirty minutes later, the auctioneer, "knocked down" the lot, the winning bid, a hammer price of five million declared. A small elderly woman in the front row, a slight smile on her powered and rouged face, lowered her hand, placing her paddle in her lap. Next to her, a businessman, tight in his Armani suit, pursed his lips and looked at his phone. Lloyds of London calling. Lowering his head, he placed his paddle on his seat and left the room. Watching him, the large man in the back smiled. Nudging the young woman beside him, he jerked his head towards the door for an early exit.

Standing outside, the young woman looked up at her companion, her eyes full of concern. A small scar on her forehead, a childhood mishap, followed the arch of her eyebrows. "What will you do with the money?"

"Donate it. Maybe the Sierra Club?" A slow smile played at the edges of his mouth.

Gently pushing him backwards, she laughed at the irony. She could just see the headlines, "Heir to Timber Fortune Saves Forest," as he pretended to fall over, her blow too much. "No seriously?"

"Well, I have to pay Lloyds first. They hold a claim for three quarters of a million. And then there's Uncle Sam. Won't be much left after that.

"Yeah, right," she said, her hand gently on his shoulder.

"Oh, I almost forgot." Reaching into his suit jacket, he pulled out a small package. Wrapped in protective paper, Sarah could see it was old, a frayed and faded ribbon held it together. "For you. To keep."

Sarah held the package carefully and looked up at her friend. "It was in the old trunk," she said, her eyes slowly widening. "The old farmhouse, I mean, your farmhouse."

"Way back on the family tree, my father's side, Josephine. Letters. All in French. Maybe while you're in Paris, new material, something new to write about? You know us Jacksons, there's always a story hiding somewhere."

Sarah raised up to her tippy-toes and planted a kiss on his soft and billowy cheek. "Hey, you know, you can write too?" her voice ending on a high note.

"I have an old man to see first." Leaning in, he gave her a warm hug, enveloping her slender frame and inhaling her light fragrance. "Lilacs?" he asked.

"Yes. They're my favorite."

He waved good-bye and watched, as she bounced down the street, her strong, athletic legs taking long, quick, strides, her ponytail blowing in the wind, slowly gaining freedom and falling to her shoulders.

Turning in the opposite direction, he saw a mob of reporters moving towards him. Squaring his shoulders and rising to full height, he walked straight into the mass of people, lights, and cameras. A giant among minions, full speed ahead, he never slacked his pace. As he met the mob, he sailed on, parting a sea of suffering, years of pain and resentment, and passed right through unscathed. Leaving behind a smattering of dazed and startled paparazzi, flashing cameras and furious pens against paper, Steadman filled his lungs with fresh air. He let the moment fill him and for once, let someone else do the writing.

BOOK I

MOMENTS OF METAPHORS
Year 2008

Chapter 1

It was later known as the week from hell, the emotional rollercoaster, and privately by Katie, as the awakening. It was a week of looking back, forever remembering, every word, object, and encounter, reminding her of what she had, before. Little moments, seemingly symbolic, took on new meaning, becoming bittersweet metaphors. It was a week she wished she could forget, but held onto, always remembered. Folded into the fabric of her life, it all began with a strange woman.

It was a Friday, forever etched into her memory. It was the first day she saw the woman and, for a long time, the last day she really enjoyed living. She will never forget that day, thanks to the red notebook. Katie wrote everything down. Still has the notebook. Worn and faded. Red cover. 70 sheets. 1 subject. Wide ruled. The edges are dog eared and there is a funny little caricature in the corner that John drew. He was always doodling. Drawing while deep in conversation, he never knew Katie scooped them up and kept them in her jewelry box. Little pieces of paper, keepsakes. Katie wrote everything down in the red notebook, after, to record the whole day, all that happened before, hoping that if it was written down, she would never forget.

It was a beautiful April morning. Katie was rushing Sarah, so she wouldn't miss the bus, again. Sarah was six years old and a terrible eater. It took almost an hour just to finish a small bowl of cereal. If she pushed too hard, Sarah would fall apart and the bus would be gone, again. It wasn't that Sarah didn't want to go to school, she loved Elmwood Elementary; she just didn't do well in the morning.

Katie was placing Sarah's lunchbox in her backpack when the doorbell rang. She looked through the window and saw Mrs. Cook with three little ones in tow.

"Good morning, Mrs. Marshall, you know," she began, trying to catch her breath.

Mrs. Cook was their elderly neighbor, a widow, who took in children before and after school. She was a rather large woman, more than twice as wide as tall, quite funny when you considered what she lacked in height was made up in width. It was as if she was resized to fit a screen, if turned on her side, would appear more correct. More often than not, she was out of breath. She had flaming red hair, a pale complexion, a baby powder scent and she always wore something purple.

When Katie asked her about the purple, not too long after they moved in, Mrs. Cook replied, "Oh, my Harold loved purple, you know?" One day it was her socks, another a blouse, the next a headscarf. "It feels like he is with me, you know?" she would say. That was another thing about Mrs. Cook, she always ended her sentences with "you know?" It seemed the more she knew about Mrs. Cook, the more things she realized she always did. By all appearances Mrs. Cook was a merry widow, but Katie often wondered if all the repetition and happiness was real.

"I have to be at church this morning for adoration, you know? Can you bring them to the stop for me?"

"Sure." Katie looked over her shoulder and saw Sarah staring into her cereal.

"Sarah," Katie called. "Time to leave. The Anderson boys are here." Like a flipped switch, Sarah jumped down from the table and grabbed her coat and shoes.

"Yippee," Sarah screeched.

"A miraculous transformation, you know?" Mrs. Cook chimed in. "You never know what the Lord will send your way." Making the sign of the cross, a wide one if you considered the distance traveled between the Holy Spirit, Mrs. Cook waved goodbye.

Sarah loved the Anderson boys. So close in age, she spent hours and hours playing with them. An only child, they were ready playmates. She did have an older step-sister, John's daughter, Kylie, from his first marriage, but they hardly saw Kylie. She was married and lived halfway across the country in Colorado. John visited several times. Katie and Sarah never went. John made trips coincide with work, but given the residual hostility surrounding her

7

parents' divorce, a younger wife, and a new sibling to boot, Kylie wasn't all that warm and fuzzy where Katie and Sarah were concerned. As for coming to Michigan, in the beginning there was always an excuse. Then Katie stopped asking.

Sarah was intrigued by the boys. Matthew, Mark and Luke were identical triplets. Not that she had any idea of the biological odds at conceiving identical triplets (150,000 to 1, according to some internet expert), she just loved having three of the same friend. It was three times the fun. Even more exciting than triplets was that their mother was from Spain. Educated in America, Mrs. Anderson spoke perfect English, yet the speed caused one to lose track of what she was saying. Often, it was a second or two after she finished speaking before Katie or Mrs. Cook would burst out laughing.

Katie thought that Mrs. Anderson was wonderful. She found her enthusiasm and zest for everything in life infectious. She loved listening to her call the boys home. *"Ven aqui, los ninos de mi Corazon,"* Mrs. Anderson sang out her front door. Waving goodbye to Katie and Sarah, the boys would run home, hungry for dinner, a flurry of Spanish peppering the evening air.

The triplets were bilingual, but with a priority. They spoke only English to their father, a third-generation Michigander, and their American friends, only Spanish to their mother, and a funny mixture of both to each other. Sarah alone was allowed into their bilingual circle. A quick study, she was always coming home with a new word or phrase.

"Mommy, Matthew says that we live in *'un casa'* and that his father likes *cerveza*." Katie would nod and smile, understanding the simple vocabulary. But when the four of them were playing, the English and Spanish banter was too much.

Mrs. Cook loved calling the boys by their first names, often ending with a John, forgetting it was the boys, not the four gospels. Katie found the whole matter amusing.

The boys loved Sarah and treated her as a sister. Usually, it was Sarah at the bottom of the pile of a snowball fight or when someone stole first base and the pitcher wasn't looking. Sarah could more than handle the contact. She was in all ways what

Katie never was, athletic, strong, confident, and physical. Sarah was all John.

With the exception of mornings, Sarah tackled everything fast forward. Sneaking a peek at the clock, Katie watched Sarah slip her shoes on, holding her tongue about unlacing them first. They didn't have the time and it was a worn-out battle. Countless shoes were discarded in disrepair, the heels squashed down and ruined.

"*Hola*, guys," Sarah greeted the boys with her hand raised. A few high five's later they were out the door.

Katie watched Mrs. Cook negotiate the driveway in her old boat-sized Buick. Reverse was never a good idea when it came to Mrs. Cook, especially the final bend in her driveway just before the street. She always covered as much distance as possible on the way down, something akin to the popular orange rickrack that hemmed Katie's favorite dress as a child. Katie wasn't sure how Mrs. Cook remained accident-free. Maybe it was all the adorations.

Slap, slap, slap, eight little feet pounded the driveway. Katie turned back to the boys and gently nudged them along. Sarah was showing off, doing cartwheels, her backpack picking up slack against her back mid-turn, while the boys flanked her with karate kicks.

Katie loved their bus stop walks. Less than half a mile, the road meandered a little, taking a final turn to stop just barely out of view of the house. A short walk, it was just enough to wake you up in the morning and make for a good break in the afternoon.

To anyone passing by, they appeared to be the typical American suburban family. Katie wasn't the youngest of mothers, having put her nursing career first, but with her trim physique, her appearance was deceiving. Topping out just over five feet and barely over a hundred pounds on a fully dressed day, Katie was the envy of many middle-age mothers. Long, curly black hair, often swept up in a careless bun, gave her the look of a student. She would turn forty-six this year, a surprise to many parents who fell well below her age.

Just as they made the final bend, Katie could make out the shape of the bus, flashing lights, and an open door.

"Oh boy, you better run," she hollered, shielding her eyes from the rising sun.

Pounding up the steps, their too large backpacks made a thumping sound hitting the back of their knees as they ran down the aisle. Sarah turned to look back at her mom, her blue eyes sparkling. Katie felt her heart swell. She watched the bus pull away.

That was when she saw the woman. Katie was startled. Half-hidden by the glare of the sun, Katie shielded her eyes and stared. Standing on her left, the woman watched the bus leave, dark sunglasses and a stern expression. Was there a new family in the neighborhood? she wondered. She was about to say hello, when the woman turned abruptly and headed up the hill. She watched her walk away. So odd, she thought, dressed a little warm for the morning. April could be unpredictable in Michigan, but a trench coat and boots? And that headscarf, tied below the chin was, well, dated. Katie made a mental note to ask Mrs. Cook about the strange woman. If only Katie knew how strange things would get.

Chapter 2

Katie never trusted memories. Like laying down tracks, the more you recalled a memory, you laid them down, over and over again, one on top of the other. But, what if, unknowingly, you made little changes each time you laid them down? A little to the right or left of the truth, might leave you with a different story in the end. And what about those events that you don't recall, feel are insignificant, only later to wish you could remember? Katie never trusted memories; she always wrote things down, always in the red notebook. She had a sense for making things right or true and writing made her feel better.

It was a busy Friday. A few phone calls, run to the grocery store and the bank, then back home in time for the bus. Katie wondered how she ever managed work and family. With John's travel, it became so hectic, she decided to take a few years off until Sarah was older. Rushing around, she forgot all about the strange woman and didn't see her again for a few days.

Sarah came home, did her homework and watched a few minutes of television. The sun gave way to clouds by late afternoon and as swiftly as the weather raced in, it abruptly stalled to drop a deluge of rain that was forecasted to continue for the next week. It was an easy dinner of soup and salad. John was traveling and would be late tonight. Landing after nine, he wouldn't be home until after ten. Sarah was anxious to read Charlotte's Web. Her ability to read was improving, but she still preferred to read together, out loud, with her mom. Katie loved this time together. It was as if they were right there on the farm, watching Charlotte spin her web and the animals come to life.

About eight thirty that night, Katie sent Sarah off to bed, and did the same herself, except, she switched books. It was Fanny Flag who was occupying Katie this week. Katie loved any story with quirky characters and Fanny was a great writer. She turned on the television and hit the mute button. As usual, she fell asleep reading.

Suddenly, she opened her eyes and saw, "Special Report" flashing on the screen. She removed her reading glasses and a serious reporter came into focus. Grabbing the remote and turning up the volume, she could hear the reporter, "...no real details, as of now. All we know is the plane is not responding to air traffic control. It is believed there were seven passengers, three crew. For now, the names are being kept confidential. Last known communication was over the Gulf of Mexico." Katie saw the ticker at the bottom of the screen and laying there, deep within the covers of their bed, still, her breathing shallow, she felt a wave of nausea. "Due in Oakland County Airport at nine this evening, the flight is still on schedule," the reporter stated. "Hoping this is a false alarm, we will be in constant report regarding this matter." The newscasters continued with a discussion about jet safety. Rolling to her side, Katie placed her head on the top of her knees and took a few deep breaths. Her heart began to race ahead of her mind, thoughts tumbling over thoughts, fear building. Suddenly, the phone rang. She jumped out of bed and screamed. Grabbing the receiver, she placed the phone to her ear.

"It's me, Katie, I heard the news."

Sinking down to the floor, she cradled the phone with her shoulder, her hands covering her face.

"Katie? Are you there?"

"I'm here, Mom. How did you know?"

"John said he was going to Brazil and that with any luck he'd be back in time to catch the end of the Tigers game."

A few minutes of silence passed. Katie's heavy breathing filled the connection. Barbara cleared her throat.

"Katie," she gently said. "This is not your father. Small planes like your father flew were much more dangerous than these big corporate jets today. They take all kinds of precautions," she insisted. "Remember, no news is good news."

Katie let out a small sound.

"I'm coming over," Barbara said. "Unlock the back door." Katie dropped the phone. The dial tone filled the room.

Barbara lived northeast of Katie in a little town on the St. Claire River. They moved there when Katie was sixteen, after her father, Edward, died, his small plane's propeller failing in a terrible thunderstorm. Barbara and Edward spent their honeymoon in a quaint hotel on the St. Claire River and they talked about retiring there. Pasted into their wedding album, photos showed tree lined streets and stately homes by the river. A faded but well preserved wedding announcement held a first page place in the album.

> Miss Barbara Crawford, daughter of Buck & Annie Crawford of Frankfort entered into blessed nuptials with Mr. Edward Stanton of Louisville, son of the late Mr. Charles Irving and Mrs. Leigh Irving on Saturday, June 4th, 1960 at the First Methodist Church of Frankfurt. The newlyweds are recent graduates of Kentucky State University. Mr. Stanton has secured a position with Foster Real Estate & Co. Mrs. Stanton will teach art at Frankfort Elementary School. They will reside in Frankfort.

A park and walkway bordered the little strip of land, otherwise known as St. Claire, Michigan. Plunging into the river, this little strip of land marked the last land foothold between the US and Canada. Edward teased it would be life on the border, the border of love. If only they knew just how quickly they would cross that border.

Suddenly, her father gone, it was just Katie and her mother. They were definitely over the border, but it wasn't love. Lost in grief, the only border they knew was the one that separated time, the time before and the time after Edward died.

Barbara's safety net, thanks to Edward's careful financial planning, gave them the means to make the move. With a full bank account and empty hearts, they left Kentucky and moved north to Michigan. It wasn't hard to do. They had little family and the friends they did have were too emotionally spent to hold ties. There were too many reminders in Kentucky.

Sitting on the bedroom floor, the dial tone breaking her thoughts, Katie found herself back over the border again.

In disbelief, she murmured, "It can't be John. Please don't be John." Down the hall, Sarah's door opened and her soft, little footsteps raced towards her. She reached back and hit the off button on the remote. The serious reporter left the screen in a flash.

"Mommy?" Sarah rubbed her eyes with the back of her small, chubby hands. Katie slowly picked herself up and replaced the phone in the cradle. "Where's Daddy?"

"Hi, sweetheart. Grandma's coming over. She said she can't sleep, so she's coming over to have a sleepover. Isn't that great?"

Katie picked up her little girl and kissing her gently on the cheek, started down the hall to put the sleepy child back to bed.

"Mommy, where's Daddy?"

Taking a deep breath, Katie delivered what she hoped wasn't the first of many lies.

"He's working, honey. Daddy has a lot of work to do."

Coughing to cover the break in her voice, Katie gently wrapped her arms around Sarah, holding her close. She tucked her into bed and pushed back the hair from her face. Kissing her goodnight for the second time and watching her fall asleep, she prayed the little girl would forget she even woke up. Katie didn't want her laying down any tracks tonight.

Chapter 3

Saturday morning came, grey and dismal. It was hard to tell the earth made a full turn. Katie woke to the ceaseless pounding of rain and the smell of fresh coffee. Disoriented, she patted the side of the bed, thinking John had risen early, as usual. Downstairs, his hair a mess, wrapped in his favorite flannel bathrobe, he'd be catching up on e-mail. She rolled over, closed her eyes, relishing the warm comfort, when she heard her mother's laughter. Lying there, she fought to keep her eyes closed, willing the tears back and the memories of last night away.

It was last night, Friday, when they lost sight of John's plane and Barbara found her daughter curled up in bed like an overgrown infant. Slipping in behind her, she wrapped her arms around her and began telling a story, the soft soothing words floating over Katie's shoulder.

"I remember when you were just two years old, Katie," she began. "You were the most beautiful baby in the world. For such a little thing, your hair hung down to your waist, curl after curl, like a beautiful cascading waterfall of black ribbons. Your little mouth was always smiling, and your eyes, so bright and clear blue, it was as if they were made of glass. Daddy called you his precious gem. He said it the first time he saw you. Said he could look into your eyes forever. You grew into a wonderful child, an earnest and kind young woman, and now a strong and loving wife and mother. I love you, Katie." Katie and Barbara drifted off to sleep riding the waves of her declarations.

"Mommy, Grandma's here." Sarah came charging into her bedroom. "Good Morning Mommy," she yelled as she jumped up and down on the bed and on top of Katie.

Sitting up, Katie placed Sarah on her lap. "Big surprise, huh?" Well, at least she didn't remember waking up last night, Katie thought.

Sarah jumped off the bed and ran away shouting, "Big surprise. Big surprise." The patter of her little stocking feet descended the stairs. Katie sat on the edge of the bed and stared.

Wrapping John's robe around herself, a little tighter than usual, Katie made her way downstairs, holding the banister, a little tighter than usual.

"You're awfully cheerful for a morning, Sarah."

"Grandma's taking me back to her house for the weekend. You can come too, please," she begged. "And Mommy, the T.V. broke." Sarah's lower lip stuck out, her little chin dimpled.

"Oh, I don't know honey, let me get some coffee first," Katie answered, thinking she would have to call the cable company and how long would that take?

Katie's mother was sitting at the kitchen table smiling. She looked into Katie's eyes and mouthed the words, "How are you?"

Katie lowered her eyes and tried to keep her hands from shaking. She walked over to the coffee pot and pulled out a cup from the cabinet, John's Detroit Tigers cup. The one with the chip in the handle, broken the night he found out Katie was expecting. Gripping the counter, she steadied herself.

Knowing her mother's coffee, Katie would need more than one cup. Her father called it, "dirty water" and teased Barbara, whispering in her ear. Katie remembers her mother playfully swatting him, giggling like a teenage girl. Understanding little about their banter, she loved their play.

As a child, Katie was so happy. There was always teasing and laughing. Just the three of them, they made a perfect trio, a healthy and happy family. It wasn't until a teenager, blindsided by her father's sudden death, that Katie realized just how happy her childhood was. In time, Katie did begin the laugh again.

Her mother was another story. For years, after Katie's father died, Barbara didn't laugh. She'd chuckle at something funny and if more down than usual, just smile. But it wasn't until Katie met John that she started to laugh again, really laugh. John told jokes and she would just about fall off her chair, almost choke herself to death laughing. It was such an about-face for her, that Katie wasn't

16

sure what was going on. Given that John was pretty much smack in the middle of Barbara and her age, Katie was angry. She had had enough and had told Barbara so one day.

"What are you trying to do?"

"Excuse me dear, I don't understand," Barbara replied. She was sitting in her favorite rocker watching the birds outside her window. A commune of chickadees took up residence in her birdhouse, offering entertainment to anyone who would feed them.

"You act like a school girl in love around John," Katie hissed. Her face was flush and her voice shook.

Barbara didn't say anything for a few moments. She just sat there. Katie was more than ready for her. She rehearsed the whole conversation. John was hers, she found him and Barbara could just butt out. It wasn't fair, her mother already had the love of her life. John was the first man Katie truly ever loved.

After what seemed too long of silence, Barbara asked, "Do you love him?"

"What? Of course." What a stupid question, she thought. Why would I be so mad, if I didn't love him. This was not going as she planned.

"That's why I laugh," Barbara said, a tear made its way down her cheek.

Katie's arms fell to her sides and her fortitude crumbled. A few seconds of silence passed. "Now, I don't understand."

"Maybe it's because we relied on each other so much. After your father died, we became so much closer than most mothers and daughters. I should have forced you to be more independent."

"No, Mom. It's not your fault. I'm the one who should be apologizing."

Lifting her chin, their eyes meeting, Barbara said, "Katie, seeing how much you and John are in love and how good you are for each other, makes me so happy."

Katie held her mother's gaze. Barbara's smile broke into a grin, her eyes sparkled. "Jealous of the old lady, are you?" she giggled. "Why, that makes an old girl feel good."

Katie kissed her mother on the forehead and they had a good long laugh.

Forcing herself to focus, the sound of pounding rain filling her ears, her hands gripping the counter, Katie looked at her mother. Sarah on her lap, she was reading the funny page out loud, her finger tracing the words one by one. It was all too much, such normalcy in the face of disaster. Oh John, why? Katie brewed some espresso, dumped the dainty cup's contents into John's big cup, big enough to serve soup, and topped it off with some of her mother's dirty water. She gulped the first swallow, blanching at the heat, and slouched against the counter. Looking out the window, she spied a few birds pecking the ground for leftovers. Too bad I don't have Mom's window feeder, she thought. Then, I could actually see the birds. She thought of Barbara's little harem of chickadees and how they seemed so frantic all the time. Barbara and Sarah were making plans for the weekend, something about a movie and lunch, and Katie wondered why her mother wasn't frantic. No one said a word about the plane since last night. Maybe it was all a bad dream? But then, why was her mother here and why was she taking Sarah away for the weekend?

Barbara turned around to look at her, her face hidden to Sarah, and Katie saw worry and concern. Katie looked into her coffee cup, hoping to find something, anything, when it dawned on her, she didn't have to call the cable company. Barbara was shielding Sarah, hoping to keep her safe from bad news. She was doing for her what she could never do for Katie. No news is good news, Barbara always said. Except when Edward died, Barbara didn't say anything. They had all the news and there wasn't anything good about it.

Packed and ready to go, Katie held Sarah a little longer than usual and kissed her goodbye. Barbara smiled weakly, pressed a note into her hand, and squeezed tightly.

"I love you, Mom," Katie whispered, watching them go. Closing the door, she opened the note and in her mother's perfect penmanship was written:

Flip the breaker in the basement, you'll have T.V. and phone.

The news this morning said "no further developments." Call 1-800-555-1212. Information for family members of passengers.

I love you

Katie placed the note on the counter and slid to the floor. Her knees fell open and her head rolled to the side. Taking a slow breath in, she felt an ache deep in her abdomen. Reaching, she opened a drawer with Sarah's school supplies and pulled out her old red notebook. Phone messages and reminders filled the first few pages. Katie hated when she forgot something, lost something. Suddenly, she thought about John being lost, lost somewhere between Brazil and home. She sat there in the kitchen, the corner cabinet door behind her pulling left, then right, John's chipped Tigers cup in her hand and the red notebook.

"I'm lost too," she cried out loud. "What about me? What about me?"

Tears blurring her vision, Katie opened the notebook, pulled out a pencil and began to write. Although nursing was her career of choice, it was writing that soothed her when troubled. It helped to put things down on paper. Only after she wrote things down, could she stop agonizing. The first day she wrote to relieve was the day her father died. Mrs. Woods, her high school English teacher, encouraged her to write every day. She explained that sometimes writing is the only way to understand your emotions. The first week after he died, Katie felt so alone, her mother distant, lost in grief. In time, writing helped sort out her feelings, to acknowledge them, to express them.

The sound of pouring rain filled the room. It was as if a deep cleansing was needed, and Katie felt relief in the white noise, the drowning out. Pencil to paper, she filled page after page. Beginning with Friday morning, she recorded everything that happened, right up to when she woke up to the news, the awful, horrifying news that John may be lost. Nothing was left out, not even the most mundane or typical of things. She recorded conversations and tasks. She wrote about the bus stop, Mrs. Cook, the triplets, and the strange woman. An hour later she stopped writing and looked up. The rain ceased. Grey angry clouds filled the window. The Tigers cup was still beside her, coffee long cold. What am I to do now? she agonized, knowing answers would not come quick enough. Staring at the red notebook, pages and pages filled with frantic writing, she turned to the beginning and at the top of the page, wrote "Before." Flipping past her words of desperation, pages and pages of release, she turned to a blank page and made a list.

1. Flip Breaker
2. Call 1-800 number
3. Buy window bird feeder

Katie needed something other than angry, grey clouds and bad news. It seemed trivial to buy a bird feeder while she painfully waited for news about John. But somehow, the thought of doing something, anything, was a comfort. If she could buy a feeder and the birds flew home, then maybe, just maybe, she could figure out a way to fly John home too.

Chapter 4

Leaning back against the kitchen cabinet, the hard floor beneath her, Katie stared at the red notebook. At the top of her list was, "Flip Breaker." The smell of stale cold coffee gave her stomach a lurch. Grabbing the edge of the counter, she pulled herself up. Homes built in the sixties did not have large and spacious basements. The lighting was minimal and the ceiling low.

Katie paused at the top of the stairs and thought about their house and the day they had spent house hunting.

Katie and John's house was a classic beauty, perched on top of a sloping yard, facing east. A development of stately homes, mature gardens and beautiful yards filled the landscape. Full sun at the back of the house, great for barbeques and pool parties, was well received during the warmer Michigan months of summer. It was a mix of retired couples and young professionals. Due to the high price of real estate at the turn of the twenty-first century, many young families didn't have the means to buy into the neighborhood. There were a few others with children, besides the Andersons, but they lived in smaller homes.

They were only married a few months when they decided to sell the condo in town and buy a house. The condo was John's. He purchased it after his divorce, long before they met, and no matter what Katie did to add a feminine touch, it still retained its bachelor qualities. It was a nice place to start a marriage, no overwhelming household duties, lots of opportunity for quality time together. But soon, they grew bored with their surroundings. A residential realtor, someone John knew from his fraternity days, was taking them to see a few properties. A few turned out to be a few too many. New to this area of Michigan, Katie was unfamiliar with the neighborhoods and after a while her back-seat position, although very soothing in the leather-bound Mercedes sedan, became as mundane as the muffled banter between the front seat occupants. The stretch between the front and back seats, as well as the division between the frat boys' conversations and herself, left her at a loss for words and bearings.

After what seemed a cross-country trip of the highest rural kind, Katie unbuckled her seatbelt and lunged herself across the abyss between the outs and the ins and asked no one in particular, "Are we looking to buy a home or the whole damned county?"

"Excuse me?" John asked.

She was about to repeat herself, much louder and closer, when frat boy jammed on the brakes. Katie's right shoulder slipped over the smooth full-grained leather and her head began its forward descent towards the windshield when a forearm caught her in the throat, sending her back into the abyss of the backseat.

"Damn deer," frat boy said. "Better keep your seatbelt on, just in case, sweetie."

Choking back her reply, that she wasn't his sweetie, and that it wasn't the deer's fault, Katie felt the car slow down to turn. Re-buckling her belt, she saw out the window two deer standing at the edge of the road. A family, she thought. Grateful they didn't hit the deer, she said a silent prayer for their safety.

Once in the quiet, serene neighborhood, Katie was immediately speechless. Long lazy ranches gracing tops of small knolls were surrounded by beautiful mature maple trees. As they drove deep into the neighborhood, each home more appealing than the next, she overheard pieces of the front seat conversation.

"Well-established…influences…esteem…no, no, not too many…" frat boy offered.

"That's good…we're not…any…no need for that," she heard John reply.

At the last turn, she saw a bus stop sign, well-worn and partially hidden by an extremely large blue spruce.

"Here we are," frat boy said as he pulled into a meandering drive that led to a classic cape cod. Everything about the curb appeal said comfort and style. Katie knew before they were even out of the car, this was home.

"I see you've recovered," John said as he opened the back door and took her hand.

"Looks like she's home," frat boy chuckled.

Walking up the drive, Katie smiled. The house reminded her of old postcards from the shores of New England. In fact, it was as if she could hear the crashing of the waves, when she saw the van, Johnson's Pool & Co. in big green letters.

Katie started laughing and John asked, "Inside or outside first?"

"Outside, definitely, outside," she replied, leading them to the rear of the home, one cobblestone at a time.

They made an offer that day and moved in four weeks later. Katie didn't pay attention to the fact that there were no signs of children in the neighborhood. Far from young in love, she wasn't thinking about children. John and Katie had discussed children before they married and agreed that their family would remain at two. John already had a daughter who was still very angry with him and an even angrier ex-wife. He didn't want any more children and on that subject, Katie was in agreement. Growing up a very happy only child, she was comfortable in small circles. Two was what she was used to, was what she was happy with, and the arrangement seemed natural. That is, until the morning she woke up and had to throw up.

Chapter 5

Flipping on the light switch at the top of the stairs, Katie spotted the little green flashlight. John always kept a flashlight at the top of the stairs. Remembering how the little flashlight came to its permanent place, her hands began to shake. That was the night she had witnessed John's deepest fears.

It was their first big fight. They had only been in the house a few months and Katie was very busy. Between her work schedule at the hospital and sudden increase in John's traveling, their time apart was lengthy. But given John's tendency to not hold onto material things, Katie was busy enough just furnishing their new home. John kept the barest of belongings in his condo. He said he didn't care for furniture or things, and never collected anything in his life. Barbara affectionately called him the thrower-outer. Katie put down the law that he was not to throw her things out. It wasn't that Katie was a hoarder, she just liked to hold onto things a little longer, just in case.

When Katie moved into the condo, all the dishes in his kitchen cabinets fit in the dishwasher with room to spare. At first, Katie figured this was typical of a late-aged bachelor, but as time went on, she realized it ran deeper.

The only mementos that John kept from his past were a childhood photo of Kylie from their ski vacation and an old footlocker. Squinting into the sun and blinding white surroundings, Kylie was smiling, her cheeks red and rosy, casually holding her skis like the great skier she would one day become.

When Katie inquired about the photo, John explained, "That was the first time I took her skiing. She made it down the hill without falling and hasn't stopped since."

The footlocker was an old army type that belonged to his father. It was quite large with brown leather straps, cracked and faded, that once buckled down the front, holding the cover closed. It smelled like old tobacco, a hint of pine. John showed Katie the footlocker when they first fell in love. It was a big step in their relationship and knowing how detached John could be, Katie realized he was sentimental, after all. The people and possessions he cherished, no matter how few, he valued beyond limits. It was at that moment; Katie knew she was hopelessly in love.

On the evening of their first big fight, Katie finished up her shift at the hospital and drove home. She was tired, planned to eat and head straight to bed. Working the three to eleven shift had its benefits, especially with John's traveling. He often flew back in the evening, they'd stay up late, then sleep in until late morning. Knowing he wouldn't be home until tomorrow, canned soup was on the menu. Katie found cooking for one lonely.

Katie loved to cook and now that she had someone she loved to cook for, she was outdoing herself. She even made up a menu on cardstock for when John returned from traveling. "Welcome Home John," was written at the top, followed by the night's fare of appetizer, soup or salad, main course, and dessert. The best part about cooking for two was that she could buy fresh ingredients, just enough for that evening. She'd take a drive by Harold's Butcher Block and choose fresh cuts and then onto Cifalagio's for her daily fresh fruit and vegetables, cheeses and other specialty ingredients. It all fit into one small reusable grocery bag, waiting for her to create something wonderful.

Pulling into the garage, Katie pressed the button for the garage door to come down. Just as the door closed, the overhead light went out and Katie found herself plunged into darkness. That's strange, she thought. Power outages were not common, at least not in the few months they lived in the neighborhood, and it was weird the electricity went out right after she closed the door. Not one to panic, Katie lived alone most of her adult life, she locked her car doors and calmly tried to open the overhead door again. No luck. She flipped on the flashlight on her keychain, took a deep breath, and whispered, "Okay, here goes nothing." Guided by the miniscule beam of her little flashlight, Katie made her way into the house, testing the light switches in vain on the way to the kitchen. The full moon outside the window illuminated the kitchen in an eerie sort of manner, casting an obtuse rectangular view of the kitchen table and chairs. Shadows at angles, receded into the dark recesses of the room, looking like amateur black and white still photography.

Placing her purse on the counter, Katie felt her way to the basement, following the helpful, although terribly little, light her keychain offered. Just before the last step, the flashlight died. Only a few feet to the breaker box, Katie felt for the main and in comparison, to those below, for she never remembered which direction was on or off, she determined that it was indeed in the, "off" position. She flipped the switch and light fell down the stairwell. Exhaling, Katie felt her shoulders relax.

When John came home the next evening, she greeted him with a long, warm hug and kiss at the back door.

"Welcome home John," she said, melting herself into him and holding just long enough for him to catch the aroma of his surprise.

"Ooooh, that smells wonderful, but I think the appetizers are served upstairs tonight."

"Oh, they are, are they?" Katie teased, pulling away to turn off the stove. Dimming the lights over the dining room table, Katie remembered the power problem and as she was following him upstairs, she said, "John, remind me to tell you something later."

"And just what would that be? That you missed me? You can't live without me?"

Laughing, she placed her hand on the small of his back and let it rest there. "No, just a power outage." Katie felt his back stiffen and almost ran into him when he stopped short.

Turning, his face serious, he asked, "What power outage?" his tone was hard and Katie flinched.

"The main breaker tripped. It happened after I pulled into the garage and put the door down. I just went down and turned it on. It hasn't happened since, but,"

Interrupting her, John raised his voice, "You did what? Are you crazy? You let yourself in? What if there was an intruder in the house? You could have been killed. And I would have come home to,"

Putting her hands up, Katie squared her shoulders, her voice quick and angry, "I'm sorry, John. I didn't think about that. What else could I do?"

"How about using your cell phone? The one you always forget in your purse? The one you say is only for emergencies? You could have locked the car doors and called the police."

Katie began to cry, realizing she did just that. She locked the car doors by instinct, but for some reason ignored her own safety. John sunk down next to Katie, his face fell and anger subsided. He pulled her to him.

"I could have lost you. I would have come home and found you and my life would be over. I can't go through that again," he whispered.

Katie placed a hand to his cheek, felt the wet of his tears. "Can't go through what again?"

"Come home to nothing."

John explained the night his first wife left him. She took everything, except for the nails in the walls and his father's footlocker. He had no idea she was going to leave. They had their troubles. She accused him on more than a few occasions of being an absentee husband and father, but he never expected what he found when he came home that unforgettable night. Turning his key in the door, he paused, waiting to hear Kylie's little feet running to greet him. When the door swung open, his mouth fell open. He thought he had the wrong apartment. The power was off and it was completely empty. Winter branches outside scratched against the window, mournfully throwing shadows against the stark walls and floors. Nails, hanging from the walls, somewhat random, were the only tangible witness to the act of abandonment he was denied.

"I was devastated," John said, his eyes lowered, face impenetrable.

"I'll be more careful," Katie murmured.

That night, "Welcome Home John" was served cold. Wrapped in blankets pulled from their bed, before a raging fire, they had a quiet and somber meal, finishing off the latest of Katie's culinary creations.

Standing at the top of the stairs, Katie gripped the banister. She felt a tear run down her cheek and painfully tore herself away from those sweet memories. She was running back up the stairs when her cell phone rang. More for emergency than regular use, she forgot to check it on Friday. John hardly ever called the cell phone, but it was listed as an emergency number and the house phone was turned off since her mother showed up.

Katie ran upstairs and grabbed her purse. Dumping everything out, she flipped open the phone. Two missed calls. Shaking, she turned off the phone by mistake and dropped it to the floor. Once again she sunk down, waiting the interminable time it took to power up.

"Two new messages," it flashed. She carefully pressed one for voicemail then punched in their four-digit code, 2000, for the year they met.

The first message rang out, "This call is for Mrs. John Marshall. We are calling to inform you that your husband, John Marshall, was not on flight 777 from Brazil to Detroit. Our manifest shows that he did not board the plane on Friday, April first."

Katie dropped the phone again. Pressing nine to save the message, the second message began, "Hi Katie, this is John. I have to stay in Brazil and won't be home until, at the earliest, the end of the week. I am up to my neck in trouble here with this deal and have to straighten things out. I'm sorry if you didn't get this earlier, I didn't want to wake you, so I called your cell phone. Things are pretty bad here right now, not much time. Poor cell coverage, so don't worry if you don't hear from me for a few days."

The phone was giving instructions about deleting or saving a message and Katie hit nine to save. She knew she would need to hear this message again.

Pulling herself up to sit at the kitchen table, she took a deep breath. The tension in her shoulders eased and a big smile broke out across her face. Realizing he had no idea about his near-death event, Katie vowed she would give John a good dose of hell for changing plans and then kiss him like never before. Just a few days, less than a week, she thought. Straightening her shoulders and stretching out her arms overhead, Katie eased the muscles of her back and neck. No problem, she thought, she vowed, she promised.

Katie knew her mother would still be on the road. Barbara never used her phone while driving. It was turned off and in her purse. Given her slow and careful driving, especially with Sarah, Katie knew it would be sometime before she could call her mother. I might as well just join them, she thought. A weekend away with my two girls may be just what I need. After a long shower, she packed a bag and jumped in the car. Backing out of the driveway, she saw Mrs. Cook pulling up the dead from her flower beds. It was a purple sunhat this time.

Katie lowered her window and called hello. "Going to Mom's for the weekend," she said raising her voice so Mrs. Cook didn't have to get off her knees. Two knee surgeries and the woman still refused to give up gardening, refused any help, even Katie's.

Turning around, Mrs. Cook smiled. "I'll watch the house for you, you know. Give my love to Barbara."

Grabbing the cell phone, Katie dialed John's number, knowing she would only get voicemail. Listening, the greeting intoned, "This is John Marshall. Please leave a message and I will call you back when I am available." Katie left him a message and then paused at the end of the driveway. Taking out the red notebook, she opened to her list. With a sigh of relief, she smiled and checked off the first two items and added a fourth.

1. Flip Breaker   X
2. Call 1-800 number   X
3. Buy window bird feeder
4. Welcome Home John

Chapter 6

Barbara left with Sarah as planned and spent most of the drive to her house answering questions. Sarah was at the age of inquisition and rarely came up for air before firing off another round of whys and how comes. Was it possible to concentrate on driving, suffer the cross-examination of a six-year-old and still be lost in thought about Katie? she wondered. Leaving Katie at the house was a hard thing to do, but Barbara felt it was more important to get Sarah away. She didn't want Sarah to have to go through what Katie went through when her father died. A high-profile tragedy, reporters and newsmen besieged their house for days. They couldn't go anywhere without cameras and microphones.

Looking into her rearview mirror, she saw Sarah staring out the window, her eyes sleepy, and smiled. Barbara knew Katie wouldn't do anything rash, she handled more than her share of tragedy, both personal and as an emergency nurse. Sometimes the two mixed, and in a small town like St. Claire the emergency room nurse was often your neighbor or closest friend.

Barbara thought about the time Katie came home from the hospital and broke down in tears. Katie didn't cry easily and as for breaking down, it never happened. Having built a wall around herself as a young woman, she handled tragedy well. It was processed and out the door before feelings could get into the equation. However, this night, things had been different.

As a teenager, Katie had made many new friends when they moved to Michigan. A few from school, some from her part-time job, and others from their church youth group. But it was the girl down the street that became her closest friend. Jessie was six years younger than Katie and at a time when she needed to feel loved, Jessie was still young enough to love her friend without all the drama of teenage friendships. Jessie loved horses and drawing and taking photographs. Katie loved tagging along. To most, it looked like Katie was the mentor, older and wiser, spending time with a younger girl. But, Barbara knew better. Katie liked the simplicity of her friendship with Jessie and without the competition typical to teenagers and the all-too-close questions, she could relax and be herself.

It was years later, her third year at the hospital and still somewhat new to the emergency room, when Jessie was brought in on a stretcher. Even before she was through the door, Katie knew it was Jesse. As the calls for staff rang out and the doors flew open, pungent smells of hay and horse filled the air. Katie reeled. The doors closed and a flurry of medics rushed in, calling out stats. Jesse's breathing was shallow and quick. A slight moan escaped and her eyelids fluttered. The stats were not good. Collapsed lung, multiple broken bones, falling pressure, contusions. Her riding helmet was unscathed and there was no evidence of head trauma. Without her helmet, they would have entered the hospital using different doors. Katie felt a slow buzz build within her and she grabbed the side of the stretcher.

She whispered in Jessie's ear, "Hey sweetheart, it's me, Katie. We are going to take good care of you. Everything will be okay." Knowing the next twelve to twenty-four hours were critical, Katie gave her hand a squeeze and moved behind as they wheeled her into surgery.

Others worked on Jessie. Katie was allowed to stay nearby, but given their friendship, protocol called for taking a step back. Taking a few deep breaths, Katie sat in the hallway and listened to the mundane sounds of an all too quiet emergency room, a low volume television, the sound of water running. Katie knew the unknown was the concern, internal bleeding. Jessie came through the surgery, critical, stable. Vital signs were good. Color was returning. Jesse opened her eyes and asked for water.

Katie tip-toed into post-op and checked on Jessie.

"Go get some rest, Katie," the nurse said. "She'll be alright through the night."

Katie kissed Jessie on the forehead, felt warmth and smiled. She squeezed Jessie's hand and Jessie squeezed back. "See you in the morning," Katie whispered. Leaving the room, she took a long look back and the nurse waved her on.

She was upstairs sleeping in the nurse's lounge, when suddenly, she woke, her eyes flew open. Running down the hallway she bypassed the elevator, skirting around crowds of silent visitors, and slipped into the stairwell. Two steps at a time and it wasn't fast enough. The buzzing began again, her hands tingling, head spinning. Picking up the pace, she busted through the double doors and stopped. Down the hall, outside Jessie's room, the surgeon, a stern expression, his hands at his sides, was facing her, and Jesse's parents, falling into each other, were slowly crumbling. There was no need for explanation. Katie read the death certificate, heart failure. She thought of all the other heart failures that didn't result in death, Jessie's family, her friends. Sometimes dying was a little too neat.

Walking in the door to their house, Barbara watched as Katie had dropped her purse and keys onto the floor, fell into the couch and fell apart.

Barbara gripped the steering wheel and looked into the rearview mirror. Sarah was awake, her little eyes fierce, brows knitted, mouth working.

"Grandma, Gramma," she hollered for the millionth time.

"Yes, Sarah. Yes, what is it?" Barbara stammered.

"Grandma. You missed the driveway."

"Oh my. Oh Sarah. It's a good thing you keep an eye on me."

"Funny Grandma. I have both of my eyes on you." Kicking her feet, Sarah giggled and Barbara laughed, even though all she wanted to do was cry

Chapter 7

Monday morning arrived with a deluge of rain. Even so, Katie felt refreshed after the nice weekend at her mother's and looked forward to John's return at the end of the week. Sarah was dragging out breakfast as usual. They were running late again and would probably miss the bus. Yet, it felt good to be back home, without the terror that imprisoned her just a few days ago. Still, every now and then something would catch her off guard and the uneasiness would return. Simple, unrelated things would trigger a memory or a train of thought and she'd find her knees buckling and her mind going back to last Friday night.

Over the weekend, blindly reaching into her mother's kitchen drawer for a pen, Katie grabbed a handheld electric screwdriver instead. Feeling its weight in her hand, she looked down. The panic began. The screwdriver was John's. Why was John's screwdriver in her mother's drawer? Not one to leave things behind and quite particular about keeping his tools in order, Katie thought it strange. How many times had she reached into that drawer, never noticing the screwdriver? It must be from last Christmas, she thought, when John helped Barbara hang up the painting. It was a beautiful old, oil painting, typical of traditional Kentucky homesteads, not just any homestead, but a very special one. Staring at the screwdriver, Katie thought back to that day, Christmas morning and the painting they had given Barbara.

The painting was a surprise Christmas gift for Barbara. They had sworn Sarah to secrecy. Barbara always spent Christmas eve with them, staying the night. Barbara and Sarah were in the kitchen, preparing the after services supper. Perched on a stool, her chubby hands reaching for this and that, Sarah chattered along, while Barbara deftly deterred and avoided unwanted ingredients, answering questions one right after another.

"Grandma," Sarah shouted. "What about the hot pepper? You forgot the hot pepper," she said, reaching over the pot to deliver a dash.

"Oh, that goes in later, sweetheart." Barbara intercepted the unwanted item and placed it out of reach.

"And what about some of this stuff, c-u-m-i-n?" Sarah asked, opening the top, about to take a big whiff.

"That's for Indian food Sarah. Indians from India, not Kentucky," she answered, sweeping away the bottle before Sarah could inhale too much.

"Yuck," Sarah complained. "That stuff smells funny." Rubbing her nose and wrinkling up her little face, she fired off the next round of questions, "Are Indians from India funny, Grandma?"

"I don't know, but you sure are." Barbara gave her a big squeeze. "Now let's get down to business, young lady. Southern food needs time to cook and we have to be ready in just a few hours for church."

Jumping down, Sarah did a little dance and ran from the room, yelling, "Mommy, Mommy where's my dress? My pretty red dress? Can I wear it now? Please? Please? p-l-e-a-s-e?"

Taking advantage of her absence, Barbara quickly got to work, preparing the meal and putting away all of Sarah's ingredients.

Every year, finding a gift for Barbara was a challenge. Independent and self-sufficient, anything she wanted, she bought. So, when Katie and John had stumbled upon the painting, they knew it was a must.

After spending a hot July day at the Detroit Zoo, watching the animals sleep and thinking humans didn't have much over animals, Katie convinced John to stop on the way home. Just a short distance up Woodward Avenue, they turned into a quiet little town. The faint sound of music in the distance, children laughing and dogs barking, made Katie lower her window, the hazy heat a good feeling against the chill of the air conditioner. Leaving their car at the edge of town, they decided to walk. John held Sarah on his shoulders, bouncing her up and down, her little giggles like hiccups.

"Yippee," she yelled. "Bounce me, Daddy."

Katie spotted a side street with vendors and artists. Painters were busy at easels, people stood around watching. Placing a hand on his arm, Katie said, "John, look. This way."

Halfway down the street, Sarah stopped giggling and bouncing. "Mommy," she whispered, pointing at a large oil painting across the street. "Grandma's house."

John and Katie looked at each other, eyebrows raised. About to ask her what she meant, they were interrupted.

"Grandma showed me in her picture album. Her house, when she was a little girl, like me. There's the swing on the front porch. That big red barn, that's where Great Grandpa kept the horses."

Katie stared, her eyes wide, jaw dropped. She stepped forward, but John held her back.

"Let me." Holding her at the elbow, they crossed the street. John casually inquired about the painting. A reasonable amount was agreed upon and paid. John looked at Katie and nodded.

"How did you come to paint this home?" she asked.

"I found an old newspaper article. I love history. Spent a summer in Kentucky drawing and painting old homes and buildings. This one was on the outskirts of Frankfort, I think, although I don't recall the name."

"It's beautiful," Katie whispered, her voice trailing off.

"I agree. It makes you want to walk right in, doesn't it?"

"You have no idea."

After reminding Sarah a thousand times this was a big secret and not to tell Grandma, the painting was forgotten, wrapped up and placed in the back of Katie's closet. Months later, gathered around the Christmas tree, Katie had the large gift, wrapped in Christmas cheer, placed before Barbara.

"Merry Christmas, Mom."

"My goodness, whatever could this be?"

Unwrapping the gift, Sarah's eye grew large as she remembered what was under the wrapping. "I know grandma. It's," she began.

John quickly covered her mouth and whispered in her ear, "Shhhh, secret, remember?" Nodding with large eyes and a big grin, Sarah giggled.

"Hmm, a secret, huh? Now, aren't all Christmas gifts a secret?" Barbara asked, as she continued to unwrap. Looking over at Sarah she smiled. Not thinking about the gift, but her granddaughter, she pulled the last of the paper away and stared at the painting.

"Oh my," she murmured. Tears filled her eyes. Covering her mouth with trembling hands, she stammered, "How? When? Where?"

Katie explained how they came across the painting and that it was Sarah who recognized the home. Barbara was amazed and kept coming back to stare at the painting throughout the day.

For Barbara, there was only one place to hang the painting. Voicing opinions about how high or low it should go, she directed John as he stood over the kitchen table, an array of tools from home spread beneath his feet.

Handing John the electric screwdriver, Katie asked her mother, "Mom, you want this in the kitchen? How about over the fireplace?"

"I want it where I spend my time and that's in the kitchen. Besides, what better place to remember old memories than in the kitchen, after all, that's center of the family."

Standing back, the three of them admired the painting, each lost in their own thoughts.

Sarah came dashing into the kitchen, took one look, hollered, "Hi Great Grandpa," and dashed out again.

They all looked at each other, shrugged, and then stepped closer. Of one-mind, they peered in the windows, shook their heads, and laughed. Feeling silly, they chalked it up to childhood imagination. If only they had known the fine line they walked between fact and fiction.

Chapter 8

Back in her kitchen, lost in the past, Katie stood there, the angry rain, too much. She looked over at Sarah, her breakfast a cast of imaginative characters. It was unnerving, the things Sarah sometimes said and did, so intuitive, so adult. Her stomach lurched nervously and her hands shook. John, where are you? she whispered. Gripping the counter, she imagined his arms around her and felt a fresh spring of tears.

Katie worried about Sarah. Just this weekend at her mother's, Sarah continued to address the painting, but in a more familiar fashion. Having never said anything to Barbara, she made a mental note to ask her mother, after John came home. After the uneasiness was gone and she could stop looking at everything and remembering, then she would ask, when reaching for a pen no longer made you think of Christmases, old paintings, and strange childhood behavior.

Pushing back her uneasiness and a dreary Monday morning, Katie willed herself to focus on Sarah and the morning at hand. Seated at the kitchen table, in some gymnastic variation of sitting, Sarah was holding her string cheese in one hand and a hard-boiled egg in the other. A heated conversation was going on between the two.

"Whatever do you mean? Mr. Egg?" asked Mrs. Stringy Cheese in a high stained voice.

"Hmm, well, I mean, after all, I am the most important part of breakfast. You, as beautiful as you are, Mrs. Stringy, are really just cheese and um...well...cheese is for lunch," Mr. Egg offered sheepishly.

"Well, I never," exclaimed Mrs. Stringy. "I ought to teach you a lesson," she promised and soon Mrs. Stringy was diving through the air for Mr. Egg, who was bouncing across the table in a hasty retreat.

"I'll fix you," Mrs. Stringy screamed.

With one hand, Katie intercepted Mr. Egg and Mrs. Stringy.

"Oh No," Mr. Egg begged. "Not the hatch, p-l-e-a-s-e," Sarah mimed.

"Down you go, Mr. Egg," Katie said and proceeded to place Mr. Egg down the hatch, while Sarah frowned and chewed and reached for Mrs. Stringy.

"One at a time, young lady," Katie said, handing Sarah back the string cheese, which immediately died a tragic death upon her plate.

Amidst a full mouth, much in need of a drink to wash it down, Sarah mumbled the last suffering words of Mrs. Stringy, "Oh Mr. Egg, I'm afraid I'm right behind you." Down the hatch she went, riding on a wave of juice and giggles.

"Wonderful performance, Sarah, but look at the time. We better get a move on or you're going to miss the bus," Katie warned.

Laughing to herself, Katie buckled Sarah in the backseat and backed out of the garage. Over the sound of the garage door opening, Katie could hear the rush of rain, the pelting of her car roof, a deluge of nails. In her rear-view mirror, she could see Sarah's mouth moving, silently, drowned out by the wind, rain, and beating of her wipers. The only time Sarah's mouth was not moving was when she was asleep.

Pulling up to the bus stop, Katie saw the bus approaching and the yellow lights flashing.

"Okay, sweetie, unbuckle, and we'll make a run for it."

Katie helped Sarah jump in-between the front seats and follow her out the driver's door. Sarah held fast to her hand, jumping to stay under the umbrella. Passing Mrs. Cook's car, Katie could see the boys in the backseat, getting ready to run.

Mrs. Cook rolled down her window and yelled after the boys, "Have a nice day, boys. Oh, and to you too Katie. Just fit for ducks, you know?" she added, rolling her eyes and her window.

The bus pulled away in a river of rain water. Katie turned around without looking and almost ran smack into the strange woman.

"Oh my. Sorry, I wasn't looking," Katie said, stepping back and peering under her umbrella at the woman. She was dressed as the first time. Thinking back, she remembered their vintage, almost retro look, the long raincoat, boots, scarf and sunglasses, all black. The umbrella had an old wooden handle, like her father's when she was a child.

The woman appeared indifferent, looked right through Katie, her eyes fixed on something beyond. A shiver ran down Katie's spine.

Offering her hand, somewhat timidly, she said, "Hello, my name is Katie."

Turning abruptly, he woman proceeded to walk up the hill, water running off her umbrella like a mountain waterfall. Katie stood there and stared, her jaw dropped. She watched her walk until she disappeared over the hill. Why am I always surprised by the rudeness of others? Katie wondered. Standing there, wind and rain continuing its onslaught, she felt her pant legs sticking to her, her shoes drenched. Returning to her car, she turned up the heat and rubbed her hands together.

Katie pulled forward to make a U-turn and go home, but at the last moment, made a left and headed up the hill. As she made the crest, she saw the woman turn into a long driveway on the left. Katie always wondered about this property. The house was a mystery, not visible from the road. There were rumors, a family tragedy years ago. But, Katie never trusted rumors. Just like memories, they changed, ending up far from the truth. Katie thought about Mrs. Cook and the time she had asked her about the farmhouse.

She had wandered over to admire Mrs. Cook's tulips, a deep blue, almost purple. Mrs. Cook was down on her knees, folded in two, hell bent on eradicating some very unlucky weeds. Looking upon her wide brimmed hat and full-coverage clothing for sun-protection, she reminded Katie of a cartoon character, as if at any moment, she would pick up a bush for cover and twinkle-toe away. Katie covered her mouth and began to giggle.

"I hope I'm not that amusing, you know," Mrs. Cook said as she turned to greet Katie with a smile.

"Oh Mrs. Cook, how do you find so many outfits in purple?"

"You'd be surprised," she answered, her voice light and airy. "If it makes you smile and helps me to remember my Harold, then so be it."

"Mrs. Cook, I was wondering, is it true what they say about that old farmhouse?"

"Well, now, that depends on what is being said, don't you know?"

Not sure if she should press on, Katie paused. Mrs. Cook was not one of the first homeowners in this neighborhood; however, she knew most of the history, if not all. Even so, she wasn't one to gossip.

"You know, I only spread good news, Katie," Mrs. Cook said with a smile.

Katie studied her fingernails and considered her reply. "Well, I was just curious, I didn't mean to,"

"For sure, sweetheart, "Mrs. Cook interrupted, rising and placing an arm around Katie's shoulders. "I'll tell you the true story, if you want to know. Let's have a seat on the porch. I'm ready for something to wet my whistle."

Mrs. Cook disappeared into the house and Katie took a seat on the glider. She looked around admiring the beautiful surroundings. It was the kind of porch that made you feel as comfortable as if you were inside, yet, at the same time, made you happy to be outside. Katie loved the outdoors and in Michigan it was a tough love. The warm seasons were short and if you didn't take advantage of them, the next thing you knew, it was blowing and snowing.

Mrs. Cook returned with a tray of cool lemonade and some shortbread cookies.

"It feels wrong to talk lightly of such a tragedy and thankfully, over the years' people seem to have forgotten. When Harold and I first moved here, it was all the neighborhood gossip. A haunted house, a preacher turned bad, an unfaithful wife." Mrs. Cook folded her hands in her lap and looked at Katie. "Nonsense."

"So it wasn't built with the rest of the homes?" Katie asked.

"Oh no. I'm getting ahead of myself here. Cart before the horse and all, you know," Mrs. Cook said, a slight lift in her voice.

"The Jackson family were a wealthy Michigan family, going back for generations. Timber, I think. The farmhouse was built at the height of the wealth of the 1920s and for miles around land was part of the estate. Over the years, parcels were sold, houses built. But, it wasn't until the late 1970s that the remaining acreage surrounding the farmhouse was sold to a developer and our neighborhood was built."

Katie looked at Mrs. Cook thoughtfully. "How do you know all this?"

"Oh, my Harold was a bit of a history lover. Spent hours poring over old deeds and maps, don't you know?"

"But why leave such a beautiful home empty, forgotten?"

"Well, that's where the gossip comes in. All I will say is, there was trouble, a terrible tragedy. In the end, both family and home were torn apart. The surrounding land was sold to a developer and that's when the houses started going up." Mrs. Cook looked into the distance, her eyes dreamy. "Don't you know, when Harold and I first moved here, we would wander the woods for hours. Harold found old fence posts, part of foundation for a barn, and even a few horse shoes. Oh, my Harold liked anything old." Letting out a deep sigh, she turned her gaze on Katie. "I always thought it strange how they left the old estate so secluded. Harold said it was part of the contract that all the surrounding trees remain around the original home. I always suspected they were hiding something back there, but the trick worked, don't you know? Sometimes, even I forget that old house is back there."

"So, who owns the house now?" Katie asked, her eyes wide.

"Well, as far as I know, an heir. The last known Jackson is a best-selling author, goes by the pen name Steadman Steinenbach, kind of a recluse, lives in California."

"Wow," Katie whispered.

"Have a cookie, Katie. More for you means less for me," she had said, patting her own plump self, good naturedly.

Watching the woman disappear down the driveway, Katie followed her. Gripping the steering wheel, her hands felt funny, her stomach queasy. She pulled into the end of the driveway. Up ahead, she could see the outline of the woman and her umbrella and then suddenly, she was gone. Closing and opening her eyes, Katie stared ahead at the empty driveway. Slowly, she let the car roll forward, the wipers thumping back and forth, her beating heart keeping time. The driveway veered to the left, opening up to a large expanse of oaks and evergreens. In the center, stood the farmhouse. It was difficult to see clearly, but, she could tell someone was living there. Katie admired the full-length cottage windows and the wrap-around porch, the dark brown clapboard, freshly painted white trim. The whole place had a nostalgic, Americana postcard quality. Buckets of pansies dotted the steps and a bench swing pendulated back and forth in the driving wind and rain. Strange woman, strange house, Katie thought.

Turning off her wipers, rain running down the windshield and windows, Katie sat in silence, her view slowly enveloped in mist. Making a small circle with her fist against the window, she peered at the farmhouse again, squinting her eyes, nose against the cold glass. A few moments later, she sat back against the seat, her hands falling to her lap. Oh John, she thought closing her eyes, please hurry. Katie stared at her hands. Suddenly, pursing her lips, she turned on her wipers, put the car in reverse and headed home. Back and forth the wipers beat. Forget about it, Katie thought, just forget. Back and forth the wipers beat. Wipe away, she prayed, if only I could wipe away, wipe away, wipe away.

Chapter 9

Tuesday morning, Katie woke to bright sunshine and the sweet sounds of spring. The finches returned, along with other wayward fliers, singing an arrangement of parts as if madly orchestrating an avian opera. Lying in bed with her eyes closed, she smiled. It was Tuesday, only three days until John would return. If he was flying back Friday, then she should get a call Thursday night, Friday morning at the latest. John always called and gave her his flight plans before boarding. That's how she knew he was scheduled on the flight that went down just four days ago. Thank God he changed his plans. Not even a week later and it felt like a lifetime. She rolled over, peeked at the clock, and smiled again. It was early. Katie loved waking up early when she didn't have to. Sleeping late made her feel behind the ball, and often the whole day played out that way as well. Relishing the quiet time, she rolled onto her back and sank deeper into the covers. Pulling her knees into her chest, she felt her lower back relax and her thoughts return to John again and the first time they had met.

It was not long after Katie was promoted to head nurse at Our Lady's Nursing Home, that Katie had met John. A hard worker and quick on her feet, it was a smart rise up the ladder since she took the job two years before. Some would say a switch from the hospital to nursing home care was a step down, but Katie preferred the older patients. Even at the hospital, she found herself gravitating to senior care and was often reprimanded for taking too much time with them. It felt as though the pace of the hospital was a detriment to those with a lifetime of wisdom and so little opportunity to share. And, Katie had enough of sick children. It broke her heart every time they lost another child. Having moved from the emergency room to the intensive care unit, she saw more and more children with respiratory problems in life threatening situations. The last child they lost was unforgettable, convincing her she had to make a change.

Olivia Patterson was only three years old when she was rushed to Detroit Mercy and came under Katie's care. A poor child, abandoned by her mother and father and raised by her eighty-year-old grandmother, she had a host of economic problems that only complicated her medical problems. Still suffering the consequences of her mother's drug addictions, she was underweight and susceptible to everything contagious. Added to the misery was the ultimate heartbreak of cystic fibrosis, a strangling life sentence of respiratory therapy and drugs. Katie worked to get Olivia stable and then pulled up a chair next to her bed. Lying with her eyes closed, the little girl's chest heaved up and down as she struggled to breathe, her own viscous fluids choking off precious oxygen. Katie heard footsteps behind her, light and quick, and she knew it was Craig, the Director of Nursing. Katie's shift ended hours ago.

"Katie, you do know it is okay for you to take a step away. We all need a break sometime," he offered.

Katie did not turn around.

"Every time I decide I can't do this anymore, I think of all the kids that will be here and need me." Katie hung her head and closed her eyes.

"Think of it this way. If you are not your best, then are you giving your best? Maybe moving to a type of nursing you are more comfortable with will make room for someone who is just perfect for this work and make room for you where you are really needed," he said softly.

Katie held Olivia's hand. Her grandmother would be here shortly with their pastor. They were going to lay hands. Katie knew Olivia would be lucky to leave the hospital. She prayed for a miracle and then prayed for guidance. Somewhere in the silence of the room, the background chorus of mechanical rhythmic intonations and Olivia's rattle-like breathing, Katie knew this was her last sick child.

By the time her grandmother and the pastor arrived, the only hands laid were those of grief. Katie grabbed her things and signed out. She went home and typed her resignation. Economically stable, she took a much-needed respite and did some soul searching. Two weeks later she entered elder care.

The change in Katie and her work was such a revelation, even Katie surprised herself. She woke up happy and came home feeling good about herself. Her energy increased and she found herself engaging in conversations with others she normally would shy away from. As the depressing clouds of loss and heartache waned, Katie brightened. Barbara sat back and watched the transformation, hoping this opening of her daughter's heart would be deep enough to allow love.

In her new position, Katie spent more time with her patients than most head nurses. A managerial position in the majority, she made time in her heavy workload to get to know the patients. She could have remained in direct patient care. Yet, she liked the heavy workload, found it energizing. Katie felt that in a supervisory position she could take care of all the patients by ensuring their direct care was of the highest quality. It was as if she was the umbrella, protecting them all, staff and patients. Spending extra time after her shift, she knew more than just names. Sometimes incoherent and unable to communicate, Katie interacted with family members or for those alone, she did a little library research.

It was such a patient, an enigma, that Katie was visiting one evening. Madeline Marshall was eighty-five years old and still beautiful. She had shoulder length, pure white hair, thicker than most women have in their prime. Sweet in nature, she communicated her gratitude with smiles and bright eyes. All the staff loved her and took pleasure in brushing her hair and caring for her. Katie knew little about Madeline, except that she was born and raised in Lexington, Michigan and lived in Michigan all her life. Her only son lived just outside of Detroit and made the long trip to visit his mother every evening. Katie was not present when Madeline was admitted. The file had minimal information and she was unsuccessful searching the internet and the library.

"How are you, Ms. Madeline?" Katie asked as she brushed the hair from her face. Madeline opened her eyes and fixed them on Katie. A smile broke, making Katie laugh. Katie squeezed her hand gently and Madeline's eyes twinkled, her grin a little lopsided.

"Oh, well, well, aren't we the happy camper?" The conversation went back and forth with Katie catching Madeline up on recent events and Madeline alternating smiles and frowns. So engrossed, Katie didn't hear the footsteps behind her.

"She can't hear you," a gruff voice said behind her. Startled, Katie turned and Madeline's smile faded.

Standing at the door was a tall figure of a man, cut in what appeared to be quite expensive attire. Blocking the light from the hall, it was difficult to distinguish features in the dimly lit room. Katie sighed. She saw her share of responsible, yet detached sons. Obligatory visits, spent mostly in silence, checking their phones, it was unclear who the visit was for. It was the successful children who had the hardest time dealing with aging and failing parents, as if somehow going up the corporate ladder, compassion became a liability.

"Excuse me?" Katie turned.

"My mother, Madeline, her stroke left her unable to hear or recognize anyone," he said, crossing the room to stand on the opposite side of his mother's bed. He continued to stare at Katie, as if his mother wasn't even between them.

Not dropping her gaze, she now saw clearly who was addressing her so forcefully. Her body stiffened and defenses rose, yet, when she looked into his dark brown eyes, she saw a deep sadness. This man loves his mother, she thought. Why was it that million dollar deals and boardrooms were a breeze, yet a tiny frail woman, the one who loved and cared for you from the time you were born, renders them so helpless? she wondered. Thinking back to her own father and his death, Katie realized that everyone had their vulnerabilities, even powerful men.

Katie turned back to Madeline and saw her eyes travel to her son. The smile was gone, brows furrowed, eyes serious.

"I'm sorry. Let me introduce myself. I'm Katie,"

"I know who you are, Katie Stanton, head nurse. I've seen you with my mother several times." Clearing his throat, he relaxed his posture. "I admire you," he said softly. "I only wish, if only I knew, if only she knew me," his voice trailed off, forcing a cough, he lowered his eyes and turned towards his mother.

46

Katie took a long look at the man before her. Good looking and powerful, he was probably use to controlling situations and yet, Madeline was beyond his control. His thick, dark brown hair and fair complexion were a nice contrast. He seemed genuine, as if his presence was more than obligation, as if there was hope. Maybe the best way to help Madeline is to help her son, she thought.

"Thank you," Katie said. "It is hardest on those who love them. To see the little signs, I mean." She walked over and stood next to him. Madeline looked up at both of them, her eyes searching.

"It's as if she is going to say something and then, well, nothing. It breaks my heart, but I can't just leave her here. She means so much to me. I can't let her go, even if she isn't really there."

Placing a hand on his shoulder, Katie spoke softly, "Just talk to her. Don't ask for anything in return. Tell her about your day and how you have been. Mothers need to know about their children and now is her time to listen."

Katie placed the back of her hand on Madeline's cheek. "Bye, Madeline," she whispered.

Raising her eyes, she looked at John. "It was nice to meet you, John." As Katie walked out of the room, she could feel his eyes following her. They were always surprised she knew their names.

A few weeks later, Katie was walking by Madeline's room and paused. She could hear John's voice, soft and intimate, rising and falling, a cadence typical to close, familial conversations. It wasn't the first time she overheard him talking. Many evenings, saying good night to her patients, she would hear his voice, at first abrupt and staccato, slowly melting into soft and easy tones, finally finding comfort in his mother's presence. More than once, Katie found little napkins with cartoon characters scribbled on them. They were actually quite good, and although the proportions were distorted, she could usually guess who they were. John F. Kennedy, Martin Luther King, and Mahatma Gandhi made their way into Madeline's trash can, along with The Three Stooges, Lucille Ball, and even the cast of The Wizard of Oz. Katie tucked away these insights to John, knowing he wasn't all that serious all the time and she liked that.

It was well after seven one evening that John sought her out. Katie had a few important things to do on the way home. Grabbing her keys and sweater, she pushed against the door to leave, the wind working against her.

"Katie," an urgent, yet, deep voice called her name. Turning, she saw John rushing towards her, and her heart raced, Madeline? He stopped a few feet short of the door and stammered, as if distracted by something.

"Is it Madeline?"

"No. Well, yes." Not meeting her eyes, he shoved his hands in his pockets and looked at the floor. "I'm sorry. I didn't mean to alarm you. I wanted to ask you about my Mother. Oh, you're on your way out," he fumbled.

Seeing how uncomfortable he was, Katie spoke up reassuringly, "That's okay, John. I have all the time in the world when it comes to Madeline."

John raised his eyes to meet hers and breathed deeply. Her steely blue eyes were in such contrast to her dark, unruly hair and fair complexion. Finding it hard to focus, his heart raced, palms tingled.

He too overheard conversations with Madeline and many others in Katie's care. Like a snapshot into her true character, John was drawn in by her compassion and dedication.

Taking a mental step forward, one he was sure would never happen again, John held her gaze and ventured, "Are you hungry? That is, if you know of somewhere to go. I am famished."

Katie let the door close and her heart open. Forgetting about what was so important just moments ago, she smiled.

"Sure, there's a cafe just down the road."

Two hours later, they were still sitting in the booth, the waitresses given up on refilling their coffee. Their conversation started with Madeline and somehow made its way around their lives, hopes, and dreams.

Throwing his head back to laugh, John reminded Katie of her father and how he would shake the windows with his deep rolling laughter. Katie thought of her mother and a deep understanding of her loss shook her. Closing her eyes, she took a deep breath.

"Are you okay?" John asked.

Blinking, Katie smiled and took notice of his untouched food.

"So you were famished?" she asked, teasing this new and wonderful friend.

Looking down at his plate, he shrugged. "Different kind of hunger, I guess," he said, his eyes serious.

"I know what you mean." Katie reached across the table.

Her hand curved in his palm, Katie felt strength and warmth. John felt tenderness and vitality. Both knew this meant dropping defenses and risking trust, something neither would have considered just weeks ago. Love was slowly eroding their walls like a rainstorm on a sandcastle, walls carefully built and fortified over the years. Content to watch them slowly crumble, Katie felt they had all the time in the world. John, on the other hand, was not a watcher. In the weeks and months following, he had not only demolished what stood between them, but had rebuilt foundations, erected new structures, adjoining walls, hearts, and lives.

Chapter 10

Going through the motions, Katie was holding up pretty well, if only for Sarah, just to crumble, as the bus pulled away. After her strange encounter following the woman to the old farmhouse in the driving rain, Katie was determined to focus on her own family, as if in doing so, she could somehow will John home.

Wednesday morning, rushing back from the bus, waving to Mrs. Cook, smiling just a bit too much, Katie ran into the house, closed the door and burst into tears. Clenching her fists, she felt her anger rise, her resolve return. Suddenly, she remembered the cell phone. Punching in the code, she waited. "You have no new messages," the matter-of-fact voice stated. If only the voice was a real person, I would reach in through the phone and strangle them, she cursed.

Katie dialed John's number again, knowing he was out of range, just to hear the sound of his voice. "I'm sorry, but the number you are trying to reach is either out of service or out of the calling area," the operator stated. Expecting to hear John's voice, Katie was startled. She stared at the phone a long time. Just about to put the phone away, she paused and dialed the number for John's office. Maybe his partner, Jim, would know something.

"Good morning, Marshall and McGlaughlin," the receptionist sang.

"Hello, Kelly. May I speak to Jim, please?"

"Good morning, Katie. How are you and little Miss Sarah?"

Kelly was their new and very young receptionist. She was fresh out of high school and sweet through and through. Still new to the position, the learning curve was going to be a steep one. Even so, neither he nor Jim, his partner for the last thirty years, had the heart to let her go. The job was simple enough and the clients really warmed to her sweet demeanor.

"Is Jim there?"

"Yes he is. I'll put you right through."

Knowing her luck with the complex telephone system, Katie braced herself for a long wait. As the seconds turned into minutes, her anxiety over this new development began to rise. She paced the room, opening the blinds, only to close them again.

"Top of the morning," the familiar, loud and boisterous voice, that could only belong to Jim McGlaughlin, blasted through the phone.

Pulling the phone away, she could hear Jim bellowing like a voice travelling down a water well, "Hey, Katie, what's up my love?"

Katie liked Jim more than she would admit. His abrasive nature and loud personality, not to mention his attire, was more than most could take in a first meeting. Yet, somehow he grew on you, so much so, that in no time, casual friends became lifelong fans.

Katie considered what to say to Jim, how to begin. Although Jim and John worked independently, all travel plans were made through the office. Most likely, Jim never knew the difference, never realized how close John came to being on that first plane, the one that crashed into the gulf and into Katie's slumber just five days earlier. Jim would have known of John's change in flight plans, before the first plane went down. So would have Katie, if, she checked her cell phone. Yet, given the last few days, her seat on the so called emotional roller-coaster of John's absence, Katie needed some reassurance. Wrestling with the urge to cry, the need to scream, she took a deep breath, and thought back to how Jim and John's life-long friendship had developed.

Jim and John's friendship went back many years, long before they had a business together. Son of a navy man, Jim lived all over the country, giving him a concoction of dialects and mannerisms that reminded one of this area or that, but not distinctive enough to place any label. Jim was like one of those suitcases with the travel stickers covering the outside. Clearly a mixture of here and there on the surface, yet, what lie inside, his true self was hidden, enclosed, locked away. John always said Jim was a puzzle and everyone likes a good puzzle. True enough, Katie thought. Jim was complex and yet, easy. More than a few women tried to solve him, to piece him together. Katie shuddered, some women will never learn, she thought. Without a doubt, Jim was a confirmed bachelor and as challenging as he was for even the most aggressive of women, when he was through, it was through, which kind of explained the revolving door on their receptionist.

John handled the personnel end of the business and typically hired more experienced, older women. They tried a few young men, but women were just nicer to listen to on the phone and whether naturally attuned or something innate, women were just politer than men, especially when faced with a rude caller. Regardless of marital status, it wouldn't be long until Jim was taking breaks chatting up the new receptionist, surprising her with his tall tales and flashy, yet almost quirky style. Cowboy boots and a ten-gallon hat one day, Hawaiian shirt and sandals the next. Each outfit had a story to go along, the time he saved a whale while reeling in the largest marlin on record or when he was in Key West and warned all the islanders about the unknown hurricane, single-handedly. Whatever the tale, he was the hero and it was all about Jim. Soon enough they'd be an item, long lunches and late night hours would lead to too much time together, another broken heart, an empty chair out front and the front office phone ringing off the hook.

It amazed Katie how any woman, who with even the littlest of experience in the real world, and some of these women were married several times, could fall for Jim's almost plastic charm. To her, he was a broken record, stuck in the 1970s. He even had bell bottom jeans and a tie-dye shirt to go along with his Woodstock story. John said Jim was more genuine that Katie realized, that she should give him a chance. Katie wasn't wired to give chances.

It wasn't that Jim was unattractive. If he stood still and didn't say a word, he was actually quite good looking, much to Katie's chagrin. For a man with such height, well over six feet tall, he was rather burly too. Broad chested with dense, muscular arms and legs, he looked like two of John when standing beside him. He had a full head of wavy red hair, "From my dear Irish Mum," he often said, and quite amazingly, could grow a beard over the weekend, should it match his Monday attire and fiction. Katie did admit his fair, green eyes were astonishing, and refused to believe they weren't contacts until he took out his contacts and held them up to the light one day.

"Gen-u-ine emeralds, my dear Katie," he said, gloating over her embarrassment.

"Well, what do you expect me to believe? After all, you do have more than ten pairs of glasses, fashion accessories or story props you call them, that don't even have a prescription," she replied, a bright pink color coming into her cheeks.

"Oh Katie, you're such a smarty. That's right," he said drawing out his words, "it was you that walked in, while I was, uh, busy, shall we say?" he laughed, knowing he caught her again.

Such nerve. Jim knew how embarrassed she was, yet, he never let an opportunity pass to remind her that it was she who had barged into the bathroom without knocking and almost ran smack into him, into the back-side of him, actually, as he was standing, facing the other way and um, taking care of business. It was the array on the bathroom counter that caught her attention, several pairs of glasses, a contact case and saline, and men's toiletry bag with enough paraphernalia to make any teenage girl drool.

Turning only his head, he shouted, "Top of the morning, Katie."

Realizing where she was and who he was, Katie screamed and ran out of the bathroom.

John thought it was hilarious and gently told her to get a little sense of humor. "If you laugh, then it's just funny. If you run, then the joke's on you."

Still, it was several months before Katie would step foot in the offices of Marshall and McGlaughlin again.

John knew that Jim had no interest in young women. Early on in their partnership, after the third receptionist, John asked Jim about his age criteria for women.

"How come you go for the vintage ladies?" John asked one evening as they headed down the street for a quick beer after work.

"What would I want with a child?"

"Well, lots of men like younger women. I'm not talking about children, Jim."

"I prefer a little seasoning," Jim said, a smile playing at the corner of his mouth. "Always have, it's just that now, well, they're not much older."

John laughed out loud. "Oh man, we could have doubled dated, mother and daughter," he teased, playfully sucker punching his big friend in the shoulder. It still amazed John how solid this guy was.

Jim grinned, not even registering the blow and said, "Besides, these young women today could be my daughter, for God's sake. That's just plain wrong, even for a playboy like me."

"An old playboy, remember, old? With old playboy bunnies," John replied, laughing so hard, he didn't see Jim's right headed for his shoulder. The easy blow landed and John almost fell off the sidewalk, except for Jim's left holding him steady.

Which is why John had hired Kelly. She was young enough to be Jim's daughter. Finally, he had closed the book on a headache that had plagued their human resources department since the start of their business. Jim barreled into the office every morning, barely taking notice of the young bunny at the desk, other than to watch her jump, with a loud and gut wrenching, "Top of the morning, my dear."

Still holding the phone and pacing the room, Katie's daydream vanished as Jim bellowed, "Still there, my love?"

Grimacing, Katie stopped pacing and stood still. Typical Jim, she thought, a slow smile forming. She looked out the kitchen window, her new bird feeder a host to hungry chickadees and nuthatches and thought, where to begin? Taking a quick breath, she condensed her concern down to one simple question.

"Have you heard from John since he left for Brazil?"

"Sure did. Got a message. Staying on until Friday this week. Ran into a few snags with the deal."

"I got that message too, but since then, I only reach his voicemail and now, this morning, the phone is out of service." Katie exhaled and pressed her fingers to her temples.

"No deal is too complicated for John, Katie. And, he's about the safest guy around." A few moments passed, Jim lowered his voice and continued, "I'll call our partners in Brazil. See if I can get an update. How's that sound?"

Katie continued to watch the birds outside her window, their frantic feeding, typical, predictable. She expected Jim to make fun of her concern, but he was surprisingly matter-of-fact and helpful.

Turning away from the window, she felt a flood of relief. "That would be great," her voice small.

"Keep the phone close, little lady," Jim replied. "Keep the phone close."

Chapter 11

John and Jim were graduates of Dearborn High School, class of 1963. Yet, at the time, they were far from a first name basis. Quiet and studious, John spent most of his free time listening to music, reading, and sketching. His plans after high school were foggy. His father owned a small, successful real estate firm, specializing in residential sales, and he knew there was a place for him. But, he wasn't sure about that. Having spent so much time around the business growing up, it was all too familiar. He wanted something different, only he hadn't figured out just what different would be. He loved the Beatles, The Rolling Stones, and anything Motown. He loved art and losing himself in a good book. His parents, Madeline and Ted were patient and gave him a long tether. As long as he was working at something, he could stay at home and help out when needed.

In high school, guys like Jim were just who John avoided. A lineman who instilled fear and more than a few cases of injury on the football field, Jim was as big in the halls as he was on the field. Loud and good natured, he had a following of admirers, girls and guys, that completed his social circle and calendar. John didn't trust guys like Jim. Figuring no one can be that golden, he kept his distance and his dislike to himself.

The only thing they did have in common was NHS, National Honor Society, and no one was more surprised to see Jim inducted than John. Only increasing his distrust of this too-perfect guy, John purposely avoided Jim. It irritated him that Jim crossed the lines he drew. Disliking Jim was easier when he didn't know him, when he could place himself higher on the academic scale. Being in the same circle at NHS, John had to face the fact that Jim wasn't all that bad. Actually, he was quite bright, quite alright.

Unknown to both of them, they shared a trait few possessed, a photographic memory. Academics came easy and college was an open door. John's indecisiveness left him living at home after high school, while Jim went off to the University of Michigan to crush some Buckeyes. John registered at Wayne Community College and breezed through enough courses in the first year to graduate with his associates in liberal arts. He registered for the fall semester at the University of Michigan, trying out political science, business, and history as possible majors. Taking a job as a tutor seemed to balance his somewhat demanding course load and he found he liked helping other students.

It was less than two years after they left Dearborn High School that Jim and John ran into each other again, leaving them more than a little surprised.

Since high school, John went from being a skinny, gangly teenager, to a full-grown man, just over six feet and two hundred pounds. Rather than indecisiveness, his deep brown eyes and quiet demeanor now reflected confidence.

Jim, for all appearances looked the same, yet, the changes inside were drastic. The recent and sudden death of his mother left him struggling. Grief was overwhelming and he became quiet and withdrawn. No longer the life of the party, his girlfriend dumped him and his posse of followers disappeared. His grades were falling and his place on the Wolverine's line was in jeopardy. Knowing his failings were unopened books and empty classroom seats, he considered tutoring a waste of time. Going against his will, he was angry. Anything less than a C was considered academic probation and a warm seat at game time, so Jim found himself in the library one brisk October Sunday, bright and early. A room was reserved in his name by the athletic department. His instructions were to sign in at the main desk and proceed to room 6A. Jim looked at his watch. Angry at himself for ending up here, angry at his mother for dying and leaving him with his father, and angry at everything else, he stomped into room 6A, and dropped his books on the table, loud enough to question the sound-proof room.

"I don't need a tutor," Jim stated. He looked at the man sitting at the table, not recognizing his old schoolmate. "I'm not some stupid athlete," he added, shoving his hands in his pockets and staring down at John.

John was taken back. Not that he was surprised by Jim's actions. This wasn't the first time he was assigned to an unwilling student athlete. John couldn't believe the student before him was Jim. He looked down at his file and placed his finger under the name at the top of the page, Rosy J. McGlaughlin. Trying to stifle the laugh tickling his throat, he faked a cough and peeked up at Jim. Even more surprising was that Jim didn't even recognize him.

"Jim?" John asked, rising from his seat he offered a handshake. "You don't remember me, do you?"

Taking his hands out of his pockets, only to shove them back in again, Jim took another look at his tutor. There was something familiar, and yet the beard, the height, he wasn't sure. Standing there, he let John's hand hang in between them like an unwanted child. He saw the file on the table and his given name clearly typed at the top of the page.

A smile spread across Jim's face as he remembered this quiet and nice guy from Dearborn. He thought about his own mother and how she refused to let anyone call him Rosy, even if it meant taking the heat from his father. No one in high school ever knew his nickname, thanks to his mother. Rosy was short for Rosenthal, his father's name. It was only after too much to drink that his father called him Rosy, nasty and demeaning. Jim's smile faded and his eyes grew dark.

After his mother died, his father drowned himself in beer bottles, too many to count. It was a slow way to die and an even slower way to watch someone die. Jim knew there was little he could do. When he found out his father registered him at Michigan as Rosy J. McGlaughlin, Jim gave up. His athletic scholarship covered tuition and living expenses, giving him economic freedom. He declared himself an adult, packed his childhood belongings, and announced he was leaving. Dodging a stumbling and cursing father as he walked to the door, Jim grabbed his mother's photo and her rosary. Opening the front door, Jim looked over his shoulder, only to see the blessed mother coming his way, her plaster cast dead on for his head. The old man had pretty good aim. Jim ducked for the last time, negotiating the door just in time to see Mary hit the door, and shatter to pieces. Jim walked away and no one picked up the pieces.

Shoving his hands deeper into his pockets, Jim thought about the chances of meeting up with John at Michigan.

"John," he said trying to smile again. "I guess I need some help after all." Jim sat down and placed his huge hands flat on the table.

Realizing this was not the same Jim and that the name on the application was a closed subject, John relaxed and offered his hand again.

"Well, let's see what we can do, okay?" John said, taking hold of Jim's hand and giving it a good shake.

Jim's step for help had opened the door for a lifetime of friendship. Playing opposites to each other, they made a good team. John helped Jim with his academics and Jim helped John with the ladies. Doors opened all over.

After college, John took a position with a large commercial real estate firm outside Detroit. He found the shiny, high-rise building overwhelming, office politics nauseating. Preferring behind the scenes to big boardroom deals, he locked himself away for hours, crunched numbers, wearing down his number two pencils and himself. John loved the challenge of commercial real estate, but found the dealings right up to the line between good and questionable ethics, leaving him with too many questions. Just because you could legally get away with a huge profit, should you? At what dollar value, does honesty disappear? Where do I fit in? And finally, what am I doing here? Sharpening pencil after pencil, John knew he could call his dad, join the family business, but he never made the call. Deep down, John yearned for something more.

Jim started selling, anything and everything, anywhere. Wherever Jim worked, sales skyrocketed. Newspapers, office furniture, cars were all out the door when Jim was on deck. A large presence, big smile, easy manner and firm handshake made prospective buyers lifelong customers. Followed up with good hard facts and an undisputed sales pitch, all that was left to do was sign on the dotted line. And although successful, Jim felt something was missing. All those sales going out the door didn't add up too much, other than a nice fat paycheck. Never one to care much about money, Jim wanted more. He needed more to make work worth working.

Jim and John kept in touch, meeting a few times a week to jump start their day at the local coffee shop. Early risers and regular customers, it was no surprise to see them waiting by the door for Cindy to open up.

"Well, look who's here for my morning coffee," Cindy said with mock surprise. A handful of years older, she was warm and friendly in a big sister kind of way.

"Bright and sunny, just like the morning, my dear," Jim bellowed with a twinkle in his eye.

"Speak for yourself," John added.

"Just come on in and we'll get you wide eyed before you know it, Johnny boy."

Mumbling something to himself, John grabbed the newspaper off the sidewalk and found himself a seat. Jim went to fetch their mugs and continue warming up Cindy. Oh God, John thought. When will he ever learn. She's not interested. It's been more than six months and Cindy was still turning him down, albeit sweetly. Jim approached women head-on, full attack. Any hint of interest was a wide-open door and the harder the better. Sometimes John thought Jim was more into the challenge than the girl.

"Just another sale," Jim said, sliding into his seat and sliding a smile across his face. "My kind of paycheck."

"Snake." John shook his head and straightened out the paper before him. Even if I could bring on the charm, I'd never hand myself out like that, John thought. Still shy with women, he spent a lot of upfront time observing before he even dared to approach a woman.

"Look at how many you lose, man," Jim said, slurping his coffee. "By the time you get around to clearing your throat, they've cleared out. What if one of them was your one and only?"

"Yeah, like you believe in anything one and only."

"Just looking out for you, buddy."

John looked up at Jim and started chuckling. Instinctively, he turned to the back section to the real estate ads. Looking for a few he posted, as well as the competition, a large tax sale ad caught his attention.

TAX SALE VACANT LAND. Eastern Colorado, Southern Wyoming. Inquire 1-800-222-2222.

John knew all about tax liens and the vultures that bought the liens in anticipation of making good out of someone else's financial misery. But commercial real estate was different. No babies on the sidewalk there. And anyone buying commercial land knew the risks of buying and not paying your taxes.

John looked up. Jim was back at the counter, working the sale.

"Hey, Jim boy, can I get my coffee while it's hot?" he called out.

Pretending not to hear him, Jim laughed a little too loud and Cindy giggled.

"You better get old grumpy his coffee soon or there'll be no cheering him up today," she said looking in John's direction, her eyes soft.

Jim shrugged and grabbed the coffee. With a big smile, he gave Cindy a wink and made his way over to Mr. doom and gloom.

"Great timing, buddy. I was getting close."

"Yeah, right."

"What's the big hurry?" Jim asked, folding his oversized frame into the dainty, coffee-shop chair.

"How about a trip out West?" John pushed the paper in front of him and watched his eyes widen.

"You know, I have an uncle, my mother's side, who always bought these things. Vacant land only. He said people were more likely to default on vacant land, less attachment. He said, waiting for people to screw up a good thing didn't take much waiting."

"So, you're in?"

"Buy the plane tickets, my bag's always packed."

Rubbing his hands together, Jim turned his attention back to the counter and his ongoing negotiations.

That was the first of many trips out west, bidding on tax liens. Over the next few years, Jim and John acquired in patchwork fashion a number of parcels that scattered their first right to purchase, in the event of default, land all over the Colorado and Wyoming border. Pouring over tax records and maps they would plot out their strategy for buying liens and connecting the parcels.

With the gasoline crisis hitting American pocketbooks, liens became sales and Jim and John's stake became larger and larger. Still buying, they held out for a turn in the market and ten years later, in the height of the mid-1980s real estate boom, along with many technology transplants to the mountain region, they cashed in their chips at an enormous profit. Sheltering under a 1031 exchange they avoided large taxation on their gains and hand selected some very desirable property around the country.

Smart enough to hold onto mineral rights and a few properties in Southern Wyoming, they made additional gains in gas wells. Changes in the FLMA, Federal Land Management Agency, regulations, allowing gas wells on federal properties, brought necessary infrastructure to the area for their underground investments to be realized. Money rolled in faster than they could count.

What had started with a morning grouch, a cold cup of coffee, a relentless flirt, and a small ad at the back of the paper, had ended up with two young, single businessmen reaping in a bounty. Good business sense, some hard-earned seed money, and a lot of tenacity played parts as well. Jim had found a reason worth working. John had found answers to his questions. Together, they had found a partnership, grounded in like minds, sound ethics, and a lifetime of friendship.

Chapter 12

Thursday morning, Katie watched Sarah board the bus, the doors close, and the bus pull away. Pulling out her cell phone, she checked for missed calls. No call from Jim. Since her call yesterday and Jim's promise to contact the Brazil partners, Katie had indeed, kept the phone close. Sliding the phone in her back pocket, she sighed.

"Beautiful weather at last, don't you know?"

Katie slowly turned around and smiled. Silently, she chuckled at the ensemble before her. Purple biking shorts, windbreaker, and helmet. Where in God's name did the woman ever find this stuff? she wondered. Even her bike was purple.

"Going for a bike ride, are you?"

"Oh yes. You know, I was out in the shed last week and stumbled across this old bike. It brought back such good memories. Harold and I loved bicycling on a sunny day, don't you know?"

Katie's eyes narrowed as she took in the overall stature of Mrs. Cook and the condition of the bicycle.

"Hmm, just how long has it been since you've ridden a bicycle?" Katie asked.

"Oh, my goodness. Well, I have no idea." A broad smile showed just a touch of lipstick on her two front teeth, purple lipstick. "Listen here young lady, don't go getting all mother hen on me. I am as fit as a fiddle, and no fool either. You can rest assured I will not be doing any tricks this morning."

Katie laughed. "Well, you are right about one thing, you are fit as a fiddle. I don't think I've ever seen you take it easy."

Mrs. Cook adjusted her helmet strap and paused for a moment.

"John's traveling again, isn't he?"

"Yes," Katie answered cautiously. "He's in Brazil until Friday." Kicking a stone across the street with the toe of her shoe, she stared at the pavement.

"You look a little forlorn, my dear. You know a little distance is good every now and then, makes you appreciate each other more."

Katie continued to stare at the pavement.

"You're probably right, but I hate it when he travels. I rush the clock until he returns and then I wonder about all the things I've ignored, forgotten."

"Take it from me, sweetheart, you don't want to rush time," Mrs. Cook replied, laying a soft hand on Katie's shoulder.

Katie gave Mrs. Cook's hand a squeeze and started to turn towards home, when suddenly she remembered something. "Didn't you say the old farmhouse house was vacant?"

"Well, yes. I believe so."

"Well, could anyone be living there? Maybe, taking care of the property?"

"I don't think so. Why do you ask?" Mrs. Cook looked at Katie, eyebrows raised.

"It's that woman, the one at the bus stop on Monday. I forgot all about seeing her last Friday," Katie stopped mid-sentence and looked the other way.

Something kept Katie from telling Mrs. Cook about John's near fatal plane crash and delay in travel plans. After her mother, Mrs. Cook was her next best confidant. And yet, she couldn't bring herself to open the subject. Telling herself she was keeping quiet for Sarah's sake, she had willed herself this far. Tomorrow was Friday. Down to the last day, Katie welcomed any diversion and the strange woman would suffice.

"What woman?" Mrs. Cook asked, her eyes narrowing.

"The one at the bus stop, black clothes, sunglasses," Katie's voice cracked and her hands began to shake. "Oh, I don't know. Maybe she's new. I've only seen her twice. Friday and then Monday in the pouring rain. You didn't see her?" Katie looked at Mrs. Cook incredulously. Mrs. Cook never missed anything.

"No." Mrs. Cook tilted her head and continued to look at Katie. "You think she has a child on the bus?"

"I guess so, but I didn't see a child."

"Hmm. And you think she has something to do with the old farmhouse?" Mrs. Cook asked, her voice serious.

"Well, I followed her," Katie whispered. Turning her head, Katie looked up the hill towards the old Farmhouse.

"Oh my. You followed her?" Mrs. Cook's voice was serious. "What is really going on here, Katie? You can't just go following people," Mrs. Cook scolded, her lips forming a fine line.

Katie's face fell and a floodgate of tears ensued. Mrs. Cook abandoned her bicycle and gathered Katie in her arms. Deep sobs, and a low wailing escaped. Holding her close, she looked up the road over Katie's shoulder. Katie's sobs subsided.

"There's always something deeper, my dear. Why don't you come back and we'll have some tea?"

"What about your bike ride?" Katie asked, pulling away, her voice small.

"Nonsense. Come. Let's get this thing settled." Mrs. Cook retrieved her bicycle and led Katie back towards the house.

Later that day, the phone rang and Katie jumped. Finally, it was Jim. He placed the call to their Brazilian partner. Something about Western Brazil and power outages, bad reception was causing a delay in communication. He hoped to hear something this afternoon or tomorrow morning.

Hanging up the phone, Katie looked out the kitchen window. A flurry of cardinals and finches were working the feeder. More birdseed, she thought. At this rate, I'll be filling up the feeder daily. Her thoughts turned to Mrs. Cook, and the talk they had earlier that morning.

They weren't even in the house and Katie had spilled the events of the last few days, starting with the news Friday night. It was almost silly, how she was so afraid to say anything and yet, once she started talking, she began to feel better. It was as if John would be home tomorrow and everything would be set right again. Although Barbara called her every day that week, they spent most of the time skirting the issue, not wanting to break the spell. As the week wore on, they both found the subject harder to broach and easier to avoid. Katie knew her mother was worried and reliving her own anguished moments when Edward's plane went down.

Katie wasn't surprised there was no news of John. Many areas in Brazil were so remote, they took all-terrain vehicles. Always with a guide and security guard, Katie knew John played it safe. Katie absorbed the latest lack of information. Oh John, she thought, if only I could hear your voice.

Mrs. Cook had told Katie to forget about the woman and to focus on John coming home. Whoever this new and strange woman was, she wasn't worth the anguish, nor worth the risk of following. With a wave of her hand and a smile plastered to her face, Mrs. Cook made Katie promise to stay away from the old farmhouse.

Pulling herself away from the busy birds at her kitchen window, Katie looked at the clock, grabbed her keys and pulled on her jacket. In a few moments, the afternoon bus would arrive and Sarah would need her attention. Mrs. Cook is right, Katie thought. I need to focus on my family. Pulling paper from the drawer and a pen, she wrote, "Welcome Home John".

Leaving the menu for Sarah to decide, Katie walked out into a beautiful April afternoon. The forecast for rain was pushed out, replaced with a bright and sunny day. Still a slight chill, Katie zipped up her jacket and dug her hands into her pockets. Buoyant, as if a weight was lifted, she bounced down the driveway to meet her little girl.

But her resolve was short-lived. Standing there, like an omen, was the strange woman. Still dressed as before, she stood stock still as Katie approached the corner. Ignore her, Katie thought. Mrs. Cook is right. Looking over her shoulder, Katie saw Mrs. Cook's car making its way out of the garage. Katie stopped halfway to the corner and folded her arms over her chest. Stuck halfway between avoiding the woman and willing Mrs. Cook to hurry up, she watched the bus approach. The lights came on, door opened, and Sarah and the three little apostles came running off.

Sarah was calling out to Katie, halfway through a story before she even reached her, jumping up to give her a big hug.

"Mommy, Mommy, you'll never guess who came to school today," Sarah shouted. "Guess, guess," she asked, turning Katie's face towards her and searching her eyes.

"Hold on sweetheart," Katie pleaded.

Placing Sarah on the ground, Katie gave a wave to Mrs. Cook. The three boys raced down the street, past Mrs. Cook's car and up the driveway, leaving a bewildered Mrs. Cook to turn around, negotiate yet another crazy three-point turn, and head back home.

"That little girl is happy to be home, don't you know?" Mrs. Cook called from her car with a wave.

Katie couldn't help but look back up the street for the woman. Surprisingly, she was still there and was looking directly at Katie. Holding her gaze for a moment, the woman stared hard and then turned, placing her right arm out at an angle, as if she was guiding a small child. Making the corner, it appeared as if she was deep in conversation. And yet, she was all alone. Could it be, I missed the child for a third time? Katie wondered, an all too familiar weird and uncomfortable feeling filled her gut.

Hollering now at full volume, Sarah's cries pulled Katie back, "Mommy, you're not listening to me."

"Okay, Okay. Honey, I'm sorry. I was just thinking about that woman."

"What woman?" Sarah asked, looking up the street. "Mommy, you're silly, there's no woman, it's just me, Sarah. Listen to me. Guess who came to school today? Guess. Guess."

"Who? Please, do tell me." Picking Sarah up again, she twirled her around, relishing the child's squeals of joy. Pushing the woman out of her mind, she dove headlong into Sarah's story and together they headed home.

It was a quiet afternoon. Sarah finished her homework and they tackled the Welcome Home John menu. Sarah, so familiar with the ritual, ran to the front desk to get the stationary. An old drop-leaf desk, it was one of the few pieces of furniture they brought with them from Kentucky. It belonged to her father's grandmother. Katie loved the smooth surfaces and deep grains of cherry, the high gloss.

"I'll get it Mommy." Sarah ran full speed into the foyer and yanked open the desk drawer, spilling its contents all over the floor.

"Oh no. I broke it, Mommy," she began crying, her little fists bunched up in anger.

"No worries," Katie comforted.

"But what about Daddy's Menu?" Sarah asked, looking at the few remaining pieces, wrinkled and ripped on the floor.

"No problem, honey. We will just have to make our own. It will be our new menu and you can draw the pictures."

"Really? Little animals and cartoons, like Daddy draws?"

"Sure." Katie sighed, thinking of all the little cartoons in her jewelry box.

"Can I make the little circles, too?"

Katie tilted her head and looked at Sarah. "Circles?"

"For the wishes, Mommy."

"Circles?" Katie murmured, "Wishes?" Suddenly her eyes brightened and she smiled. "You mean bubbles. Bubbles for what they say?"

"Silly Mommy. Bubbles are for the bathtub. You can't put wishes in a bubble." Sarah's face suddenly changed and her eyes lit up. "Hey Mommy, can I have a bubble bath tonight? Please, please, please."

"Slow down little girl," Katie said playfully. "Dinner first."

Sarah took off running for the kitchen. Katie picked up the papers, carefully replacing them in the old drop-leaf desk. A little piece of paper floated to the floor, falling in the fading sunlight of the day, it shimmered, catching Katie's attention. One of John's little doodles, it was funny little Genie floating on a magic carpet. His big belly took up most of the drawing and his little cap was covered in tassels. A little lamp lay at his feet. Katie smiled and thought about wishes. Rubbing her thumb across the little lamp, she made a wish, folded the paper in half and placed it in the front pocket of her jeans. This one stays with me, she thought. Maybe then, little genie, my wish will come true.

Chapter 13

That evening, Sarah chatted through dinner, so much so that Katie found herself lost in thought, rethinking the past week. Despite all her experience as a nurse, numerous tragedies, countless trials, she never experienced the upheaval, the roller-coaster of emotions, of the last few days. Many of her patients were dear to her and hard to lose, especially the children, but knowing the odds against them, she prepared herself. When her father died, it was shocking, but final. They knew he was gone within hours of his plane disappearing. It was the not knowing of John's absence that tormented her, the timeless interim of waiting, everything a heart wrenching reminder, wishing, hoping for news, good news, and finally, just any news.

The, "Welcome Home John" menu lay on the table, an array of markers and crayons, scissors and glue nearby. Sarah continued her chatter and Katie, deep in thought, her torment. Dinner was cold and forgotten. Although Katie felt the crest of the roller-coaster now, something told her the ride was not over, the biggest drop yet to come. Bracing herself, she thought of Mrs. Cook and her mother, widows for years, their strength and courage in meeting each day. Oh John, where are you? she wondered. If only I could hear your voice, lay my head on your shoulder, hold you close.

And that strange woman, her mind raced. Where in the hell did she come from? Am I the only one who saw her? she wondered. Am I going crazy? Just forget about her, just forget, just forget, Katie repeated to herself, over and over.

After dinner, Sarah begged Katie to go on a bike ride and with the sun setting, spreading red and orange hues over the horizon, Katie agreed. Bundling up against the wind, they set out with Sarah first, her training wheels teetering on and off the pavement, counterbalancing her against a fall, first right, then left, with Katie watching from behind. They made a left at the bus stop and headed up the hill.

Katie couldn't help but think about the last time she went up the hill, following the strange woman. Suddenly, she remembered Sarah's fixation on the old property. Sarah called it the woods.

From the time Sarah could speak, she talked about the woods. Given her vivid imagination, Katie never gave it much thought. Until one day, riding home in the car, passing the old farmhouse property, Sarah pointed and said very clearly, "Mommy, the woods." It was a pretty accurate description. Thick, densely populated with evergreens, the property differed from the surrounding neighborhood houses, manicured lawns and green leafy trees. Yet, it was odd. It was this particular woods that held Sarah's attention. Passing many landscapes in their travels, she made no mention of other wooded areas. What was it about this property, woods, house, family that drew her in? Drew them in?

Trying to ride slow enough to stay behind Sarah and still stay upright on her bike, Katie listened to Sarah's endless chatter as they climbed the hill.

"I like...and she has a baby doll that...what do you think Mommy?" Sarah asked turning around to look at her mother, teetering way too far to the right.

"Sarah," Katie cried as she pulled hard on her brakes to stop, just in time to avoid colliding with Sarah, but not soon enough to catch her from toppling over.

Katie dropped her bike and ran to her. "Are you okay, Sarah? What hurts? Oh, I'm so sorry."

"Mommy, I'm okay." A small cut on her forehead began to bleed. "Oh no, my bike. It's all muddy," she cried and more tears ensued.

Katie pressed her thumb against the cut, applying pressure. Taking her hand away, Sarah saw the blood and began to wail. Pulling her close, Katie felt hot tears on her cheek, her soft little hands around her neck.

"Let's pull over here and take a look at you and your bike."

Up righting the small bike, Katie noticed the bleeding slowed, but given the gap, a small scar would remain.

Suddenly, Sarah brightened. "It's the woods, Mommy. Can we look? Can we? Please? Maybe there's a castle?"

Katie looked down the long driveway and thought about her promise to Mrs. Cook. Still, it did look like a good place for a castle and Sarah could use a rest from her bike for a few minutes. The tall evergreens cast deep shadows in the slant of the setting sun. The magic was enough to tempt Katie.

"Sure, just a quick peek. It will be dark real soon."

"Yippee," Sarah cheered and took off running down the driveway.

Left with the bicycles, Katie moved them aside and rushed after Sarah. Out of sight already, Katie rounded the bend, calling out, "Sarah, slow down, I can't see you." So intent on finding Sarah, she didn't even notice the farmhouse. Sarah was standing still in the clearing, staring straight ahead.

"There you are, you little devil. You shouldn't run ahead like that. It scares Mommy," Katie scolded. When Sarah didn't respond, Katie walked around in front of her and knelt down. "Hey sweetheart," she started, but was interrupted by Sarah's stern and serious expression. Staring, as if straight through her, Sarah was fixated on the house.

"I don't like this place, Mommy," Sarah said, her voice trembling, chin quivering.

"Oh, don't be silly," Katie said. "It's just an old house." Placing her hand on Sarah's shoulder, she turned around and couldn't believe what she saw.

There in front of her, was the farmhouse, old and tired, but much different than before. It was as if the house aged a hundred years in the last few days.

"What the," she started to say. "Where's the flowers and the porch swing?" she stammered.

Looking up to the roof, she saw that the northern side all but collapsed. Vines covered the southern side and were growing in and out of the cracks in the crumbling clapboard. The front door was closed, but the screen door, held askew by only the upper hinge, opened and closed with the wind, making a swoosh and a bang as it careened back and forth. Stepping closer for a better look, she stopped. Sarah began to cry and was pulling on her jacket.

"Mommy, let's go." Letting go of her mother, Sarah ran away.

Taking one last look at the house, Katie whispered, "Where in the hell are you, John? I'm losing my mind. I need you."

Tears falling as she ran after Sarah, Katie picked up the pace, knowing she was running away from more than an eerie old farmhouse and a strange woman. If only she knew what she was running into.

Chapter 14

At eleven o'clock that evening Katie climbed into bed and looked around the room. She didn't feel like watching T.V. or reading Fanny Flagg tonight. The red notebook was laying on the nightstand. She definitely didn't want to open that tonight. Turning out the light, she sunk down into the mattress and stretched her arms out wide. Her fingers grasping nothing but empty space, she quickly curled up, retreating to her own side of the bed. First, the old farmhouse, the banging screen door and growing vines, then the strange woman, her stern expression and severe clothing, invaded her thoughts, prevented sleep. Tossing and turning for the next hour, she finally turned on the light and sat up.

This is useless, she thought. Why can't I get that woman or that house out of my head? I'm beginning to imagine things. Sitting on the side of the bed, she dropped her feet into her slippers, pulled on her robe and made her way downstairs to the kitchen. She could hear Sarah's soft breathing, fast asleep. Thank God I have Sarah, she thought. It would be hard to imagine life without her and yet, she remembered John's reaction when had he found out they were to be three.

They were still newlyweds, had just celebrated their second anniversary. Two years of late night dinners, movies and trips to Lake Michigan. Two years of the kind of life they both wanted. Two years with just the two of them, never yearning for more. And yet, in spite of all precautions, Katie found herself one morning, sick for no particular reason. As the week went on and her indigestion became worse, she recalled a little poem her mother often recited.

> Sickness out of the blue,
> A special morning hue,
> Is bound to be,

Nine months you'll see,
A new baby.

Katie was floored. Yet, her biggest concern was breaking the news to John. They thoroughly discussed children and given their late marriage, John's estranged relationship with his only daughter, and Katie's torment in pediatric critical care, they decided the best decision was prevention. Her lack of maternal yearning worried her more than their decision not to have children. Shouldn't I want children? Is there something wrong with me? During the first year they were married, these insecurities would pop up, shifting the ground under Katie, leaving her with questions without answers. At the gynecologist, expectant mothers filled chairs, smiling secret smiles she would never understand, belonged to a club she could not join. And now, a member of the club and owner of the secret, she was afraid to share the secret.

Four weeks later, finding it harder and harder to hide her fatigue and nausea, Katie understood she must tell John. Katie knew he would never turn away his own child. It was his reaction that scared her, stalled her, immobilized her. Katie knew she was being unfair. John had a right to know, now. Agonizing over when to tell him, the news was delivered without her consent.

Saturday mornings were for staying in bed and reading, at least for Katie. John, an early riser, liked his coffee with the Detroit News. Propping up her pillows, Katie reached for her reading glasses and her latest escape, John Irving and a Prayer for Owen Meany. There was something about Owen Meany that made her want to save him, so little and lost without a mother. Katie wondered if a few months ago, would she have felt the same? Sounds from downstairs echoed through the house. The coffee pot dripping, scalding water on the hot plate, John never could wait for the pot to finish, the opening and closing of the front door, dust sweep dragging on the wood floor as John reached for the morning paper. Katie smiled, picturing his robe, bare legs and the cold assault of a chilly Michigan morning. Willing her heaving stomach to settle, she unwrapped a caramel candy, popped it into her mouth, and prayed.

The front door closed and the phone rang. Reaching for the receiver, Katie knocked Owen Meany to the floor. A familiar voice said hello and asked for Mrs. John Marshall. Katie announced herself and before she realized that John picked up the phone downstairs, the nurse informed her that the test was positive. Ceramic on ceramic rang out from downstairs as well as the phone to the floor.

"Is everything alright, Mrs. Marshall?" the nurse asked, her voice a high pitch.

"I think so. Thank you," Katie answered and quickly hung up.

Katie placed the phone back in the receiver, rolled over, and groaned. I don't blame him if he's angry, she told herself, I may as well get this over with.

John was in the kitchen crouched down, sweeping up broken pieces of the handle of his favorite coffee mug. The phone was back in the cradle. Coffee was dripping from the counter and pooling on the floor forging little rivers. Katie grabbed a sponge and knelt down beside John to clean up the mess. John reached over and placed his arms around her, pulling her to him.

"I thought you'd be angry," Katie whispered, burying her head into his shoulder.

John lifted her chin and placing a kiss upon her forehead, looked into her eyes, his expression unreadable. "Yes," he answered, somewhat flatly.

Crushed, Katie dropped her head and began to cry, when John gently lifted her chin once more. "My Tigers cup." A big smile broke out and he began to laugh. Crouched down on the kitchen floor, amidst shards and spilled coffee, Katie laughed too.

"What are we going to do? I'm too old to have a baby."

"You?" he laughed. "What about me? I could be a grandfather."

"I was afraid to tell you. I'm sorry you found out this way." Katie searched his face.

"Well, I had my suspicions. You do look a little, well, green these days. And since when do you like anchovies?"

"You knew. Why didn't you tell me?" Katie leaned over and playfully punched his shoulder.

"I was afraid you didn't want the baby. I wanted you to tell me on your own."

"So, you're not unhappy?" she asked, dropping her hands to her lap and looking down.

"About my Tigers cup, yes. About the baby, no. My baby is having my baby. I am the happiest man in the world."

Nine months later, they had a new member of the family and somehow three made a perfect family.

Katie paused on her way to the kitchen and drew in the sleepy sounds of Sarah's soft murmurs. It seemed like only yesterday they were sitting on the kitchen floor, spilled coffee and ceramic shards at their feet, their lives about to change forever. Turning into the kitchen and turning on the light, Katie looked to the corner where they knelt that day, realizing that in many ways, they were still afraid to be honest with each other. Had it really been six years? No doubt Sarah had a lot to do with the quality and comfort of their marriage. Three is complete, she thought, feeling the pang of John's absence. Tomorrow is Friday and still, no call, she thought, her jaw clenching, eyes stinging.

Katie turned on the coffee pot, grabbed John's Tigers cup, fired up her computer, and opened up internet explorer. Typing into the search engine, she began, "Jackson Farmhouse Steadman Steinenbach writer." Two results popped up on her computer screen.

> FAMOUS WRITER, Steinenbach, Steadman, heir to Jackson-Saginaw Timber Co. fortune, murder orphan…. Detroit Free Press, society archives….

> JACKSON FAMILY HERITAGE…. North Oakland Historical Society……Estate archives….

Selecting the first hit, Katie filled her coffee cup and inhaled the warm, bitter aroma. Well into the morning she worked over the subject, finding various sources and piecing together the mysterious story of the Jackson Family. What a life, she thought. Like something out of a great novel, it made her wonder how many other true life stories, so romantic and tragic, were long forgotten and unknown. But what did this all have to do with that strange woman and the farmhouse? And why am I so obsessed with finding the answers?

Katie sat back in her chair and stretched her arms. Shadows cast across the room, elongating chairs and tables, backlight by the night's full moon. Well past three in the morning, Katie knew if she was going to sleep, it wouldn't be at the computer. Shutting down, she marveled at how modern technology brought not just the world to your fingertips, but also those lives, laying and waiting to be rediscovered. And yet, with John, there was little or no information. Jim promised to call as soon as he heard. She knew he was good to his promise, but the waiting was agony. Barbara would know what to do. She always knew what to do. I'll call her in the morning, Katie thought. We'll have lunch and maybe I can get some sleep. Tomorrow is Friday. One more day, twenty-four hours, 1440 minutes, 86,400 seconds.

Chapter 15

Just before noon on Friday, Barbara was sitting at a table for two in the back of the room. It was early for lunch and Say Jay's was empty. Earlier that morning, when Katie called, Barbara was sleeping. So unlike her to sleep in, Katie wondered if something was wrong.

"Mom, hello, uh, did I wake you?"

"Oh yes. That's okay, sweetie, I have to get up anyway. I was up late watching old movies, couldn't sleep. No call from Jim yet?"

"No. He doesn't seem to be worried," Katie replied, her voice catching in the back of her throat. "Hey, Mom, are you up for lunch today? I know it's a long drive, but I can meet you in the middle?"

Katie readjusted the phone and sorting the laundry, she came across her jeans from the night before and found John's drawing of the little genie. Carefully, she placed the little piece of paper just inside her bra, next to her heart. Here's wishing, she said to herself.

"Sure, honey. No problem. Let's meet at Say Jay's in Lapeer," Barbara suggested. Say Jay's was a busy little cafe on the main street where Barbara and Katie always stopped when passing through town.

"If you're too tired, I can come up there," Katie offered, wondering if her mother was having trouble holding up with John's absence.

"No, not at all. You know me, a little lost sleep won't slow me down. Let's meet at eleven."

Say Jay's cafe was typical of a small Michigan town like Lapeer. Although the County Seat, the town had a bygone nostalgia that gave credibility and longevity to small mom and pop type businesses. From the hardware store to the local grocer, friendly faces and local products were abundant. Having avoided and survived the onslaught of mass-produced franchise retailers and large-chain department stores, the main street area of Lapeer was a welcome place to spend a nice afternoon. The owner's name was Jay and the cafe name came from his wife, Edna's newspaper column, "Say Jay, Whatta' Ya' Say?" A weekly column about the social side of Lapeer, it included the goings on of the locals and lots of information that was funny, but not necessarily useful. Like how to keep your cat out of the bread basket and where Mrs. Wilkonski got her new highlights. Not surprisingly, most conversations at the cafe ended up, with a little editing to fit her opinion, in the column and Jay never had much to say. Edna and Jay owned and operated Say Jay's for the last forty years. Petite and dark, true to her French ancestry, Edna was a whirlwind of motion and words. Her family came to Detrioux in the late 1800s as fur traders and eventually settled in the historic Grosse Pointe area as ribbon farmers. The family moved north in the early part of the twentieth century and ran a small dairy farm. Edna was born and raised on the farm and felt there was nothing better than a full day of hard work. Busy at home and the cafe, Edna also organized the quilting group at church and babysat during services. She volunteered at the elementary school and drove meals on wheels on Wednesdays. All this, in addition to the weekly column. When asked how she did it all and write a column, she'd reply, "Well, I have to do something with all the goings-on around here. Life is too interesting to keep quiet."

Jay moved to Lapeer as a young man, having lost a bet with his uncle. A man of few words, he made his presence known with his size. Standing at six foot four, Dutch through and through, he had hands as big a frying pans and feet like battleships. Topped off with a shock of hair the color of straw and a serious demeanor, he was formidable. In his youth, he was ridiculed for his size, until others no longer found it wise to do so. On the day of his sixteenth birthday he found himself, once again, being tested because of his size. His father's brother, a notorious gambler and risk taker, just won his hand at a local poker game. The losers were far from happy and out to reclaim their loss, by any means. Hiding behind his overgrown nephew, his uncle promised Jay that if he could take care of his pursuers, then he'd split the winnings with him. Too good to be true, Jay ended up before a judge, his uncle behind bars and the winnings part of a sting operation. Jay apologized to the court and asked for leniency. Losing the bet was the best thing Jay ever won. Sent to Lapeer to work on a dairy farm, he met and fell in love with Edna. It was Edna's idea to start the cafe, showcasing farm fresh milk and other local grown items and Jay took to running the kitchen like a professional. Strawberry and gooseberry flapjacks, bacon/tomato/egg grinders, chili/spoonbread soup, hot turkey over fresh cut fries were a few of his inventions. Working alone in the kitchen, he'd come alive in a way he never could with conversation. Content to let Edna do all the talking, the cafe name was a brand of local humor.

Regulars let the door slam behind them, calling out, "Whatta' Ya' Say?" with Jay always hollering, "Ask Edna."

Anxious to see her mother, Katie made her way over to the table. "Hey Mom. Thanks for meeting me." She leaned over and gave Barbara a big hug. Clasping hands they sat down opposite each other, arms outstretched across the table. "People will think we haven't seen each other in years." Katie forced a small smile.

"Well, it feels like years, doesn't it? This has been an awfully long week," Barbara said, squeezing Katie's hand and releasing it.

Taking in her daughter's appearance, Barbara's heart lurched. Her normally flawless hair was a mess, makeup forgotten revealed deep dark circles, and her hands shook uncontrollably. But it was her choice of clothing that made Barbara pause, actually John's clothing. Way too big for her trim petite frame, she was swimming in John's Detroit Tigers shirt. Katie never wore John's clothes.

"Hey Mom," Katie began, "I didn't ask you here to talk about John. I have something else to tell, well, ask you," she trailed off, looking out the window.

The waitress came and took their order. Fajita Quiche for Barbara and a Very Berry Lemonade, plain BLT for Katie and a glass of ice water.

"It's about some things that have, well, happened, in the last week. I forgot all about it at first, with John's plane and then his message, but then I saw her again in the rain and then the farmhouse. It's this woman, so weird," Katie's voice faltered. "I'm sorry. This isn't making much sense, is it?" she apologized.

"Well, not really, but start at the beginning. Tell me about the woman and when you first saw her."

Katie thought about the red notebook and all she wrote, about sitting on the kitchen floor, and John's Tigers cup. Everything was so mixed up. How could she possibly explain, when she didn't even understand it herself? Starting with Friday morning, before, when all was right with the world and her husband was not missing, she recounted the last week, her encounters with the strange woman, and the eerie transformation of the farmhouse. She explained her findings on the internet about the Jackson family and the reclusive writer Steadman Steinenbach.

"This is crazy, Mom. What is going on?" Katie looked at her mother, her eyes wide.

The waitress brought their order and asked if they needed anything.

"Just some silverware, sweetie," Barbara replied. Blushing, the waitress promised a quick return. Tired from talking, Katie looked at her watch, surprised at how much time passed. She looked around the cafe and noticed all the bustle. The tables were full and there was a line at the door. Barbara sensed Katie's confusion and trouble. She knew this was the hardest week of her life. Even harder than her father's death or any loss as a nurse. Katie looked exhausted. Her hands were still shaking and she kept readjusting her hair behind her ear, a nervous gesture so familiar to her mother.

Waiting until the waitress returned with the silverware, she urged Katie to eat and remained silent herself for a very long time.

The chatter of customers filled the room with a buzz, punctuated by a laugh or surprise greeting among old friends. The kitchen doors banged open and closed as orders were delivered, letting out the heat and energy of the kitchen in fragments of words and movements. A woman settled in behind them, requiring more room than most, and an adjustment in space was needed.

"Excuse me," the woman apologized, laughing, not so much for having done anything, but for the amount of space still required. Placing her oversized purse on the floor, the woman encroached far too close for Katie's comfort, her perfume too strong for Katie's taste, and her laughter too loud for Katie's mood.

Barbara pulled the table away from Katie, yielding a sliver of space and room to move. She was not at all surprised at Katie's story nor her encounters with the strange woman.

Barbara took a deep breath and began, "I should have told you years ago. Your father and I, we were determined not to keep it a secret. We were waiting until you were old enough to understand, and then well, your father was gone." Barbara looked down at her hands and noticed that they were shaking too.

"What are you saying, Mom?" Katie interrupted.

Barbara raised her hand and exhaled. "It all started when you were in grammar school. I don't know, maybe five or six years old. You knew things, Katie. Things a kid just doesn't know. Like who was lying or not and if someone was hiding their feelings. It became a problem, and your teacher asked for a consultation with the school psychologist. You accused someone of lying, rather matter-of-factly, and the teacher was at a loss to explain. So, we met with Dr. Rosenthal. I'll never forget his face, such a kind face, and he told us that a very small percentage of children have an extra sensitive sense of feelings and emotions. Whatever you call it, sixth sense, e.s.p., basically it is a child's intuition far beyond those reaches of the norm. His suggestion was to let it run its course. That most children outgrow the sense and it gets buried in life's accumulations of experiences. Dr. Rosenthal said that adults who retain this ability, and it is truly rare, cultivate the sense. In his experience, it was best to let you be a child. We continued to see him for the several years and eventually, it did seem to run its course." Barbara reached for Katie's hand.

Katie stared at her mother, her eyes widening. "I remember meeting with a nice old man. He wore a grey sweater, right? But, I didn't know he was a doctor," she trailed off, withdrawing her hand from Barbara's, she let it fall to her lap.

"I'm so sorry sweetheart," Barbara said, tears beginning to fall. "I never meant to keep this from you. I just wonder, now, with everything going on and all the stress you are under, if maybe this sense of yours is, I don't know, heightened?"

Staring at each other, Katie let out a small grunt and closed her eyes.

"Katie," Barbara pleaded. "If you're the only one to see this woman, there must be a reason. Maybe she knows you can see her and she is asking something of you." Barbara looked at Katie hard. "Katie, you are not crazy. Whatever you are experiencing is real."

Katie sat there, eyes closed. A slow wave of nausea overwhelmed her. White noise filled her ears and she felt herself fall, slowly into a trance. She thought about all the things in her life that seemed so strange, how tragic news was more often than not, not a surprise. Her struggles with love, wanting so much to be in love and yet, knowing how untrue it would be, meeting John and the feeling that all in the world was right. Her struggles in the pediatric ward and personal attachment to the very sickest and terminal of cases and sweet Jessie, Oh God, she knew even before they brought her in on a stretcher. Suddenly, she opened her eyes. Looking around the cafe, so many faces, so much activity, her head began to spin, throat began to close. Standing up, she stepped on the woman's purse behind her and almost fell.

"Oh, I'm so sorry," she cried.

Barbara reached out, but Katie stopped her. "No, Mom, stay."

Outside the cafe, she looked at her watch and realized she was late for the bus. Oh no, Sarah. It dawned on her, Sarah and the painting, Sarah and her all too adult understanding. Grabbing her keys from her purse she ran to her car.

Just about to pull out, she saw Barbara running after her. Rolling her window down, Barbara stood before her, breathing hard, pleading, crying. Her face was red and her hair a mess, blowing all around her face.

"Katie, this is all too much, but you can't run away." Gripping the open window, her soft hands blanching, she looked at

Katie hard, saw her anger and resentment. "I'm so sorry, Katie. I should have told you. I was afraid."

Katie placed her hand on the gearshift. She turned away and stared out the windshield. A light sprinkling of rain began to fall. Barbara's soft sobs and heavy breathing filled her ears and melted her heart.

"Mom, I have to go. Sarah."

"Oh Katie, sweetheart, take it from me, running away is like digging shallow graves. You never escape," her breath short, raspy, she continued, "the problem with shallow graves," she paused gasping for air, "what you bury never stays, always rises to the top." Looking at Katie's profile, she pleaded, "Life is hard, Katie. You have to dig deep. I know you understand. Dig deep, Katie. You owe yourself that much."

Katie looked at her mother, so upset, her eyes wet, cheeks raw. Katie understood. She knew she didn't want to be her mother, a widow with a child. A deep ache pierced her gut, long and hard. Wincing, she put the car in drive.

"I'm sorry, Mom," she cried. "I'm so sorry."

Katie called Mrs. Cook to get Sarah off the bus. As the miles began to pass, she felt her tension ease. She began to organize her thoughts with this new information. Even if what her mother said was true, even if she looked at life a little differently now, what did it really mean? The doctor said adults must cultivate the sense. Well, she certainly never did any cultivating when it came to emotions. If anything, she swept her emotions away. She buried herself in tasks, felt the satisfaction of a job well done, and hoped the issue would go away. Shallow graves, she thought. Oh, I have a few of those. I'd probably fill more than a few graveyards in that department.

But with John, things were different. It was all she could do this week, to keep from falling apart, crying at the sights or sounds of something that reminded her of him, and her hands, dammit, if they would only stop shaking. Gripping the wheel even tighter, she thought about the strange woman. Could she possibly be asking something of me? Why me?

It certainly was a puzzling story, the Jackson family and that mysterious farmhouse. Katie's thoughts drifted to her findings on the internet. There was a lot of information about the original Jackson family, their children, and the next generations of Jacksons that lived in the house. The Jackson heir inherited a timber fortune earned by the hard work and ruthless practices of his father, grandfather and great-grandfather. Their millions, only exceeded by the number of trees felled whose purpose it seemed was solely to print Jackson money, was held privately and safe from the stock market crash of the 1920s. There was a notation about his fortune in spite of the depression. Must have kept his money to himself, Katie thought. There seemed to be a lot of secrecy in this family story, because all of a sudden, the story just ended. It was as if they vanished from the historical archives altogether. There was mention of a wedding in 1968, Daniel Jackson, a preacher strangely enough, to a Victoria Emerson and then one very brief article about the tragedy, murder and money and a little boy orphaned. Katie connected the dots easily enough.

The little boy, heir to the Jackson fortune, was now known as Steadman Steinenbach, a famous writer and recluse. Every search about a Victoria Emerson came up blank. Thinking back to the strange woman at the bus, Katie thought about the name, Victoria. If only I had a picture to go with the name, could she possibly be the woman from the bus? It was all so strange.

Turning onto her street, Katie could see the bus already came. One of the Anderson boys dropped his lunch box. Scooby Doo was lying in the middle of the street, face up.

Katie stopped to retrieve the lunch box, when she saw the rear end of a car in her driveway. Too far away to guess the owner and just out of line of sight, she wondered who it could be. Her thoughts were still on the old farmhouse and the Jacksons when she pulled in behind the car.

Taking up the entire left portion of the vehicle, it could only be Jim. One leg emerged, crisp jeans and fine leathered cowboy boots. As he unfolded his frame, Katie noticed how strange he looked, so tired and serious. Katie stepped out of the car, leaving the engine running and the door ajar. Her knees threatened to buckle and her legs melted.

Jim crossed the short distance between them in two long strides, wrapped his arms around her and enveloped her in his huge embrace.

"Katie, I'm so sorry. They can't find him. Found the vehicle, the driver and bodyguard on the side of the road, dead. Recovered all his belongings, cell phone, laptop, duffle bag." He squeezed her even harder and Katie felt herself go limp.

"The consulate is working with the Brazilian government, no ransom note, very unusual, three days they think since the ambush," he whispered, hot words, like liquid fire seared deep into her brain. "I've got international legal and a private investigator on this, Katie. We will find him. I will find him. I promise." Pulling away, she lifted her head. Tears ran down his face, his eyes angry, chin firm.

"I can't do this," she cried out. Placing her hands flat on his chest, she pushed him away, surprising him with her strength.

Breaking the embrace, Katie caught the edge of the door and her shirt ripped. Looking down, the bottom half of John's Tigers shirt, hanging by a thread, she stammered and fell a step back. Turning, she jumped back into her car and took off down the street. Water ran from her eyes, nose and mouth. Her hands, slippery on the wheel, turned at the corner, her vision, blurry and streaked, evergreens and the old farmhouse up ahead. "No. Oh God no," she cried. "You were coming home, today. Why? John, why?" she screamed, banging her fists against the steering wheel. Making the turn at the evergreens, the car slowed to a crawl, drifted to a stop. Stepping out into the bright sunshine, she looked up, clouds dotted the sky, birds flew, dogs barked. Towering evergreens along the long driveway created a tunnel-like illusion, the clearing ahead, a light at the end. Katie felt drawn to the clearing, drawn to the light. Closing her eyes, she let the warm breeze run over her, the bright sunshine soak in. Take me away, she whispered and giving into the pull of light, she relaxed.

Taking small and steady steps, Katie walked down the driveway towards the house. There was the brown clapboard and white trim, the screen door fit snugly, tight against the wind teasing at its corners. The same pansies in a pot and the porch swing. Rocking back and forth it appeared to be occupied. The whole place had a surreal and strange magnetic feeling. It was exactly as before, when she followed the strange woman. Katie felt safe, yet drawn to the house. She noticed two cars parked to the side. They were new, and yet, she was pretty sure they were made in the seventies. One, looked just like her mother's old car, a red Ford Mustang, the first car Katie learned to drive. Taking a deep breath, she let her hands drop to her sides, and with eyes wide open, walked straight into the glaring sun and onto the porch.

To her left, a row of rocking chairs moved back and forth silently. The wind picked up, rustling a stack of discarded newspapers and Katie turned. Picking up a page, her mouth fell open and she placed a hand to her forehead. Blinking a few times, she took in the front page, "Sunday Free Press, May 29, 1977." The ink, only days old, left her fingers black. Dropping the newspaper, she felt her bearings loosen and a somewhat familiar strange feeling in her gut. The squeak of a swing caught her attention and slowly, dazed and dream-like, she turned.

There on the swing, swinging, was a small boy, fast asleep. Chubby, in the way of a loved child, he appeared to be five or six years old. Dressed in a bright red, two-piece polyester leisure suit, a wide-collared Hawaiian shirt underneath, his socks mismatched, he made Katie pause, fleeting images of the Bee Gees, disco, and Motown reminding her of her youth. Katie stared at the little boy and felt a deep and piercing sadness. White planks on the porch floor amplified the bright sun, making the child on the swing appear as if he was mid-air.

A floorboard creaked and the child stirred. He was lying on his side, his arm stretched out, his little hand, palm up, a tight fist. Tilting her head, Katie peered closer to get a better look. Swinging back and forth, the boy came within a few feet from her. On the backswing, he disappeared into the bright and glaring sunlight, only his outstretched fist visible, as if bearing a secret.

Opening his eyes slowly, he looked at Katie and smiled. In the dying wind, the swing came to a stop. Slowly, his little fist uncurled.

Raising one hand to shield the blinding light, Katie touched his outstretched hand. She felt a tingling sensation up her fingers, converging at her wrist. As she wrapped her fingers around his hand, she felt a pull, deep within her soul, like a newly born child, first at the breast, the soft folds of a child's hand, and the promise of a small and delicate key.

Eyes locked, hands clasped, breath held, they crossed a barrier, an incomprehensible dimension, a crossing Katie never believed possible, a small boy would never understand, and a strange woman so desperately needed. Bridging more than a thirty-year span, Katie and the small boy held fast, the moment frozen in time.

Suddenly, the child's eyes widened at the sound of gunshots.

Katie felt her grip loosen, her vision blur. Sounds disappearing into wind, sights lost in illumination, Katie floated, amorphous, warmed by the loving touch of a child, she let herself fall. Falling on moments of metaphors, diving into waves of the past, searching, searching, and for once, no longer running away, she began the beautiful process of digging deep.

BOOK II

THE DEEP PAST
Years 1870 – 1920

Chapter 1

In the early nineteenth century, Michigan's forests were a vast and untapped natural resource. Native Americans, French trappers, and European missionaries most familiar with the land, had little impact upon the forests. However, by the 1830s, commercial timber production began with Michigan's most common and favorable tree, the white pine. Growing straight and tall, some reaching several hundred feet in height and almost ten feet in diameter, these 300-year-old beauties were the first to go. Saginaw boasted over three million acres of white pine and more than 1500 miles of navigable rivers and streams. Too early for rail, water was the method of transportation. Felled in the winter, the timber was cut into logs and transported by horse drawn sleds over snow. Stacked on the frozen rivers, there they remained until the spring thaw brought the rivers to life and the logs to fruition, where the sawmills would sort, claim and cut.

For those determined enough to work under the harshest of winter conditions, there was money to be made. Sprung from absolute poverty, American immigrants were put to the test, some making fortunes far beyond dreams. Daniel Arthur Jackson was destined for such a fortune. So eager to claim his new country, he made his arrival far earlier than expected. Sailing upon an angry and miserable Atlantic Ocean, the "Saint Elizabeth of the Seas" register was amended, 28 days into the voyage, to add one additional passenger, "boy, Daniel Arthur, son of Samuel A. Jackson and Elizabeth Marie Jackson, this twenty-eighth day of February, in the year of our Lord, 1870."

Daniel's father had come to America for the same reasons every other Scot-Irishman left Ulster behind. Irish in the geographic sense only, the Ulster people were protestant descendants from the Scottish and English who colonized the Ulster Province of Ireland in the seventeenth century. Two centuries later, although the immigration more of an ebb than flow, the reasons remained the same, freedom and opportunity. And although poor, he did have one advantage. Samuel Arthur Jackson had an invention.

From the time he was ten years old, Samuel spent long days working alongside his father and uncles, felling trees for a living. It was the potato famine that brought the men back to the forests. An old trade belonging to their fathers and grandfathers, they learned the trade as youngsters. Depletion of the forests sent them home to farm, yet at the mercy of English rule. Landlord-tenant laws limited the size of a farm to little more than an acre and a half, leaving no other choice but to cultivate potatoes. In 1839, the potato crop in Ulster failed. By 1845, crops were failing all over the island, the "taint," the "dry rot," or the "curl," cruel adjectives responsible for the starvation of entire populations, so casually applied to describe the deadly virus, applied equally to its victims and their hideous symptoms. And yet, they were so much better off than the Catholic Irish who were starving by the thousands. When farming became futile, Samuel's father and uncles returned to the trade of their origins, travelling far distances to fell what trees were left, filling the bellies of their famished families back home.

Hard work for a young man, Samuel bore those relentless, tortuous hours dreaming of almost anything other than his cold feet and food starved stomach. Fashioning fairytales in his head, he would fell thousands of trees with one blow of the axe, clear hundreds of acres, all for the glory of a warm bowl of soup and his mother's loving embrace. In the little time he had to himself, he fashioned tools and odd looking axes, all designed to save time and labor. Most of his inventions went to naught, yet his mother encouraged him to continue. "The good Lord gave you a mind for a reason, Samuel, and there 'tis no sin in using it wisely."

It was on a miserable, cold and rainy March day that Samuel's father and uncles gave him the measure of his manhood.

"Seeing how 'ur as big as a man now and right strong enough as two, we think 'ur ready for the cross cut, my boy," his father's eldest brother said.

Samuel looked at the men gathered around him. Bright beady eyes, toothless smiles, and weather worn visages fixed him with their attention. Taller by two heads than most, Samuel was a giant by Ulster standards. Long days of hard physical labor lent his fifteen-year-old frame the power and strength of a man. His father, the youngest of twelve, was also on the tall side, and standing now beside him, Samuel thought they looked like the leaders of elves. Years of back breaking work reduced his uncles to bent and sinewy old men, yet one never underestimated their strength. And like the trees they felled, these men were a dying breed. With less than two percent of the island belonging to forests, they knew their days in the woods were numbered, just like the men, just like the trees. But to Samuel, they were the heroes of his fairy tales. They could fell evil trees ten times their size and thousands of pounds in weight. Magic with the axe, just the right cut would send the giants crashing, the echo of their fall reverberating through the forests, like the cry of the conquered.

"We're in the big ones now, my boy," His father said, referring to the section of the forest where trees were three, sometimes four men around. "Time to pull 'ur weight."

Samuel was impressed by this promotion and eager to show his worth. The cross cut was one of the hardest, requiring brute strength and hours of endurance. After the tree was felled, it was cut into cross sectional lengths for transport out of the forests. Hundred foot trees required ten or more cuts. In teams of two, the men would line up opposite each other and work across the log making precise cuts with their axe until they met in the middle. Unlike felling a tree, where gravity was a bonus, cutting a felled tree in cross section was all hard work. Samuel knew there must be a better way. He knew, if he could combine the strength of two men, the cuts would go faster and easier. It was just as he met his partner in the middle, the clash of their axes ringing through the forest, sparks rising, that the idea was born. What if there was one axe, long enough to cut through, made for two men? he thought. Samuel envisioned them pushing and pulling, a tandem back and forth with strength of two men. He couldn't wait to get home to tell his mother, to get to work on this new axe, the cross-cut axe.

Heaven may belong to dreamers and the world to doers, but with the design of his new cross-cut axe, Samuel had heaven on earth. In bringing his dream to life and then to the minds of business, Samuel opened the door to the new world. Papers were filed and tickets purchased for him and his new wife to travel to America. They were headed to Michigan, America's largest timber producing state. Five years after the end of the civil war, the new country was beginning to heal. It was the future America was looking towards and for Samuel Arthur Jackson there was no turning back.

"Blame it on the boat. He's been restless from the day he was born," she said moving from the stove to the table. Pouring his tea, she took a step back to avoid the steam intent on escaping.

Samuel wrapped a long arm around her waist and pulled her to him, "Come 'ere my love," he begged. "Sit a while with me, dear."

Elizabeth felt herself melting into his embrace. Even after all these years, more than ten since they left Ulster, she found his gentle and loving pursuit of her inescapable.

"And what will I get done today, if all I do is sit in 'ur godforsaken lap?" She asked, her stern attempt falling short of the mark.

"Hmm, let me see," he replied, his voice trailing off, muted by the soft folds of her neckline.

Closing her eyes, Elizabeth relaxed, her body mending to his, but her mind wandering. Oh, she loved her husband, more than she ever thought possible. A fixed marriage it was, a way to solve a problem, so to speak. What with ten daughters and no sons, her father grabbed every opportunity. Samuel was something of a legend in their village, and inventor who attracted the eyes and ears of those with money and power, those with interests in the new world, where endless forests meant endless opportunity. Too busy in the forests and tool shop for love, he was already nineteen when he found fortune and then fortune found love. Elizabeth thought back to that day, her mother had gently brushed her long hair, taking more time than usual. Her sisters at her feet, touching her, searching her eyes for something to keep of her. Her father, nervous and short, "Hurry on, Woman," he repeatedly stated, making large strides back and forth across the small room, avoiding all eye contact.

The minister, his long robe and gold gilded bible so out of place in their small makeshift home. A knock on the door, the rush of cold air and then, Samuel, tall and lean, a thick cap of blond curly hair, turning his hat around and round in his hands, nervous, searching her face for something. It was his smile, warm and inviting that stilled her racing heart.

Samuel gave them hope, their families, the village, and then growing in the way of folklore, to all those of Ulster who needed a dream. The old ways were killing them at the hands of the English and yet, as if in spite, here was Samuel, a young, poor, unknown, uneducated man, God given with the brilliant mind to save them all, rising above. And on top of it all, he only had eyes for her. From the day they were married, they were kindred. Ten years later, they had more children than she could count on one hand, and all it took was one look in her eyes for her racing heart to still.

"What he needs is work," Samuel said, rising from his chair to look out the window. "I was quite a handful to my own mum, that is, until my da took me to the forests."

"Oh Samuel, but he is so small for his age," she pleaded.

"A boy becomes a man by hard work, Elizabeth. You have your hands full here and he is of no help at all, running amuck with a bunch of sisters. Even in the New World with all its new inventions, there is hard work to do," he finished, closing the subject for good.

Daniel may sit on a bed of gold, his father thought, but he won't appreciate any of it, unless he starts at the bottom. In Saginaw, the bottom meant long hours of hard labor in the dark, cold forests. But, Samuel would be there to guide him and watch over, just as Samuel's father and uncles did for him. Samuel knew that money changed men, it could make them cruel and careless with those who toiled under them. Yet, if a man walked in their shoes? What Samuel wanted most for Daniel was for him to appreciate his fortune and have compassion for those he would have the means to master.

A year younger than his father was when he went to work, Daniel was unfamiliar with the hardships of life. Being the first born and the only son lent him special privileges his sisters and even his mother didn't enjoy. All too often Samuel would feel the pull of his own age upon him and yet, Daniel was so small he hated to put too much strain on his small frame. But enough was enough and pregnant again, Elizabeth was short on patience for his antics and troubles.

At ten years old, Daniel was the smartest pupil in Saginaw Primary School. Within a few months of his start at the little red schoolhouse, he mastered his alphabet and numbers. Within six months he was reading primers and working complex addition and subtraction problems. His teacher, Miss Windall, placed his desk in the front row and as soon as he finished one task, she placed another before him. Daniel was a machine. He could work for hours at a time, so focused, not even a ruckus amongst the other pupils could detract his attention. Yet, should his hands and mind become idle, they didn't remain long. Comfortable in a home of the opposite sex, Daniel would start first with the little girls, playfully pulling their hair or making eyes at them. Soon the other boys would join in and Miss Windall would have to call outside recess just to break up the commotion.

This was not the first-time Elizabeth was called to the classroom.

"What has my lad gone and done this time?" Elizabeth asked, gasping as she lowered her heavy frame into a chair.

"Oh Mrs. Jackson, I am so sorry to have called you all the way down here. If I knew, well, I would have made the trip to you." Miss Windall reddened, hiding her surprise and astonishment that such a small woman could have such an enormous middle.

Elizabeth stood at exactly four foot six inches or more precisely three-quarters of the way up her husband's frame. She had flaming red hair that seemed in constant motion, bright green eyes etched with brown, and a quick and ready smile. Walking together, Elizabeth and Samuel appeared as one, for they fit like a jigsaw pieces with her head snug up under his arm.

"No worries, my dear, it seems I am winded all the time these days. A little deep breathing never killed anyone. Besides, the air feels good. I spend way too much time at the stove. You know, on the way over, I saw at least thirty juncos feeding at the bottom of the big pine tree. Thirty, can you imagine that?" Elizabeth exclaimed.

Not quite sure what to say about juncos, for Miss Windall felt the most out of place out-of-doors and the last person you'd find walking amongst the pines on a cold January afternoon, she nervously walked over to the stove and began poking at the fire.

"Are you warm enough, Mrs. Jackson?" she asked, turning just slightly over her shoulder to see Elizabeth holding her head in her hands.

Hurrying to her side, she begged, "Are you feeling poorly? May I get you a cool drink? The baby is not due anytime soon, I hope," she stammered, feeling foolish and yet hoping she wouldn't have to do anything "mid-wifely" for worse than the out-of-doors for Miss Windall, was the sight of blood. All it took was one drop and drop she would, right to the floor. Having a father for a doctor, Miss Windall should have been used to the sight of blood and yet having fainted every time, she never had the opportunity. It was her brother who would follow in father's footsteps.

Elizabeth raised her head and smiled.

"Oh dear child," she said, grasping Miss Windall's cold and clammy hand, "I think it might be me who should be offering you a cool drink, no?"

Miss Windall took a seat next to Elizabeth and sighed. "I am a little out of sorts today, it seems."

"And a wee bit young for so many little lads and lassies?" Elizabeth inquired.

"Yes, yes, well, maybe just a few. But I love them so, Mrs. Jackson. I just wish I had more experience with so many children."

"Ah, yes. Experience is something. But ya' know, it takes more than that. I have enough of me own kids and plenty of experience you might say, but when it comes to book learning, well, my stick is a little short, ya' know." Elizabeth giggled, pushed back her unruly hair, and placed her hands on the next little Jackson-to-be.

"Mrs. Jackson," Miss Windall began.

"Please, dear, call me Elizabeth, now that we've confessed our weaknesses to each other." Smiling brightly, her green eyes danced.

"Elizabeth," Miss Windall took a deep breath. "I need to speak frankly with you about Daniel."

Elizabeth's expression turned serious.

"Please forgive my introduction to this matter, it is just that Daniel told me that he will be leaving his studies to work in the forests."

"Ah. Yes. That would be his father's wishes."

"And yours, if I may be so bold?" Miss Windall inquired, somewhat warily.

"Well, we don't have all day to cover a mother's wishes, now do we?" Elizabeth answered quite matter-of-factly.

"No, I suppose not," Miss Windall replied. Rising from her chair, she returned to the stove to gather her thoughts more than to pick up the heat. Turning around, she stood before Elizabeth.

"I will be honest with you, Elizabeth. Daniel is the brightest student I have ever taught and although I am young, I do know the difference between smart and bright," she explained. "I hope you do not mind, but I took the liberty of sending some of his work to the Brothers at Detroit College. They have replied with an interest in his education."

Elizabeth remained silent. If Miss Windall was going to plead her case for Daniel, she may as well do so without interruption, she thought.

"Do you know of Detroit College?" Miss Windall asked carefully.

"I have heard it 'tis a long way off from 'ere and that a bright lad can get a lot of learnin' there."

"Yes, that is true. It is just that Daniel has so much to offer. It won't be long before he will outgrow what I can teach him here at our little school. And I know about your husband's good fortune. I know you are better off than most families around here."

"So," Elizabeth began slowly, "You want me to go on home and when my husband comes in from a long 'ard day in the forest, when he is short on patience and long on temper, you want me to ask 'im to send his only son, his first born, far away to be raised by the *Catholics*?"

Miss Windall's eyes widened. So, she knew more than she let on. Quite a puzzle, some of these families, Miss Windall thought. By all appearances Elizabeth and Samuel seemed like plain and simple people and yet, when she spoke with her father, he knew about Samuel's invention and how he amassed such a fortune with so little education. "There is always more, if you're willing to dig deeper," her father said. Strange words for a surgeon, she thought. But, she understood. Her father knew that understanding your lack of understanding was sometimes the greatest understanding of all.

"Elizabeth, I too am a protestant, and yet I was educated by our Roman Sisters. Don't let the differences of church get in the way of a young boy's future. We all serve the same God and yet, who better to teach a young man the ways of the world than the Jesuits. They are the brightest minds, have traveled the world over," she pleaded. "The world is changing and if our children don't change with it, they'll be left behind. Daniel has the mind of a leader, the energy of a catalyst, and the compassion to do all in the name of God." Miss Windall finished, took a deep breath, and folding her hands in front of her, she relaxed against her desk and waited for Elizabeth's reply.

"I do hope this one is a boy," Elizabeth said, patting her middle, eyes cast downward. "You know; I fear for the girls. Life is so 'ard for them. A woman lives at the mercy of men. And to hope for so many good men to take care of me girls," she said turning serious. "But, a boy is different. A man can make his way in this world. He can be independent and choose his way, if he has opportunities." Taking a deep breath, Elizabeth looked up at Miss Windall. "You are right. Daniel is a bright boy and there is little here for him at school or home. But, he is a boy and before he can choose what he will do with his life, he needs to know his choices. He needs to know there is more to this world than the God forsaken forests." Setting her chin firmly, Elizabeth placed her right hand on the desk and pulled up to a stand, a somewhat off-balance stand, but up-right all the same. "So what do I say when the man of the house comes home, Miss Windall?" Elizabeth asked, a slight smile forming at the edges of her mouth.

Miss Windall placed her arm around Elizabeth's shoulders conspiratorially and whispered, "Tell him Daniel has won a scholarship."

Chapter 2

"Good morning, Mr. Jackson. What a nice surprise." she greeted Daniel with a quick smile, her fingers typing furiously, somewhat of their own accord.

"To you as well, Melinda, but please, shhh, I hope to catch the old man off guard," he whispered, a finger to his lips as he silently turned the doorknob to his father's office.

"Oh, now Daniel, it has been a rough morning so far. Tread carefully," she cautioned, typing away.

Melinda was a real beauty and as a young boy, Daniel would lose all track of time watching her type, while he waited for his father. Her petite frame was crowned with the palest of green eyes and rich, deep auburn hair. Swept up in a neat pile upon her head, it gave a beautiful view of her long slender neck as it plunged deep into the hidden recess of the conservative business dress of the day. In the hot summer months, a young Daniel would watch beads of sweat form on her brow, their slow descent down her cheek and neck, making him wish he could alleviate her distress, and his, in some way. Too young to understand his infatuation, he vowed devotion to no other than Melinda, that is, until his father's deep and commanding voice broke his reverie, commanding his attention.

With the door cracked barely an inch or two, hard voices escaped, as if they wished nothing other than to get away.

"What do you mean, you can't finish the job?" his father's voice boomed. Silence followed with tension as thick as an Irish morning fog. "My suggestion is this, go back to your drawing board or whatever the hell you call it, pray for a good measure of intervention and come up with a better plan," Samuel bellowed, closing the subject for now and dismissing the unfortunate messenger.

Quick, determined footsteps sounded a hasty exit. Daniel moved behind the door, catching a glimpse of a small, bespectacled man, an armful of papers and a face full of woe trying his best to hide and escape at the same time.

Melinda continued to type, her eyes following the man in miniature as he left, coming almost full circle in her chair, never missing a key.

"Poor man, you can't help but feel sorry for him," she murmured, shaking her head. "What fool would send such a man before your father?" she clicked her tongue.

I wonder if she types in her sleep? Daniel thought. Blinking a few times and nodding his head, more to clear the enticing visions of Melinda in slumber than in agreement with her observations, Daniel peeked around the door and into the room. Met by his father's broad back, he silently slipped in and took an empty seat.

Daniel watched his father from behind. Still tall and imposing, he was a man many feared. His hands clasped behind him, such a familiar sight, made him appear like a general surveying his army before battle. Daniel admired and loved his father.

A deep exhale, followed by an attempt to control his unruly hair, Samuel stood at the window staring out at the beauty of the Saginaw River, a symbol of all his success and fortune. The mid-morning sun shimmered off the water, making it easy to daydream of warmer days, yet Samuel knew the truth. April was still winter in Saginaw and although there was no snow this particular morning, one couldn't be so sure about tomorrow. One thing for sure, this beauty he admired from afar was not to be so appreciated experienced firsthand. Many cold and miserable days he spent laboring in the forests and even though now he climbed his way out and beyond, he felt for those who toiled in his favor on this cold and deceptive morning. It was because of this appreciation, those who worked for Samuel considered themselves fortunate. Fair, yet firm, he demanded a hard day's labor for a good return in wages. So dedicated were his workers, they placed their sons' names on the work list to be sure of a safe and reliable future for their families.

Samuel came a long way from Ulster, much farther in economic and metaphorical terms than in distance and a great distance it was. His invention led him to crew leader, then section manager, soon followed by partner and then in a windfall year to buy out the entire company. Saginaw Timber Incorporated became Jackson-Saginaw Timber Company in 1885. Samuel hung his first cross-cut axe over his desk and at Elizabeth's urging replaced his suspenders and flannel of the forests with more fashionable attire. With "wings" on his shirt collar and a "four-in-hand" for a necktie, Samuel appeared more like a bear dressed like a man than a man in the popular "ditto suit" of the day. Regardless of how sudden this change appeared to those familiar with his casual side, it didn't take long to see how easily he could successfully command a board room and direct a company, making millions out of wood.

Unable to suppress a tickle in his throat, a squeak escaped and a shy smile emerged across Daniel's face, betraying his presence. Samuel turned to see Daniel's smile and surprise met pure joy.

"Daniel, my boy," Samuel bellowed and in two giant strides he made his way from the window to bear hug Daniel right off his seat. "What a wonderful surprise," he exclaimed, placing his son's feet back on the floor, he held him at arm's length, looking at him up and down as if to be sure this was indeed his long-awaited son. "We didn't expect you for another month, my boy. To what do we owe this early return?" Samuel asked, pulling him once again to embrace.

"Well, I finished up my term early. Professor Hardy allowed me to test on the remaining subjects and return home to clerk until I could take my final exams."

"And have you found a judge worthy of your measure?" Samuel asked, both a twinkle and a tear in his eye.

"Ah, for that, you'll have to wait, dear Da," Daniel said, falling back into his childhood Irish intonations. "I have a lot to tell you and Ma, but for now I was hoping we could see the work?" he asked, raising his eyebrows, a smile playing at the edges of his mouth.

"Oh, what the hell," Samuel said. "All this paper will be here tomorrow," he bellowed with a broad and infectious smile.

"If you keep cutting down trees, it will," Daniel chided.

"You mean, we, my boy. Now that you're home," he said, slapping Daniel across the shoulders, a little heartier than Daniel expected.

The old man was still an ox, Daniel thought admiringly. Samuel pulled two pairs of work boots from the closet and some cold weather gear.

"Melinda, my dear," Samuel said opening the door to his office. "Please have the wagon brought around. Daniel and I are going to meet the cutting crews."

"Should I cancel your afternoon appointments?" she asked, her fingers still working the keys.

"And those of tomorrow also," he shouted, grinning from ear-to-ear.

Melinda's fingers screeched to a halt. Looking up at both men, she saw a similarity she never noticed before. The unruly hair, combed back into submission, the strong chin and square set of shoulders. A smaller version Daniel was, yet appearing as if there was more to come.

"To think you left here a scrawny and wee little boy," Melinda said to Daniel. "And look at you now. A handsome and right young man." Still focused on the men, she began to type, the unusual break in her rhythm restored.

Daniel's face reddened. He pulled his eyes away from Melinda enough to see his father looking at him.

Hugging him once again, Samuel gave Daniel another smack on the back and said, "Let's go, my boy. Let's go."

The last ten years of the nineteenth century brought great change for Americans and especially the Jackson Family. The introduction of the narrow-gauge railroad offered a more navigable rail. Lighter in construction, it afforded higher climbs and greater horseshoe turns, resulting in a more economical means of transport over the traditional rail lines. Cheaper to build, it was a favorite of those where commodities were being transported in sparsely populated areas. Michigan's timber industry fit the formula for such rail lines and in 1894, the Detroit, Bay City, and Alpena Railroad was incorporated into the Detroit and Mackinac (D&M).

The D&M expanded north giving Jackson-Saginaw Timber Company a direct link from Cheboygan all the way to Bay City and points south.

Having survived the Panic of 1873 and the long depression of 1873-1879, where over 15,000 businesses, hundreds of banks and several states went bankrupt, Jackson-Saginaw Timber Company was regarded in the industrial business sectors with great respect. Samuel had an inherent distrust of the banking system and therefore, a cash-minded business sense. Samuel speculated with tangible collateral only. Memories of local lenders of his homeland calling in their loans with more brutality than panache kept Samuel firm in his resolve to never put his family and hard earned success at risk for the chance of some glorious profit or gain.

Even so, doing business was becoming more complicated than ever. No longer a local clientele, Samuel was dealing with fortune makers of the new America. Railroad, banking, steel, and mining were all expanding at an unprecedented rate. Survival and fortune was there for those who could set and keep the pace. With one eye on the forests and another on retirement, Samuel needed Daniel. Not just for his youth and vigor, but also his legal expertise. Transactions were becoming more and more legally intricate and although good counsel could be found, Samuel wanted the security only a trusted son could offer.

Torn between the accelerating pace of business and the slow drag of education, Samuel felt as though he was holding his breath these last few years. Now that Daniel was finished with his education and soon to join the company, he saw a bright and beautiful future for himself and Elizabeth. Securing just the right judge for Daniel to understudy was imperative. Law was still a balance between reputation and expertise, with neither ever out of the equation. Anxious to hear his son's news, Samuel held his tongue, praying that his son's choice would be both ethically and politically advantageous.

While Daniel was away studying the ever-changing law of this expanding country, Samuel and Elizabeth were putting their dream of a quiet life into action. The last few summers were spent on Mackinac Island. Soaking up the warmth, only available midsummer, Samuel and Elizabeth rented several different cottages around the island during the last week of July. Free from the crowds during Independence week, they could walk the bluffs and relax by the lake.

Less than four miles' square, Mackinac Island holds a rich history both in trade and war. Strategically located for both, most of the land was federally owned until 1895 when it was turned over to the State of Michigan. Designated in 1875 as a national park, second only to Yellowstone, this beautiful island still retains much of its natural beauty. During the 1800s, fur companies exporting beaver pelts gave way to commercial fishing for whitefish and lake trout and finally rounded out the century with sport fishing and a more tourist based economy. Hotels and restaurants catered to vacationers coming by train and then boat to the island. Just before the turn of the century, motor transport was made illegal, leaving the horse and carriage, bicycle and foot the way to go.

During the summer, Daniel would join them for a few days, making the most of the social scene, especially the ladies. Only a few hours of sunshine and his hair would shine like gold and his skin like bronze. Although swimwear of the day required knee-length trousers and a sleeveless woolen shirt, Daniel's good health and masculinity radiated like the sun. It was Daniel that convinced his parents to invest in the island, a small piece of heaven to be treasured for generations to come. In typical painstaking fashion, Samuel covered most of the island's available land for the best views and most precious timber, especially the beautiful Tamarack. Settling on a somewhat meandering lake-view property line, their new summer cottage was built high upon the bluffs overlooking the southeasterly point of the island. Considered an eastern bluff cottage, it was built rather conservatively compared to the multi-storied, turreted Victorian-style mansions of the day. Only two stories of living space with function rather than fashion in mind, Elizabeth and Samuel made one concession, a large master bedroom with an expansive view of the water. Placing her sewing machine directly in front of the window, Elizabeth spent hours working and gazing at the beauty of the island and its surrounding waters. Long morning walks and late night tea on the porch would round out their days, all too short, for leaving came long before it was desired.

Daniel knew his days of youth and frolicking were numbered. What was once an escape to the island for pure fun and abandon was now tempered with his future in mind. Focusing more on the details where the ladies were concerned, it was the Jackson family's first summer in their new vacation cottage that Daniel fell in love for the very first time.

Chapter 3

Although Samuel and Elizabeth's cottage offered solitude and peace from the bustling tourists landing daily at the docks, Daniel's favorite place on the island was the very place his parents avoided. Walking the shoreline, watching the water traffic, ambling along the main street, side stepping the powerful and majestic carriage horses, Daniel loved the vitality of man and beast. The cries of tourists, smells of fresh baked goods, and the cool fresh breezes off the straits that left summer tourists in want of warmer attire was where he was most. Many mornings, Daniel would rise with the sun and work his way down to the docks. Lost in thought, it was a carriage driver's cry that broke his reverie and saved his step in the wrong direction. Accustomed to his negligence, the drivers knew Daniel and his family and would chide him, waiting until the last moment to herald their cries, just for the chance to watch his surprise. Good humor was found and Daniel became a friend to both driver and horse.

One morning, early, the chill biting, Daniel was out walking. The harbor was shrouded in fog, a mixture of remaining warm air from the night before and a cool front moving in from the northwest. It was the last weekend of summer and typical to the island, the weather was one of a cold tease and belligerent warmth. He heard the horn of approaching vessels and cries of tourists, the lap of their wake. The sounds were subdued and far off, yet the clarity afforded by the invisibility of the surroundings, the lack of background noise of quiet early mornings, made Daniel feel as if the communication was personal.

Shoving his cold hands deeper into his pockets, he lowered his head to the wind and paused at the sound of horse and carriage, before crossing the dense fog that almost erased main street. Snorting and the clacking of hooves filled his ears, the wet smell of animal hair and the unmistakable odor of that which must be cleaned off the streets at regular intervals, assaulted his senses making him impatient to cross. The sound of tourists approaching from behind, soft female laughter interrupted his thoughts and made him turn. White cotton, soft and flowing, appeared and receded from view as the light and tilting soprano sounds approached. Yet it was the red, untamed and ethereal, that made him stare. Something was not right. The inflection was to one of class, the dress customary for one on the way to a family cottage, as well as the arrival time. Yet, such freedom of tress was not seen. Blinking to bring focus amidst the fog, Daniel stepped back an inch too far. A cry went up. Horses screamed. Reaching, grasping for something, anything, hot animal breath, and the sound of panicked hooves pierced his senses. Horse hair, musty, upon his cheek, pungent street water splashing, the groaning of wooden wheels and the carriage pushed past. Sitting in the street, amazed at his narrow escape, Daniel felt the gentle pull of a small laced hand and looked towards the figure shrouded in white and fog.

Blue eyes and red hair, so much red hair, a smile like the sun and laughter greeted, "Why, Sir, you must be Irish, for who else has the luck of the leprechauns to escape such disaster?"

Pausing a moment more than normal, Daniel opened his mouth to speak. Looking at his wet and muddy hands, Daniel stood, clasped his hands behind his back and straightened.

A horn from the docks sounded, as shouts began to announce their arrival. Sun filtered through fog, slowly releasing its hold on the morning, leaving small traces of chill and the promise of a warm and welcoming day. Morning deliveries, ready for transport began to fill the street, drivers calling out to each other in greeting and friendship.

"I will bring your bags over directly, Miss McGough," a voice called from behind.

"That would be wonderful. Thank you," the young woman answered. Turning back towards Daniel, she said, "Pleased to meet you. My name is Lucille."

At the laced hand, once again offered, Daniel reached out, this time finding himself, he answered, "Daniel Jackson. I do apologize for my foolishness and yes, I am Irish. You must be too. Who else would deem a clumsy escape the luck of our elves?" A slight smile played at the corners of his mouth, his eyes dancing.

A group of young ladies, dressed in similar attire caught up with Lucille, their conversation rising and beckoning, until they saw Daniel. Shushing the others, a tall brunette, reached back with authority and waved her hand, silencing them.

"Time to go. Mother is waiting. She will be worried, should we be late." A firm and serious expression told Daniel their encounter was over.

Lucille's smile became a fine line. Releasing Daniel's hand, she said, "Jackson, a funny name for an Irishman."

"Ah, well, yes, that would be the Scot in the Scot-Irish."

The tall brunette gave a snort, her posture ramrod straight, arms folded firmly across her chest. A serious older sister for sure, Daniel thought.

Turning to go, Lucille leaned towards Daniel and whispered, "This is our first and last weekend this summer. Mother is nervous with the weather and our traveling alone."

"Lucy, we need to leave now."

"Perhaps I will see you again?" A smile returned, her eyes softening. "There will be music tonight in the park," she dared.

A threatening voice called and she disappeared into the glare of the rising sun.

Daniel looked around him at all the commotion of a busy morning. The quiet reverie was gone. Placing his hand at the nape of his neck he felt the sting of his injuries, a burn in his side, rough bite at his hands. The wind abated and he lifted his head to the warm and bright rising sun. A bit of a wash, I need, he thought, smiling. "Lucille McGough," he whispered. Lengthening his stride to match the rise of the road, Daniel quickened his pace and his heart too.

Chapter 4

While Michigan was making strides in advancement and civilization in the last decade of the nineteenth century, across Lake Michigan there was a tempest and fury of advancement. Chicago, the French translation of the native Miami-Illinois word *"Shikaawa"* or "stinky onion," aptly named after a common plant that grew along the Chicago River, was the fastest growing city in America, its population exploding from about 300,000 in 1870 to over 1.7 million in 1900. Strategically located for both rail and water transportation, it became the hub for manufacturing, warehousing, commerce, education, and music. Rich farmlands attracted Yankee settlers, their produce and grain shipped east up the Erie canal, down the Hudson and onto the dinner tables of New York City. To the west and south, from the Great Lakes to the Mississippi River to the Gulf of Mexico, Chicago expanded its worth, including millwork and lumber from the forests of Michigan and Wisconsin, and refrigerated rail cars carrying fresh meat.

The Great Chicago Fire of 1871, destroying the central business district, led to stringent fire safety codes and the replacement of wood with masonry as the main building material. An influx of immigrants, first German, Irish, and Scandinavian, then Jews, Poles, and Italians, fed the machines of a city that never slept. In less than a century, from the first filing of the city plat in 1830 and a population of one hundred, to the turn of the century with almost two million, Chicago's explosion onto the American scene set the pace for the emerging industrial age with steel mills and the rise of the first skyscraper.

Just short of thirty years into its infancy, Chicago became the standard for American ingenuity and its can-do attitude. Because of its low-lying topography and intense flooding, the entire city was raised four to five feet, including the twenty-two story Briggs Hotel, which continued business as normal while the job was completed.

A melting pot of ethnicities, religions, and social-economic standings, Chicago was a filthy and often very violent city. Anti-immigration and anti-liquor policies clashed protestant citizens with the masses that spent their only day off work at the pubs. In the mid-1850s the mayoral election of Levi Boone by the Know Nothing Party led to temperance restrictions aimed at the German and Irish population that included higher license fees, shorter terms and an enforcement of an old ban on Sunday liquor and beer. Tensions mounted. While eight Germans were being tried for liquor ordinance violations inside the courthouse, Chicago had its first civil disturbance outside that resulted in one death, sixty arrests and the drawing of political party lines. This event mobilized the immigrant voter, bringing elections to light. The following year, a heavy German/Irish turnout reversed the election, restoring order to previous regulations, forever changing Chicago's political scene.

With the emergence of ward-based political machines, militant labor unions, violent strikes, and high wages, the Chicago businessman had a reputation of winning at all costs. Doing business in this city was sometimes akin to warfare. Having a judge on your side didn't hurt either.

Downwind of such a tumultuous economic atmosphere, Michigan and the outlying haven of Saginaw was another world. And yet, the reaches of Chicago and its whirlwind had a real effect on the commerce of the day, regardless how peaceful a haven. Jackson-Saginaw Timber Company depended on rail and as the new century approached a good portion of business was headed west and south, the only route through Chicago. Cargo fees, taxes, and labor delays all reduced the bottom line, adding to the general dislike of doing business with their western neighbor. A commitment to steel and reduction of wood didn't help matters.

Samuel felt the need to stay abreast of Chicago politics, but could not help the bile that rose when he considered the complexities. With summer over and Daniel home for good, he felt his nerves abate. A plan was made. Elizabeth and Samuel dined with a gentleman, a Detroit judge, who was looking for a young lawyer like Daniel. Schooled in the ethics of Michigan and modern commerce of the time, he would learn a sound Christian base for the law and its application. Samuel trusted his influence and knew that although like-minded, his young, impressionable son would trust the judge more so than his father. Little did Samuel know he and Elizabeth were not the only ones plotting a future. Daniel too was dining in secret.

Chapter 5

The trip home from the island was long. More than 200 miles by steamboat and rail meant an early rise and a long weary day. Having packed the night before and made the cottage ready for winter, the Jackson family was patiently waiting to board the boat. Elizabeth with treats and games for the little ones, Samuel with a stack of papers to review, and Daniel, his eyes searching the crowd, they looked like any other well-to-do family returning from what was a lovely weekend on the island. Without the excitement of beginning a trip, the sentiment was melancholy, not only for the long day ahead, but the last of summer on the island. Other families waited in line, checking and rechecking their tickets, securing last minute baggage, and taking stock of errant children. The morning was cool and the wind much fiercer than normal, as if willing tourists home with a push of good riddance. Elizabeth pulled her shawl closer around her neck and tucked her hands inside her sleeves. Standing next to Samuel, she leaned into him and saw his smile as he turned her way. The children, using their parents as a break, huddled deep together, giving little shoves and pushes to each other for position. Turning away from the wind and water, she saw Daniel making his way through the crowd, his head high, bright blonde hair blowing, turning left and right, as if searching. Just a moment ago he was behind us, she thought and reached up to tell Samuel, when Daniel stopped. It was difficult to see, being short in stature, and the milling of the crowd, but she could tell it was a young lady he found. Daniel turned in their direction for a moment and then it was his back again. A few moments passed settling a quarrel with the children, who would sit next to whom once aboard, when a deep voice was heard in greeting.

"Good morning, Mr. Jackson, Mrs. Jackson."

A very stout and solid man stood before them. Dressed in the finest, his wife beside him, a beauty herself, wearing a bright, solid blue traveling suit with a matching hat of silk. A beautiful brooch arranged with emeralds of the deepest green held together a shawl of hand-tatted lace. They made a picture of wealth and success.

Feeling a little out of place, her shawl lovingly knitted those cold Saginaw winters sitting before the fire, Elizabeth cringed at the disparity. Although successful beyond their dreams, all the money amassed could not erase the country frugality bred into their bones. Gripping Samuel's arm, she felt him straighten, his welcoming hand outstretched.

"A good day for leaving," Samuel answered, tilting his head towards the onslaught of the wind.

"Yes. Yes, it is," the round mighty gentleman beamed rocking back and forth on his heels. "So wonderful we could meet before she blows us clear off the island. I get the feeling the islanders are tiring of us."

Elizabeth watched Samuel open his mouth to laugh. How good he is, she thought. Never second guessing himself to that of others. Feeling the children pressing up behind her, she thought of Daniel. Searching the crowd, she saw nothing but families huddled, rocking for warmth. A slight spray of water dosed the crowd and cacophony of voices exclaimed their surprise.

"Henry McGough, and this is my lovely wife, Josephine."

An awkward silence passed. Josephine smiled warmly at Elizabeth, while the two men eyed each other. Samuel opened his mouth to reply when suddenly, Daniel appeared with a push from the crowd sending them all up against the rail. Josephine lost her balance and reached for Henry, just as her hat sailed out over the water. The crowd watched blue silk, braided with fine feathers and peonies catch the current and float slowly down, down, down. A murmur went through the crowd, when a blast of wind picked up the sailing millinery, bringing it back to rest playfully upon Daniel's head.

The crowd erupted in cheers and laughter, including Daniel, a slow red creeping up from his collar. Elizabeth reached into her pocket and pulled out a few hat pins.

"For when we are safe aboard," she offered, standing a little straighter, her eyes bright and warm.

"*Merci beaucoup*, dear friend," Josephine answered. Pieces of thick black hair began to blow about her face.

Elizabeth felt a shift in the crowd again. The deck hands were calling away to place the plank. A feeling of relief was felt as they would board soon and be rid of the weather. Memories of a warm weekend were fleeting.

"Father," Daniel began, "this is Mr. and Mrs. McGough and this is," he paused smiling at his companion, "Lucille." Appearing from behind her father, Lucille held her hat fast to her head, red tresses escaping in long tendrils.

Elizabeth took in the scene before her. She felt her husband stiffen and knew his sting at being the last to know. So, that's where Daniel was all weekend. Not one to miss family time, Daniel was curiously absent on some such account, this or that without much of an explanation. Given his age and now that he was a man, Elizabeth didn't question. It was all too clear. Lucille, with her mother's beauty, with all the trappings of a life of luxury, but something about the girl, something simmering beneath the surface, made her look towards the father. Ah, yes. She is her father's daughter. Confidence, bold and daunting, held in check by a good upbringing. Not once did the girl try to control her floundering locks, which by now were almost completely free of their bindings.

Smiling, Elizabeth offered her hand, "Pleased to meet you, Miss Lucille."

Lucille returned the favor with a nod of her head to both Elizabeth and Samuel. She met their gaze head on, her bright blue eyes shining, despite the torment of the wind. Standing almost a half a foot taller than her mother and Elizabeth, she was more in line with the men. Elizabeth wondered just how much she measured up in more than height. Looking at Daniel, she saw he saw nothing but Lucille. Elizabeth peered up at Samuel, his eyes fixed on Daniel, his expression serious. Elizabeth dropped her gaze. A deep sigh escaped. Saying a silent petition to Saint Patrick, she prayed for peace, she prayed for all of them.

Chapter 6

It was early morning. The first hues of daybreak were creeping through the kitchen curtains. The stove was full of wood, the fire at full throws. In the warm kitchen, Elizabeth drew back the curtains and placed her palm against the cold pane. Bringing it back to the nape of her neck she felt the cool wet of the morning and shivered. Little voices chattered at the table, the girls teasing and playing. Elizabeth looked over her shoulder, hiding a smile. Six little legs swung back and forth, six little hands clapped with glee, three little mouths laughed and the breakfast, fast going cold, remained untouched. My three babies, she thought, and my littlest, almost six. Pausing a moment, she held her tongue in scolding and watched their play. With Daniel, a man on his own, and the older sisters married with families, Elizabeth held a little tighter to the strings that tied these young ones.

"Oh my, Daniel. What beautiful blonde hair you have," a little voice exclaimed.

"Who me? Oh, it is nothing compared to your b-e-a-u-t-i-f-u-l rose red hair, my love," mimicked another.

Turning serious, the youngest of the brood, Lizzie, cried, "My Daniel," her eyes filling with tears, her tiny mouth trembling.

A double for Daniel, bright blonde hair and the bluest of eyes, Lizzie adored her older brother. As a toddler, her first steps still fresh upon the wood floors, it was Lizzie who met Daniel at the front door, always playing nearby, waiting for him to come home. Now, no longer a toddling little sister, she wavered between keeping up with her two older sisters and falling back to play the baby of the family. Typical of the last in a big family, her emotional predilection was as varied as the wind, changing with little notice.

Elizabeth placed a comforting hand upon Lizzie's head, picked up the corner of her apron and dried her tears. "Now, now," she scolded the older girls. "You'll get her all worked up. There'll be no getting her to school."

116

The older sisters looked at Lizzie for a second and suddenly they erupted in laughter. Kissy noises and giggles ensued, little feet kicked the table and forks and spoons clanged like the lovers they pretended to be. Elizabeth shook her head and returned to her task.

Hearing the fall of heavy tread upon the stairs, Elizabeth turned to the girls with a look of warning. "Shhhh. You'll have the wrath of the men upon us all, if you don't hush your silly ways, girls," scolded Elizabeth.

A stern voice erupted on the other side of the house and all went silent. Pausing at the kitchen door, Elizabeth motioned for the girls to finish up. A muffle of footfalls came to a halt and Samuel's angry voice bellowed, full of accusation. Elizabeth heard Daniel's high-pitched reply, emotional, resentful. The front door slammed and facing the girls, Elizabeth placed her index finger to her lips. She put Daniel's plate in the warmer. Suddenly, the door swung in with a rush, and Samuel's full frame filled the doorway, his brooding and angry brows knitted.

"Say good day to your da, girls," Elizabeth rushed. The eldest girls looked timidly at their father, grabbed their books and ran out the back door. Lizzie, in a wave of deep emotion, hugged Elizabeth fiercely, kissed Samuel quickly on the hand and ran after her sisters. A cool blast of air filled the room, giggling and teasing, the sound of little footsteps faded away with the girls leaving, as they ran down the path towards school.

Elizabeth opened her hand towards Samuel's chair. "Your food is getting cold."

Taking his seat, he stared in silence. Lifting her eyes to the heavens, Elizabeth took a deep breath, pursed her lips and sat in the chair opposite him.

"You know," she began, "sometimes the very thing you hate becomes the thing you love the most."

"I have no use for riddles, woman." Samuel set his palms down on either side of his plate and his jaw firm.

"It's the girl, Samuel."

His face expressionless, he asked, "What?"

117

"The red hair girl, Samuel. Lucille. Have you got eyes in your head, man? Didn't you see that all Daniel could see was Lucille?" Exasperated, Elizabeth leaned back in her chair and looked into Samuel's eyes. "He's in Love. Where do you think he was all weekend?"

"Making a deal with the devil," Samuel exploded.

"Oh Samuel, you forget your son. This is Daniel. Kind and loving. The one you sent to the forest to toughen him up. He's not you, with your inventions and barely a pair of britches traipsing the world to make a name for yourself."

Placing his head in his hands, Samuel's voice softened, "He is going to leave."

"Oh Samuel, you are a great man, but sometimes a great man is too much for his son. Don't be so hard and for God's sake, just tell him."

"Tell him what?" Samuel asked, his eyes searching.

Rolling her eyes, Elizabeth silently asked herself, why is it the angry words come so easily with men, but the ones that last, really last, are beyond them?

"Tell him you love him. You don't want to lose him."

"Anyone, but McGough. Why McGough? A godforsaken Catholic. Daniel has his pick of any judge, Michigan or Illinois. Why McGough? Self-made millionaire, they say. Hardly. He and his family hail from North Carolina. Made their fortune in emerald mines, selling out just in time. He is the one behind masonry and steel, the reason all my wood in Chicago is sitting on the rails, the money outstanding. The fat, obstinate bastard."

Elizabeth reached across the table and placed her hand in his. "Loosen the harness, Samuel. You have done right by your son. He needs to see the world. How can he make his own choices when all he has ever seen is what is under your hand? He'll come back to us and maybe," she smiled, "with a brood of little red heads."

Samuel sat in silence staring at his hands. A few moments passed. Slowly, he raised his head. "Well, you would love that, now wouldn't you?" he asked, his eyes meeting hers, searching, his voice a little lighter.

"That is true."

"Even if they're half Catholic?" he asked, his eyes searching.

"Even if they're all Catholic," she answered, her look serious.

Samuel pulled a little harder on Elizabeth's hand and stared into her eyes.

"What?" she asked. "Now your wanting me on that side of the table?" she laughed. "Oh no." Rising to place his hat on his head and push him out the door, she felt the tension ease. "It will be noon before I get you out of here and I have work to do, what with a brooding son on the lam and a gang full of giggly little girls beating the door down in a few hours."

Kissing her on lips, Samuel grabbed her around the waist and pulled her off the floor. Swinging around, he held her tightly, gently setting her down in his chair.

"Looks like you get the cold grub today, my dear," he laughed, letting the door slam behind him.

Elizabeth took a deep breath and sighed. Running her hands through her hair, she readjusted her hair pins and took off her apron. Cold food can wait, she thought. So can dirty dishes. Down the hall, she made her way into the parlor. The sun, beaming through the windows, chased away the morning chill. Sitting at her desk, the one Samuel made himself for their tenth anniversary, handpicked cherry, Jackson grown, she reached for the key and paused. Her fingertips coming up empty in the tiny, almost transparent china bowl, ivory with tiny red roses, Elizabeth frowned. Keyed for a tiny brass key, Elizabeth was forever misplacing it. Shrugging her shoulders, she pulled out a hair pin and unlocked the desk. Female ingenuity, that's what's in order, she thought. Paper in hand, she dipped the quill in the well and began to write.

Dear Josephine,

It was such a pleasure to journey in your company. If I may be so bold, I do believe we are two of the same mind when it comes to family matters. Perhaps, it would be prudent for the

Mothers of the two young in love, the wives of the two in opposition, to meet somewhere in the middle? There is a lovely resort on the shores of Lake Michigan. Travel by steamboat is possible from Chicago. My driver will meet you, should you be able to make arrangements. The favor of your reply is anxiously awaited,

Sincerely,
Elizabeth Jackson

Elizabeth closed the desk and replaced the pin in her hair. Running her hands across desk, Samuel's fine and delicate engraving, she paused. Such careful and patient work, she thought. If only, he was this patient with his son. Along the top of the drop-leaf, small landscapes of Ulster meadows were met by the great Atlantic. Placing her fingers in the deep grooves, she continued down the side, the St. Lawrence Sea Way leading to the Great Lakes and at the bottom, the tall majestic forests of Michigan, white pines, giving depth and breath, all created by a man and his imagination. Holding the letter to Josephine in one hand, postage affixed to the upper right corner, the other hand resting on the desk, Elizabeth felt the pull of the past, deep and comforting, and the need of the future, anxious and quick. Shaking her head, she placed the letter in the box on the front porch for the postman and headed back down the hall. Pushing through the kitchen door, the heat of the kitchen met her full force and she smiled.

Chapter 7

It was a beautiful day to travel. True to its promise, this July morning was warm, the sun teasing its way over the horizon. Rising early, Elizabeth found comfort in her routine, despite the chaos of the last few days. Busy birds outside her window made her smile at their earnest industry, fluttering this way and that. Cardinals, goldfinches, and wrens took advantage of her morning offering of seeds and suet, saying thank you with a melody of calls and song. What a whirlwind the last few days were, last few months, she thought. *This time last year, I was praying for peace and mending fences.* Adding wood to the stove, her thoughts turned to Josephine. What a true friend she found in Josephine and what a surprise at that. So different in temperament, style, and demeanor, they were much the same in marriage, both bound to men who ruled their world. Elizabeth marveled at Josephine's quiet and reserved composure, her delicate French intonations and peaceful ability to turn Henry towards her way of thinking. More of a head-on approach, Elizabeth usually battled it out with Samuel until they found a middle ground. With the ends justifying the means, their ways of maintaining a happy marriage were proven. Indeed, they both were right where they wanted to be, right beside their men.

Today they would travel. Tomorrow they would marry. The children were so excited. It was the wee hours before they fell asleep, their little voices finally lost in dreams and slumber. It was their first time to Chicago. Elizabeth awoke in the middle of the night and unable to sleep, she peeked in at each bedroom, hoping for glimpses into their mysterious and imaginative dreams. The girls were all curled up together in one bed like a nest of newborn kittens yet to open their eyes. Lizzie, her little blonde curls, a mass of ringlets against her sister's shoulder, were caught in the moonlight, almost white. Always the last of the three, her outside position left her cold to the touch. Elizabeth pulled up the covers, gently tucking them in, planting silent kisses upon their foreheads.

The other beds gave testimony to the day before, the dressing and redressing of what to wear, the dilemma of choosing. Discarded items, on and off the bed, took on lifeforms in the nighttime shadows, a crinoline skirt here, a trail of taffeta there, hats and gloves littering the heaps, left in the haste of silly giggles and glances. Down the hall in Daniel's room, he was more off the bed than on, so big in his boyhood bed. Lifting the sheet to his chin, she brushed back a lock of hair and kissed his forehead. The heat of his sleep rose up to meet her and she smiled. Daniel always was a hot sleeper. Many times, when he was a child she would find him sound asleep, red cheeks and hot little hands and feet, covers thrown to the floor. It was nice to have him home again, even if just for a short week. Unlike the girls, his bag was packed, his room in order, his tuxedo hanging by the door, patiently waiting for the new life that awaited.

It was a hard time last fall when Daniel left for Chicago. Elizabeth missed his cheery disposition, the funny stories he told at dinner, the way he teased the girls, getting them all wound up, yet bringing them down with a song or a story before bed. Daniel not only remembered the old Scot-Irish songs of the forests, those handed down from Samuel who learned them working the Ulster forests with his father and uncles, he had them memorized. Whistling throughout the house, belting them out as he walked in the door, Daniel brought cheer and smiles to any room he entered. Not so with Samuel. In Daniel's absence, Elizabeth tried to keep their spirits up, but Samuel with his long face and harsh words always brought them down again. It wasn't until a surprise visit home last fall that Samuel had emerged from the depths of despair.

It was Elizabeth and Josephine's idea and Lucille's mastery that had Daniel make the trip home to see his father. Parting with harsh words just a few months before, neither man would budge in the direction of reconciliation. Samuel was angry and let down. He felt deserted and worst of all he missed Daniel. True to the young, Daniel was hurt and resentful, but the excitement of clerking for a famous judge, a new city, and new love helped to soften the jagged edges of loss. It was in the quiet moments that

Lucille saw his regret. Celebrating his success, she'd see his bright blue eyes excited and dancing, dim for a moment, his facial features go silent and mournful. One evening walk, while taking in the autumn splendor, Lucille threw out the bait and went fishing.

"You know Daniel; Chicago has the most beautiful autumn colors. I doubt that any state could match its beauty," Lucille boasted, casting her line deep into waters uncharted, unsure if Daniel would bite.

Daniel drew his shoulders back and smiled. Looking straight ahead, he chided, "Now when did you travel outside Chicago this time of year?" He knew, up to now, Lucille spent this time of year in finishing school, on the Chicago side of Lake Michigan.

Dangling her bait, a little this way and that, Lucille puffed up her posture and ventured, "Well, Charles says Chicago has the highest density of maple and oak trees, all because,"

Cutting her off with a short, hard laugh, Daniel bristled at the mention of Lucille's childhood neighbor. He didn't trust Charles, especially when it came to Lucille. Knowing her perceptiveness, he remained silent.

Taking a quick peek at Daniel's profile, Lucille reeled in a little, mitigating her position. "Oh, you know Charles, always boasting. But, who needs to travel when perfection is right before your eyes."

Leaning down to kiss her lips, he paused in step and conversation. Beginning again, he conceded, "I would have to agree with you on that my dear."

Shaking her head away, her cheeks reddening, Lucille re-casted and tried for a more direct approach. "I just don't see how you can even consider any other place. Only Chicago is protecting its forests and its citizens. We let our trees be trees here and build with stone. Never again, such a fire, except of course if you consider autumn colors, fiery red, burnt orange, crimson leaves." Feeling his hand stiffen, Lucille knew she had set the hook.

"So, it is a tree lover I have here?" he asked, his narrowing, vibrant eyes belying the light tone of his question. "Well, that is a noble stand, my love. But, perhaps, even a lady as sheltered and protected as yourself would consider another view, should you

123

have the chance to see real forestry at work? One must always be careful of neighboring opinions."

Before he could admonish her completely, Lucille jumped up and threw her arms around him. "Oh really, really?" she exclaimed knowing he was hooked for good. "I would love to go. When do we leave?" she asked, her long hair falling down her back, her smile bright.

Not quite sure what just happened, but feeling as if something larger was going on here, Daniel gently set Lucille down before him. Holding her at arm's length he considered this beautiful and yet so unconventional girl. What woman would want to go into the forests? Muddy and dark, wet and dank, it was no place for a woman, let alone the daughter of one of the most influential and prominent judges of the day. And yet, this was why he loved her, why he spent most nights awake and longing. She was different and unpredictable and equal to his own. She was a challenge for sure, yet one he looked forward to meeting at every opportunity. She was interested in his cases and held opinions on proceedings. Daniel knew her father proudly humored her vitality and intelligence, her inquisitive nature, knowing it reflected well on him. He wasn't so sure about Josephine, there were reservations on her part. But the strange mixture seemed to work for the McGough family. Could it possibly work for them too? he wondered.

Drinking in her broad and enthusiastic smile, Daniel conceded, "A trip home to see the colors would be wonderful. I am sure Da would give us personal tour." Having said it out loud, there was no turning back. Tucking the crown of her head under his chin, Daniel knitted his brows and paused. Meeting his father wouldn't be easy. Lucille leaned into him, his chest broadened, and shoulders set back. Feeling his courage rise, he had buried his face in her hair, exhaled deeply, and letting go of more than breath, he felt his horizons rise.

Lost in thought, Elizabeth stood before the kitchen stove, in her hand a few small pieces of wood. A ray of morning sunshine broke through the horizon, washed the kitchen in gold, and intruded into her thoughts. Letting out a small sigh, Elizabeth lit the stove and replaced the cover. She rubbed her hands together and reached for the flour. Bread making was her favorite way to start the day. Her hands kneading, the feel of warm dough, the yeasty smell filling her senses, making bread was a beginning, just like the sun rising, the children waking, even a new marriage. Such happiness at the start of things. A chance to be good and real and make a difference. A smile began to emerge as she thought of Daniel as young boy and how he would pester her all morning until the bread came out of the oven, the first slice just for him. Sitting at the table, his little legs swinging back and forth, he would talk non-stop, his mouth full of bread, butter, and jam.

New beginnings, she thought. Like Samuel and Daniel. Elizabeth thought back to Daniel's surprise visit last fall. Flour tickled her nose and she looked up, her mind lost in the past, her hands kneading.

Oh, how she had feigned surprise at Daniel and Lucille's visit last fall. Seeing his son before him, Elizabeth knew Samuel was speechless for more than the typical male reasons. Not only did Daniel show up unannounced, but he brought Lucille and Josephine.

Pins and needles all morning, Elizabeth ran out of excuses to look out the front door. It was a Sunday, warm and breezy. Samuel was sitting on the wide front porch at the table, reading the paper, or trying to read the paper, his eyes tiny slits.

"Samuel, your spectacles. Have you lost them again?" Elizabeth scolded, letting the porch door slam.

Samuel jumped in his chair and turned. "What's taken hold of you, woman? This is the tenth time you've been in and out here, slamming the door. You've got my nerves in a jumble," he complained.

Staying behind him, Elizabeth placed her hand on his shoulder, more to steady herself than him. A ray of sunshine gleamed under the table, revealing the lost spectacles. "Right there you go, under the table," she laughed. "We may just have to tie them to you," she teased, rising to her tippy toes to kiss the top of his head.

The sound of horses and the rise of dust up the road made them look. Elizabeth stiffened, quickly holding her breath. Samuel rose as the carriage turned onto their property.

"Now, who could that be?" he asked, turning around to look at Elizabeth, but she was gone. Already down the porch stairs, she was pulling on the carriage door all smiles and tears. No doubt, the work of the women, Samuel mused, shaking his head.

Daniel, Lucille, and Josephine spent a lovely week with the Jacksons. Father and son soon warmed to each other and Elizabeth could see a little of the old banter so normal to their relationship. Josephine was great company for Elizabeth, as the main event was when the men took Lucille to see the forests.

At first, Samuel wasn't so sure about Daniel's reasons for coming home. Years more experience with the ways of women, sublime ways of women, he was a little suspicious of the deals made in Daniel's ignorance, and even his earnest in reconciling. But soon enough, the feeling of family and good company, laughter and joy began to soften his regard. They had a wonderful dinner Sunday evening. Elizabeth prepared enough for a feast, with roasted turkey, fall squash, sweet potatoes and cold cabbage slaw. It was no surprise to Samuel that Elizabeth prepared more than enough food nor why she was up earlier than usual that morning, fast at work in the kitchen. Knowing Elizabeth, Samuel didn't ask, but played along as usual.

Sitting on the porch that evening, the women retired to handiwork inside, Samuel quietly regarded Daniel, passing him a brandy and offering up a toast.

"To you're being home once again."

"Yes, Da, I will toast to that."

Silence filled the air. A gentle breeze blew across the porch, a row of empty rockers moving ever so slightly back and forth.

"I love sitting out here," Daniel observed. "All the rockers, made from our trees." He looked down the long porch that wrapped around the front and sides of the house. Long rows of perfectly laid plank lined the ceiling and floor, with rail and post enclosing all but three entrances, one at the front and two on the sides. Painted a pure white to match the house, the bright red shutters stood out like a male cardinal on a blanket of snow.

Samuel caught the word "our" and felt his back muscles ease.

"That would be your mother's work. She said one for each member of the family. I think she planned to fill up the front and both sides with rockers, but the good Lord made us stop at seven."

Seeing Daniel's confusion, Samuel added, "Children, my boy."

Laughing, Daniel shook his head. "Sometimes I get the feeling that we men are ruled more than we know."

"You are right about that, my boy, " Samuel hollered, slapping him on the shoulder. "Look at you, all grown up, a brandy in your hand and lady love pulling your strings."

"I think Ma has a few strings of her own, you know," Daniel chided, "or of your own, I should say." A smile broke, a silent laugh escaped.

"To women and strings," Samuel offered, tapping his glass against Daniel's. "Now, tell me the real reason you came home and brought this fine young woman."

Daniel told his father about the walk and Lucille's sudden interest in forestry. Somehow, in its telling, the story held new meaning.

Looking into his father's eyes, he said, "You know, Da, I was always coming home. I just wasn't sure how to tell Lucille. She is so close to her mother and father." Hanging his head, he whispered, "I don't want her to choose. What if she doesn't choose me?"

Reaching over to grasp Daniel's hand, Samuel sighed. "Well, we will have to make it one hell of a trip to the trees, won't we, my boy? You know, the Jackson men have a long history of dealings. I think we can come up with a few strings of our own, pull them just so and in no time your pretty, red headed filly will love it here as much as we do."

Daniel's eyes came to life again, bright blue and sparkling.

"To the Jackson men," Daniel toasted, tapping his glass against his father's he waited until both glasses were raised and in one motion, the Brandy was gone.

The morning of the trip to the trees had arrived. It rained the night before, torrentially. Samuel greeted them in the kitchen with long overcoats and boots. Daniel looked across the table and saw Lucille hesitate. Recovering quickly, she finished her tea in one gulp and standing to take the offered gear, she threw back her shoulders and sailed a defiant stare his way.

They took the carriage to the office, but from there they switched to an open wagon. Warm and snug in the polished and upholstered interior of the carriage, the wagon looked more weary than welcoming. Wet, vibrant leaves fell in the morning midst, taking place on shoulders, hats, and boots. Lucille picked up a large, maple leaf, red and orange swirled together like leftover watercolors on a pallet.

"Up front you go," Samuel directed Lucille. "Daniel will sit behind us."

Lucille glanced at Daniel, her eyes wide. Taking her seat, she pressed her hands into the bench and peered down. It was a lot higher up than she imagined. Seated behind her, Daniel was all grins. Pursing her lips, Lucille gave a little snort and turned to face front. Once settled, Samuel took the reins, giving them a quick snap. "High yah," he yelled. The team of great horses took off with a jerk and Lucille almost fell back. Placing his hand against her back, Daniel gave a little push and she straightened up. Shaking her head, red curls bouncing out from under her hood, Daniel heard a little gasp escape and saw her tightly grip the bench.

This is working out perfectly, Daniel thought. Watching them from behind, Daniel could hear the soft words of his father, the cadence a slow trot like the horses and the pull of the wagon. Swaying left and right with the terrain of the path, the wagon meandered along, leftover rain giving up its hold on the trees, showering them now and then in a hail of drops. He knew the stories. How the forests were formed, the cycle of birth, life and death. Old forests and new, the symbiosis with God's creatures, living and giving, taking, and making new generations. Closing his eyes, Daniel could see himself as a small boy, his father teaching him. Looking out into the rich colors of autumn, he felt a feeling of home and realized how much he missed this place.

The wagon lurched and Samuel reached out to steady Lucille, his large hand bringing her back to center in one motion. Lucille's shoulders shook a little and Samuel threw back his head, a hearty laugh thrown to the tree tops. The sound of the horses snorting, the wheels groaning and moaning over ruts made it hard to hear what was so funny. Daniel saw Lucille reach over and brush a leaf from Samuel's hat. His father turned and smiled.

Daniel thought about his father, his imposing frame before him. It was his mother who confided in him. "He's working too hard," she said. "The doctor said it will be the death of him. I told him he has to take it easy. He just grumbles. You know, Daniel, he never smiles anymore," she said.

Daniel lowered his eyes and felt the weight of his own absence. A behemoth of a man, his father always seemed invincible. Thinking about him in the years to come, he couldn't imagine frailty, forgetfulness, or immobility. Watching him now, his broad back straight and strong, his mastery of such a team of horses, he shook away the fears, the worry.

They were laughing now, and suddenly, his father began to sing. At first softly, just so Lucille could hear. Keeping time with the music, her hands softly clapping, encouraging, soon he was belting out a full chorus of Irish songs.

Oh, she has him eating out of her hand, he thought and joined right in. The sun breaking through the trees, Lucille's wet curls bouncing, as they clapped and sang full force, Daniel felt as if his heart would burst. Now this is happiness, he thought. Lucille, my family, and the forests. Daniel knew what he had to do.

The morning came and went, followed by a quiet lunch on a bluff overlooking the river, hard boiled eggs and sliced ham. A few crisp apples and loaf of Elizabeth's bread filled their hunger. Daniel and Lucille took a stroll, while Samuel took an unacknowledged nap. As the sun began to move towards the horizon, they reluctantly took seat in the wagon and headed back.

The trip home was quieter, no songs or loud laughter. Even the horses seemed content to slacken the pace, prolong the beauty. Just before they reached the barn, Samuel turned to look at Daniel. A wink of his eye and he snapped the team to a full trot. Daniel slid on the bench as far right as he could safely go, ready to spring forth. He felt his pulse quicken and his palms tingle. He ran the motions over in his mind. They planned it down to the second. First a wink, a change in pace, then a quick dip to the right, just enough to send Lucille over the side and into Daniel's saving arms.

Suddenly, the team turned right instead of left, a steep hill before them and the horses picked up pace. Samuel pulled back on the reins, hollered to halt, but the horses were startled. The pace quickened, faster and faster. The wagon flew over the crest. This was not the plan, Daniel thought. As he watched in horror, Lucille's hands, blanching white, gripping the bench, his father's demeanor, serious and grim, pulling as hard as possible on the reins, he pressed his feet up against the kick plate and held his breath.

Daniel reached forward to grab Lucille, when all of a sudden, he felt himself sailing backward, the team finally coming to a hard stop. Flying over the back of the bench, autumn colors overhead blurred as if in motion. Daniel let out a yell and landed in a bed of leaves. His thoughts raced to Lucille. Grappling to rise, his face covered with leaves, he reached out and felt the soft touch of her hand. Shaking the leaves loose, he saw Lucille, standing full before him, covered head to toe in leaves, a grin from ear-to-ear. His father, rushed over to them, stopped, and placing his hands on his hips, reared back, letting loose a laugh that could fell a thousand trees.

"How did you? What?" Daniel asked, breathing hard.

"Is it the luck of the leprechauns again, Mr. Jackson?" she asked, her eyes light, but her breathing hard.

Daniel thought about the first time they met, Mackinaw Island, his near miss with the carriages, her small outstretched hand in rescue. Reddening through to his scalp, Daniel wrapped his arms around her and buried his face in her hair, leaves, twigs and underbrush.

Samuel righted the team and helped Lucille settle back into the wagon. Standing beside Daniel, he placed his arm around his shoulder. They looked down the hill they narrowly avoided and shuddered at what could have been.

"From savoir to saved," Samuel whispered. "Does it really matter?" Giving Daniel a tight squeeze, he pulled him closer and said, "Look at the lady." Daniel turned and saw Lucille looking towards him, her face full of concern. "A right trip to the trees, you had, my boy."

"That wasn't the plan, Da." Daniel looked at Lucille and tried to smile.

"When it comes to women, it never is, Daniel. You can thank your leprechauns for your lady, my boy. A job well done."

With Samuel's cry and snap to the team, Daniel grabbed the wagon bench a little tighter than usual and took a deep breath. Leprechauns, he thought, don't leave me now. We have one more job to do.

That evening Daniel found his parents in the parlor. A lazy fire burned in the fireplace. His mother busy, at needlework, sat close by the fire in her favorite straight back chair. Licking the thread with her lips, she expertly threaded the needle and began a quick succession of stitches so nimble Daniel barely caught a glimpse of the needle before it plunged again into the cloth. A cadence took over her movements as she added color and design to the plain cloth, her head moving ever so slightly as if keeping time for the task. His father, deep in thought by the desk, was working through a large stack of papers.

Clearing his throat, Daniel rocked back and forth and waited. Elizabeth looked up and smiled, Samuel, barely turning at the interruption, grunted a reply.

"Don't mind your da, Daniel," Elizabeth said lightly, "He's deep in his numbers."

Daniel placed his hands behind his back, then in front, then in back again, clasping them hard. Elizabeth watched him and reached over to Samuel and patted him on the shoulder.

"Samuel, best if you take a moment. It looks like Daniel has something to tell us."

Samuel sat up straight and squared his shoulders. He removed his spectacles and placed them on the desk. Rubbing his forehead, he said, "Anything has to be better than running godforsaken numbers." Turning around, he looked at Elizabeth with a question and she shrugged.

Taking two strides into the room, Daniel took the chair opposite his parents. "I want to ask Lucille to marry me," he blurted out. Sweat dripped from his brow, his hands, shaking and nervous tried to find a steady measure.

"A little nervous, are you?" his mother asked, a slight smile on her lips.

"He looks like he's going to his grave," his father teased.

Blowing out air, Daniel dropped his arms. "I need help."

Laughter lightened the load and Elizabeth offered, "You know, having something in your hand, helps quell the nerves."

"And what would you know about asking a girl to marry?" Samuel exclaimed, turning to look at Elizabeth.

"Hush, dear man, it is Daniel we are talking about here." Reaching over to quiet Daniel's hands, Elizabeth began, "It is an old country tradition that the mother of the groom gives something from the family to the bride at the engagement. An heirloom, welcoming her new daughter. It is given to the father of the bride for safe keeping, until the wedding. Kind of like a blending of the families. A little bit of Jackson in the McGough home."

Elizabeth looked to Samuel and their eyes met. Slowly, their gaze shifted to the drop-leaf desk. Samuel's eyes grew soft. Elizabeth gave a slight nod to her head and they turned to Daniel who watched their movements, his eyes wide.

"Oh, Lucille will be touched," Daniel said softly, his hands quiet.

Rising, Samuel cleared his throat and said, "There is another tradition. This one is for the man, my son."

Quickly leaving the room and returning, Samuel held in his hand a small velvet pouch. Taking his place next to Elizabeth, he placed the pouch in Daniel's hand and sat back silently.

Daniel opened the strings slowly. He could feel the weight of the contents, their irregular shape filling the bag. Peering in, he gasped, "Diamonds?"

Samuel reached over and pulled out a stone. "Irish diamonds, Daniel."

"Irish diamonds?" he asked, a funny look on his face. "I never heard of such a thing."

"'Tis a well-kept secret," Elizabeth whispered.

"How? What? I don't understand?" Daniel asked, his eyes searched their faces.

"They are not to be sold. Handed down, father to son, they are ages old. Most likely from a mine in Africa. Your great-great grandfather, Nathaniel Sampson Jackson, traveled the world, had quite a collection. My da gave them to me when I asked your ma to marry."

"And I no wiser to them until many years later," Elizabeth half-heartily accused, giving Samuel and little shove.

"But, why diamonds?" Daniel asked, shifting the pouch this way and that, the firelight refracting like magic.

"The Battle of the Diamond. Not that it had anything to do with diamonds. A few years before the turn of the century. Your great-great grandfather and his brothers fought for the right to be Catholic. The Protestants ruled County Armagh and controlled the industries. The Diamond was a cross road in Armagh and protestant held."

"Did they win, Da?" Daniel asked, his small voice more like a child than a man about to marry.

"Nah, it was a massacre," he said, his voice flat. "But, it is the reason you come from Ulster. After the battle, many Catholics scattered, including your great-great grandfather the only man left in the family. The story is, old Nathaniel, he was quite a story teller, brought back the diamonds from one of his travels many years after the battle. Making up his own version of history, he would bring the diamonds out to show the young lads, sit them in a circle and by firelight, tell them stories about the battle, scaring them half to death."

"So," Daniel began slowly, "You mean we're Catholic?" Daniel thought incredulously of all those years he studied with the Jesuits.

"Not anymore," Samuel replied, shrugging his shoulders, "Your great-great grandfather settled in Ulster, fell in love, and married a Protestant. The rest is, as they say, history."

A few moments passed, Samuel sitting quietly and Daniel staring into the small pouch. Elizabeth leaned over and patted Daniel's hand. "That's life, my sweet boy. Things are forever getting mixed up. It's how you sort them out, that matters."

Daniel pulled the strings tight on the bag and looked at his parents. "Wow. I can't wait to see Lucille's face when I tell her. Part Catholic?" Looking up at his parents, a small smile tugged at the corners of his mouth.

"God's children," Elizabeth answered.

Placing the pouch in his pocket, Daniel's face turned serious. "I will keep them always."

A tear fell on Elizabeth's needlework. Suddenly, she jumped up, "Oh my, I've lost the key," she exclaimed. "I've looked everywhere."

Pulling her back to her chair, Samuel, kissed her lightly on the forehead and said, "Keys can be made, my dear. Keys can be made."

"The diamonds are yours Daniel. 'Tis up to you how you keep them in the family," Elizabeth said picking up her needlepoint off the floor.

"You could make a right nice engagement ring, my boy." Samuel stood, reaching out his hand to Daniel.

Taking his father's hand firmly, he had stood and agreed, "And a pretty little key too."

Standing in the kitchen, lost in thought, her arms floured to the elbows, Elizabeth didn't hear Samuel come in. Quietly he placed his arms around her waist and she squealed in surprise, waking from her daydream.

"Ah, a right surprise this morning," Samuel teased, wiping the flour from the tip of her nose. "Nothing for me, my dear. It is breakfast with the boys this morning." Samuel prepared and served breakfast once a month to the crews. It was his way of showing his appreciation. It was also a good way to stay connected at the deepest level of his business.

Dreamy, her thoughts still pulling at the past, Elizabeth said goodbye and returned to her task. It was a lovely visit and a wonderful outcome. Elizabeth knew more was at work than the quiet dealings between women and that amongst men. God gave his blessing and in that blessing, new love grew. Father and son were closer than ever, Josephine proved be a devoted friend, almost a sister, and Daniel and Lucille were to be married.

Lovingly patting the circle of fresh dough, she said a silent prayer for this new beginning, for Daniel and Lucille, for love and kindness, patience and forgiveness, for happiness and security. High spirited Lucille, she thought. She was her father through and through, much like Samuel. Well, Daniel had a lifetime of such a father, but a father was to be obeyed. She wasn't sure about a wife, even Lucille. Elizabeth loved Lucille. She was full of life and love, just a little short on patience and who knew about forgiveness. They will just have to grow up like me and Samuel, she told herself.

Scoring the loaf, she opened the oven door and tested the temperature. Too hot for rising, she placed the loaf on the window sill, covering it first. Just like our two lovers, she thought. Too hot in the beginning, but the heat does subside, lending a warm glow, as long as there is enough yeast, vitality, to make things rise and stay. And that's what a good marriage needs, she thought, the warmth to stay. Much like baking a perfect loaf of bread, it doesn't always happen. Too much heat, too little yeast and things fall apart. Unleavened bread. It was good enough for the Jews, good enough for Jesus, she considered, and good enough for us. So, you eat a little unleavened bread along the way, start over fresh with flour and yeast, warm water and a little lard and after a few years, a few children, a few fights, a few lovely nights, and a few fallen loaves, somehow you end up with the right recipe, a good combination, and a smattering of ingredients.

Breaking through the curtains, a stream of sunshine filled the kitchen with light. Little dancers of dust floated above the floor, pirouetting and rejoicing in the bright and radiant light. Wiping her hands on her apron, Elizabeth pushed back the curtains to either side, her face lifted to the sun, and sighed. Time to start this new beginning, she promised to herself. Pausing a moment longer, she took a deep breath in and exhaled. For love and understanding, patience and forgiveness, and enough warmth to stay, for these I pray, dear Lord, for these, I pray.

Chapter 8

It was a beautiful evening for a wedding. A rare occurrence, the clouds parted in the Chicago sky, revealing a vast depth of dark unknown glittered with thousands of stars. White linens draped tables, dotted with hundreds of small candles and evergreens. It was Lucille's idea to bring a little of the trees to the tables and Samuel was all smiles. The warmth of the day still lingered, leaving the guests comfortable in the evening air. A slight breeze off Lake Michigan flickered the flames, sending firelight dancing among the seated guests.

Daniel scanned the room. While keeping a serious conversation with an aging senator, his thoughts were with Lucille. He felt at a loss in her absence, like the lingering chill after a long, warm embrace. In the months and weeks leading up to the wedding they were inseparable. Never did he have such conviction, as he did about their impending marriage. All the world was right with Lucille by his side. And yet, in the days and hours leading up to the altar, he was kept at a distance. Even their brief interlude of promise and pledge before God, seemed fleeting, dream-like. Upon their arrival at the reception and grand announcement as the new Mr. and Mrs. Daniel Arthur Jackson, Lucille was whisked away by her bridesmaids. Only moments ago, they stood there, hand in hand before the world, just enough time for the men to surround him with nudges of good cheer and the passing of cigars. Yet, it seemed like hours.

Bringing him back to the conversation at hand, the old senator was laboring the subject of property rights and eminent domain, his equally aging wife, smiling placidly, though Daniel was quite sure she was expertly adept at sleeping on her feet.

"It is a dilemma, my son, one that requires much thought and deliberation," he intoned, his voice gravely, legato.

"Time, Sir," Daniel replied, slightly rocking on his heels, "I will agree to that." Turning to smile at the senator's wife, he peaked over her shoulder, his eyes searching. Uncanny, he thought, I don't believe the old lady has blinked once.

"Take your time when it comes to law. Too many young men in too much of a hurry these days. Onto the next item, before the ink has dried on the first. It takes years to undo a poor decision, more so than to do it proper the first go around."

The old man leaned heavily on his wife's arm, her eyes widened at the change in balance, her smile lost its fix and faltered, and at last, Daniel saw her blink.

Daniel reached out his hand to steady the aging couple, just as another long termed consummate politician garnered their attention. Daniel found humor in those, given their age, with obviously so little time, pondering the very idea of taking so much time to discuss, well, time.

In the corner of the room, he caught a glimpse of red hair, piled high, a few tresses escaping white crinoline and lace. The old senators began debating a matter of agricultural legislation and Daniel felt himself split in two, one half deep in the technicalities of law, the other wandering back to the first time he met Lucille. Red hair and white lace. Pulling at his collar, his face felt flush. Would it be like this always? He wondered. This feeling, warm and weakening?

Waiting for the opportunity to gracefully leave his present conversation, he was rescued by his father-in-law and a sudden change in music. It was time for the bride and groom's first dance. Whisked away, the old senators and their wives pushing him gently forward with good wishes, Daniel found himself, suddenly, face-to-face with his bride.

Handed off by her mother and father, Daniel placed his hand in hers and pulled her close. His right lightly against her lower back, hers on his shoulder. As decorous as possible, Daniel felt his blood run hot and his heart pound. The smell of roses and fresh talc overwhelmed his senses, as they began to waltz, first slowly, then a little quicker, until they were moving, seamlessly, with the quartet's rhythm, as if sound, light, and matter were one.

Lucille pressed her cheek to his and whispered in his ear. A slow red crept up his neck. Daniel pulled his head back and considered this woman, his woman. I will forever be surprised, he thought. Alone on the dance floor, all eyes on them, Daniel applied pressure to her slender waist and leaned forward.

"How will I stand the long evening with such promises?"

Light laughter and the turn of her cheek, "Oh Mr. Jackson. I am sure you have negotiated many long and laborious contracts. Do tell, is the reward more so, when promise is say, very promising? Or should I say, enticing?"

"Oh yes, enticing. Please do say enticing, again, softly, closely," he teased. Throwing his head back to laugh, he felt the quartet pick up the tempo as did he, their dance now a fast and furious twirl. Heat rising, cheeks reddening, they swirled and twirled before family and friends, loved ones and business associates.

Suddenly, Lucille came to a halt. Raising her hands overhead, she gave a swift, smart clap. Daniel stood still as the dance floor cleared and the quartet paused. A trio came forth with fiddle, whistle, and flute. Elizabeth and Josephine, full of smiles, lined up on either side of Lucille, linking arms. Faced with such formidable women, impish and daring, Daniel retreated into the masses of men on the opposite side of the room.

The reel began in typical four/four measure. Hitching their skirts and kicking their heels, Lucille, Josephine, and Elizabeth raced towards the men, a challenge to their partners. Just about to clash, the women kicked up their heels, made a quick dip of the hip, and turned in a flurry of skirts to the other side of the room. Laughter exploded, applause thundered, and the trio picked up the pace.

Now it was the men. Standing tall, arms across shoulders, they challenged with a rise and dip and a kick across the room, a barn dance version more typical of the highlands. Seconds from colliding with his bride, Daniel swooped down a kiss upon her nose, plucked a flower from her hair with his teeth, turning with a kick, victorious. The room was at a roar with clapping hands, stomping feet, and the fast and furious pace of the trio. The excitement spread with the challenge and the answer. Sixteen measures to a step, eight for the right foot, another eight for the left, the reel continued until the older guests took leave and the younger took over. Reel changed to jig, giving way for displays of youth and vigor. A large circle enclosed the dance floor with the middle for those brave enough to show their Irish pride with dance.

Daniel grabbed Lucille's hand and pulled, winding through the crowd they ran outside the celebration. The large expanse of lawn led down to a reflecting pool, the moon holding its discourse with the stars in perfect harmony. Holding her close, he felt the heat of their dance blend and dissipate into the cool evening air. Standing still, their hearts racing, he found her lips, chin, and eyes.

"Lucille," he whispered. Placing his hands in her hair, he felt their edges soften, bodies melt.

Pulling back just a little, Lucille reached inside her bodice to reveal a chain. A tiny gold key, encrusted with Irish diamonds and McGough emeralds twisted in the dark, a flash caught in the light of the moon and danced across the water like tiny fairies.

Daniel's eyes widened, his mouth sought hers again. She remembered. She understands. She knows, he thought.

Shouts from the celebration brought them back to the present. Their name, called out from the crowd broke their respite. Lingering a moment longer, Daniel held Lucille's hand to his lips. The ring, so beautiful, a mastery of gold and Irish diamonds stood for today and tomorrow, a promise, like a circle, eternal, their marriage. Placing the key back in her bodice, Lucille kissed Daniel softly. Slowly, they walked back. Daniel looked up at the stars and wondered if there ever was a more perfect moment.

The celebration continued into the early hours of the morning. Elizabeth and Josephine, closely knit like sisters, were deep in conversation on the bench by the reflecting pool. Months of wedding preparations led to many long letters and weekend trips across Michigan and its great lake. Having left her sisters at such a young age, Elizabeth craved the closeness of female companionship, the comfort she found in Josephine. Quiet and soft spoken was not to be confused with meekness when it came to Josephine. Deep down a strong and determined woman, she was a pillar of support in friendship.

The last few guests could be heard at the carriages, the horses snorting and stepping in the quiet, misty morning. Samuel was wrapping up with the establishment, his tie long gone, shirt sleeves rolled up, collar askew. Looking around at the tables, an overturned chair here, a forgotten shawl there, a few candles still burning, their wicks liquid, long overdue, Samuel thought the night a huge success. Who would have thought, a Jackson and a McGough? he mused. It was through the work of women and the genius of Henry that what was once an unforgeable margin was now steeped in friendship. Samuel, too, found a friend in the McGough's. With Samuel's eye for detail and Henry's aptitude for large scale solutions, steel did not have to replace timber. With the ever-expanding rails, Chicago was not the end of the line.

Henry saw a place for timber in Chicago. High quality, high priced Jackson timber with short transportation costs soon decorated the expansive mansions of Lakeshore drive. Artisans, expert in crafting relief in wood, requested Jackson Timber alone for its beauty and durability. Using a method of qualities, Daniel devised a scale of sorts, separating the timber on the basis of color, grain, strength, and absorptivity. With the scale, the timber was sold at its highest price and targeted distributions reduced unnecessary costs due to delays and returns.

Lucille and Daniel decided long before the wedding day that unlike the tradition of the time, to be whisked away amidst a big send off, they would remain at the celebration. With their whole lives ahead of them, they wanted to be with family.

Lucille and Daniel were winding their way between the tables hand in hand, pausing here and there for a table or chair in the way, an errant shoe, a forgotten jacket. The celestial discourse between moon and stars ended long ago and an emerging dawn, a slight brightening amongst remnant shadows of the night took place. Lucille looked across the room and saw Samuel shaking hands with the owner of the establishment. Turning towards them, he thrust his hands in his pockets and with a grin pulled them inside out.

They laughed, slow and easy. Lucille, covering her laugh with a yawn, opened her eyes wide, blinking a few times.

Looking around, Lucille turned towards Daniel and squeezed his hand, "Have you seen my Father?" she asked gently. Looking down, he kissed her on the nose, a lazy smile plastered across his face.

Over Lucille's shoulder Daniel could see their mothers on the bench at the reflecting pool. The heat of the celebration long gone, left what was a cool evening, an even chillier morning. The damp dew rose to a thick, low-lying fog, so that the mothers appeared as if upon a floating bench for two. Just in the last few moments, the emerging dawn brought the ladies into view, going from black night to grey twilight, and now with a thin bright line of light across the horizon, the promise of a blinding morning.

Daniel placed his hand above his brow and looked out over the lawn. Suddenly, he stiffened. Lucille felt his hand release. Surprised, she looked up, saw his face slacken, eyes widened. In a second, he was running through the tables, knocking chairs, jumping over obstacles. Samuel wheeled around at the commotion, paused to look at Lucille, his eyes soft, mouth down turned, and was off chasing Daniel. Catching up with him on the lawn, Samuel and Daniel stopped short and knelt down. Lucille, gathering her skirts in her hands, held back, leaned her head to one side and peered through the thinning fog. The bench at the reflecting pool empty, Lucille turned back towards the men, when an awful cry filled the air.

Morning broke in reds like never before. Looking towards the sky, Lucille whispered, red sky at night, sailors delight, red sky at morning, sailors take warning. Faltering, her knees weakening, palms releasing, her skirts billowed around her, rendering her immovable. Sinking to the floor, the scene on the lawn took hold. Banishing dew and mist, this new day, their first of day of the rest of their lives, began with a revelation. Her father, lying on the lawn, colder than night before, was whisked away without warning, quietly, in the night. So sure and secure just moments before, their charted course was forever, devastatingly altered.

Red sky at morning, sailors take warning.

Chapter 9

A honeymoon forgotten, a funeral remembered, marked the beginning days, weeks, and months of their marriage. Utterly changed, their plans so carefully made before the wedding, every detail painstakingly deliberated, now seemed unimportant, immaterial with the passing of Henry. Agonizing over how long he suffered, just beyond reach of all that loved and cherished him, such suffering in the midst of such celebration, there was little solace.

They planned to stay in Chicago. An apartment was secured, furnishings purchased, a place at the bar for Daniel. Agricultural law with an eye on the senate. Henry, with his vast breath of vision saw beyond Daniel's limited aspirations, into the future and the generations of the Jackson-McGough legacy. Dreams of children, a brood of strawberry blond babies, filled their talk of family.

Now, nothing was the same. Chicago was too big, too busy. The apartment was filled with unopened wedding gifts, the reminders too painful. The job, an office with a view, now felt cold and harsh. With broken hearts, they held onto each other and their dreams of children, hoping, wishing for the news of new life, so needed by this sad and grieving family.

Although married in the Catholic faith at the McGough family parish, Daniel and Lucille, surprisingly, never talked about choosing a faith after they married. During their courtship and engagement, Daniel's time in Chicago, they went exclusively to the Catholic church, never setting foot once in a Protestant church. Daniel felt welcome and with Lucille by his side, his worship was fulfilling. With the gloom of Henry's passing, the subject was buried under layers of grief and depression. Although absent from the thoughts of the newlyweds, there was one person who needed the question of faith answered. Little did the newlyweds know, the answer, non-negotiable as it was, would set the course of the new Jackson-McGough lineage in a different direction and the one who needed the answer most, leading the way.

Without a son, Henry's fortune came down to dollars and cents. Wise enough to know that passing his fortune to those with the means to double or even triple its worth was the way to go, Henry designed his will with the industry and intelligence of his sons-in-law in mind and his lovely wife, Josephine, well cared for. With only two girls, the estate was divided equally. Josephine and Henry's home would pass to their first born, Margaret, with the stipulation that Josephine held life estate. Everything was as planned, until Margaret's husband, Tor, was offered a position abroad. Off to England, a measure of stair-step children to follow shortly after, Margaret and Tor opened up an opportunity for Daniel, his thoughts turning to home, to Michigan. Daniel knew he wanted to return to Michigan, the end was clear, it was only the means or the method he lacked. How could he convince Lucille to leave her home, the only home she ever knew and loved?

It was late in the afternoon on a Sunday. Daniel and Lucille came to the McGough home to have dinner with Josephine, Margaret, and Tor, a farewell dinner, for they were to leave in only a few, short days. Warm August breezes blew the curtains inward, as Daniel ran his fingers along the rows and rows of bookshelves of his late father-in-law's office. The heat in the room was stifling. A trickle ran down his neck, and Daniel stopped, running his fingers inside his collar, he pulled against his necktie. Staring at the spines of old law books, Daniel still couldn't believe Henry was gone. It was apparent in the calm and quiet of the house, in the sad faces of those he sought, and especially in this room. Yet, if he closed his eyes, he could almost imagine Henry, just outside the door, stomping his feet, shouting out greetings of good cheer, about to barge in and lead Daniel in some new direction or decision. Henry became a second father to him and Daniel felt lost without his guidance and leadership. In the complex world of Chicago politics, Daniel no longer desired a place, no longer looked up the ladder. It was as if he was led blindfolded halfway up the ladder, safely, only to have his eyes opened, fully seeing the horrible danger for the first time. Not able to go back down, he was stuck, his past and future slowly shrouded in fog, with only the rungs of

144

the present left in view. A throat cleared behind him and Daniel turned.

"Daniel, may I have a word with you?" a soft voice inquired.

Josephine was a soft-spoken woman to begin with, but lately she hardly spoke at all. Crossing the room, they met in the middle, Daniel, reaching his hands out, gently placed her hands in his and looked into her eyes.

"It seems nothing will be the same," she whispered.

Daniel opened his mouth to reply, deciding otherwise. Josephine was a mystery. Such a beautiful woman with exceptional composure, he often wondered from where she drew her strength. Yet since Henry's death, underneath her mask of acceptance, Daniel saw signs of struggle. A tear escaped, a too bright smile, a faraway look. Waiting for her reply, he thought of Lucille and how she too, since the death of her father, struggled below the surface.

"Margaret and Tor leave in a few days. I will be busy with the children until they can send for them," she stated.

"Do you need help here?" he asked cautiously.

Daniel knew if they moved into the home with Elizabeth, Lucille would never leave. Moving to Michigan would be out of the question. Releasing her hands, Daniel turned, looking anywhere but Josephine's eyes.

"*Non.* No," she reassured. "Margaret has hired a nanny who will accompany the children and stay with them in England. I have no interest in traveling."

Daniel exhaled softly. Thoughts returned of home and his mind began to race, questions upon questions. A few moments passed and Josephine gestured for them to sit. Daniel thought about Henry, his constant motion and commotion, and realized this is how Josephine got her way. Nothing was at chance with this clever woman. Like an expert chess player, she knew where each piece would go, controlling the game from the beginning. Soft spoken and quiet, she downplayed her request, leading them to believe it was a matter of nominal importance. Daniel could see Henry becoming restless and bored. He would be pacing the room by now, his mind elsewhere, ultimately, agreeing to whatever Josephine wanted just to get on with things. Josephine knew her

145

Aesop. It was the tortoise and the hare all over. Daniel leaned to his right and looked out the window. The children were playing, calling and running to each other. Someone fell and began to cry.

Changing gears, Josephine looked down at her hands, "I was thinking how beautiful Michigan must be in the fall."

Whipping his head around, Daniel's heart stopped. "Pardon?"

"What do you think about Michigan, Daniel? Maybe Margaret is right. I need a change of venue." Josephine locked her eyes on his. He noticed her firm jaw, unwavering stare and understood what was not said.

"This is your home," Daniel whispered.

"Was our home," she replied. "Henry's blood was Chicago, not mine."

Daniel tilted his head and considered this new information. Not that he ever thought about Josephine's beginnings, he always assumed she was born and bred Chicago. As his mind began to question her past, her beginnings, Josephine spoke abruptly, interrupting his thoughts.

"Lucille," Josephine said, her voice flat.

"Lucille," Daniel muttered and lowered his head, stared at his hands, helpless in his lap. Daniel saw the three of them on the ladder, Josephine a few rungs up, Lucille a few below. Both were just out of reach, just barely visible in the developing fog.

"You see," patting his hand, Josephine stood, cleared her throat and continued, "Lucille has it all figured out, my dear. All we need is your blessing and by October we will be 'in the trees', as your father says."

Daniel opened his mouth to speak, his eyes wide, and for the second time, decided otherwise.

Pressing her hands against the folds of her skirt, she looked Daniel in the eyes hard, "I am told there is a beautiful Catholic church in Saginaw."

Lowering his eyes, her stare too much, Daniel hastily agreed, "Yes, yes, I do believe there is."

What a clever woman, he thought, dangling the prize, just out of reach. She learned a lot from Henry, he mused, or did she?

Josephine smiled. "What do you litigators call it?" she paused, "Oh, a real estate term, when the value of deal is uneven, the amount of worth of one side over the other?"

"Oh," Daniel ventured cautiously, pretty sure the price for returning to Michigan was at hand, "the boot?"

"*Oui*. Yes, that's it. Henry always loved, 'the boot of the booty,' as he would say." Her eyes clouded just a little. Placing her hands on her hips, Josephine lowered her voice and continued, "Daniel dear, it is very important that my grandchildren grow up in a Catholic family. I guess you could call this request, payment for the boot. Do you understand?"

Daniel let out a quick rush of breath. So, that's the price. A fleeting thought of his parents, their full acceptance of Lucille, never once raising the question of faith, crossed his mind. Meeting her eyes, Daniel rose to full height. "I will follow Lucille anywhere, anyhow, anyway."

"You know," Josephine said with a smile, "I have to agree with Lucille, when it comes to women, you are a bit sharper than my Henry." Her smile fading, she turned to towards the door, pausing to add, "I'll tell Lucille, you said yes."

The next few months went by in a flurry of activity. September arrived with a series of departures. First, it was Margaret and Tor, planning, purchasing, and packing. Then, two weeks later, the children, and finally, with the house to herself, Josephine. Lucille and Daniel had their share of arrangements, but as newlyweds and with a sense of returning home, it was less to handle.

Josephine wanted time to go through Henry's things, to reminisce, to say good-bye. A moving date of October third was decided. Henry would have turned forty-five that day. Josephine was firm. She wanted to be anything but idle on the first hurdle as a widow. "I need a running start," she said. "Two weeks in this big house alone is enough." Lucille and Daniel agreed and with no one else to argue, the case was closed. Daniel began to see that the litigator ran deep in Josephine.

147

Back in August, Daniel had written to Samuel of their plans. Samuel telegrammed a one-word reply, "overjoyed." From there, the women took over arrangements on the domestic side. Elizabeth found a nice two-story home just blocks from downtown Saginaw for Lucille and Daniel. It boasted large windows and beautiful oak floors. Samuel went along for the inspection. One look at the front door, a beautiful cherry, and his mind was made up. The owner was a retired craftsman who built the home with love. They raised their family and now, in their late fifties, they were heading south to be closer to their children. A daughter lived outside of Detroit, a son near Toledo. The kitchen was bright and sunny and looked out over a large rose garden. Elizabeth thought of Lucille and hoped over the years to come she would draw comfort from such a view. A wrap around porch offered escape in the warmer months and a far-off view of the river with its countless vessels and their cargo. A washroom off the kitchen, a formal dining room and living room, and parlor completed the first floor. Up the cherry red staircase were three bedrooms with expansive views of the river, downtown, and neighborhoods to the rear. The house felt loved. Walking out onto the porch, Elizabeth could hear the children of long ago laughing and playing. Hands shook and the deal was complete.

Stepping off the porch, Elizabeth linked her arm into Samuel's. He turned and smiled. The day was sunny and warm, a late September present. Leaves, crimson reds and yellows covered the ground, filled puddles and even idle carriages. Their feet swishing through leaves, made rustling sounds, flying up in little eddies around Elizabeth's skirts, only to slowly drift down, down, down.

"Oh, how I love a warm and breezy fall day," Elizabeth warmed.

"It sure gives a man a lot to look upon."

"You know, we women have a couple of eyes ourselves," she teased, her voice a little breathless.

"There is proof of that," he answered with a low and slow nature. He eyes, rooted to the horizon, scanned the river, taking in the cargo, his mind on profits.

Elizabeth chuckled and squeezed his arm a little tighter. Putting pressure on his arm, she tried to match her stride to his, but there was no use. Even at his leisure, she hurried to keep up, his long legs taking one for every two of her steps.

"It feels good, " Elizabeth started, feeling her heart beat faster and her breath shorten. Stopping at a cross street to let a carriage pass, Elizabeth caught her breath and began again, "It feels good to have the newlyweds taken care of. I know Lucille will love the house. It's just, well, Josephine," pausing to catch her breath. "I worry about Josephine."

Feeling as if she was almost at a trot and soon to cantor, she pulled on Samuel's arm hard. Samuel came up short and almost fell backwards. Turning around in surprise, he was faced with a stern expression, hands on hips, and although he lowered his gaze considerably to meet her eyes, a formidable and opposing wife.

Raising his hands, palms forward, Samuel took a step back. "What about Josephine? She's coming with them." Shrugging his shoulders, he dropped his hands to his side, his face full of question.

Shaking her head back and forth, Elizabeth blew out her breath, her hands still rooted to her hips. "Where's the fire, husband of mine? Will you tell me that?" she asked, cheeks more vibrant than the leaves around them, eyes fiery than the sun upon the river.

Samuel looked around and kicked a few leaves. A few moments passed and Elizabeth walked passed him. Now he was the one catching up, although not too earnestly. A few penitential paces behind, he held his features firm, trying not to show the humor that was threatening the corners of his mouth. Elizabeth was mumbling something about how many years they were married and he should know better. A block from their home, Samuel could see their front porch, rockers lined up and waiting. Quick as a wick, he strode the distance between them and before Elizabeth was any the wiser, she was up in the air and over his shoulder. Her fury turned to indignation, her fists pounding on his broad and strong back as he ran up the porch and halted at the door. The three youngest girls, just a few moments before chasing each other home from school, were standing still staring at the scene before them, mouths open, eyes wide. A few giggles from Elizabeth and she was flipped over like a flap-jack smack into Samuel's arms. Samuel opened the door and crossed the threshold with all the flourish and drama of a newlywed man, taking the stairs to their room three at a time. The girls stood outside the door, staring, pressed against the screen, little cross hatches making memories upon their little noses, their astonishment turning to laughter at their typically stern father's shenanigans.

Ever so gently, he laid Elizabeth upon the duvet, kicked the door closed with his heel, loosened his tie and looked Elizabeth in the eyes. "What was it you wanted to know? Something about a fire?" Leaning over, his breath hot on her neck. "You, my dear, Elizabeth, fire," he whispered, breathless.

The sun blazed red through their window, the wind abated and falling leaves paused. Daniel and Lucille were coming home. A dream come true. Yet, pulling at her heart, tendrils of guilt made Elizabeth pause. Josephine, she wondered, what to do about Josephine?

Chapter 10

"What can we do about Josephine, Mother?" she asked, her long black habit blowing in the wind, one hand to her to her veil, the other hidden in the many layers and folds of dark, woolen fabric. The sound of her voice, a sweet and lilting French, peppered the air surrounding them.

"I have prayed for guidance, Sister, but so far He has been silent."

"Silence does not feed hungry mouths or quiet a crying baby. Surely, there is an answer." Closing her eyes, she let out a small sigh.

"Sister Celestine, God helps those who help themselves. I will speak with Reverend Gillet."

Standing at the mouth of the river Raisin, the two Sisters looked out upon a grey and dismal morning. Clouds were building overhead and a bite in the air threatened snow again. Lifting their skirts an inch or two, the bottoms already covered in snow and ice, they began the slow walk back to their log home. Just six weeks since the founding of the Congregation of Sisters, Servants of the Immaculate Heart of Mary at Monroe, Michigan, they were a small group, Sister M. Celestine, the first novice. Their days were long and hard, but with open and loving hearts, they toiled with the peace and grace of God.

The year 1845, Michigan and the United States still much of frontier, was finishing up as a year of many surprises. A twenty-seventh and twenty-eighth star was added to the American Flag with the admittance of Florida and Texas, President Andrew Jackson died, only eight years after leaving the White House, anesthesia was used for the first time during childbirth, and Edgar Alan Poe published The Raven. Adding to the list of God's benevolence or trials, the Sisters of IHM had the biggest surprise of all left at their very doorstep.

Just yesterday, Mother Maxis leading the way, a French litany or two sent up to the heavens on a blustery and cold December morning, the Sisters were returning from their morning walk. As they approached the cabin, the wind began to blow harder, sideways, slanted, upside down, back and forth. Pulling their veils around their faces they hurried along the path. Having walked this way almost every morning, a benediction at the river, a ritual for the Sisters, crooked roots and stones, frozen mounds of ice and snow, were navigated with ease. As they neared the clearing of their cabin, they stopped short. A cry was heard, small and staccato, a pause, then another cry, muffled, tiny, high pitched. Sister Celestine's heart lurched and her mind raced. Thoughts of her baby sister, the night she died, all her mother's attempts failing until all they could do was hold her until she breathed her last, crashed into her reverie and she began to run. Flying past Mother Maxis with a "Forgive me Mother apology," she raced towards the sound, finding a tiny baby girl, an infant, wrapped in a rough woolen blanket, the edges torn and icy. Quickly, they brought the baby into the cabin. She was perfect in every way, quite possibly only a few hours old, as the umbilical cord, roughly severed, was still warm and soft.

"Wolves. It is a wonder you found her first." Sister Ann rushed to heat a pot of water.

"Glory be to God," Sister Celestine exclaimed. "What in the world was He thinking? A tiny baby?" Rocking back and forth as close to the fire as safely possible, she looked up searching Mother Maxis' eyes. The baby cried, little spurts of high pitched wails that wracked its body. Sister Celestine, using the soft pad of her thumb, gently wiped away the purple sticky afterbirth, crusty now over the infant's eyes. *"Fils de Dieu,"* she whispered. Sister Ann returned and agreeing with Sister Celestine, she too prayed for the infant, this child of God.

"What was she thinking, the poor soul," Mother Maxis muttered low and slow under her breath. She placed her hand against the baby's face and felt some warmth return.

"May I name her, Mother? *S'il vous plait.* Josephine? She has the spirit of a survivor."

"*Oui.* Your baby sister. I remember. Josephine. She will need a mother's milk."

"And baptism. I fear the angels will not hear her cries," Sister Celestine worried. *"Mon Dieu."*

"God hears the cry of the poor, Sister. Sister Ann, fetch a nurse at once."

Josephine Theresa Renauld Gillet entered the world, nameless, with a violent birth and abrupt dismissal. Abandoned by her mother, she was thrown at the mercy of the Immaculate Heart of Mary. This little order of Sisters, with everything a hardship and all odds against them, did not fail this blessing from God. Listening to the inner voice of God's spirit, they poured all their love into her being. Their mission was two-fold, fidelity to God and to bring faith to the French-Canadian immigrants, which with Reverend Gillet's blessing, fit perfectly with the task of nurturing a baby into a young Catholic woman.

At the age of five, a precocious and energetic child, the topic of what to do with Josephine became a constant source of tension among the Sisters. Equally divided on the matter, they both loved her beyond reason and questioned what was best. Although orphanages were becoming more popular with the Canadian Catholic Ministries, education was more the point than a home.

Over the next few years, reports of a new vision in the city of Toronto had the Sisters looking north and to the recently consecrated Bishop Charbonnel. The founder of several important Toronto ministries including an orphanage, hospital, youth hostel, homes for the elderly and The Society of St. Vincent De Paul, Bishop Charbonnel created a wave of conversion with his dynamic preaching and by bringing two orders to the city, the Christian Brothers/Basilian Fathers, and the Sisters of St. Joseph. In the ten years of his episcopate, he built twenty-three churches, brought thousands closer to God, among them, a young motherless girl from Monroe, Michigan.

Mother Maxis agonized the most over the question of Josephine. A position of authority in the order, she had to consider her head as well as her heart. Changes within the order, as well as great growth in numbers, left Mother with the need to secure a future for Josephine. Bishop John Nueman of Scranton, Pennsylvania expressed interest in starting an IHM order in the east. It was only time before she was invited to leave this frontier and return to where her life as a Sister began.

Mother Delphine Fontbonne and the Sisters of St Joseph were having great success in Toronto with the Irish poor under Bishop Charbonnel's loving embrace. However, it was their dedication to the education of young women, unique at this time, with the creation of St. Joseph's Academy, a private day and boarding school for young women from elementary through high school years that caught the attention of Mother Maxis. More than a finishing school for rich, young women, the Sisters were dedicated to educating the whole person in physical, creative, intellectual, spiritual, and social abilities within a faith-filled community.

A parcel of valuable east coast land, Mother Maxis' grandfather's bequeath for financial security, became Josephine's divine intervention and the means to a promising future. Fluent in French and English, a ten-year-old Josephine and her few belongings were packed up and ready to part for Toronto.

The sendoff was one of blessings, tears, and joy. Waiting to leave, Josephine was unusually quiet. The warm winds of summer abated during the night, leaving a wet and cool morning. Pulling her shawl close around her neck, a gift from Sister Ann, lovingly tatted throughout the winter, she took a long look at her surroundings. This little log cabin, the only home she knew, the big oak tree, one of many hours of hiding and climbing and scolding, these women, her mothers, her family, Josephine realized how lucky she was and just how much she would miss them. She was well prepared for secondary school, already far beyond her years in education. Mathematics, philosophy, biology and chemistry, and of course, literature were her foundations.

"Something for you. To remember us," Sister Celestine offered and placed a small parcel in Josephine's hands. Small, sad, smiling eyes looked at her from numerous black and white habits. Smiling back, Josephine felt the weight of the parcel and thought of long, cold winter nights in the cabin and Sister Celestine reading to them from their bible. Their only bible.

Looking up, Josephine opened her mouth to object, holding out the parcel in her upturned palm.

"You know we have it memorized. Only the weight of it, holding it in your hand, an opening of the Word. Besides, we each marked passages for you." Mother Maxis redirected the parcel back into Josephine's embrace. Reaching into the endless folds of her habit, Mother pulled out a small gift. Wrapped in a purple ribbon were several sheets of precious paper, a small bound journal, pen and ink. "Write to us and write to Him, " she said with a twinkle in her eye. *"Bonjour, mon cher."*

"Bonjour, Mere Maxis," she managed to return. Forcing a small smile, Josephine nervously stepped up into the wagon that would bring her to the ferry where she would meet the family, her chaperones, and begin the arduous five-day journey. The wagon pulled slowly away. Josephine watched the Sisters, identical except for height and girth, waving and crying, get smaller and smaller until the wagon turned and they were no more.

Chapter 11

Josephine grew into a beautiful and well educated young woman under the guidance of the Sisters of Saint Joseph. In the mid-1860s, residing in Canada became a blessing, as the United States now found itself at war with itself. Torn apart at the seams, this once great nation turned inwards, pitting north against south, state against state, neighbor to neighbor, friends, and families. Divisions cleaved as the casualties mounted, and the great organism of war raged on.

When going to war seemed imminent, families far outside the conflict, with the means to do so, prepared alternate plans. One such family, prominent in the Chicago Southside Irish community, was determined their one and only son, Henry, was not to be lost to a conflict with which they held no conviction.

Unlike other American cities, well established many decades prior to the great influx of immigrants, Chicago was a prairie until the 1800s. It was during its infancy that the Illinois and Michigan Canal was built, connecting the Great Lakes to the Mississippi river and the Irish immigrants to Chicago. Arriving at the city's emergence at the middle point of the nineteenth century, the Irish avoided much of the anti-Catholic, anti-Irish sentiment that so deeply polluted other, earlier founded American cities.

James Lane, the Cork native who would go down in history for the success of meat production in the United States, began so in Chicago in 1836. Joining the first St. Patrick's Day Parade in 1843, he led the way for other Irish immigrants to rise to the top. Another Cork native, a shrewd young man, William McGough, arrived in Chicago in 1837, grabbed onto the shirttails of the rising Mr. Lane and secured a place for himself in the economic engine of one of America's fastest growing cities.

Although better off than their fellow Irishmen in New York or Philadelphia, the Chicago Irish still dealt with the cultural and ethnic politics and grievances typical of the time. True to their clan origins, they stuck together and became not only the majority ethnicity in Chicago, but also a worthy and intimidating opponent.

William McGough, scrappy and fist ready, was blessed with the gift of language, appealing to both the ignorant, starving Irish and those who rose above. Sitting smack in the middle of the Irish social equation, he was the perfect answer to Mr. Lane's personnel problems and a way for those counting the cash to keep their hands clean. Ten years into the position, it was William's hands that were now washed, his eyes fixed on the cash being counted. An elegant wife and five beautiful daughters, added ease and comfort to the social scene. Yet it wasn't until the birth of his son, Henry, in 1850, that William finally felt he made his mark.

Spoiled by his sisters and especially his father, Henry knew no hardship. Yet, all this love and attention led only to good nature, a ready smile, and a sweet disposition. In the warmer months of summer, Henry's sisters would take him to the river to watch the boat races. Pretty, in their summer hats and dresses, Henry, in his knee britches, vest, and tie, they were a sight to see. Strong, young men, their muscles taut and sinewy would lean and pull, drawing oars deftly, the boats gliding across the water, as if flying. The coxswain, tiny at the bow, called out commands, directing and correcting their course and the crew in the art of rowing. Outriggers held the oars far beyond the vessel, allowing for a lighter, more streamlined shell. Just two years after the advent of shell racing, they were preparing for an exciting event. The events of October, 1858 would prove the better oarsman. In a five-mile course, The Metropolitan Rowing Club of Chicago and the Shakespeare Rowing Club of Toronto would square off in four oared shells for the unbelievable purse of $1,000. Much to the dismay of a large and overly excited Chicago crowd, Toronto took the lead early and claimed the prize. Henry never forgot that day and dreamt of nothing but rowing, water, and wind.

About the time of Henry's tenth birthday, the unrest brewing over the question of slavery was beginning to boil over. No pot was big enough to keep the conflict contained. Burning, scalding, erupting, the issue refused to remain inert, rising to unforeseen heights, escaping its confines and ultimately, running over the

157

sides, no means effective enough to stop the boiling concoction of hatred, resentment, and anger. America's civil war was soon to begin.

The Irish were a hard-birthed people. Even those riding the waves of fortune were not that far from the bottom rung to remember their toil. In a time when physiognomy was the method of discrimination, as apparent as the nose on a face, some Irish separated themselves from the issue of slavery. They carried enough on their backs. William McGough felt no obligation to the question of slavery nor the division of North and South. Although economics certainly caused concern, William counted enough cash, to think only of Henry, his one and only loving, gentle son. Inquiries were made and a place secured at the Community of De La Salle Brothers for a young Henry McGough. At the corner of Lombard and Jarvis Streets, Henry would learn French, excel in academics, and to his delight, learn the art of rowing. It was his obsession of rowing that would lead him to his other obsession in life, a beautiful woman, five years his senior and one step away from final vows.

Soon enough, Josephine was invited by the Sisters of St. Joseph to join their family on a permanent basis. This time, there was no question about Josephine. As the novitiate, Sister Marie Fontenbleu, she was following the only road in life she ever knew. A voracious reader, avid writer, and dedicated follower of Jesus Christ, she easily took to teaching and life in a religious community. The structured environment gave a sense of security and belonging, something a young woman with unanswered questions needed. Morning prayers, a humble breakfast, and community chores marked the hours before sunrise, which led Josephine to her favorite part of the day, her morning walk to the market.

List in hand, the cook's scrawling French penmanship covering every inch of precious paper, Josephine took the long way into town. It was early September and the summer was falling fast. Down the large expanse of lawn, she inhaled the fresh smell of hay, allowed the sounds of waking animals to wash over her. Leaves, rising and falling with the swish and sway of her three-layered skirts, her feet chilled by the damp and dew of morning, Josephine felt her step lighten, her eyes brighten. Turning at the barn, she took the path down to the water. A stiff breeze picked up her veil like a sail unfurled to the sea, and she was forced to remove her hands from the warmth of her wools and hold the veil close to her face. The sun, just a painter's stroke on the horizon, held promise of warmth and friendship. Josephine felt her connection to God through nature. Maybe it was her beginnings in Monroe, their hard scrabble existence, dependence on nature, and gratitude for any and all blessings that rooted her to the earth. Thrown into this world, her first moments and breaths at the mercy of nature, Josephine was a child of the earth, her very being symbiotic with all of God's creation. Happy to dwell on the beauty of the morning, Josephine knew there was a schedule to keep and a price to pay if late. Cook did not tolerate tardiness.

Picking up her pace, she rushed past the busy crowds of the wharf, eyes downcast, hands lost in the hidden recesses of her habit. A busy place in the morning, she took the far side of the road, casting small glances at the water, the sea gulls fighting for fisherman's bait, the sun now a few more touches of color and shape. Her navigation almost complete, the sounds of the wharf, vessels straining at their ties, the lap of water against hull and dock, a shout, "All hands on deck," receded and new calls of sellers shouting out wares, hopeful and enticing, took hold. Just about to cross the divide between those who bring in and those who give out, the crowd abruptly stopped. All eyes turned towards the reef and a new drama unfolding, unfurling, afloat from its moors. The crowd, open mouthed and wide eyed, went from silent to raucous as laughter built, shouts teased, and overall hilarity was exhibited at the expense of a young, embarrassed and naive oarsman. The Toronto Yacht club, it's club building a refitted freighter, in the spirit of independence, broke from its moorings and was headed out to sea. Given the morning task of preparing the floating foundation for daily meetings and merriment, this unfortunate young man was outmatched and outmanned for such a worthy opponent. As if recalling the glory days of past, the freighter was making great speed to sea, defeating all its demons and winning it all in a single sail at the expense of an unfortunate young Henry McGough.

Young men in fours jumped into sleek shells, wrestled oars into the water and raced to the rescue. Like the beginnings of rowing, any two boats running alongside with good wagers to place were game. Coxswain were screaming orders, muscles straining, cheers flying. It took long enough to return the errant freighter to its moors to attract a large crowd, the young men exuberant in their success, with the exception of poor Henry, who like his floating kidnapper, was defeated, deflated, and dejected.

Josephine took notice quickly of the handsome young man so downcast and depressed, running from the wharf. Her heart went out to him and she wondered, what would he do now? Under her breath she said a quick prayer for fortitude. Hurrying to finish her errands, she was lost in the negotiations of the day, using her religious station and habit expertly for the benefit of the best price, the seller's allowances a vain hope for grace or forgiveness. It wasn't until on her way back home, that she realized the voice booming on the wharf was the very young man of her prayers. Halting just a second or two, she glanced upwards, the sun now fully formed and framing the young man standing before a crowd. In expert storytelling, he retold the events of the day, as if part of a dervish fairy tale. The freighter, a mind and heart of its own, was the spirits of the sea, the moorings, its forgiving mother, and Henry, the young Gilgamesh epic in his mission. The crowd was roaring and in full form. Josephine saw not only fortitude, but genius. With his crazy tale, full of past and present archetypes, the day was his. His eyes met hers and he paused for a moment. Quickly turning away, Josephine hurried, the wind at her back, like the hand of God. Pushing her towards devotion, she felt the pull of those eyes, the will of a young man, and all the unanswered questions she could not escape.

Henry sought out Josephine at every opportunity. Her white veil was a clear sign to him that negotiations were still underway, exit doors were still ajar. It wasn't until final vows that she would wear the black veil and white coif. A true yarn-spinner, Henry felt he could turn any situation to his advantage, and proved so at the wharf. From that very day he recreated his mishap, Henry thought of nothing but the young novitiate. It took two weeks before she would acknowledge his presence, greeting her every morning on her way to the market. A quiet *"Monsieur"* was the limit for another two. At six weeks, she looked him in the eye for a moment and smiled. Josephine walked and Henry talked. He told her everything, his life story, all his hopes and dreams. Early on, he learned if he pushed too far, asked too many questions, she would whisper *"adieu"* and quickly leave. Like a silent confessional, Henry bared his soul. Something told him, maybe the tilt of her head, the fact that she did not divert her route, even the cold, white puffs of breath, that she was more than a listener. It wasn't until he announced that he was leaving that she revealed her true feelings.

"Sister, *Bienvenudo.*"

Josephine nodded, walking briskly beside him. Her woolen shawl was sprinkled with snow, white on white like linen and lace.

"I must tell you, Sister, I am to leave tomorrow," Henry stumbled in French, his speaking skills far behind his comprehension.

Unaware she was fluent in English, his mind scrambled for something to say. Halting, he realized she stopped and was staring out at the water. It was a cold, clear morning. Ice and frost covered the ground, cold forbidding waves frothed and foamed, glittering in the sunlight. Walking towards her, he saw a tear escape, her beautiful brown eyes, deep and warm in a vibrant pool of emotion.

"*Non.* No, *Monsieur,* the market. I cannot be late," she muttered under her breath. Drawing inside herself, almost hidden in the white folds of her habit, Josephine began to tremble.

"I don't even know your name. Sister, please, if only your name, I will have someone. Someone to pray for me."

"Not to war?" she asked, this time in English, her lips trembling. The wind picked up off the wharf and Josephine buried her face in her hands.

Henry's eyes widened. Realizing his struggling French was no longer a barrier, he gently placed his hand at her elbow and guided her behind a large oak tree, out of the wind and eyes of others.

"I must return. The draft, it cannot be avoided. They say the war will not last long. A dispensation may be granted. I can only hope and pray. But, your name? How can I pray without your name?" he begged.

Josephine raised her head and for the first time since that day at the wharf, fully looked upon Henry. Her heart lurched and she felt the ties of her habit bind, the rules of her day harbor, and the answer to her questions shipwrecked in an empty ocean. Removing her hands from her deep pockets, she gently cradled his face and began to cry. Here before her was everything she ever wished for in a man.

"How?" she asked. "When all is against us?"

Laying her head upon his chest, Josephine felt the beat of his heart and felt a comfort, a place where she belonged. It was as if her roots, so wild and reaching before, now longed to deepen.

"Do not pray for me, but hurry back," she pleaded. "When you come, you may ask for Sister Marie Fontenbleu, but Josephine will be waiting."

Although history would prove Henry's quest for love and marriage a success, Josephine would always keep a part of herself secret. Both relegated in their youth to the auspices of Father Charbonnel for safety, their journey north was of the same intent and direction. However, there the similarity ended. Henry, for all his love and devotion would never learn of the beginnings of Josephine, the root of her heart and the core of her conception. Only the IHM Sisters, their letters to Josephine, lovingly written in French, every one saved, a small stack bound in purple ribbon, and her little black bible, held the answers to her past. Josephine had no need to hide these things, Henry was not a man of the past. Always looking ahead, he reached out and Josephine, holding fast, learned that fairy tales need not a beginning to come true.

Chapter 12

It was an unusually warm and sticky July morning, the temperature well above eighty degrees and only just before sunrise. Wet morning moisture hung between the escaping night and the emerging morning like the overdue curtain call at the end of a long drawn out performance. Lucille, after a night of little sleep, more of a morning sleeper than riser, was up and dressed before Daniel even stirred. Sitting at her desk, a wedding present from Elizabeth, she ran her hands over the fine wood grain, fingered the clear glass knobs and delicate carvings. Depicted in relief, as if illustrating a story, were the Irish meadows falling down to meet the great Atlantic, its waters leading, as if with purpose, to the meandering St. Lawrence Seaway and ultimately, the vast forests of Michigan. Pausing, her hands resting on the very wood of the trees depicted, Lucille let out a small sigh.

Looking up, her eyes drifted to a family photo, their twentieth anniversary, her mother, Daniel's parents, the children all laughing and fooling around, hung above the desk on the wall. It had taken over an hour to get the picture taken and Daniel had to pay double. The photographer was not pleased. Six girls and at last, a boy, Charles. Today was a day to reminisce. Many years passed since the day she married Daniel and had lost her father. There were many reasons to look back. Melancholy, she turned and stood, walked over to the window and pulled back the curtains. A faint glow was beginning to highlight the river, its color washed out by the light fog holding on like a newborn clasp. The rustle of covers and soft, breathy sounds of Daniel waking made her turn. This man, she thought, I am so lucky. Elizabeth and Samuel, like parents of her own, and of course her mother, Josephine, all of them so close, so precious.

She'll never forget the day her mother had arrived in Michigan. Just one suitcase, pink with peach blossoms, and a large black umbrella. It was raining, torrentially. Standing at Samuel and

Elizabeth's front door, water running off her like a spring rain set on amassing new rivers, she surprised them all. Not expected for over a week, Lucille answered the door, never guessing it would be her mother.

"Mother. You're here," Lucille stammered.

"*Oui.* Yes, it would seem so."

A few moments passed. The sound of battering rain on the porch roof and the drip of Josephine's umbrella filled the awkward silence. Taking a step inside, Josephine set down her suitcase and placed a hand upon Lucille's shoulder.

"Wake up, darling. Please tell my dear friend, Elizabeth, I am here."

Josephine had walked in the door that wet and windy day, everything she cared about in one suitcase. Moving in with Elizabeth, just blocks from Lucille and Daniel, Josephine positioned herself for busy hands and a full heart. She and Elizabeth were inseparable. With each new child, another bed, chair at the table, shoes at the door, it soon became clear to the keen grandmothers that Daniel and Lucille's home was too small. When Charles was born, Elizabeth and Josephine invited them to move into the big house. "Empty rockers need little children," they said. After Samuel died, Elizabeth and Josephine had moved into adjoining bedrooms and now, many years later and well into their seventies, they were like tiny identical china dolls, finishing each other's sentences and correcting each other's mistakes.

Sitting at the desk, her thoughts in the deep past, Lucille felt unusually sentimental. She walked over to the bed and leaning over, planted a kiss on Daniel's forehead. Warm and damp like the emerging morning, she felt the urge to crawl back in bed and forget the past, wrap her arms around this wonderful man and hide under the covers. Daniel opened his eyes, dreams washing away, blue upon blue focusing, waking.

"My, look who's up with the crows." Daniel let out a sigh and closed his eyes.

"Sleep was not kind to me, again." Lucille's face was placid, her eyes unreadable.

164

"No doubt, the wedding." Reaching his arms around her, he pulled her towards him.

A ray of sunlight streamed through the window, blinding, for a moment. Startled, Daniel sat up. Too close, heads knocked. Daniel fell back with a thud, threw his head to the side and stuck out his tongue with a flourish of theatrics. Opening one eye, he saw Lucille's unchanged profile.

"You're a murderous woman," he teased. "What time is it?" he asked. "I will be late."

"Plenty of time. They won't be here until noon." Lucille thought of pretty Pearl. Charles certainly waited to marry and in doing so, found what appeared a perfect partner. Yet, Lucille knew her son, his tendency to harbor sullen moods, his difficulty with happiness. From the time he was a small boy, what seemed immaterial to his sisters, often struck Charles deeply, his sensitive heart striking out, anger the first emotion. Lucille said a silent prayer for the new couple. One week away, the family would arrive today to stay before the wedding.

"Going to be a boiler of a day, I see," Daniel said as he rose from the bed. "Reminds me of another hot July day, long ago, a handsome young lad and a beautiful little red head." Taking a swipe at her seat, he laughed, stopping short. "Why so sad?"

"I too was remembering, but of father." Sitting on the side of the bed, she stared at her hands.

Daniel sat beside her and reached out. "Charles is our baby, Lucille. It feels like loss to me too. I see him and think of Da. But, then I see our mothers together, the children, such wonderful people they've become, and you, my lovely wife, and I feel good."

"But, why so far? It will take a full day's travel to see them. That is, with good weather."

"We will have to find ourselves a little cottage. One on Mill Pond maybe, where we can cozy up to the Roosevelts and Fords. Maybe even try out one of those new automobiles." Daniel gently nudged Lucille with his elbow and looked at her, his face full of question.

"It is lovely there."

"Clarkston, where vacation is your home," he mimicked. "Chin up, my dear Lucille," he said, gently placing a finger under her chin he pulled her towards him, planting a quick kiss upon her forehead. Rising, he stretched his arms up high and let out a long, slow breath.

Lucille looked out the window. "I decided to give Pearl the desk." Reaching into her pocket, she pulled out the small gold key, Jackson diamonds and McGough emeralds glittered in the bright sunshine, throwing diamonds of dancing light across the dark mahogany floor. A tiny pink ribbon was tied to the top.

"I think," he dropped his hands to his sides, "that is a splendid idea. It will be a tradition, and that, my dear, makes looking back looking ahead."

Daniel pulled Lucille to her feet and began to twirl them around. Tripping over his feet, she was soon laughing, Daniel belting out an old Irish wedding song. Lucille felt something release and her smile widen. Soon, the room was spinning, objects appearing and disappearing on fast forward. Lucille threw back her head and relishing the feeling of freedom, for a moment, left the past behind. There was a wedding on the way, things to do, and lives to live.

In the early 1920s, the little Village of Clarkston, saw much change. Almost a century old, this quaint little hamlet of lakes, woodlands, and farms, was the era of new living. Young couples looked to live where their home was a place of pleasure as well as work. A place to escape for residents of Detroit and Pontiac since the introduction of the railroad in early 1850s, Clarkston was well established for respite with several hotels, scenic recreation areas, and an opera house. But it wasn't until the automobile that came the greatest change. Saginaw Trail, a native American pathway, was widened and paved to accommodate this new, emerging form of transportation. Main Street followed a few years later and soon it wasn't just summer visitors that filled the downtown streets and shops.

Charles and Pearl moved into a little apartment on Main Street until their farmhouse on Holcomb road was completed.

Less than a mile outside of town, this sprawling yellow and white two story beauty included all the latest of new home construction with a sleeping porch and a breakfast nook. At a time when building trends were leaning towards more affordable housing and the bungalow style, Charles and Pearl decided on a mixture of the two. Keeping the two-story, wrap-around porch of the nineteenth century, they designed a more cost effective home without the maid in mind, used the latest, more efficient heating and cooling methods, the finished product a home with plenty of room for guests on the second floor, a nice family flow on the first, and all the grandeur of the house on the hill. Filling the wide front porch with rockers, summer evenings were spent overlooking the busy Village of Clarkston, appreciating the natural beauty of their large estate, all from the quiet and peaceful haven of their new-fashioned home.

Charles was to supervise the expansion of the family business southward. Well-traveled to Chicago and its points south and west, Charles saw a new method of transportation on the horizon for the Jackson-Saginaw Timber Company and this time, it was not limited to the confines of rails, the schedules and tariffs of the railroad machine, and the disasters that plagued profits. Automobile transport, although still in its infancy, held the allure of independence and the beauty of freedom, something that appealed greatly to the entrepreneurial businessmen of the roaring twenties.

Riding the waves of newlywed bliss, Charles was staying well above the dark depths that threatened his happiness. With the confidence of a beautiful and adoring wife, he was well known and liked, a gregarious young man with a good mix of Daniel's steady hand, Lucille's passion, and Samuel's inventive genius. Well-read on the inventions of the day, he knew about the "horseless carriages" that became "trail mobiles" that became "semi-trailers". Although, in the years to come, economics and the intrusion of war would delay the application of this new method of transport to the logging industry, Charles filled journal after journal with ideas for breaking confines of rail and blazing new pathways for the Jackson-Saginaw Timber Company. Many years later, these journals, long forgotten by the hardships of life and the injustices of war, became a reminder of failure, a reason for resentment, and a permanent wedge between a father and son.

With Charles at the helm of the family business and Pearl at the hearth of a new brood of Jacksons, Daniel and Lucille, Elizabeth and Josephine spent their days a comfortable step away from the pressures of life, enjoying their well-earned fortune. Sticking to Samuel's non-speculative practice of investing within, their land and timber increased, their money in regional assets such as ore, they rode out the 1920s with the ability to stay afloat of the financial crisis. Adjustments were made. Many furnishing and clothes were donated. The house on Mackinaw Island was closed, travel reduced, clothing mended and food stores scrimped and saved. More fortunate than others, Charles helped local businesses with free labor and materials and Pearl volunteered with local charities in soup kitchens and food donations, tending to the elderly and sick, and educating children. Applying his inventive mind to the trials at hand, Charles learned how to do much with little, passing down more than a few valuable lessons to his young sons. Tagging alongside, they watched with wide eyes as hundreds of men lined up for work each morning at the local lumber mill on Holcomb Street. Knowing most would be turned away without work, Charles arrived with a wagon full of warm fresh baked bread and hot coffee. For those interested, he held instructive classes, teaching unskilled workers how to process raw timber from long, rough cuts to fine pieces of woodwork. Charles knew with little else to do but agonize over the hunger pitting their stomachs, they would fall prey to the depressing evil of idleness, the despair he fought every day, its claws so often within inches. Even without the promise of payback, many signed up for the prospect of staying busy, both mind and body, and the sliver of hope for rising above the bindings of poverty.

Yet for all their industry and good faith, the Jacksons were not immune to tragedy. Although medical practices were far more advanced than the dark blindfolds and bindings of the 1800s, childbirth was still a dangerous process. Just a few years before the crash of cash, Pearl gave birth for the fifth time to boys, this time twins. A girl was not in the cards, nor were identical boys. Walter, the first to emerge, took his first breath, howling at the injury of being expelled, followed by Charles, his head cradled between Walter's feet, silent and still. The loss of a child and physical injury to Pearl was more than she could take. She would bear no more. It took months for her to rise from the bed and over a year for the diagnosis of polio. Yet, the tragedy was not for her alone. The guilt of delivering a disease to one child and death to the other quieted her. Surviving the depression, only to jump headlong into WWII was a source of anguish and a true test of faith and character for Charles and Pearl, one that would yield very different results and in the end, prove the true character of each.

Walter, never releasing the hold on his brother, dragged his Polio wracked feet behind him and persevered. Throughout the hard times, snug on his father's hip, Walter took in the misery of poverty, the hungry and drawn children, their outstretched hands, their faces defeated, took note of his well-kept clothes, full belly, and warmth of his father's embrace and believed he was blessed. This foundation of appreciation and compassion, this witness to outreach would change course for the Jackson family faith, a change causing anguish and upheaval at the very root of their hard working, Irish beginnings, a change never believed possible. But Walter was different, never firm footed, never having stood rooted to the ground, he led with his heart, and in doing so changed the lives of generations to come.

BOOK III

THE NEAR PAST
Years 1975 -1977

Chapter 1

"Come here, Steady," she said, sweet and slow, her arms stretched out wide, her smile inviting.

Steady, a fitting nickname for the stout and sturdy little man he was, ran into the arms of his gramma. Her soft, billowy dress, deep purple lilacs on white, a fashionable pattern for a gramma in the mid-1970s, gave a comfortable landing to the troubled little boy.

"Now, now, what is the matter, darlin'?" she asked gently, holding him close, the smell of fresh cut grass, dirt, and sweat filling her senses.

Steady let go of the strap holding his books and they fell to the floor with a thud. Just home from school, he was breathing like a freight train, as if he, unbelievably, ran the whole way up the hill from the bus stop. Letting silence fill the room, Gramma Weddington gently rubbed his back, placed her hand at the nape of his neck, his little body hot and tense.

It was she who gave the little boy his nickname. Steadman, a name too big for most men, a mouthful for any gramma lovingly whispering her grandchild's name, she held her tongue when they named him. It was holding him for the first time, her first grandchild, that she felt her heart return to normal, its beat steady for once. "Steady," she whispered, and the name stuck. Now, his stout little legs and sturdy frame, passive nature and gentle heart all in agreement with this endearing nickname, he answered to no other.

As his sobs subsided, Steady lifted his head and looked into his gramma's soft and gentile face. "They make fun of Father." With his large brown eyes pleading, tears brimming, cheeks ruddy, he didn't have to explain what happened.

Iris knew the trouble of her only son, Daniel. A Methodist preacher, just like her beloved Walter, he too walked as far left as possible when it came to conflict. And with Vietnam, the wounds refusing to heal, there was plenty of conflict. Too many boys came home wrapped in black bags, paying the price for political mayhem. Just another body in what was not a war, not understood, not wanted, and yet, the boys kept going and the boys kept dying. In speaking out, speaking truth, Daniel became a target. The Methodist church, cutting ties that bound two generations, turned away in fear. If Walter were here, he would be livid. It wouldn't be just Daniel speaking the truth. But Walter wasn't here. Only six years ago, just after the birth of his first and only grandchild, they placed him in the ground. Iris shuddered, thinking back. Cold and miserable, the winds blowing and rain biting, they huddled around the empty, gaping hole that held what she loved most in life. A private ceremony, it was just the four of them, Steady a swaddled bundle, close to his mother's breast. They tried to reach Walter's father, Charles, left several messages with a woman, each time an empty promise for his reply. Even then, Walter's father was absent and Walter, his last son to bury. On the way home Iris requested the baby was raised to call her Gramma Weddington, her family name. Never a Jackson, she buried the name with Walter, once and for all.

Not two months after they buried Walter, the church elders removed Daniel's rights. Still mourning, he proudly held his ground and started his own church. A few of the wealthier, braver members stood with Daniel, offering the funds needed and joined him in establishing a new church.

Now, five years after the founding of Faith Mission Church of God, holding her precious grandson, she found joy, in spite of all the turmoil. Although two full years since the official end of the US involvement in Vietnam, the country was still at war, this time with itself. Divisions created and resentments harbored still held neighbors, families, and generations apart. They were a nation in need of healing, Daniel preached. Running her finger across her forehead, as if to wipe away the finely etched lines, she knew enough of life to know peace was fleeting. Yet, thinking of Daniel and his new church, she smiled. A proud mother is not without worry or joy, she thought.

Reaching behind her, Gramma Weddington picked up the family bible and placed it on her lap. Large and heavy, covered with a deep, rich, engrained, red leather, it was their present to Daniel at his ordination. Walter spent weeks choosing, weighing each one in his hand, running the tips of his fingers over the covers, inhaling the new and crisp scent of fresh paper, the deep musty smell of leather. A family tree page in the beginning was a must, Walter insisted, for God's word is rooted in family.

Patting a place beside her on the sofa, she asked, "How about a story, honey?"

Seeing the familiar family bible, Steady's eyes brightened and he giggled. Jumping up to sit beside her he started, "Samuel and Elizabeth were born in the old country, Ulcer provedend."

"Ul-ster prov-i-dence," she gently corrected. Opening the book, she placed her finger at the top of the family tree where Samuel and Elizabeth's names began the Jackson legacy.

Their fingers followed the generations down. Reading aloud he continued, "Daniel and Lucille, Charles and Pearl, Walter and Iris. That's you. Gramma, Iris is you." Steady beamed, a chubby little index finger wiggled in her direction.

Only six, he was already reading and writing. A bright and eager little boy, round and soft like the plush leather chairs in Walter's study, he was a delight to his gramma. Unfortunately, what delighted his gramma made him a perfect target for the cruelty of children.

"Gramma," he asked, "you and Grandpa were married at the end of the war, right?" Steady pictured a long, dark and gloomy battlefront, men hiding on either side, entrenched, smoke and fire lifting and there at the end of the battlefield stood his gramma and grandpa, she in a long white gown, he, a dark suit, looking up from the confines of his wheelchair, a preacher with a bible standing before them.

"That's right, Steady," she replied, her mind reeling back in time.

Their wedding day, it was Walter's walk down the aisle that held all eyes, his familiar crutches, almost permanent appendages, left at the altar. Meeting in the middle, they held hands, his grasp a little too fierce, brought tears to eyes already awash in emotion.

Now, many years later, tears again stinging the outside of her eyes, she continued with her finger down the page.

Steady reached up and turned her face towards him. "How? Grandpa wasn't in the war. Grandpa was in a wheelchair."

Suddenly understanding, Iris hugged him fiercely, crushing the book between them. "Sometimes I forget what a youngin' you are, little man. Grandpa wasn't in a wheelchair during the war, but Uncle Sam didn't want him, on account of his polio. We were married after the war was over. Oh Steady, it was such a beautiful day." Looking away she paused, lost in thought.

Grabbing her hand, Steady placed it back on the page. "Daniel and Victoria, that's Mommy and Daddy." His voice firm, he stared at the page, missing Iris' face cloud over, her lips form a thin line.

"Yes sir," she agreed. "Daniel is your Daddy, my little boy. And Victoria," clearing her throat she paused, "Victoria is your mother."

Cocking his head, Steady looked up at his Gramma. "Don't you like Mother?" he asked, already keen to the tensions that undercut their daily lives.

"Of course, sweetheart." Placing her arm around him, she gave a little squeeze. "Victoria is just fine."

Feeling a little guilty, Iris thought about her mysterious daughter-in-law. There were many unsettling things about Victoria. She was quiet and withdrawn and her dress, always black, the whole outfit, including sunglasses. And whenever Iris asked her about her family or childhood, she clammed up. Yet, she was kind to Iris. Moving to the carriage house, when Daniel and Victoria married and took over the farmhouse, Iris held a side-view into their lives. It was clear Victoria loved Daniel and could not be a more devoted mother. Yet, there was something. She was always a step back, no matter how hard Iris tried. And try Iris did. Layered on all the southern charm a well-bred Kentucky woman could muster. No matter, Victoria was still the same, quiet, a mystery. Even Daniel understood, said so on more than one occasion. Victoria has her own way, "Mom," he would say. "It's just not your way." Not anyone's way, Iris thought.

"And Aunt Isabella was your little girl," Steady said, looking up at Iris, his eyes twitching, hovering just below her chin. "I wish she grew up like Daddy, Gramma."

"Me too, honey," Iris answered.

Many times, they read the family tree and every time, when they came to Iris' first born, Isabella, Steady nervously searched her out. Isabella, only a baby when she died, was the first of many holes that would tear their hearts apart. Squeezing his little hand, Iris knew the routine.

Placing his chubby finger at the bottom of the family tree, Steady smiled. "Steadman Jackson, now that's me," he hollered, jumping off the couch and clapping. "Hooray. Hooray."

Iris laughed at his wonderful innocence and kissed the top of his messy, little head. "Well, do I have a story to tell you," she began.

Seeing him pause, his look of wonder, Iris knew Steady was all hers. Pulling him on the couch next to her, she began, "One day, long ago, must have been the hottest Kentucky day ever, your grandfather and I went swimming. We jumped in the cool, clear water and were having a great time. It felt sooo good and my, was Walter sure a good swimmer. The sun was shining and not a cloud in the sky. All of a sudden, dark clouds rolled in, thunder and lightning crashed all around us. We knew we must get out of the water, on account of the lightening. We weren't fixing on being bacon, crispy, fried up and all," Iris smiled and continued. "I should have known better, born and raised in Kentucky. Of course, it never occurred to Walter. All around us, the banks were covered with rattlesnakes."

"Snakes are cold blooded, Gramma," Steady whispered, his eyes wide as possible, cheeks quivering. "They need sunlight. What did you do? "

"Yes, they are, Steady. You are such a smart little man," she patted his chubby hand and continued, nice and slow, "Well, snakes hate lightening and usually they head straight for their den, but a pack of vultures were roosting right nearby."

"Gramma, Vultures don't eat live snakes. They eat dead snakes," Steady looked up at Iris, his lips pursed and eyes half-mast.

"Well, now that is true, Steady. You are such a smart little man, but you see, there was a pile of dead snakes, right smack in front of their den. They were halfway between one place and another and downright confused. They weren't the only ones confused. Your grandfather and I, well, we were in a pickle for sure."

"What - what - did - you - do?" Steady asked, his eyes bright, jaw firm, barely open.

"The only thing we could do," she exclaimed.

"I know, I know," he shouted. "Grandpa jumped up and tied those vines together, the kind that hang down, just like Tarzan, and swung you right out of there," he declared, pumping his fist in the air. Stopping suddenly, he stared at his gramma all smiles.

"How did you ever know?" she asked, emphasizing each word, her jaw dropped and eyes played merrily. Narrowing her brows, she pretended to be serious. "You've heard this story, haven't you?"

"No, Gramma, never," Steady exclaimed, slowly moving his head right and left.

"Well, then, it must be Grandpa Walter's blood in you. I do declare, you are a right smart little man, just like my Walter." Pulling him close, Iris laughed a little laugh. "Now it's your turn. Tell me a story, Steady."

Steady screwed up his face, his eyes intent and chin firm. He swung his little legs back and forth and tapped his knees. Coming to a standstill, he looked up and smiled. "Oh boy, do I have a story for you," he began.

With the sun setting and the smell of dinner cooking, Steady and Gramma Weddington passed the early evening in what was their favorite pastime. Spinning a yarn, telling stories, letting their imagination run wild, the seeds were planted for the years ahead. And like most plantings, a few seeds blew away and strayed, rooting firmly in places never imagined.

Gramma Weddington and Steady finished their stories, Steady now fast asleep. Victoria called from the kitchen, dinner was ready. Closing her eyes Iris exhaled long and deep. This room, the formal living area, was her favorite. Paintings, purchased over the years, hung with care. A wide and deep fireplace, rich walnut mantle held the center of attention. To the right, stood the beautiful drop-leaf writing desk, perfectly placed for long letters to far away family on cold Michigan nights. Family photos and treasures from years of marriage were here and there, so many memories. Long cottage windows, ceiling to floor on all sides let in sun and stars. So many nights she spent here, Walter traveling, the windows open like French doors, curtains blowing, the moon and stars casting shadows throughout the room. After she moved to the carriage house, it was Daniel who said to leave this room untouched, a place for her when she came to visit. Referred to as Gramma's room, the study across the hall, was Grandpa's, Walter's, also untouched. Entering the front door, Iris on the right and Walter on the left, visitors were greeted with a true history of the home and a warm and welcoming spirit.

Chapter 2

Walter and Iris were married in the summer of 1946 when the boys were coming home, hearts were mending, and love was blossoming. At the onset of the draft, denied for service because of his handicap, Walter was dejected. Although, spiritually less suited for service than most, he was at a loss staying home with women and old men, waiting, worrying, only to deliver one after another report of bad news of sons, brothers, fathers lost, heroically, tragically in saving the free world.

In desperation, he thrashed out. Only sixteen when the US joined the fight, Walter felt abandoned by his God, his country, his family and friends. Just like the legs that barely held him, his convictions fell, leaving him without a foundation, a worthy way to contribute. Stubborn, he turned against the Catholic church and his parents. Charles and Pearl, devout, holding onto their faith, their last lifeline to four boys at war, did not understand. But it wasn't until Walter packed his bags and left, a note neatly written, left on his mother's drop-leaf writing desk, a Jackson family heirloom, that his father's heart hardened.

Iris knew little of the real story behind Walter and his father's falling out. She knew Walter walked away from the family and the business. She knew his father, Charles, was difficult and struggled with alcohol. Never one for money, Walter held no interest in the family business or high stake finance. Young and impulsive, he followed his heart, one step at a time, all his belongings slung over his shoulder, ultimately ending up at a Southern Methodist revival in Kentucky. More for the meal than the service, serendipity intervened and he fell head over heels for Iris, finding a fit for his faith and his heart. The first time Iris saw Walter, she wanted to feed him, hug him, and marry him all at once. Completing his seminary, Walter married his true love and headed straight home to Michigan to win over hearts and heads with his new bride and faith. Only, it was too late. Four brothers lost to war and his mother, fresh in the ground, a victim of tuberculosis, Walter found an empty, abandoned, and cold home. On his mother's cherished writing desk was a note, this time to Walter. Her last deed, a sign of unconditional love, Pearl turned over the farmhouse to her only living son. Walter was shocked. His father, Charles, holding onto his anger, his hand firmly wrapped around the bottle, got up one day, moved to Los Angeles, never to return. The sins of the son became the sins of the father, except for one difference, greed. Jackson-Saginaw Timber Company moved to Los Angeles too.

Only once, did Iris ask about the Jackson fortune. She knew there was more than the farmhouse. The family business was bigger than ever, with a publicly traded stock, board of Directors, and a CEO. Aunts and great aunts of Walter's held a small percentage, and Walter's father, the last Jackson at the helm, held fast to the largest interest, the corporation now registered and domiciled in the state of California. Walter told her his family was well off, but she had no idea how well, until one afternoon, going through boxes in the attic, she came across an old scrapbook filled with newspaper clippings about the Jackson-Saginaw Timber Company. Sitting there, surrounded by things of the past, she was shocked. Everyone knew the Jackson family. They were right up there with the Vanderbilt's and the Rockefellers. But, why? she wondered, why was Walter so silent about his wealth? Especially, when as a minister in the Methodist church, he made barely enough for them to survive. Knowing the reason must have deep roots, Iris had waited until the right time to ask.

It was a beautiful summer Sunday night. The sweet scent of honeysuckle had filled the air and fireflies danced, their rhythmic illumination punctuating the darkness. After a full day of church services and meetings, Walter retired, as usual, to his study to review finances. The quarter-moon glowed, stars twinkled, and candlewicks burned low. Ready for bed, Iris stopped by the study to kiss Walter goodnight and beg him to retire.

Tense and irritable, he waved his hand at her and pleaded, "Please leave me be. I cannot sleep until I figure a way. I must find some money."

Iris knew Walter's usual easy going manner was tested late at night when his polio flared and his legs ached. Pressing her lips together, she turned to go, stopping suddenly. Walter was crying, softly. Throwing her arms around him, she was about to ask the question, but Walter interrupted her.

"Oh Iris. How can I support a family on such a pitiful allowance? The church knows I am resigned against my father's money, yet, they sit back and wait, as if I will give up my convictions and crawl back to the old man, begging. They are testing me," his voice was angry, words wet with tears and anguish.

Iris hugged him harder. Placing her head upon his shoulder, she waited.

"I will never take a penny from him," he cried. "Letters, so many letters I wrote home. No reply, ever. I never told you. All my mother's letters, I found them in her desk, sealed and stamped. Never got past the old man's hands. He is a cruel bastard. Angry at me for leaving. Angry at mother for leaving the house to me. Well, he sure landed the last blow."

A few moments passed. Walters hands hung at his sides. Iris lifted her head and ran her hand down his broad back. Making slow circles, she felt the tension of his muscles, the heat of his anger.

Taking a deep breath, he whispered, "I didn't know she was dying. I would have come." Slowly, his sobs subsided, his head heavy upon the desk.

"We will depend on God," Iris comforted, hoping the firmness of her voice belied her lack of conviction.

Hot, blustery winds blew in through the open windows. Cloud cover raced in and the sky went black. Flames flickered their last breath, extinguishing the moment and the last time Walter had ever spoke of his father.

In spite of all the loss, Iris and Walter were happy. They had each other and their faith. Fresh faced, earnest, and hardworking, they spent hours painting and sanding, fixing up the farmhouse. With the house a deep brown and trim a fresh coat of white, the old farmhouse took on new life. Walter found an old porch swing behind the shed. Hours of sanding revealed a beautiful cherry wood. Hung on the wide front porch it was a prized possession.

Most of all, Walter couldn't get over the carriage house. First, a place for the horses, then for the prized automobile, in his absence it was converted into a lovely cottage for his mother, Pearl, for her internment. All throughout the small and quaint little house were touches of Pearl. Early in their marriage, Walter could be found in the carriage house, walking the rooms, gently touching his mother's things. He insisted on only two changes. All icons of the Catholic faith were removed, boxed away and placed in the attic and his mother's cherished drop-leaf writing desk was moved back to the farmhouse, a posthumous present from Pearl to Iris, a maternal Jackson tradition. Inside the desk was a small note.

Lovingly made by Samuel Jackson for his bride, Elizabeth. Handed down Mother to daughter, a Jackson Legacy.

The only problem was the key was missing. His mother always kept the key in her jewelry box. As a young boy, his legs too tired and heavy to play, Walter would sit on the floor and watch her work, writing for hours. Rising from the desk, she would carefully close the leaf, and reaching deep into her pocket, pull out the tiny gold key. Placing the key into the lock, the little stones, green and white sparkled, throwing dancing diamonds against the wall. Pearl led the way to her bedroom, up the stairs, an arduous task for the little boy, his hands holding fast to the banister, Walter stayed close behind, stared at the little gold key in her hand, the dancing diamonds making it a threesome. Knowing her son needed encouragement to walk, she dangled the key, her pace slow and easy, one step at a time. Walter remembered those walks, her jewelry box and the way she carefully placed the key in the tiny wooden drawer.

Turning to face him, his mother would cover her smile and feign surprise, "Oh my, Walter, you little mouse. Now you know my secret hiding place." Placing a finger against her lips, she would finish with, "Shhh, it will be our secret, just you and me."

The key was not in the jewelry box. Walter was furious. Searching the carriage house for days, he blamed his father. "It wasn't his to take," he ranted. Several years later an insurance adjuster came snooping around the property asking questions about a diamond and emerald key belonging to Charles Jackson. A claim for mysterious disappearance. The adjuster stated the estimated value and Iris' eyes widened. "Did Pearl hide the key?" she whispered. Over the years, the key became part of the Jackson family legend and local history. Blown out of proportion, it went in and out of fashion, rumored at times to be worth millions. Walter felt the whole affair was bad business. Kindling for his anger and resentment, the fires of which smoldered, always ready to ignite, these thoughts turned him from his faith. Walter refused to discuss the subject. Understanding the frailty with which her husband stood and the demons that threatened his balance, Iris never spoke of the key nor Jackson money again.

Chapter 3

"The road of the righteous is a lonely road." Leaning on the podium, Pastor Daniel's clear blue eyes burned brightly, sweat poured down from the crown of his head, his blonde, curly hair forging wayward designs. It was the middle of September, summer hanging on with a vengeance, as if the cold Michigan winds of winter weren't right around the corner. "But, you are not alone. God is with you. He holds the faithful in his arms and protects them from harm." His voice rose and fell, like the arms of a conductor leading an orchestra through a slow and melodious arrangement. Lowering his voice, barely a whisper, his large hands gripping the sides the podium, knuckles white, raising up to full height, he murmured in a low and deep bass, "My brothers and sisters, we are the faithful and with God, we must walk the lonely road."

The small room was filled far beyond capacity. Bodies crowded in the sweltering heat, the choir humming in the background, gave the room a hazy, meditative atmosphere and their burdens the tangible weight deserved. The crowd, spilling out the door, stood still, listening, praying for what they so desperately needed to hear. The word spread and Faith Mission Church of God was growing in leaps and bounds. Fed up with a government that left wounds too large to heal, Americans were searching for answers. The events of the last decade, civil rights, Kennedy assassinations, and Vietnam were catalysts to many giving up on their church and state. Looking for change, they sought out those who preached and spoke out against the wounds that plagued. Daniel preached against convention, but as much as he went against the established lines of party and denomination, never did he stray from non-violence. Preaching for peaceful opposition, he spoke out against flag burning, riots, guns and power plays of extremists who were gaining unprecedented ground during this time of need and upheaval.

Standing in the middle of the conservative status quo and the far-reaching extremists, Daniel was a saving ship to those adrift, those who believed in serving and respecting your country, but still grieved uncontrollably for sons lost or missing, empty graves and empty answers by a government that was incapable of closing the gaping hole that held them apart. Those who by the very grain of their souls, would not and could not venture to extremes, found Daniel's moderate opposition a home for their growing discontentment and restless energy.

Looking out among the faces of his followers, Daniel found Victoria. Their eyes met. Reading each other instantly, Daniel felt her strength infuse his soul, energize him, validate him. Dressed fashionably, a dress in black lace, she was a picture of elegance and beauty. Her strong facial features, high cheek bones and wide set eyes radiated strength. Set off by her white, alabaster complexion, her deep black eyes, long eyelashes and straight, long black hair, she was unique and exquisite. The women were drawn to her, men nervous, almost weak in her presence. Yet, it was her demeanor, so quiet and calm that made her different. Good deeds endeared her to many. A knitted baby blanket for a newborn, a warm meal for a shut-in, a few hours helping in the kitchen after services went a long way where words failed her.

As the choir began a three-hymn intercession, Daniel's mind drifted back to the first time they met. Traveling through the south, deep in the Smokey Mountains, Daniel had been a young and passionate minister on the road for the first time. Evangelization was key to his drive and dreams of spreading the word of God and the impoverished south was the perfect place to start for an overeager and compassionate young man of the cloth. Born and raised in the fold, his father a prominent Methodist preacher in Michigan, Daniel had much to prove. Year after year, Sunday sitting, listening to his father's words, Daniel longed for the chance to blend his own message. His mother, Iris, a woman of endless and restless energy, never left a moment idle, filling up his days with music, art, outings, and gatherings. As a young seminarian, only a few days on the road, his former life still pulsing through his veins, Daniel pulled up to a small cafe deep in the mountains. He was hot, hungry, and his head was throbbing. His 1963 Chevy Nova, white when he left Michigan, was covered in dust and dirt, the front grill quilted with turkey feathers, remnants from his foggy encounter with a flock of hens somewhere south of Missouri. Pushing open the door, a bell clanged. Grimacing, he raised his hand to his forehead, smearing dirt and grease across his brow.

Taking in the tiny cafe, he chose a booth in the corner, placed his arms on the table and dropped his head. Footsteps approached, coffee pots perked, and the smell of ages old bacon grease hung heavy. Nat King Cole crooned, chairs scratched, and spoons rang out ceramic syllables. A bad rendition of happy birthday, sung at the counter, caught Daniel's attention. Turning around he watched as eighteen turns on a stool a beautiful young woman was serenaded by a strikingly handsome older man and a team of waitresses. As the stool made its last few turns, Daniel's baby blues met Victoria's coal black, and his heart lurched. A slight smile from Victoria was his reward. A year later they married and a year after that, they returned to Michigan. Now, nearly eight years later, they were a family.

Changing keys, the choir deepened its chords and switched from Amazing Grace to How Great Thou Art. The organist, seated on more than enough of a firm foundation, swayed back and forth, tandem with the choir. More than anyone else, Daniel knew what held Victoria captive. Late one night, shortly after he proposed, her father, Victor, had poured out his heart and all their secrets. Victoria was different.

Victoria *Awinita* Emerson was the child of an American Cherokee woman and a traveling salesman of mixed immigrant heritage. Living on the reservation until the age of six, Victoria's memories of her Native American upbringing were fleeting, snapshots that came and went when nature showed its hand. Northerly winds singing at her window, a bleeding red sunset, the fresh musky smell after a heavy summer rain assaulted her senses and invoked emotions of her Indian spirit. Whisked away by her father, she spent the next twelve years of her life moving from one town to another, one school to another, one friend to another.

Never knowing how long they would stay, Victoria learned at a young age to rely on herself. Her father, a warm hearted, generous man, who fell in and out of love like the rising and setting of the sun, spread his big heart clear across the country. Selling vacuum cleaners, Victor Emerson left a wake of clean carpets and love sick women, empty bank accounts and little bundles of joy from north to south and east to west. When Victor became restless, he packed his bags and off they went. It wasn't until Victoria was ten that she understood her cousins were half brothers and sisters, the women who welcomed her, step-mothers. Somehow she knew this all along. Victoria had a strange understanding of things, a sense of others true feelings and it made her cautious. What she didn't understand was why she left too.

Victoria's mother was full blooded Cherokee. Known by the Cherokee as *Tsistunagiska*, wild rose, her strong facial features, lithe and lean body, graceful movements and peaceful presence were more than Victor could resist. He fell hard and fast. When she told him they were to have a child, he promised to stay, promised to be faithful. But before his will could be tested, she fell ill. Doctors gave her six months. Victor did what Victor did best. When the going got rough, Victor got going. Burying his grief in the welcoming arms of women, he made his way across the south, until he could stay away no longer. Returning two days after Tsistunagiska died giving birth to a little girl named Awinita, the Cherokee word for fawn, Victor was wracked with guilt and shame. Victoria was left in the care of her aunt and Victor resumed his vagabond life for months at a time, always returning to the child of his one true love. When the aunt suddenly died, Victor fulfilled his promise of faith. Awinita joined her father, two days after she turned six. Sitting on a diner stool, deep in Southern Louisiana they celebrated. Baptized that morning, Victoria, in a little Baptist church, miles off the beaten path, she began a new life. Two pieces of chocolate cake, a glass of cold milk, a cup of black coffee sat before them. Spinning her around on the stool six times, Victor and a group of swooning waitresses sang her Happy Birthday. About to blow out her candles, Victoria looked up, her expression serious. The little cross around her neck, a present from her father,

"You are a child of God now, honey," he said, twisted this way and that, reflected in the endless deep black of her eyes, as her stool found its way to a stop.

"Make a wish, Sugar," the little redhead cried, eyes glued to Victor.

"Hurry up, now, or you'll have nothin' to blow," the big, buxom blonde begged, sucking in her midriff and pulling back her shoulders.

"You can't tell nobody," a little brunette sang, as she passed by with a tray full of food. "Won't come true."

Victor, built like a god with the face of an angel, beamed down at Victoria. Placing his hand upon her shoulder, he leaned in and kissed her cheek. Never taking her eyes from him, she made her wish. Keeping it a secret was easy. Victoria was a quiet child. She could go days without speaking. Leaning over, she thrust out her chin and blew out her candles. As everyone celebrated, she surveyed the strange scene before her, cheers, clapping, laughing, all because of her. Her father, his eyes dancing, broke into an enormous grin, just for her. Reaching down to touch the pretty little cross, Victoria had closed her eyes and for the first time, she smiled.

Now, sitting in the front pew, listening to her husband, many years later, Victoria was a picture of formidable composure. Only Daniel knew her past, her fleeting foundation. Ramrod posture and strong shoulders, led to graceful hands and long fingers. Folded in her lap, they remained palms down. Looking to his son, Daniel felt his heart skip. Fast asleep in the crook of his mother's arm, Steady's bright red cheeks, long beautiful lashes, his plump little boy body slumbered, dreaming. Unlike his mother, Steady's hands were open, palms up, a picture of vulnerability and innocence. A fierce jolt surged through Daniel and he felt a deep need to protect his son.

"These are our boys," he bellowed. "Our children, the babes we bore. They need us." Staring intently at those before him, Pastor Daniel continued, "Can we stand by while our boys are forgotten, prisoners in hell, while our leaders go deaf? Can we stand by, while the ones who came home are humiliated and mistreated, our leaders blind to its heroes? Where is their reward? Let us stand together for liberty. Let us stand for honor. Let us stand for peace. Dear Merciful God, please rain down your love, your peace, direct us on the lonely road of the righteous, we ask this through Jesus Christ your son, Amen."

"Amen." The congregation was on its feet, as the choir began We Shall Overcome. Daniel wiped his brow with his handkerchief and stepped down. Victoria gracefully slid her arm into his, as did Steady, a few sleepy steps behind. The congregation spilled out into the bright sunshine and gathered around, the warm feeling of fellowship, burdens slightly lifted, lingered like the crowd hesitating to part.

Shaking hands and blessing children, Victoria and Steady by his side, Daniel felt gratitude seep into his bones. When the crowd cleared and they were about to leave, a tall man dressed in a blue three-piece suit stepped out of a bright red Ford Mustang. Daniel welcomed the stranger, his confident swagger, a surprise.

Well over six feet tall, the presence of this man was felt more by his long and determined movements than his height. Hands, size the size of frying pans, seemed almost too large for the crisp, lean cut of his high-priced suit. An open collar, a fashion too trendy for a small Michigan town, strained in holding back the fair, red, hair that threatened to spill beyond the small buttons of his smooth, white, silky shirt. A small, red, coat-of-arms crest was embroidered into the cuff of his jacket. Thick, wavy, fire engine red hair, slicked back to show wide cheekbones and a strong square jaw, framed his almost shockingly friendly face.

"Matthew O'Leary" he said, giving Daniel a firm handshake, his grip, a tad tighter than his smile. Drawing out his syllables, he gave special emphasis to the letter a.

Victoria watched the stranger with passive features. Behind her dark sunglasses, she took some liberty and observed the conflicting details. His dress was fine, but his movements were rough. Hands well groomed, a large gold university ring on his left and expensive watch on his right, yet, the palms of his hands were rough and worn. His shoes gleamed perfectly in the bright sunshine, but there was missing a button on his vest. On the side of his neck, emerging from his collar, was a scar, a thin red line, made more prominent by his pale and freckled complexion. His accent was Boston Irish, but his manner was smooth and southern. Growing up on the road, Victoria knew people and places, what made them different, unique. Lean and tall, he was handsome, too handsome. Victoria pulled Steady behind her and squared her shoulders.

"Nice to meet you," Daniel offered. "My wife, Victoria, and our son, Steady."

The stranger briefly tousled Steady's hair, smiled at Victoria, lingering, his stare intense. A bee flew in between them, buzzing, breaking the hot and stifling silence. Stiffening, she pulled her hat down, and placed a hand on her husband's shoulder.

Daniel's voice redirected the stranger's gaze, "What brings you to Michigan? You don't sound Michigan."

"What wouldn't bring me to Michigan?" he asked, his gaze shifting back towards Victoria. Before Daniel could respond, Matthew added, "Accounting. Certified."

"That's interesting," Daniel looked quizzically at the stranger. "We need a comptroller."

Matthew O'Leary slowly pulled his eyes away from Victoria and pumped Daniel's hand.

"Monday morning, then? Eight o'clock."

Giving Steady's shoulder a little squeeze he turned and in two full strides, disappeared into the blinding sunlight.

Chapter 4

As the last hot breath of summer faded, autumn colors and cool evenings returned. October bled into November and with the approach of Thanksgiving, Daniel and his staff were busier than ever.

A board of directors was elected, Daniel as president, Mrs. Eva Thompson, a retired school teacher with over forty years of service in the Detroit Public School System, as vice president, Victoria as secretary, and Matthew O'Leary, as treasurer. Several other community church members were elected to the remaining four positions for a total of eight. Controls were put into place to adhere to a consensus, such as quorum thresholds, signing rules for funds, ratification regulations, among others. Daniel engaged a local attorney for the charter agreement and the board ratified the agreement on their first meeting. Rules of order were followed and as the secretary, Victoria kept the minutes. A feeling of goodwill pervaded all, as they started off on excellent terms.

With numbers continuing to grow, their lean and sparse conditions, a rundown recreation hall, became more and more of an issue. Talk naturally turned to building a new facility. It was the second meeting, when it became a surprise agenda item, included under Hopeful Endeavors.

The meeting began as usual with a little small talk and light refreshments. Iris loved to bake and arrived early to set up drinks and finger foods. After ten minutes of fellowship, Daniel called the meeting to order with the beginnings of prayer. Taking their seats around a folding table in the worship/activity/board room, metal chairs scratched the vinyl floor and groaned under the weight of a few of the more well established members. Daniel sat at the head of the table.

Victoria was about to take her seat, she felt a hand on her elbow, as Matthew pulled out the second seat from Daniel for her in a gentile show of courtesy. His smile, quick and warm at the surface, turned cold as a sudden gust blew in the open windows.

Victoria stepped away, crossing the room to close the windows. Returning, she took her seat next to Matthew, placing her hands in her lap.

"Let us begin by asking for God's presence among us," Daniel began. The room became quiet. Heads were bowed and eyes closed.

Victoria, her hands still resting in her lap, felt the rough wear of Matthew's as he placed his hand over hers. As the Board began clasping and raising hands around the table, Matthew hesitated, applying pressure to Victoria's thigh. In one quick motion, before she could turn and show indignation, Matthew lifted their hands to the Lord, never opening his eyes, or breaking form. Holding her silence, Victoria let her hand go limp, a hostage in his game of tug and war.

"It is with your guidance; we begin this journey of faith. Please bless us as we do your work, Lord. Lead, guide, and direct us. Amen."

"Amen," rang out in unison. Matthew released her hand slowly, running his fingers along the inside of her forearm.

The upcoming Thanksgiving celebration was discussed. The topic of childcare, visiting the sick, and day activities for seniors were considered. A budget was approved for the next twelve months.

"That brings us to our last item, Hopeful Endeavors," Daniel said. The meeting was in its second hour and faces were worn. Saving this for last, Daniel knew they would need a little spiritual pick up. All eyes turned. "New Building Fund," Daniel announced. Faces lit up, a few smiled, as a low murmur filled the room.

Mrs. Thompson, her reading glasses, chained to the sides of her head and threatening to jump off its narrow precipice, leaned over to Mr. Wilder, a banker with more invested in his girth than considered prudent, and whispered, "I knew they were up to something."

"Say it so the whole class can hear," Daniel chuckled, his bright blue eyes dancing.

"Ha," Mrs. Thompson straightened and allowed. "Yes, please do, Pastor. We are all ears." Laughter around the room made clear her reference.

Just last Sunday, Daniel preached about "How not to be all ears, first and all mouths, second." That, "Whenever, two or more of you are gathered in my name," does not include discussing your neighbor's personal business.

"Very well said," Daniel laughed. "I may call on you in the future, when words fail me, dear Mrs. Thompson." His shoulders relaxed and placing his hands before him, he turned to Matthew.

All eyes were on Matthew. Reveling in the attention, Victoria could see this was no surprise to him. Pulling back his shoulders, he looked around the table before handing out a neatly typed three-page report. It was only yesterday, Daniel mentioned the possibility of a new building. Casually, over dinner, he explained things were going well and that Matthew hinted if the accounts kept increasing, maybe by next summer, they could look for property. Victoria knew all about the rising balances. Packed services, overflowing collection baskets, were constant reminders how much was at stake. Money made Victoria nervous. Growing up with a father for a con artist, a much-loved con artist, she knew that appearances could be deceiving and the more money involved, the more deceiving things were. In spite of this, being only the second meeting, here was Matthew with his report, with more than a few hours invested.

Matthew finished addressing the board. Daniel was impressed. The report was detailed, considerate and exact. Board members began absorbing the material, considerations for special investments of a building fund and high level risk, investing for short term gain were discussed. The jargon was highly technical, baffling most at the table. Questions were slow. Mr. Wilder, typically the first to drill, was unusually quiet. Turning the pages back and forth, he whispered to Mrs. Thompson in a show of comprehension and explanation that fooled most. Victoria remained quiet, folding her report in half. Looking over at Matthew's hands, she took note of the large university ring. Vanderbilt, she was almost certain. Making a mental note to herself, she thought about a kind and intelligent woman, Professor Thelen, Chair of Ancient Greek History, Vanderbilt University, and the time, as a young girl, she spent in Nashville.

Chapter 5

Thanksgiving dinner was a huge success. Early that morning, the Jacksons headed to church. Although Daniel preached against war, he felt that attending to those in need, included all, especially, those who served. The baking began at five in the morning and by two o'clock there was a feast prepared for local veterans. Turkey, mashed potatoes, sweet potatoes, corn, cranberries, pumpkin and apple pie were served buffet style. Old, middle aged, and young men, all veterans of the US Armed Services, along with their families, sat at folding tables, decorated with white tablecloths and colorful Indian corn. Small American flags stood on each table. Victoria and Iris served the main course, Mrs. Thompson, the pies, Mr. Wilder, beverages. Steady handed out plates at the front of the line with an enthusiastic, "Happy Thanksgiving." Daniel and a few other board members greeted guests. Matthew walked between the tables, helping where needed, tousling little heads and shaking hands. He wore a dark brown tweed jacket with an orange silk handkerchief. A bright white oxford shirt and dark green dress pants showed off his Irish coloring and bright red head of hair. Clean shaven and loaded with cologne, he drew more than a few admiring glances. Victoria saw him kneel down next to a young man in a wheelchair with both legs missing. A pretty young wife smiled nervously and twin boys, tow-headed and no older than Steady, leaned in as close as possible to their father. Matthew was telling a story and held their attention. His right arm loosely closed the circle and Victoria could see his watch, fall out from under his shirt cuff. One of the twins noticed the watch too and reaching over, ran his thumb over the surface. Holding up his palm to the mother's protests, Matthew unhooked the clasp and handed the watch to its admirer. Both boys sat silently staring at the watch, turning it over and over, playing with the dials and looking into the face. Mrs. Thompson leaned towards Victoria and blew a low and slow whistle.

"Must have money somewhere," she observed.

Victoria smiled and continuing to serve, replied, "Will you need another pie, soon?"

"Humph." Mrs. Thompson took a step away and glanced at the pies. "Plenty of pies. You know, not that I am all-ears on this Thanksgiving Day, but," exhaling for emphasis, she leaned in towards Victoria for a second time, "but, just the engraving is beyond my budget." Taking a step back, Mrs. Thompson closed the conversation, making sure she wasn't caught all-mouth.

Victoria took note of the watch, as the boys hung it in the air. Twisting back and forth, she could see the elaborate engraving. Suddenly, Matthew turned and stared. Slowly, a sneer crept up the side of his face. Taking a sharp breath in, Victoria felt the bile rise up from her gut.

The line was beginning to slack. Most of the tables were on their third sitting. Daniel came over and touching her shoulder gently said, "Let's eat."

Taking their seats, Iris, Steady, Daniel and Victoria bowed their heads and closed their eyes for a moment.

Before they could begin, Matthew, noisily dragging a chair over and placing it between Victoria and Daniel, said in his best Boston brogue, "Have a wee bit of room for a poor Irish boy?" Topping it off, he jumped up and clicked his heels together, snapping his fingers in unison.

Steady hollered, "Magically delicious. A leprechaun," giggled and squirmed in his seat.

Hiding her smile, Iris leaned over to shush her grandchild. Daniel made a show of consideration by moving over and making room. Matthew placed his chair in between them and sat down.

"Now, where were we, my maties?" he asked, his lower jaw thrusted out, teeth bared, right eye closed.

"Grrrr, Blackbeard," Steady began, muffled by Gramma Weddington's soft and gentle hand.

Making a show of surrender, Matthew raised his hands, palms up. Pressing her lips together, Victoria joined in the prayer circle. Matthew's oversized ring laid heavy on her hand and she thought back to last week and the telephone conversation she had with Professor Thelen.

196

"Victoria, what a pleasure," Professor Thelen had crooned. "But, please, call me Maria. After all, we are family."

"Oh yes." Victoria held the phone in her right hand, pacing the kitchen floor.

"How are you? And your Father? What brings you calling? Oh, too many questions," she apologized.

Victoria smiled and felt a warm glow. Maria Thelen, most likely the highest educated of all her father's conquests, was a bright, effervescent, and dramatic woman. Swooping down to pick Victoria up as a child, no matter that they were almost the same height, she would hug her fiercely and say, "I will squeeze the Greek into you, my darling. Every child needs a Greek mama." Now, standing in her own kitchen, Victoria felt a sharp pain. Leaving Maria was the worst. With no other so-called cousins, Victoria was the center of attention. They read books together, went to foreign films, cooked for hours in the kitchen. When Victor was gone, they stayed up late drinking coffee and eating cookies, bringing the blankets into her small living room, wrapping up, "Like Egyptians," Maria would say, and listening to records.

"We are doing well," Victoria assured. Holding the telephone cord, she wrapped and unwrapped it around her fingers. "I was wondering, if I gave you a name, a Vanderbilt graduate, would you be able to get me some information?" her voice small and soft, she felt like the child Maria held all those years ago.

"Oh my," she exclaimed. "Are you in trouble? Steady? Daniel?" she rattled on. "Of course, of course, please tell me there is no trouble."

"No trouble. Just a new business associate of Daniel's. A man named Matthew O'Leary." Victoria looked out the kitchen window, her brows knitted. Daniel was expected any moment.

"Ah, well, yes, that husband of yours, too good. I understand. I will see what I can find out. Let me get a piece of paper, hold on please." Victoria heard the phone drop and Maria shout in surprise, "Oh, so sorry, I dropped you."

Victoria smiled. "Excuse me?"

"No, really. I dropped you, and Daniel, and Steady, and Iris," she hollered, laughing and talking at the same time. Victoria frowned and looked at the phone. "Your Christmas card, last year. It is hanging on my refrigerator all this time. Well, was hanging, I mean, I knocked it off when the phone fell. So, you see, I dropped you, the whole family."

"I miss you, Maria," Victoria said, unwinding the phone cord from her fingers and relaxing her shoulders. "I miss your laughter."

"No tears, my dear. Got it, Matthew O'Leary. I am off to see what I can find out. I will be in touch as soon as I know something." Kissing sounds came through the phone and then a dial tone.

Holding the phone, lost in thought, she was caught unaware. Daniel, standing behind her, briefcase in hand, looked at her quizzically.

"Serious caller?" he asked.

Jumping a few inches off the ground, Victoria let out her breath and turned. Met with Daniel's boyish grin, she kissed him on the cheek, replaced the phone in the cradle and shrugged. Wrapping her apron around her waist, she handed him a cup of coffee and the newspaper and gently pushed him out of the kitchen. Daniel liked to read the paper with his coffee while Victoria prepared dinner. In warmer months, he preferred the front porch. Perusing the Detroit Free Press, he let the sections fall one by one to the floor, where they remained until Victoria picked them up. Cleaning up after Daniel was not a difficult job. In fact, although many young women were refusing traditional roles, Victoria liked the confines and roles of marriage. She felt safe, understood. Returning to her tasks, she began to pull ingredients, pots and pans together. Chopping vegetables, she paused, the telephone silent in its cradle. A wave of guilt ran through her. They were always honest with each other. Swallowing hard, Victoria pulled her eyes away and braced herself. Everything about Matthew set her on edge. If only Daniel could see. She could tell he liked Matthew. Daniel, the last remaining child, the man without a father, the pastor and good shepherd, was blind to a fault. Chopping furiously, carrots and celery flying left

198

and right, Victoria had silently begged, Oh Maria, please bring good news, please bring good news.

Now, sitting before their Thanksgiving feast, Matthew's ring cutting into her palm as hands lifted in prayer, she squeezed Daniel's hand and pushed thoughts of betrayal away. Two weeks and no word from Maria.

"Lead us, guide us, direct us, Lord," Daniel finished as always with hope and petition.

"Amen," Victoria joined the others, her wish silent on her lips.

After all the guests left and dinner was over, Daniel stood up and asked if they would like dessert. Following suit, the other men rose and served the ladies, a pleasant surprise. Holding his hands up, Daniel begged them to remain seated and turned to Steady. Matthew and Mr. Wilder stood at attention.

"Ready, Steady?"

"Right and ready," he replied, his shinning eyes glued to his father, expression serious. Iris held back a smile and Victoria gave them her full attention.

Daniel clapped and the men removed their jackets, rolled up their shirt sleeves, took off their ties and loosened their collars.

Matthew removed his ring and watch and slipped them into his jacket pocket. Placing his tie around his head, he stuck a butter knife between his teeth, made a muscle with his right arm and commanded, "All hands on deck."

Steady jumped up and down. "Popeye the sailor man."

"To the galley," Matthew called out and off they marched. Steady's eyes were glued ahead, his chubby little legs and arms pumping up and down after his father.

Staring at them in amazement, the ladies watched with open mouths and humorous expressions.

"Well, if that don't beat all," Iris remarked.

"They do say there is a revolution," Mrs. Thompson added.

"Interesting," Victoria whispered.

Enjoying their time, the ladies chatted about plans for Christmas, now that they turned the corner of Thanksgiving. Mrs. Thompson was going to buy an artificial tree. Woolworths was having a sale. Iris was hoping for a white Christmas. Last year was such a letdown. Victoria asked what they thought about poinsettias for the worship area, tall white candles and gold bows. The conversation began to lag and they looked around, their eyes settling on the kitchen door.

"A little too quiet," Mrs. Thompson observed.

Iris sneaked up and peaked around the door. Tip-toeing back to the table, she wore a bright smile. She was in the middle of explaining the situation, Steady, up on a chair, handing dishes to his father, who was washing, who handed to Matthew, who was drying, who handed to Mr. Wilder, who was doing his best to keep up, putting away the clean dishes, when suddenly, a sponge came flying out the door. Raucous laughter erupted and they all rushed over, eager to peek in, but ready to run at a moment's notice.

"So, that's the way, eh?" a deep voice questioned followed by a hearty laugh. "Me 'tinks he needs a little 'air on his chest."

Daniel, a full face of suds, leaned over to Steady, pulled out his shirt collar and placed a big scoop of suds inside his shirt. Steady grinned and puffed out his chest.

Mr. Wilder taking a step backwards, finding his fit more snug than ideal, looked warily at his companions.

"No gettin' away, bugger," shouted Matthew, placing a full round of suds on Mr. Wilder's face.

Steady peaked around his father's form at Mr. Wilder and giggled.

"Ho, ho, ho?" Mr. Wilder tried, his effort weak.

"Santy Claus," Steady yelled.

All three looked at each other and then slowly advanced on Matthew.

Backing up, he held his hands up in surrender, "Go easy, my countrymen, my country 'tis of thee," he begged.

"Benedict Arnold," Steady shouted. All eyes turned in amazement.

With a full pail of soapy water, Daniel, Steady, and Mr. Wilder, a well soaped trio, advance on Matthew.

"He's a traitor."

"Dirty rotten traitor," another chimed in.

"Me 'tinks he needs a right regular washin'." Daniel grinned and in one fell swoop dumped the pail over Matthew's head.

Water rushed to the floor and the ladies quickly returned to their seats, picked up their coffee cups, dessert forks, and conversation, as if there weren't spying just moments ago.

"How's it going out here?" Daniel asked, peaking around the door, his head wet and soapy, a grin from ear-to-ear.

"Not quite as lively as in there," Mrs. Thompson answered, her glasses perfectly pitched, frowning in all seriousness.

"Uh, where can I find a mop?" Daniel asked, dropping his eyes to the ground and turning to shush his comrades.

Iris began to rise and found both of her arms stayed by Victoria and Mrs. Thompson. "Try the pantry, it's with the soap-p-p," and they all dissolved into hysterics.

Half an hour later, the kitchen cleaner than ever, the men emerged, ties loosely around their necks, and for the most part, somewhat drier than before. Daniel carried a big box.

"I was going to wait until Christmas, but it seems as if some of us are in need of dry clothes," he stated flatly. Opening the box, he pulled out a red t-shirt with white lettering.

Steady studied the shirt front, knitted his brows and began in staccato fashion, "We're. on. a. Mission.". Turning to show the back, Daniel held out his hand. "A Mission of Faith, Faith Mission Church of God, Clarkston, Michigan."

Giving out the shirts, he looked Matthew up and down, shaking his head.

"I know, I know," Matthew answered and walked towards the pantry.

Iris helped Steady with his shirt and Victoria, placing her hand on Daniel's arm, leaned over and kissed him gently. Daniel turned and gently ran his finger over her brow, showing her a soapy finger.

"We'll try our shirts on later," he whispered in her ear, playfully.

Tables and chairs put away, Mr. Wilder was off with the leftovers and Mrs. Thompson with the linens. Daniel chuckled, telling Victoria, "Mr. Wilder was on washing down duty and Mrs.

Thompson, washing up." Iris took Steady to the car, as Daniel carried out the last few things.

Victoria spotted a pile of dirt on the floor and headed back to the pantry for the broom. The door was slightly ajar. Peeking inside, she saw Matthew, his back turned, shirt off. The red scar, before just a thin line above his collar, led down his back to a massive labyrinth of raised, red, angry scars. Victoria, drawing in a quick breath, stepped back and turned away. As she turned, Matthew threw his new t-shirt over his head, looked over his shoulder and seeing her walk away, smiled a rueful and knowing smile.

Hurrying back to the front of the building, Victoria's mind raced. Feelings of horror, compassion, and fear swelled in her gut. We know nothing about this man, she thought. Grabbing their jackets in a panic, Matthew's fell to the floor. Something fell out and she saw his ring roll away and his watch on the floor, face up.

"Oh no," Victoria said under her breath. She grabbed the ring. It was Vanderbilt alright, class of 1970. But the initials inside were not Matthew's, but T.E.M. Looking over her shoulder, she felt her heart race. She picked up Matthew's jacket and replaced the ring. Reaching for the watch, she turned it over. Suddenly, she felt hot breath on her neck, the smell of cologne, and weight bearing down. Matthew placed his hand over hers and the watch.

"Oh Tori," he moaned. "You don't mind if I call you Tori, right? Our little secret." Running his fingers up and down her arm, he leaned harder, their balance dangerously close to a fault. Victoria closed her eyes and breathed deeply. "You keep secrets, don't you, Tori? Everyone keeps secrets." Retrieving his watch, he looked towards the parking lot and saw Daniel returning. Hesitating just long enough, he met Daniel's eyes, stood up and offered a hand to Victoria.

Daniel walked in the door, keys in hand, his expression a mixture of confusion and concern. "Are you okay?" he asked Victoria.

Quickly gathering their things, she dropped her gaze and brushed past them. Daniel looked to Matthew, brows raised, eyes searching.

"Women?" Matthew stated, shrugging his shoulders. Slipping his watch into his pocket, he felt the ring, and relaxed.

"Great day, wasn't it?" Daniel said, flipping off the light switches and making way for Matthew to exit. As Matthew stepped over the threshold, Daniel slapped him on the back. "Thanks so much for all your hard work, Matthew." Flinching slightly, Daniel noticed his shoulders stiffen, eyes close for a moment.

Turning to Daniel he stretched his arms out and laughed, "Washing dishes is hard work."

Daniel locked the door and followed Matthew out to the parking lot. I wonder what that was all about, he thought. Pausing at his car, he hollered goodbye.

Through the car window, Victoria watched Matthew walk away. Something told her the engraving on the watch was not for Matthew, nor was he the same person who owned the ring, T.E.M, whomever that was. Clenching her teeth, she saw him turn and raise his right arm to wave. Slowly, a red stain began to bleed through the back of his shirt, its contours a perfect match for Daniel's handprint.

Chapter 6

The week after Thanksgiving Victoria called Maria again. There was no record of a Matthew O'Leary attending Vanderbilt. Victoria told Maria about the initials, T.E.M., engraved inside the ring. Maria said they should file a formal request for public information. She would submit the form in Victoria's name and pay the ten-dollar fee. Unfortunately, it would take weeks, thanks to Lyndon B. Johnson and the Freedom of Information Act. A letter would be sent directly to Victoria.

Preparations for Christmas were in full swing. Steady, the official twelve days of Christmas counter, ran through the house every morning, shouting out the day and singing at the top of his lungs. Victoria was busy makes lists and getting things ready for the upcoming celebrations at church and at home.

On the fifth day of Christmas, Steady woke them up with a long drawn out version of F-i-v-e G-o-l-d-e-n R-i-n-g-s. Snowing non-stop for the last two days, they were cooped up in the house, with the exception of a few short outings, lasting no longer than the time it took to get him dressed in his snowsuit. The first day of the storm, Steady and Daniel made a snowman. By the end of the second day, only a carrot nose and black eye patch was visible. A pirate snowman, he was lost in a sea of snow.

Daniel peeked out from under the covers, quickly retreating back to his shelter. "Son. The sun is not up. Go back to bed," came a muffled voice.

Victoria threw her legs over the side of the bed, sat up and shook out her long, dark hair.

"Back to bed with you," Daniel mumbled, still buried under layers of blankets, he reached for her waist.

Stretching her arms overhead she leaned over and turned on the light. "Iris is coming over early this morning. We are baking Christmas cookies."

"Iris isn't going anywhere. Look outside. Wait, on second thought, don't look outside, get back here and for heaven's sake, shut the light off," he cried.

Steady watched his father's form move under the covers towards his mother. Jumping up on the bed, straddling his father, he raised his hand high in the air and shouted, "I'll protect you, Mamma. Take that, you sneaky, slithering snake." Bouncing up and down, he landed over and over on top of his father. Groaning and moaning, Daniel threw back the covers, and counterattacked. Giggling uncontrollably, Steady fell back onto the bed, dying a slow death. "Arrrgh," he cried.

Victoria shook her head. "I'll leave you two to your bedroom brawl and please, Daniel, be careful. No stitches this morning. No trip to the hospital in this weather."

Moving through the dark house effortlessly, Victoria started the coffee and drew back the curtains over the sink. Still dark outside, the vast white landscape gave an eerie, almost space-like feeling to her surroundings. I'll call Iris and let her know Daniel will come get her, she thought. Gathering a few things, a couple of favorite cookie cutters, some red and green sugar, and a few cookie sheets, she placed them on the counter and looked out the back door. It was windy and a large drift piled almost to the doorknob.

Switching on the light over the kitchen table, she began straightening some loose papers and folders Daniel left the night before. A handful of Polaroids fell out and dropped to the floor. Reaching to retrieve them, she stopped. They fell in a haphazard fashion, face up. From Thanksgiving, shots of guests and volunteers, Matthew was in every picture. Talking with guests at the door, crouching down beside a table, posing with volunteers. Smiling broadly, he looked so confident and handsome. None of this was a surprise. What caught her attention was where he stood. In every picture, he was standing to the side or in front of others, except, for those with her and Daniel. Posing with them, he was always wedged in between, looking straight into the camera like he was right where he belonged. Picking up the pictures, her hands shook. Placing them in a pile, she pressed her hands to her abdomen and paused. The coffee pot, a full perk now, made her turn. Focusing her attention on breakfast, she decided to wait for the letter from Vanderbilt before approaching Daniel about Matthew. Yet, throughout the day, every now and then, she would stop and place her hands against her abdomen, her thoughts returning to Matthew and all her unanswered questions.

Later that evening, Victoria was cleaning up after dinner. Daniel crept up behind her and wrapping his arms around her waist, he buried his face in her hair. Leaning back slightly, she felt the warmth of his body and the soft touch of his lips against her neck.

"Only a week until Christmas," he murmured. "You know what I want for Christmas?" Slipping his hands under her apron, he pulled her towards him, eager for familiar territory.

Steady, ran into the kitchen and collided with their legs, pulling on his father's arm and shouting, "Pirate P.J.'s. Look Daddy. Look what Gramma Weddington got me. Look, look, look." Daniel and Victoria couldn't help but smile. Lifting him up with one arm, the other still buried deep under Victoria's apron, Daniel swung Steady high in the air, bringing him down for a soft landing and a sweet kiss goodnight. Iris, standing at the entry to the kitchen, watched her grandson and beamed.

"Come on, Steady. Do I have a story to tell you," she coaxed.

"Now, where were we?" Daniel asked, rewrapping his arm around her slender waist.

"Washing dishes," she laughed, pushing him away gently.

"I was thinking," Daniel began, moving in closer. "How about we invite Matthew for Christmas dinner?" Victoria stiffened and her hands went still.

Stepping back, Daniel shoved his hands in his pockets and stared at her back. "Why don't you like him? It's fairly obvious you don't."

Turning around, she said slowly, "I don't trust him. Daniel, we don't know anything about him."

"You, don't know anything about him, Vic." Gently placing a hand on her shoulder, he looked into her eyes.

"I know his type," she replied flatly, turning back around. She thrust her hands into the soapy water.

Daniel felt his blood rise. He regarded Matthew as more than an associate. They were becoming fast friends and Daniel craved the comradery. A pastor was often isolated and required to keep his distance. Everyone came to him with problems, but to whom could he bare his soul? He wondered. In times of weakness, he wanted more than silent prayer. Her tone dismissed his opinion, as if he was a child, and the insult stung. Dropping his hands, he felt his voice go hard.

"He's not your father."

Taking a sharp breath, Victoria removed her hands from the dishwater and dried them. Calmly walking over to the table, she picked up the Polaroids and handed them to Daniel.

"What do you see?" she asked.

Daniel looked at the photos, looked up, eyebrows raised, mouth slightly open.

"You only see the good in people Daniel. Even when it is right in front of you."

"That's my job, Vic. To see the good in people. What are you talking about?"

"He's lying. He never went to Vanderbilt. And his ring, it belongs to someone else."

Daniel looked at the Polaroids and back at Victoria. His furrowed brows suddenly relaxed and the tension in his face, eased.

"You know," he began slowly, "I am bound by confidentiality. I took his confession, Vic. I know about the ring and the initials." Shuffling the pictures back and forth, he asked, "You know what I see? I see a man with a burden. Thanksgiving. That was a turning point for him. You are so set on hating him, you never noticed the change."

"I notice he always stands between us. Daniel, look at the photos. Look at us. He is creating division."

A little over three weeks before, on Thanksgiving evening, when Victoria and Steady were over at the carriage house, Matthew had stopped by. Leading him into his study, Daniel looked at his new friend. He was nervous and holding back, so unlike his typical casual and confident demeanor. His clothes were disheveled and

Daniel smelled the faint scent of alcohol. Born and raised Methodist, a former Methodist minister himself, there was no place for alcohol in Daniel's church or home. Placing his Vanderbilt University ring on the desk, Matthew broke down. Daniel opened his heart and welcomed his confession, his story. He explained Matthew O'Leary was not his name. He was a draft dodger, headed to Canada, when he stopped in Clarkston for a cool drink and to fill up his tank. Hot and tired, he took a seat outside the station and chatted with a few old men. More reliable than the associated press, Matthew listened as the old cronies talked about politics, a ramped-up effort at the boarder to catch old draft dodgers, and a few local stories of interest. A little old guy, far more in years than stature, mentioned a new church down the road and how it was growing. Matthew took the hint and headed over, arriving just as services were spilling out the door. Daniel listened, thought about Matthew's arrival and felt the hand of God. Counseling his new friend, he suggested his detour was a sign, a divine sign. Matthew, a keen observer and quick study, acted stunned at Daniel's insight. From the time he was a little boy, he wanted to be a minister, he confided. Taking on this new role as mentor, Daniel promised to make a few inquiries. There were a couple of good theology schools in the area. Matthew was contrite and grateful.

Daniel's insight was blinded by his pastoral robes and the need to see good in others. He didn't see Matthew's car at the end of the driveway, waiting, until Victoria was out of the house to ring the doorbell and make his confession. He didn't know about Victoria picking up the ring and reading the initials after the Thanksgiving celebration. Shrewd as he was, Matthew figured Victoria saw something and needed a cover story, just in case. Daniel didn't see through Matthew's deception. Matthew did his homework. If accepted to theology school, he would be as good as pardoned for draft dodging and if that failed, he could always fall back on his original plan and head to Canada. Although not his first choice, there were miles and miles of unmanned border in the vast wilds of the northwest. Matthew had made sure he always had a plan B.

Now, a week before Christmas, standing in the kitchen, a handful of photos and too many angry words between them, Victoria was scared and upset. Throwing the photos down, Daniel stormed out of the kitchen and locked himself in his study. Victoria stood there staring after him. Her hands shook uncontrollably. Even if Daniel knew about the ring and why the initials were not Matthew's, what about the scars? And all the little indecencies, the way he took the liberty of intimacy, embarrassing her, implicating her. Picking up the photos, she shoved them under a stack of old cookbooks and pushed the question of Matthew away. If only I saw the back of the watch, she thought. Recalling her fear, the way he whispered in her ear, hateful, suggestive, she resolved to keep her distance. As for Daniel, so kind and loving, she forgave his remark about her father. It was true, Matthew did remind her a little of her father, but only at the surface. Who knew what lie deep within Matthew's soul. Victoria didn't want to know.

Many hours later, Daniel crawled into bed, his anger gone. In fact, he could hardly recall what they argued about. Moonlight spilled in through the window, illuminating Victoria, her black hair shinning, her fair skin the color of pearl. Watching her sleep, her back turned, guilt and regret filled his thoughts. He hated their going to bed angry. Yet, she had every right to be angry. Bringing up her father was cruel. What do I really know about Matthew? Showed up only a few months ago and now, I am taking his side over my wife. I'm such a fool, he thought. Covering his face with his hands, he racked his brain, how can I make amends?

The next morning Daniel woke with a start. A bright, white landscape and full sun filled the room. The storm was over. Almost noon, he jumped up, threw on his bathrobe and went in search of Victoria. He found her in the kitchen, reading to Steady.

Daniel, his eyes downcast, hands behind his back, greeted them warily, "Good morning?" he said, looking down at the floor, making circles with his big toe.

"You're silly, Daddy," Steady looked up. "It's almost lunch time."

Victoria greeted him with a warm smile and he felt his nerves stay. A sweet surge of happiness washed over him. Grabbing a cup of coffee, he looked around and spotted the photos, face down, under a stack of books on the counter. Racks of decorated Christmas cookies covered every inch of countertop. Shoved aside, he thought, hmm, kind of like our argument last night. Probably not the best way to go. Pulling up a chair next to Victoria, he inhaled the sweet scent of pine, cinnamon, and burnt sugar, felt her gentle touch on his knee and her lean into him. His heart melted and courage faltered. Steady handed a book to his father, The Grinch Who Stole Christmas. Fitting, he thought, there' s a lesson for every fool, including me.

Chapter 7

The year 1977 arrived in its infancy with a changing of the guards. The White House staff said goodbye to the Ford family and welcomed the Carters. Apple Computer was incorporated, men's colorful polyester leisure suits were all the rage, and unbelievably, on the nineteenth of January, Miami residents could drink Florida orange juice while building a snowman. The television mini-series, based on Alex Haley's epic novel, Roots, began its legendary run on ABC. Gary Gilmore, the first victim after the reintroduction of the death penalty, was executed by firing squad in Utah.

But the day of reckoning, a fruition of all the preaching, prayers and efforts of Daniel and the Faith Mission Church of God was on Friday, January twenty-first, when President Carter pardoned Vietnam draft evaders. Just six days' shy of the fourth anniversary of the signing of the Paris Peace Accord, the US official withdrawal of troops and end to involvement in the Vietnam conflict, this act of forgiveness was a giant step towards the healing of a nation. Signing the pardon, President Carter set the wheels of healing in motion. However, as with most things monumental, it is the first few turns of the cogs that require the most energy.

For over a month, Daniel preached forgiveness, about laying down differences and reaping the beauty of burdens lifted. Yet, the congregation, just like the nation, remained divided. Now, with the sixth Sunday since the presidential pardon just around the corner, Daniel was going all out. This would be the Sunday he would light the fires of forgiveness, lead his people down the path of peace. All week, papers strewn on the desk and floor of his study, a few crumpled, some torn in half, gave proof to his need for just the right words. His typewriter, the latest IBM Selectric model, sat patiently waiting, idle and silent, its return passive, keys hopeful. New, it was a gift from the church at Christmas. Now, only two days away, he felt his words lacking, the tone all too familiar, the message inadequate. How can I inspire the welcoming, the forgiveness of these boys, draft dodgers, lost souls who ran from the horrors of an unjust war, if I can't find the words? How can I reconcile them to those who lost loved ones and those who served, now home facing an onslaught of hate for what they did in service to their country, their freedom? I owe them, he thought, a multitude of faces, young men, filling his thoughts, pulling at his heart. Leaning back in his chair, he raised his arms overhead and stretched. The clock on his desk read seven in the morning. Two hours and nothing. Tossing and turning throughout the night, he rose early, anxious to put thoughts to paper, to ease the anxiety of forgetting the words. Spinning around in his chair a few times, he thought about his father, all the years he wrote sermons in this very chair, this very desk, the same books, pens, and papers. As a child, they were forbidden from disturbing Walter while working. Daniel, curious and emboldened, would sit outside the door, listening to the soft cadence of his father's voice as he orated his writings. So familiar, the sounds and intonations, as a boy, Daniel mimicked his father's orchestrations perfectly. Unknown to him, Iris, too, was watching and smiling, her son a perfect prodigy to the man she loved.

His chair slowly coming to a stop, Daniel grabbed his jacket and headed outdoors. A cold and cloudy morning, he zipped up tight, pulled on a woolen cap and grabbed a pair of heavy gloves. February twenty-eighth and fifteen degrees Fahrenheit. The day's light just beginning and windless, it was Daniel's favorite time of the day, even when the thermometer refused to rise. Empty branches and tall trunks stood like sentinels, wrapping the perimeter of their yard, encircling their home in a way that made one look up. Taking a trail well-traveled, he wandered down the west side of the house, taking note of a few loose boards and shingles. The fluttering of wings, soft against soft, raised Daniel's eyes to the eaves and the muffled sounds of a mother dove. Off in the distance, faint sounds of cars passing were carried over the trees, free from impedance. It was on silent mornings like this, cold and forbidden, that Daniel felt his thoughts clear. Void of everyday noise and chatter, the tiniest sounds became audible. It was in these miniscule details, the scurry of a rodent, the cry of the red hawk, the crack of a tiny tree branch, he felt the prick of inspiration, the awe of God's creation, and the clarity he craved. Alone, the reward was all his and like a sponge he soaked up all the sights, sounds and feelings of the morning. Rounding the back of the property, he kept to the tree line, his eyes on the ground ahead. Small patches of snow held at the base of trees and throughout the woods. A few footprints, stamped and cast, held memory of deer, racoons, fox, and other small animals that brave the cold months of winter. Daniel sought out and treasured these sights of the forest, elusive animals that lived symbiotically at the edge of his world. Quiet partners, they too craved solitude and peace, sustenance and survival.

Looking up, the carriage house stood in the distance. A warm glow radiated from the kitchen window. Iris was an early riser too. Now, almost to the far east side of the property, he turned, his footprints still visible, evident in the frosty remnants of a cold night's grip. At this point, the path detoured into the woods, a cool and inviting respite in warmer months, a few chains and links, and emerged at the front of the clearing, a pleasant surprise, facing the farmhouse, situated in all its splendor, like a postcard of Americana bliss. Two stories with dark brown clapboard and white trim, a wide front porch wrapping around three sides of the house, along with multiple rocking chairs, a bench swing, gave it all the red, white, and blue curb appeal it could possibly have.

Daniel decided against the woods and skirted the back of the carriage house. Long lines of evergreens, well over eighty feet tall, funneled the driveway ahead, leading away from the house and out to the road. Stopping to admire their beauty, so green in a time lacking of color and life, Daniel thought about all the hard work his great grandparents put into making their home. More than fifty years ago, Clarkston, although a haven for summer escapes, was still rural enough to require extreme effort and cost to transform the wilds of the woods to the beautiful and majestic home he and Victoria now loved. A testament to the success of generations before, it was the last link to the Jackson family fortune, ties severed by his grandfather, Charles, known only for his cruelty and bitterness.

Taking the stairs to the porch two at a time, Daniel felt his heart lighten and his spirits rise. His father told him about the Jackson family fortune and his heart-breaking discovery when he came home, a beautiful bride and hopeful heart, aching for reunion, only to find abandonment, loss and vengeance. Money, he said, although necessary, is the currency of suffering. Like a river that runs deep, it has many currents. Some light and shallow, refresh and rejuvenate. Others, hidden in the depths, quickly grab and drag, swift and strong, bringing you down, over your head, miles downstream before you can save yourself. "I lost my inheritance, but found my fortune in God," he told Daniel. "Stick with the currency of the creator, Son," were his words. Daniel knew his grandfather was still alive, still at the helm of the Jackson timber fortune. Born in 1900, he would turn seventy-seven this year. Every year, two copies of the annual report for Jackson-Saginaw Timber Company arrived in their mailbox. Each year, Iris immediately tore her copy in half. Daniel, not so sure, placed it on his desk, unopened for months, only to throw it out in the energy of creating order, cleaning up. Only last year did he open the envelope. Staring at the opening statement, the figures were astounding. More commas and zeros than he ever imagined. His thoughts turning to his mother, with nervous hands, he tore the report in two and walked away, once again, from a fortune decided against him, long before he was even born.

Daniel could hear little feet running inside the house and the soft sounds of Victoria in the kitchen. Holding the screen door ajar, he looked back at the front porch, rockers lined up and down both sides, still, peaceful. Imagining the Jacksons of old, those that held the branches of their family tree, he saw them sitting quietly, one after another, filling the rockers, looking back at him, their faces serious and silent. Color gave way to black and white and then copper as he looked down the sides of the porch, imagining the generations past. Only his father, Walter, a slight smile playing at the corner of his lips, his fingers tapping on the handrails, began to rock slowly back and forth. In the stillness of morning, Daniel felt his pulse quicken and a warm, comfortable feeling fill him. Smiling back, he made a slow and sweeping bow, offering thanks to those who bore him here, without whom he would never know the grace of God.

A wall of heat and crescendo of sounds met his cold and quiet ears as he stepped into the house. Pulling off his hat and gloves, his thoughts still on the front porch, he felt the blow of little arms around his legs.

"Daddy, Daddy, here you are." Steady hollered, holding tight to his father's legs, his face full of wonder.

Daniel looked down into Steady's face, thought of the other faces he left on the front porch and was struck by the impossibility of past, present and future, his need to deliver the perfect sermon, his struggles this past week, writing and re-writing. Reaching down, he touched Steady's mess of morning hair and felt a quick jolt, an inspiration. That's it, he thought, laughing out loud. Steady stopped and released his grasp at his father's sudden laughter, his eyes wide and searching. Deep and resonant, Daniel's laughter filled the room.

"Forest for the trees, my boy," he said, reaching down to pick up his son. "Forest for the trees."

Following the warm and inviting smells of the day's beginnings, he walked back to the kitchen. It was there all the time, right there before his very eyes, in the study, on his father's desk, etched into a small piece of Jackson cherry, "Remember to refocus, the forest is there, visible, if only for the trees."

Chapter 8

On Sunday morning, Pastor Daniel was ready. Dressed in his white robes, typically reserved for special occasions such as weddings, religious holidays, baptisms, and funerals, he met the congregation in front of closed doors, outside the church. As the congregation arrived, murmurs began to build. Huddling against the cold winds of March, questions and complaints were passed back and forth. Daniel raised his hands overhead and a hush fell over the crowd as it began to part in the center. Mrs. Singleton, the choir director, pushed through the middle, leading her choir, dressed in bright red robes. At first slow and soft, their voices began to build, the familiar Rock of Ages filling the air and overpowering the moment. Gathered around Daniel, they were a bright and beautiful sight on a dismal and gloomy morning.

Bringing the hymn to a close, Daniel dropped his hands and clasping them in prayer, began, "Red, the color of blood. It is what binds us, what divides us. White, the color of divinity. It is what saves us. Delivers us. Dear God, please enter into our hearts as we make this journey today."

Throwing open the double doors, Daniel led the choir and the congregation into their worship space. A hush fell upon the crowd, as they took in the astounding changes. Walls painted a fresh coat of white, the floors shined to a high gloss, the old shabby space looked new. Bright red drapes hung from the windows, ceiling to floor. Bright white lights hung overhead. Chairs arranged on either side of a center aisle, were covered in alternating white and red damask. A bright red carpet ran from the front doors to the altar.

Gone were the old hanging lights, the rickety metal chairs, the dingy walls and floors. Like a brand new naval ship ready for its maiden voyage, the worship space of Faith Mission Church of God was ready to be christened.

The altar was made from old stones found on Daniel's property. A large piece of slate across the top held an assortment of candles, a bible, and a hymn book. Evergreen cuttings were arranged at the base of the altar and a large rugged, wooden cross, over seven feet tall, stood to the right.

The choir was seated to the right of the altar, their old piano covered with red and white ribbons. Mrs. Singleton took her seat, hands poised above the keys, a serious, but knowing look upon her face.

Steady and Victoria took their places in the front left row, two seats nearest the center aisle. Placing a hand on Steady's knee, she quieted his restless little legs. Looking around her, the beautiful transformation, she felt her heart swell with love and pride for her husband. Climbing into bed late last night, Daniel had wrapped his arms around her. His heart raced, he was so excited. "You won't believe your eyes," he said.

They had worked through the night, the finishing touches completed just before sunrise. Iris, an expert seamstress was responsible for the ribbons, chair covers, and drapes. Matthew organized a crew of young men to paint and clean the church, replace fixtures and wax floors. Daniel had created the altar.

Opposite Victoria, Matthew sat in the first row, along with four young men. Two, dressed in army military dress, sat erect, eyes straight ahead. The other two, in bell bottom pants and silk shirts, their long hair meeting their shoulders, held an easy air about their seat. Unknown to the congregation, these four young men were attracting a considerable amount of attention.

But if all this weren't enough, one thing stood out, rendering the congregation speechless. A row of twelve empty white rocking chairs filled the space between the altar and the front row, six on the right and six on the left, facing the congregation. Daniel took his place behind the altar and turned the pages in his bible. He placed his hands onto the altar and looked into the faces of his followers.

"Welcome." Daniel gazed compassionately at his church. "Thank you for joining us today and a special thank you to all who worked so hard to accomplish what you now see before you."

Daniel's eyes met Matthew's. It had been Matthew's idea to bring in the four young men. In fact, it had been Matthew who

217

found the young men, counseled them and with their blessing, they were here today, willing participants in the drama about to unfold.

Just two days ago, Daniel had been back in his study after a brisk morning walk and sudden inspiration, when Matthew rang the doorbell. Victoria answered and hesitant to interrupt Daniel, attempted to dissuade him. Slipping out into the cold morning air, her bathrobe wrapped tight and black hair falling in waves upon her shoulders, she pulled the front door closed and faced Matthew. His train of thought broken, Daniel peeked out the study window and saw Victoria's back, stiff, arms hugged at her sides. Matthew was saying something quick and muffled. Daniel caught the end of his sentence. Did he say, Tori? he wondered. He looked different, his expression angry. Daniel strained to hear, but seconds later the front door slammed and Victoria was gone. Alone on the porch, Matthew looked at his watch and shoved his hands in his pockets. A few moments passed and Daniel watched, thoughts of his sermon long gone. Suddenly, Matthew threw open the front door. There was a knock at the study door. Quick to return to his desk, Daniel shuffled papers and with an attempt at nonchalance, he granted entry. Matthew entered, his cheeks high color as if from the cold, but his hand shake was warm. Daniel thought about the encounter on the front porch, the strange, yet personal body language and was puzzled. Matthew, holding his hand a moment longer, pulled on his arm and wrapped Daniel in a tight embrace.

"I just want to thank you," he said, his eyes suddenly misty, expression shy.

"You're welcome?" Daniel asked, pulling back, he looked at Matthew, eyebrows raised. Such a quick change of emotions, he observed.

"These last few weeks have been hard. My reasons for staying, the draft penalty, gone." Turning away, he ran his hands through his hair. "I can't explain it, but for the first time, I have more reasons to stay, than leave." Fiddling with his watch, he whispered, "This is new to me."

"What reasons?" Daniel asked, his voice flat. Recalling the encounter on the front porch with Victoria, he felt a hot pang pierce his gut.

"Hard to explain," he started and then a floodgate of tears ensued. "Please, please let me stay." Holding his head in his hands, he sobbed.

Daniel opened his arms and welcomed his friend.

That night, the second turning point in their friendship, they planned Sunday's sermon. Matthew had friends in the area and was sure they would come. Daniel would give his sermon and then the young men would stand before the altar and face the congregation. Daniel would begin his exit down the center isle with his family and after a few moments of silence, the four young men, two who chose to serve and two who chose to oppose, would face each other and embrace in an act of forgiveness. Hoping to catalyze his congregation, Daniel had it all figured out. Desperate to move his followers away from this obstacle of pain and resentment, he had prayed for a miracle.

Now, standing at the altar, Daniel's shifted his gaze from Mathew and looked at the four young men. A sea of differences separated them, their body language saying more than any demonstration could deliver. Daniel felt a quick sweat break out all over his body, his hands, placed upon the bible, began to shake. His stomach turned upside down, empty and angry, it made itself known. Taking a deep breath in he said a quick and silent prayer for fortitude and began.

Turning towards the choir and Mrs. Singleton, he gave a slight nod. The choir hummed, and as six children, between the ages of four and six, walked up the aisle, dressed in their Sunday best, they broke out into a deep and resonate version of Jesus Loves Me. One by one, the children took their seats in the rocking chairs to the right of the aisle. The music ended and Daniel looked once again at his followers.

"What you will see today is not magic, nor is it an illusion." With a wide sweep of his arm, he directed their attention to the children rocking quietly. "Before you, these young children, are our future. These rocking chairs are filled with promise, hope, all we dream and wish. Back and forth, they will go through life, making choices, committing sin, and living the consequences. We love them, care for them, guide them, forgiving their faults and errors. They are an extension of who we are, our legacy." The children smiled, a few soft giggles escaped and a few parents waved proudly.

Sweeping his opposite arm in the same fashion, he directed their attention to the empty rockers. "These chairs, they too are occupied. They may appear empty, but I assure you, they are filled with the souls of those departed. Take a good look. Now, close your eyes please." Waiting a few moments, Daniel looked into the crowd, imploring with his gentle gaze even the most resistant. Confident all eyes were closed, Daniel began again, "Imagine, sitting before you, those who have gone on before us. A father or mother, possibly a great-grandfather or great-great Aunt you never knew. Maybe it is a child, one whose absence still pierces your heart. Gathered here today, they are before us, with us."

A few moments of silence passed. "I also assure you," his voice rising, "these souls we love and miss were not free from sin. They were guilty. They were stubborn. They were sorry. Many went to meet their maker with heavy burdens."

The sound of the crowd breathing deeply filled the room.

"Now, given just one wish, this very moment, what would that wish be?" Mrs. Singleton began softly playing, Cannon in D Major. The chords swept back and forth across the room, like the conflicting emotions sweeping the congregation. Daniel let the soft notes fall over closed eyes and sensitive hearts. "One day. That is what I wish for. Just one day with my father. I wish to hear his voice, touch his face, smell his tobacco. I want to hold his hand, the rugged grain of his palm so familiar, ask all the questions I never knew to ask, tell him I love him, just one more time." Letting his voice drop, barely a whisper, he asked, "What would I give to have this wish? Everything. I would forgive him all, for just one day." Giving time for his words to sink in, find reception, and become fabric of their thoughts, he paused. A few heavy, grey clouds gathering outside, rumbled. Eyes opened, only to quickly close, safe and secure in the presence of family, friends, and God.

In a sudden burst of emotion, his voice booming, Daniel asked, "Who will join me? Who will open their hearts and forgive? If you are ready, come out of the dark, open your eyes." The crescendo of Pachelbel's Cannon rose, imploring eyes to open.

The congregation slowly raised their heads and looked around the room. A few, reluctant to leave the visions of the souls they so missed, dabbed their tears, slowly focusing. All eyes opened. The urge to see was too great, even for the most stubborn and outspoken. Between the rocking chairs, in front of the altar, stood the four young men that were seated next to Matthew. The two in military dress were on the left, the other two on the right. Serious, they stood still, looking ahead.

"We forgive our future," Daniel said, a wide sweep of his arm indicating the children. "We forgive our past." He stood before them, arms wide open. "Who does that leave?" he asked, his eyes fiery. The piano thundered. "You. Me. Us. We." Stepping down from, he stood between the four young men.

"Here before you are four of us. Two young men who served our country in Vietnam, only to come home to hatred and rejection." Turning, he motioned to the other two. "Here, two young men who stood against the war, recently pardoned. We talk about the road of the righteous, standing together, opposing all that is against God. But, we forget. The road of the righteous is not the road of the self-righteous. It is a road, shrouded, invisible by sin, failings and resentments, guilt and remorse. And only, with the grace of God, by following the words of Jesus Christ, can we forgive and be forgiven. Forgiveness is not a single act, it is a process, a commitment to journey with Christ, even when we are not sure, even when we fail. Let us journey together this road of the righteous, this road strewn with pitfalls, this road of forgiveness, this road of redemption." Bringing his hands before him, open, he closed his sermon with a reminder, "Just remember, the first step is always the most difficult." The piano began to fade as Daniel stepped away from the young men, gathered Victoria and Steady, and made his way down the aisle to the back of church.

Holding back tears, the congregation watched the four young men before them. Waves of emotion played across their faces, fists clenched at their sides. A few seconds passed. The room was silent. Standing at the back of the church, Daniel's thoughts began to race, his confidence falter. Angry, he thought. They look angry. Mrs. Singleton peered over the piano at him, her eyes searching, her hands paused above the keys, the recessional hymn but a note away. Daniel turned away from her gaze and just about to step forward, he heard a noise. All heads turned. In the middle of the congregation, a chair scraped the floor, as a young man rose. Struggling, the sound of crutches filled the room. Slowly, painfully, he made his way up the center aisle, one pant leg folded at the knee. He stood before the four young men, looking one at a time into their eyes. Wind buffeted at the windows, panes rattled. Slowly, his shoulders began to shake, his head hung. Leaning hard on his crutches, he faltered. Reaching out, the four young men came together to help. Suddenly, he lifted his arms, crutches falling. A deep cry came from within and throwing his arms around them, he fell into their embrace.

One by one, others rose and coming forward, tears fell, arms embraced, and hearts opened. Without asking, without granting, there was healing. Standing beside Victoria, Steady high upon his shoulders, Daniel stood in line, waiting to shake hands with the five young men who started the journey, led them down the road of forgiveness. Today, I follow, he thought, a slow smile forming. Taking in the view from the back of the church, the crowd before him, the altar and transformation of their building, he was struck by this unexpected unfolding of events. Daniel noticed many were wearing their red, "We're on a Mission" t-shirts. So different the view, he thought. Things certainly did not go as planned and yet, how wonderful. Bouncing Steady up and down, he felt his spirits rise. Forest for the trees, how appropriate, he thought. Never saw a forest with just one tree. There are thousands of trees in the forest of followers, and me, well, I'm just one, he thought. "Oh, but for the grace of God, go I," he whispered, "Oh, but for the grace of God."

Chapter 9

March came in like a lion and went out the same. Mother
nature was not in the mood for lambs, let alone daffodils, tulips,
baby bunnies or sunshine. Wet and miserable, April began each
day with the threat of frost and ended with a little warmth and a
false promise. Braving the outdoors as much as possible, still left
many hours inside, too many hours. Nerves were strained, moods
touchy. Victoria was anxious to receive word from Vanderbilt and
every day, she walked the long driveway down to the mailbox, to
no avail. Steady was full of energy, more than healthy for indoors,
especially for Iris, who nursing a cough for over a month, had
moved into the farmhouse so Victoria could help her recover.

It had been a hard winter for Iris. What started as a sore
throat, moved into a deep cough and overall tiredness that refused
to leave. Propped up on pillows on the sofa in her favorite room,
she slept off and on throughout the day and night. Visits from the
doctor and a myriad of remedies did little to help her slow recovery
and lagging spirits. What did help, was time with her grandson.
Steady, with all his observations, energy, and innocence brought
out the old Iris, so much so, that instructions not to bother
Gramma Weddington were amended to include several visits a day,
especially story time.

Iris, pulling herself up to a seat, would welcome Steady with
open arms, wrap them together in a layer of quilts and off they
would go, riding the tales of past generations. All the way back to
Samuel Jackson and his invention, felling trees the size of giants.
Josephine, so much more than a sister-in-law to Elizabeth, they
were inseparable, late in life, a dynamic duo heading up the Jackson
family. Josephine's delicate French handwriting adorned many of
the old family heirlooms, and Henry, his wrath upon the bench,
was a judge to be feared, a Chicago legend. Lucille, her fiery temper
and quick wit, and Daniel, tall and handsome, his love for Lucille
strong enough to jump denominations, changed course for the
Jackson devotion to God. Embellishing stories with tragedy and

dastardly deeds, Iris painted a picture, vivid and bright, where good always won and evil lost. Southern charm and a few strung-out syllables gave color and cadence to her stories, keeping a young boy's interest. Steady, always a step ahead, yelled out the familiar endings, jumping up and down, hurray, hurray.

Monday nights were finance night. Daniel and Matthew held a private discussion, usually in the study, but with Iris just across the hall and Steady climbing the walls, they moved to the Clarkston Diner. Located on Main Street, it was a hub of local activity. Serving breakfast, lunch, and dinner, they were open seven days a week, making the conversation as good as the local paper. A morning edition and sold at the diner, by the end of the day the news was ingested and refashioned as many times as the cook yelled, "Order up." It was Matthew's suggestion to move their meeting to the diner. Renting a room in a local boarding house, Matthew took most of his meals served at the counter. A pretty little redhead waitress, Leona, kept a keen eye on Matthew, commandeering his service and attention whenever he visited. Daniel considered Matthew a private person, only on two occasions did he reveal anything about himself, and even then, the details were fleeting. Walking into the diner that evening, Matthew showered with familiar greetings from staff and patrons alike, Daniel realized this could be an insight into his new and somewhat distant friend.

"Will you be sitting at the counter this evening, luv?" the petite redhead asked leaning far over the counter, her deep brown eyes drinking in Matthew's tall and muscular physique.

"Evening, Leona," Matthew answered, his voice easy. "How about a booth in the back? Private business." Stepping back, he held his expression serious.

Her lower lip jutted out and her eyes dimmed. With a flip of her hair, she grabbed two menus and called into the kitchen. "Mary, you're on counter."

Leona led them to the back of the diner, her hips moving like a teeter-totter full of children. Without asking, she poured them coffee, moving Matthew's far to the right and then throwing herself halfway across the table to fill his cup. Daniel felt himself going red, even though the display was clearly not for his benefit. Matthew took it all in stride, patiently waiting for Leona to leave, no second glance or word regarding the drama.

Pouring over the numbers, Daniel made a quick run in his head and said, "Collections are down." He flipped through the last few months, beginning with January. "I'd like to see a summary, cost analysis by month. And throw it on a line graph. Visuals always help."

"Sure," Matthew said, smiling for the first time that evening. Pulling out a stack of papers, he placed them on the table in front of Daniel and sat back, loosened his tie and waited.

Daniel looked through the papers and began to chuckle. "You're good," he said. "Oh, you are good." Following the line graph, he could see the collections peaked in February and since then, were quite steady, plus or minus a few percentage points. Daniel took a quick glance at the expenses and it all seemed typical.

"Your copy," Matthew said, draining his coffee and looking over his shoulder for the little redhead. Catching her eye, he laughed as she quickly turned away, ignoring him.

"You may have to make some adjustments," Daniel quipped.

"Excuse me?" Matthew turned, his tone flat, confused.

"Little Leona, with the not so little crush for you," Daniel said, hiding his smile behind the papers. "I think her bottom line is a little in the red."

"Ha," Matthew laughed, "No worries there, my friend. No worries there."

Daniel watched Matthew's expression go from confidence to humor to boredom. Clearly, there was some history, past history for one and not the other. Seeing his friend in a new light, Matthew reminded him of a large tabby cat that hung around the church parking lot. Arriving early one morning, Daniel caught sight of the cat with its latest prey, a tiny mouse, no more than a baby, half-dead. A few half-eaten mice were strewn around and now, no longer hungry, he was playing with the last of the litter. Batting it back and forth, reviving it a moment or two, it would pounce, only to sit back and watch. Finally, boredom took hold and the cat trotted away. Disturbing and cruel, Daniel shook the memory away.

Typically, the finance meetings were quick. Thirty minutes or so and Matthew was gone. But tonight, waiting for dinner and for the waitress to warm up enough to even take their order, they were left with time on their hands. Matthew excused himself for a moment and Daniel went back to the report before him. Everything seemed to be in order and yet, there was something missing. Not able to put his finger on it, Daniel put down the report and picked up the menu. Having established firm controls at the onset of the church's formation, he felt confident there were enough checks in place to deter poor money handling. Yet, Daniel knew, where there was money, anything was possible. And even the best controls deterred at best.

Six members of the church, including himself and Matthew made up the collections committee. A rotation, randomly assigned a month ahead, with two collecting, two others counting, and the last two verifying. No less than two ever handled the collections. Checks, withdrawals, and deposits required two signatures, one of which was always Daniel's, the other Matthew or a board member. Withdrawals over five hundred dollars required a third board member's approval and an item line at the next meeting.

In spite of this, Daniel made regular trips to the bank to reconcile the accounts with the reports Matthew filed. Making a few notes on the edge of the paper, Daniel wrote, "Feb. 1st: receipts," folded the report in four and stuck it in his shirt pocket. Checking his watch, he looked around. With no sign of Matthew or the little redhead, he threw down a five-dollar bill and scribbled on a napkin, leaving the note on top of Matthew's coffee cup. As he stepped out the door, the sunset blinded him for a moment. Raising his hand to shield his eyes, he caught a glimpse of a red Ford Mustang pulling away. He was pretty sure it was Matthew driving. Standing there, his hand on the door, feet in the threshold, his mouth opened in surprise. It took a moment for things to register. I've been stood up, he thought, his mouth a fine line. Matthew's leaving him was no big deal, he was pretty sure, given the performance tonight, the reason for his hasty departure was of the female persuasion. After all, sitting right up next to Matthew, practically in his lap, he saw a woman. As they turned the corner, Daniel looked into the car and suddenly, grabbed hold of the door. Matthew's red hair was a blaze of fire in the bright light of the setting sun. What struck Daniel, made his heart stop, was what he did not see. The woman in the car was far from what he expected. Daniel saw no flames upon her head, but long, straight, beautiful, black hair.

Chapter 10

Victoria was alone in the kitchen. With Daniel, off to the diner to meet Matthew, and Iris busy entertaining Steady with Jackson family stories, she could take her time cleaning up. Filling the sink with hot, soapy water, she looked out the window. Sunlight, just falling behind the trees, still held the day with the little warmth it harbored. A few robins, busy with their nest, hollered back and forth to invaders and took turns minding the tiny blue eggs, one on guard, the other on warming. Untying her apron, she hung it on the chair and stepped outside. The warm sun and cool ground seemed to compliment her indecisive mood and Victoria decided to go for a walk. Loosening her long braid, she let her hair fall from her shoulders in soft waves, the braid a temporary memory maker. After the hot kitchen, the promise of a cool evening felt good. Out to the mailbox and back, a quick check of the cottage, and then the front porch. Another robin couple set up house on the side of the front porch, nearest the kitchen. Squabbles ensued between the four in a flurry of feathers and calls. Looking down at their nest, tucked neatly beneath a quiet rocker, Victoria thought about roaming cats and the unpredictability of nature.

Peaking in the front porch window, she could see Iris and Steady fast asleep upon the sofa. Steady's feet stuck out from the quilts, one foot bare, the other a sock dangling by a toe. Iris, her head to the side, eyes closed, looked peaceful, the deep cough quiet, for once. The fireplace, a blazing fire hours ago, was almost out. Heading around back, she suddenly felt cold, now that the sun, almost below the horizon, left an open invitation to the night's chill. Without a sweater or jacket, she quickly hurried to the back door and went inside.

The house was quiet, water in the sink cold. Placing her hands on her cheeks, red and raw, she shivered. Grabbing her apron, she tied it around her waist, drained the dishwater, and tip-toed down the hall to check on Iris. In the doorway, she smiled at the serene sight. Steady, always a hot sleeper, threw the quilts to the floor, both feet now bare, and was completely turned over. Iris, Victoria noticed, had not moved at all. Entering the room, she stoked up the fire and throwing on a log, it came back to life. She thought to feel Iris for fever, but the sound of an approaching car, fast and furious caught her off guard. Standing halfway between Iris, her hand suspended mid-air, and the window, she leaned over to look outside. It was Daniel, but why the hurry? she wondered. A squeal of brakes and slam of the car door were followed by urgent footsteps. The front door flew open. Steady grunted in his sleep and readjusted, falling back in slumber. Victoria, frozen, looked down at Iris, then the front door. Daniel, face flushed, full of panic, crossed the foyer to the living room. His eyes, electric, took in his wife, the apron, her red cheeks, the fire, and her hair, full of waves, it floated down past her shoulders like the biblical waters of forgiveness.

"Daniel?" Victoria asked, her voice light and questioning.

Gathering his wits, his error full upon him, Daniel cringed. A smattering fool, I am, he thought. How could I think? Managing a quick grunt, he turned to go.

"Daniel?" Victoria asked again, this time, her voice faltering, her hand no longer suspended mid-air, but firmly upon Iris' brow.

Rushing to Victoria's side, he fell to his knees. His hand, full of fire, fell gently upon Victoria's and the stone, cold, brow of his gentle and loving mother.

On the morning Iris was buried, spring finally arrived. Tulips and daffodils spread their petals wide open, trees pushed forth new, green buds, and all sorts of miniature creatures, tiny versions of their parents, ran and flew among the brush. Late into the evening, family and friends remained, the kitchen full of food, lovingly prepared and brought over, every chair in the house full and the front porch, standing room only. In the corner, Steady, his feet barely touching the floor, sat rocking back and forth quietly. Daniel spotted him and politely excused himself from conversation.

Placing his finger under his son's chin he whispered, "Hey there."

"I miss Gramma." His chubby cheeks quivered, eyes watered.

"Me too, buddy." Daniel picked Steady up and taking a seat on the rocker, placed him on his lap. "I miss her voice," he said softly, leaning into his son and inhaling the sweet scent of shampoo and powder.

"Stories. Who will tell me stories?" Steady asked, his voice small, barely a whisper.

"Well, we could write them down. Do you remember them?" he asked.

Turning to look at his father, Steady's face transformed, brightened. "Yes, I do. I know about Samuel, and Daniel, not you, but Daniel from a long time ago, and Lucille and Josephine and Walter, that's Gramma Weddington's honey," rambling on, he swung his legs back and forth as they rocked to and fro. "All upstairs in the attic, Daddy, Daddy, Daddy. Are you listening?" he asked, his voice breathless.

Daniel, lost in thought, felt the rocker go still. "Yes, little man," he said, "Go ahead, what's this about the attic?"

To Daniel's amazement, Steady explained in detail the treasures upstairs in his attic, hidden in plain sight. Apparently, Steady and Iris spent many hours going through old trunks and treasures, ages old, absorbing things of the past. Unknown to him, there was a wealth of family history just two stories up. Funny, he thought, it never occurred to me to even look in the attic. I never even thought about the old Jackson family. I wonder how my mother knew? Gramma Pearl was gone by the time Walter brought her here, his new bride from the south. Making a mental note to ask Victoria, he patted Steady on the back and stood up.

"Run along and get some of Mrs. Thompson's cookies," he told Steady. "I bet they're just about gone." Steady took off through the crowd, jockeying legs and arms, letting the front door slam.

Daniel stretched his arms overhead and seeing an opening, snuck out the kitchen side of the porch. Enough small talk, he thought. Stepping over a small bird's nest, barely missing, he thought about the chances in life. One step in the wrong direction and there you go, he thought. Wishing everyone would just go home, he sought out Victoria, her gentle gaze, loving embrace. Almost dark outside, the kitchen light burned brightly. Daniel looked through the door and saw Victoria, deep in conversation at the kitchen table. Emotions of the day, raw and edgy, made him restless. All he wanted was his wife. Alone.

It had been three days since he found his wife innocent, himself a fool, and his mother gone. Three busy days and nights. As a pastor, he presided over many funerals, but never did he fathom the amount of work, the burden a family undertakes in sending off a loved one. Too little sleep, all the wrong food, and not enough solace culminated in an emotional sendoff that left you high wired, craving silence. Daniel knew, the solace he craved would haunt him for months to come and maybe that was the idea. Overwhelming, it eased you into the next phase of coping with the loss of a loved one, a phase when you would do anything to escape the loneliness and solitude of loss. Still, Daniel knew he was not alone. Victoria. Beautiful Victoria. Their eyes meeting through the glass pane, he begged. He watched as she stood up, hugged and excused herself and left the room. A warm night, Daniel stood in total darkness, his eyes blinded from the kitchen light within. Shouts of farewell, footsteps down the drive, gave telltale signs it was time to leave.

Just about to give up, Daniel felt an embrace. Arms, strong and familiar grasped around his waist.

"I thought you'd never come," he teased.

"Steady. It's almost bedtime. Mrs. Thompson is reading him a bedtime story."

Feeling her press against him, he turned around and wrapped her in his arms. "How long of a story?" he asked, his voice deep and husky.

"Oh, it will take a while," she answered, running her hands down his back, she encouraged his embrace.

The full moon, hiding behind a deep curtain of cloud cover, lent just enough light for Daniel to read Victoria's eyes. Pulling her hand, he broke out into a run around the back of the house. They giggled like teenagers. They ran tripping into the dark and hushed each other's outbursts. At the cottage door, Daniel fumbled with the key, his hands urgent, pulse quick. Victoria, breathing heavy, turned and looked back at the farmhouse. Goodbyes on the front porch and shadows of people leaving filled the front yard. Daniel dropped the key, muttered something incoherent, and bending over, smacked his head on the door frame. Holding his forehead, a moment, he closed his eyes. Just then, the clouds broke and Victoria gasped. There, in the middle of the front yard, staring, the moon an eerie spotlight, was Matthew, watching them, staring at them. Victoria exhaled and returning his gaze, saw his slow smile, cruel and haunting. Reaching for Daniel, she heard the key catch and suddenly, they were inside, falling over the back of the sofa and into each other's arms.

Later that evening, the guests gone and Steady fast asleep, Daniel and Victoria lay wrapped in each other's arms, comfortable, back in their large, four poster bed. The urgency he felt, just hours before, was replaced with a feeling of calm. Victoria's eyes were closed, her hair a wreath of black around her head.

"Hey, Vic," he said touching her arm lightly.

"Mmm?" she responded, her voice sleepy, eyes still closed.

"Have you ever been in the attic?"

"Sure." Rolling over to face him, she opened her eyes and looked up. "Why?"

"Steady said something tonight."

"What did he say?" Victoria asked, stifling a slow, wide yawn.

"Not much really. Just kept saying, 'It's all in the attic, all in the attic.' What's all in the attic? And how did my mother know all those Jackson family stories? She never even met them. I can't believe my father told her. He wasn't exactly a proud Jackson, considering his father, mean old man Charles."

"Well," Victoria began, pulling herself up to a seat and pulling the covers up to her chin, "A few times. Iris liked to go through all the old things. Boxes and boxes of Jackson memorabilia. An archeologist could make a life-long career out of just half the stuff up there."

Daniel shook his head slightly and sighed. "I can't believe I never set foot up there. Not even as a kid. There is so much I don't know. Of course, I know all the folklore. How Samuel came from the old country, penniless and made a fortune, how the fortune doubled when the Jackson's married the McGough's, a wealthy, well-established and powerful Chicago entity, and of course, the key, the mysterious key, lost or buried, worth millions. But, it's not like they are real or anything. Steady talks about them like they are his best friends. It's kind of strange, don't you think?"

"Oh, I don't know," she murmured. "Iris spun so many stories. She was a great storyteller and Steady, well, he has a vivid imagination, that's for sure."

"Funny, I don't remember her telling stories when I was a kid."

"Daniel. She was a preacher's wife. No time for stories." Smacking him across the face playfully, she readjusted her position.

"Well, I just find it interesting that she invested so much time into a family name she denied."

"Not the name, the man, Charles. She never denied your father."

"I just wish I could ask her why."

"Does she have any family left?" Victoria asked softly.

"Just a few old aunts, I think." Staring at nothing in particular, he whispered, "It must have been lonely for her, an only child."

Victoria looked at Daniel in silence.

"Oh Vic. I'm so sorry. I'm such an idiot. Was it lonely being an only child? You never talk about your childhood," he said, his voice soft and pleading.

"I loved my father more than anything, in spite of the circumstances. No, I wasn't lonely, but Iris was different. She never even knew her parents. Dead before she took her first steps."

"And raised by two mean old spinster aunts. She always said Dad rescued her." Daniel leaned over and planted a kiss on her forehead. "You know, maybe you should tell Steady some stories from when you grew up, I mean, the good stuff."

"Your mother was the storyteller, not me," Victoria said, her voice firm.

"Steady would love them, especially the Indian reservation," Daniel said, his eyes soft.

"He sure would," Victoria's face clouded over. "So would Mrs. Thompson and all the rest of the church. No, I don't need anyone digging into my past. It's hard enough being a preacher's wife. I'm not giving out free ammunition."

"I like the fact you're a woman with a past," he said playfully, burying his face in her hair and taking a deep breath. "You know, I save souls and you look like you need a little saving." Bringing the covers over his head, Daniel had grabbed Victoria and pulled her under, under the covers, away from their troubles and into his heart.

Chapter 11

The next few weeks were a struggle. The world kept turning, sun rose and set, and the rhythms of normal daily life continued, at least for some. Every now and then, Daniel would stop, and for no particular reason, think of his mother. As if stepping off a speeding train, he was jolted back by sorrow, while the blur of life sped by.

Victoria made a point of spending a little time every morning in Iris' favorite room. Carefully dusting her photos, her favorite things, she remembered and felt the warmth and love of her mother-in-law, her friend. She felt her presence, a tingle upon her shoulder or a breeze through the open window. It was as if there was a connection, between this life and the next, a feeling of love and tenderness. Closing her eyes, the smell of Iris' perfume, the faintest hint of lilac upon the room, she could hear her soft southern drawl, the musical cadence of her voice, see her perched upon the sofa, waiting for Steady to come home from school.

But for Steady it was as if every day was the day his grandmother died. Rushing to catch the school bus in the morning, busy at school, he would forget. The first week, he came running in through the front door, calling out, "Gramma," only to stare at the empty sofa, the screen door a startling slam behind him. Standing still, his books falling to the floor, his eyes would well up and his fists clench. Victoria knew it was harsh, but she stayed in the kitchen, letting him come to her and to an understanding of Iris' absence. Gradually, he remembered, no longer running home, but slowly walking, dragging his feet and staring up at the clouds. The day he came in the back door to the kitchen, Victoria knew he was coming to terms. From then on, she met him at the bus and together, they walked back slowly.

But, three weeks out, it was Daniel that concerned Victoria. Quiet and withdrawn, he spent hours alone in his study. Blank sheets of paper, a quiet typewriter and empty waste basket, spoke volumes. He was lost, going through the motions, building walls of silence. It all came to a head one Sunday after services. Daniel was at his desk, again, accomplishing nothing. Suddenly, from somewhere came a loud banging, over and over, thud, thud, thud, louder and louder until Daniel threw open the door, his face red and swollen, eyes angry.

"What the heck?" he asked, finding the foyer, living room, and kitchen empty.

Thud, thud, thud, the banging continued. Running up the stairs, Daniel followed the sound, his anger at the interruption slowly turning to curiosity and then concern. Rounding the corner at the top of the stairs, he found the second floor empty. The banging continued. Standing there, his hand on his hips, jaw firm, the noise came closer and closer. Following the sound, he turned and just in time threw out his hands. The attic door swung open and with a final thud, out fell Steady, Victoria, and the biggest trunk Daniel ever saw.

"Well, that explains that," Daniel said, his lips a fine line, eyes half-mast.

"Sorry, Daddy," Steady shouted. "Look. Look. We found it. We found it." With one hand on the trunk and the other pulling at his father's pant leg, his eyes pleading, Steady did his best to get his father's attention.

Daniel's eyes met Victoria's. "Sorry," she whispered, with a slight shrug and a smile in Steady's direction.

Daniel helped them carry the trunk downstairs, this time quietly. Steady buzzed around like a honeybee on the first day of spring. He was so excited to open the trunk and kept getting in the way, that Victoria called a halt, declaring a break, lunch. With directions to wash up to their elbows, Victoria sent the men off and sat down beside the trunk. Covered in several inches of dust, it looked untouched. A bronze plate was affixed to the front. "D. Jackson, Saginaw, Michigan," it read. Victoria ran her hand across the plate, removing layers of dust. She looked at the trunk a long time. A feeling of awe, a wish to respect the past, the dead, filled her. Of course, she knew about the rumors, but who knew if they were true. A key, covered in emeralds and diamonds, a Jackson legacy, lost or hidden, remained unfound. Worth millions, it was rumored. Iris told her the story. The key was real. A wedding gift generations ago. Handed down from mother to daughter, the key and the drop-leaf desk. Looking across the room, Victoria could see the desk, Iris' things lovingly placed, her pen and writing tablet. So, what happened to the key? Victoria wondered. Iris thought Daniel's grandmother, Pearl, hid the key from Charles, knowing it's worth and well, his worth. In a drunken rage, he threatened. Buried somewhere on the property, it was rumored. Took it to her grave, others said. Victoria thought about Pearl, her sons gone, husband a terror. Poor woman, she thought, first polio, then tuberculosis. I can't imagine knowing you are going to die, left all alone. A chill went up her spine and Victoria pulled herself up. I wonder, she thought. Must have taken some strength to go against Charles. Left the house to Walter in spite of the old man. But maybe that's not all, was there more to the story? Iris told her that when she and Walter came to Michigan, the key was missing. Walter was sure his father took the key. He refused to believe he would leave without it, the mean old miser, but Iris wasn't so sure. Maybe Iris knew something, Victoria thought. Wrapping her arms around herself, a sudden chill in the room, Victoria felt a familiar presence, the slight scent of lilac.

"Us men are hungry," Steady yelled from the kitchen. Laughter floated down the hall.

Walking over to close the window, Victoria paused, running her right hand across the front of the desk. As her fingers met the key hole, the tiniest tingle ran up her arm. Pulling her hand away, she closed the window and stared at the desk and then the trunk. If only the dead could talk, she thought. On her way out of the room, she felt sharp pain. Grabbing her hand, she muffled a cry, quickly running from the room, not stopping to look back. Following the sound of laughter, she pushed away thoughts of the past, for the moment, living for the moment.

With lunch over, they were back in the living room. Steady kept leaning into the trunk and almost tipping it over. Victoria put up her hands and Daniel, with one arm on the cover, held it in place to prevent it from slamming shut. Sitting back on her heels,

Victoria's face stern and expressionless, she pulled Steady out of the trunk for the third time and placed him on the couch.

"Okay, Mr. Ready Freddy," she said, wagging her finger at him. "This is how we are going to do this."

There was a knock at the front door and Daniel motioned he would answer.

Victoria's voice trailed off behind him, "You will sit here. I will sit over there."

It was Matthew. A little surprised, Daniel pulled the door behind him and stepped onto the porch. Sunday afternoon was their only time off from church work and as far as Daniel knew, when not working, Matthew was fishing. Fall, winter, spring, snow, rain, or shine, Matthew fished. He wasn't sure what Matthew did with all the fish he caught, living in a boarding room with no place to cook. To hear Matthew talk, he caught plenty. Matthew handed him their weekly financial report, only this time it was a day early and about twice as thick.

"No fishing today?" Daniel asked, taking the report and tilting his head, as he flipped through the pages.

"Hit my limit," Matthew said, his green eyes dancing.

Daniel met Matthew's eyes. "Ahhh," he said. "Why so early and so," holding the report on the palm of his hand, his lifted it up and down slightly, "long?"

"I wanted you to have a chance to review the numbers before our meeting on Monday." Handing him another envelope, he motioned towards the rockers, his eyebrows raised.

Sitting down, Daniel went to open the envelope, but Matthew placed a hand over his.

"Not now," he said. Leaning back in his chair, he rocked back and forth and closed his eyes.

Daniel watched him for a few moments. It wasn't like Matthew to draw things out. Upfront and frank, he said what was to be said and then he was gone. Other than Iris' funeral, this was the first time he came to see him without an agenda, or did he? Daniel thought. Matthew's sudden disappearance at the Clarkston Cafe lurked in the back of his mind. The few times he went to ask, he thought better. The image of his passenger, so like his Victoria, came to mind and all the feelings of guilt and foolishness returned. I am their pastor, after all, he thought. I'm supposed to provide peace, not drama.

Suddenly, little feet barged through the door and Steady stood before them. "A gabbel, Daddy. Look, a gabble." Swinging the gavel back and forth, too close to his head for comfort, Daniel stayed the swinging instrument.

"A g-a-v-e-l," Daniel said. "V, Steady, not B".

Matthew continued to rock back and forth, opening one eye to watch every now and then. His face was passive, except for a small turn at the edge of his mouth.

"This was Lucille's daddy's. Judge Henry McGough," he said in a deep voice and serious face. "See?" he pointed to an engraving on the side.

Before Daniel could take a look, Steady was back through the door, little footsteps running away. Daniel leaned forward in his chair and pulled his gaze away from the front door. Matthew continued to rock silently back and forth. Is he asleep? he wondered. A slight twitch of Matthew's eye and adjustment in his chair gave him his answer. Daniel placed his hand to his mouth and coughed. Matthew opened his eyes and began to speak when the front door flew open again and there before them was Steady, an old black hat perched upon his head. Draped over his shoulders was a shawl, better days long gone, and on his feet, a funny looking pair of lace up boots. A ridiculous grin spread across his face.

Matthew broke out into fits of laughter. "Steady, my boy," he laughed. "You sure are a sight to see."

Daniel chuckled, familiar with his son's antics, he leaned over and put out his hand. "Why hello, Sir, pleased to make your acquaintance," he offered playfully.

"Right back at ya'," Steady answered. "Mr. Samuel A. Jackson at your service. I can tell a tree in a single blow," he boasted.

"Tell?" Matthew asked, suppressing a laugh, his face about to fall into fits.

"Fell, Steady. Cutting a tree is felling," Daniel instructed.

Leaning over, a hand to his hat falling over his eyes, the other to the side of his mouth, Steady whispered conspiratorially, "Daddy, I'm not Steady. I'm Mr. Samuel A. Jackson."

Matthew looked away, a merry muffle escaping. Before Daniel could commit to his son's trust, the boy was off again, the front door slamming and the windows rattling. Matthew looked over at Daniel and raised his eyebrows.

"Old attic stuff," Daniel explained. "Victoria thought it would help Steady. He misses his grandmother."

Daniel went on to explain about Iris and how she lost her parents, only to be raised by spinster aunts. It was his father, Walter, who found her, at a southern revival in Kentucky, fell in love and brought her to Michigan. And even though she never met them, Iris knew all the old Jackson family stories, told them to Steady every day after school.

"I guess, since she never had any family, she felt it was important her grandchild knew his history," Daniel finished.

"Well, he sure knows his history," Matthew agreed. "Almost a first name basis."

"True," Daniel said. "It is a funny thing, the way he talks about the old Jacksons. Never met one of them. And here's another interesting piece of Jackson family history, when my father died, my mother dropped the Jackson name."

"Really? That's quite a big name to drop." Matthew's voice lifted a note or two.

"It's a long story. My grandfather, Charles, has quite the reputation. Collects grudges like some people collect coins. Took off, left his wife to die, keeping it all from his son out of spite. My father came home, new bride in tow, only to find his mother in the ground and his father gone."

"Ouch. Brothers? Sisters?"

"Four brothers. All dead. European theater."

"Wow."

"This farmhouse," Daniel said, "Gramma Pearl left to him. Everything else, gone with the old man."

"And he's still alive?" Matthew asked, his chair slowly creaking back and forth.

240

"Somewhere," Daniel's voice flattened out, bored with the same old story. Suddenly, he stopped rocking and his voice lifted, "Except, there is supposed to be a key. Crazy. A key worth a mint, lost or maybe hidden. No one knows."

Matthew continued to rock, not breaking his cadence, his eyes closed. Yet where his collar met his hairline, the thin scar flamed red. Taking a quiet breath in, he held it a moment, his heart racing, pounding. Placing his hands flat against the rocker's side arms, he stood towering over Daniel. He jingled his keys, looked towards his car, and stepped off the porch.

"Family," his voice matter-of-fact and flat. "Too bad we can't choose."

Daniel felt the mood change and rose to say good-bye.

"It's not a lottery, you know. Family, that is. God works in mysterious ways. Even if we don't understand."

"Divine is not for thine," Matthew stated. "Got that from the old man. Can't out run 'em, no matter how hard you try." Throwing his keys up in the air, he caught them and turned to leave. "Got that from the old woman."

Daniel's heart lurched and he felt an opportunity passing. Holding up a pair of work gloves he called, "Garden day today. Want to turn over a little dirt?"

Matthew stopped and looked back. Daniel stood at the top of the porch steps, his hands out front, gloves dangling. His wavy blonde hair fell over his eager face and a big smile broke out. Matthew laughed.

"Sure." Taking a look at his own clothes and then his watch, he shouted, "I'll change."

Daniel watched Matthew leave, and his heart felt light. Bouncing up and down, he felt happier than in days. The front door slammed and Steady grabbed his legs from behind.

"Hey there, Stranger," he said to the little messenger, a stack of letters held with a frayed and faded ribbon in his hands. "Who do we have here?"

"Silly Daddy. It's me, Steady." he laughed, releasing his hold. "Look," he exclaimed, "O-l-d l-e-t-t-e-r-s. Mommy says they were probably Gramma Josephine's." Screwing up his little face, he looked at the old letters, and then his father. "Daddy, I can't read this. The writing is funny."

Daniel patted Steady's head, taking the fragile letters from him. Eyebrows knitted, as he considered the fine and gentle script. Squinting, he stared at the top envelope. M. Maxis, I.H.M in the upper left hand corner gave no clues, as well as the addressee. All he could make out was the letters *Mlle* and Toronto.

"Well, look at that," he said softly. "That's French, Steady."

"Wow. Does that mean I'm French?"

"That makes both of us French, " he answered, his eyebrows high and wide. Handing them back to Steady, he added, "Be careful, buddy. They look pretty fragile."

Turning towards the door, he stopped. Victoria was standing in the house, smiling at Steady. Looking up, her smile faded, jaw set. The sound of Matthew's car leaving, dust rising, caught her attention. Daniel felt a heaviness in his gut, a wavering in his mood, so light just moments before. Why did I ask him to come back? he thought, gritting his teeth. Victoria put a lot of work into her Sunday dinners and Matthew was probably the last person she wanted at their table. Meeting her eyes, he attempted a feeble smile, his heart lurching. Victoria lowered her eyes. Without a sound, she turned, walked up the stairs and shut the bedroom door.

Chapter 12

Matthew walked into his shoebox of a room and placed his keys and watch on the dresser. Throwing open the only window, he jammed a fan under the sash and turned the dial to high. He removed his shirt and stood with his back to the fan. Opening and closing his fists, he resisted the urge to scratch, the angry, red scars irritated in the heat. Grabbing a towel, he headed down the hall for a cool shower.

Back in his room, he popped a few aspirin, sat on the side of the bed and picked up his watch. Turning it over, he stared at the back for a moment. "J.M. 40 years Lloyds of London," was engraved in block letters. Reaching under the bed, he pulled out a beat up cardboard box, coming apart at the sides. Filled with old newspaper clippings, a page from a magazine, and a few odd papers, he reached for the magazine page. A small photo fell to the floor. Matthew bent over, staring at the photo. Black and white, a young couple with an infant, stood before a row of fishing vessels. Caught off guard, she looked nervous. The man stared straight ahead and the baby was crying. Matthew picked up the photo and without a second look, placed it in the box, face down. Divine is not for thine, he thought. In his hand, he held the magazine page. "The Indemnitor, Jan/Feb 1972," it read at the top of the page. "The Key to the Missing Key," was the title of the article.

Staring at the page, Matthew thought about the old man and his watch, forty years of adjusting claims for Lloyds of London. Who would have guessed he was penniless? After all, he was wearing a Rolex and his suit, tailor made, the Lloyds coat of arms sewn into the cuff of his jacket, shiny white silk shirt, even his cologne said money. It was creepy, the way the old man had zoned in on him. Tired and hungry, Matthew pulled into a roadside bar, somewhere outside of Tucson, Arizona looking for a cold beer and a hamburger. Figured he'd fill up the car and himself and then hit the road again. But the old guy wouldn't shut up. Kept talking about his god damned forty years, his pension, and how he was going to spend it. Laying an arm on his shoulder, he sent signals Matthew was not wired for. Yet, there was the Rolex and who knew what else.

The old man was a sham. Except for the Rolex, an expensive suit and a few small wads of cash, he had nothing. He played Matthew perfectly and nobody played Matthew. Lucky for him, the suit was a perfect fit. One night, a small price to pay. Mornings in Tucson were hot and the double wide at Arizona Acres was a cooker. Just before palming the Rolex, Matthew spotted a magazine open on the counter, "The Key to the Missing Key." The smell was beginning to overpower him and he felt the need to escape. No time to read, he ripped the page out, washed his hands once more just in case, checked his fingernails, and had left the scene for someone else to find. It wouldn't take long in this heat and by then, Matthew would have been long gone.

That was almost a year ago. Now, sitting on his bed in the rooming house, Matthew placed the article back in the box. Just thinking about the key, his heart raced. Probably worth over two million today, he thought. The article focused on the finer points of insurance law and presumptive theft, most of which he did not understand. However, his keen mind figured out right away, a valuable object claimed lost and claimed on an insurance policy was still worth something on the black market. If he could find the key, he was sure he would make a fortune. The article stated in 1957, the owner of a large timber company filed a claim for a key, gold, with the highest quality diamonds and emeralds, insured at the time for $750,000 with Lloyds of London. Lloyds paid the claim under the Mysterious Disappearance clause of the policy, a new type of coverage, due to recent changes in insurance law. The article made point of the fact that the insurer failed to require updated appraisals and that the only appraisal on file was the one provided when the policy was issued in 1925. Lloyds had no way of knowing exactly when the key disappeared. Matthew quickly figured out two things, one, the key was probably worth far more in 1957 and therefore even more today, and two, since 1956, a mysterious disappearance claim did not fall under presumptive theft and therefore, only a statement of loss was required. The

244

insurance company could not require any evidence of theft. Loss was any loss, however mysterious the disappearance. The only proof of ownership was when the policy was issued in 1925. Because the insurer did not require updated appraisals, the key may have been missing for years, may still be missing. Matthew was highly suspicious that they key was in fact not stolen, but lost or hidden. The crafty old man had no idea where it was, that's why he waited until after the insurance law changed to file the claim. Most likely, as a family heirloom, it was still on the property. Matthew headed to Michigan. He needed to get far enough away from Arizona and a trailer full of evidence and closer to Canada. Hopefully, he could evade the feds looking for old draft dodgers long enough to find the key and then over the boarder he would go. His plan was to turn the key into cash and then disappear once and for all.

Only Matthew didn't plan on Victoria. From that first day outside the church, he couldn't stop thinking about her. There was something about her, something different. She wasn't your typical preacher's wife. No, her blood ran a little deeper, a little darker, just like his. She too had a secret past. She too wanted to forget. Making a few calls, he quickly discovered her story. A half-breed, motherless, she was raised on the road by a father, door-to-door salesman, peddling more in hearts and children than vacuum cleaners. No wonder she was so serious. That faraway look, nervous when he was near. Just thinking about her, his body ached. Reaching across the nightstand, he picked up a polaroid. The three of them, Thanksgiving dinner. Placing his finger over Daniel, he stared at the photo. Standing next to Victoria, wedged between them, Matthew was grinning. Victoria stared straight at the camera, as if, if she looked away, it would all disappear. We belong together, he thought. Only, it was taking too long.

Rolling his shoulders, Matthew threw on an old brown shirt and a pair of work pants. Boots, covered in dried mud were considered, but given the smell, he decided otherwise. Sticking his hands in his pockets, he pulled out a pair of old work gloves. Stiff and mud covered, he banged them against the nightstand to loosen them up. Black paint covered half the fingertips. Matthew stretched the gloves over his hands and opened and closed his fists a few times. The black paint flaked away and revealed a deep red. Pushing the cardboard box back under the bed, he pulled out a small can of black paint. Dipping his fingertips into the paint, he held them up before the fan to dry. Tiny splatters of paint flew out before the fan, covering the floor and windowsill with a good measure of paint. Shrugging, he grabbed his keys and began the drive over to the Jackson home. No problem, he thought, I've been lying to them for months. Thinking about Daniel, he drummed his fingers on the steering wheel and laughed. Such a good boy, that Daniel. Hook, line, and sinker on that one, not that I ever fished in my life. Spend my free time fishing, he chuckled. Maybe for money, he thought. And theology school, what a joke. No preacher here, unless of course it would get me into a few deep pockets and deep into a few pairs of pants. There were a few at church though that he kept his distance. Like Mrs. Thompson, shrewd old woman, stay the hell away from her, he thought. Suddenly, Victoria came to mind and his smile faded. A horn blared and he looked up, the traffic light red, tires screeching. Stepping on the gas, he blew through the light and kept going. Victoria, he moaned, how much longer? His heart raced and he began to sweat. Against the vinyl seat, his back stung, and he cursed. Just past the light, there was a sign for Port Huron, the Blue Water Bridge and Canada, left exit ahead. Split in two, he felt the urge pulling left, escape and yet, his right hand on the wheel and Victoria, her face burned into his brain, pulled harder. Blowing past the exit, he looked in his rearview mirror. If only there was a mirror to see what lie ahead, he thought. One more day, he promised himself, just one more day.

Chapter 13

Daniel and Matthew worked until late afternoon on the garden. With their shirtsleeves rolled up and a handkerchief tied around their head, they dug, hoed, and raked until a nice patch of fresh dirt was ready for planting. The five o'clock sun was beating down hard and the men wiped their brows, smearing sweat and dirt across their forehead. Steady, discontented with the mere task of delivering lemonade, changed his clothes, smeared his face with dirt, and wrapping a handkerchief around his forehead, joined his father and Matthew in the garden.

Watching from the kitchen window, Victoria considered the scene before her. Smiling at her son, she watched as he pestered his father, trying so hard to be just like him. Daniel, patient as always, stayed Steady's rake and leaned over to say something to him. Daniel was in the foreground, having cleared a good portion and was now raking clean the weeds and rocks. He looked tired. Matthew, working behind Daniel, not only cleared and hoed, but was almost done raking as well. His powerful arms rippled, his large hands wrapping around the handle. Matthew cleared more than twice the area than Daniel. He looked as if he could work for hours. Daniel slapped Matthew on the back and she saw him wince, recovering with a quick smile. As he turned his back, Victoria's eyes narrowed in on Matthew. His brown shirt was soaked with sweat and stuck to his back and shoulders. Leaning into the window and squinting her eyes, she stared. Unable to see, she was about to pull back, when suddenly, out of the corner of her eye, she saw Daniel watching her. Letting the curtain drop, she placed a hand against her heart, and took a deep breath. I have to do something. I have to get rid of that man, but how?

The men cleaned up and a light supper of salad and sandwiches was served out on the front porch. Not the usual fancy Sunday meal, Victoria's heart was not into cooking tonight. A small round table with few chairs provided intimate seating for three and given Matthew's presence, Victoria was happy to give up her seat to their guest. Steady was informing them about his plans for the garden. What they would plant and how they would begin. Daniel, wolfing down two sandwiches and a glass of lemonade, nodded his head and smiled. Matthew, not quite as famished, took a few bites, looked around and considered his company. When Victoria refilled their glasses, he sat back in his chair, fingering his ring, the Vanderbilt ring, his eyes following her, his expression blank. Victoria stared at Matthew's hands, the ring and her heart skipped. Almost dropping the lemonade, she hurried into the house.

Victoria begged off joining them and retreated to the kitchen. Two trips back and forth were enough. Why did he have to stare at her so? She could feel his eyes following her, every nerve cell on edge, all she wanted to do was hide. Back in the house, she rung her hands and worried. Closer, she mumbled. He keeps getting closer. Now he's helping with the yardwork and having supper with us. She could see how Daniel warmed to him, invited his friendship. How could he be so blind? Didn't he see the way he switched off and on, so warm and friendly with everyone else, so cold and cruel with her. I just have to talk to Daniel. Make him understand, but how? she agonized. Picturing the ring, she thought of the letter from Vanderbilt. What could be taking so long? Exhaling slowly, she closed her eyes. Tomorrow, she thought. If the letter doesn't come tomorrow, I will call them. One more day, she promised herself, just one more day.

Victoria could hear Steady chattering in the hall and the sound of approaching footsteps. Daniel and Steady, their arms full of dirty dishes, said they were going out to the garden. Victoria smiled and filling the sink, she watched them walk outside, side by side, Steady chattering and Daniel, his head leaning, was listening. She thought she heard the front screen door. The top hinge was loose again and needed tightening. Drying her hands on a towel, she walked quietly down the hall, stopping just outside the living room. Sun streaming in the full-length cottage windows cast the hallway in shadows and provided cover for her to watch.

Matthew, his back turned, was running his fingers across the desk. He kept looking over his shoulder. Placing his pinky finger against the keyhole, he paused. He turned abruptly, Victoria stepping back just in time, and looked hard in her direction. Taking a deep breath in, she rung her hands in the towel and crept forward again. Now he was bent over the open trunk. The fabric that lined the trunk was old and worn, but held well at the seams. Placing his hands flat against the insides, he pressed, as if feeling for something hidden. The backdoor slammed and Matthew stood up and walked over to the window. Victoria stepped back quickly, and gasped. Someone was behind her. Turning, she looked up and saw Daniel, his face serious, confused.

"What's going on?" he asked, taking a step back and folding his arms across his chest.

Before he could answer, Matthew stepped into the hall. "Well, there's the little lady," he said. "I was looking for you. Okay to kiss the cook?" he asked, looking up at Daniel.

Victoria turned, almost knocking Daniel over and rushed back into the kitchen. Daniel looked at Matthew and shrugged.

"Something I said?" he asked.

"No harm done," Daniel answered. "Hey, thanks for all your help."

"No problem. See you tomorrow night."

Daniel watched Matthew leave. Turning back towards the kitchen, he felt a weight pressing down. A slight headache was coming on and he halted, placing his hands to his temples. Why did she have to be so difficult? he wondered. And if she dislikes him so much, why is she always watching him? Stiffening, he felt his back rigid, his fists clench. A deep ache filled his gut and he turned again, this time away. Heading to his study, he locked the door, put a blank piece of paper in the typewriter and began typing.

Victoria knew Daniel was angry. Banging away at the typewriter, she wondered what he was putting to paper. As the night wore on, they avoided each other. Their anger, large slices of silence hung throughout the house. Daniel went to bed without saying a word. When Victoria joined him, he turned away, his back a wall between them. Quietly, she left the room.

Knowing she would not sleep, Victoria roamed the house, room by room. In the kitchen, she looked out at the garden, the fresh soil shinning in the full moon, a new beginning. Back to the front hall, she peered out the door. A pile of discarded newspapers was heaped by the front door, their pages shifting in the nighttime air. In the living room, she carefully placed the old items back into the trunk. Pausing for a moment, she held a small black bible. It was very old. The binding was breaking and a few pages fell to the floor. Picking up the pages, the moon illuminated a few lines of finely etched writing. Victoria squinted. Was it in French? she wondered. All she could read was the initials I.H.M. Inside, passages were marked, again, the writing very fine, difficult to read. Shrugging, she placed the little book in the trunk and closed the lid, running her fingers over the bronze plate, it's surface cool to the touch. Moonlight spilled in through the curtains, over the top of the trunk and angled across the floor. Refractions of light cast through a small crystal vase spun across the wall, as the night breeze blew into the room. Victoria felt the room too heavy and moved on. Across the hall, she stepped into Daniel's office. Sitting at his desk, she saw the typewriter was empty of paper, as was the trash can. A large report lay on the desk on top of a file marked, financial reports. Inside was a piece of paper, folded in four. Columns of numbers filled the page. In Daniel's handwriting, "Feb 1st," was written at the top. The day Iris died, she thought. Victoria looked at the clock, two in the morning. Two hours later, she closed the file and readjusted the report.

Leaning back in Daniel's chair, Victoria thought about what she read. Matthew was very clever. He covered his tracks well. Going back to last October, all the expenses were itemized, deposits detailed. However, when looking at the report, as a whole, there were trends. Several expenses would increase for a few months and then drop back down. It could easily be explained with an invoice. Could it be, that Matthew created fake invoices, wrote the checks and obtained the required signatures, but then endorsed them himself and pocketed the money? Adding up those expenses that followed the trend, Victoria paused. Just over $3,000, it was a significant amount by church standards, but not a huge windfall. Why would Matthew go to such trouble, stay so long, and run such a risk for $3,000? He was not the small crime type, that much Victoria knew. He must be after something else, something big, but what? She wondered.

Victoria knew she must compare the figures in this report to bank records. She needed to see the endorsements on the back of the checks, look at the signatures. There was something else too. The suspected overpayments were all made to a few specific businesses of church members. Matthew knew them, knew their full names, knew their signatures. He also knew a pretty, young teller at the bank. Victoria was pretty sure he was familiar with more than her signature.

I have to tell Daniel, she thought. Make him understand. A cold shiver went up her spine as she thought about Matthew. Even if she could convince Daniel, she knew the risk was too great. Matthew was dangerous. Accusing Matthew was dangerous. It would open them up to all kinds of scrutiny. Open her up to all kinds of scrutiny. Victoria put her head in her hands. She was tired, so tired. If only he would leave. How can I convince him to leave? I need help, but who?

Thinking about the Vanderbilt ring, Maria came to mind. I already told her about the ring, she thought. I'll tell her about the expenses. She'll know what to do. Too late to call, she spun around in Daniel's chair in frustration. Sleep will not come until I get this off my chest, she thought. Coming to a slow stop, she stared, in front of her, the typewriter, its carriage empty, almost begging for a page. Pulling out a piece of paper, she began to type. "Dear Maria, I am afraid for our lives..." Two pages later, she signed her name in pen, addressed the envelope to Dr. Maria Thelen, Vanderbilt University, Nashville, TN, affixed the stamp, sat back and relaxed. Shutting off the light, she walked into the living room and put the letter in Iris' drop-leaf desk. The faint scent of lilac greeted her and she smiled. I know, Iris, she murmured, time for bed.

Just before five in the morning, Victoria crawled back into bed. Daniel was sound asleep and did not stir. Slowly, her eyes became heavy, her breathing lengthened out, her limbs softened. Just before falling asleep, an object came to mind. Hovering, just out of reach, she struggled, fought the deep pull of sleep. Her eyelids so heavy, closed, her thoughts receded and mind shifted, a field of sparkling green, white, and gold enveloped her, taking her down, down, down, a labyrinth of slumber.

Chapter 14

Daniel woke to the remnants of a morning shower. Humidity clouded the room and as he rose, he felt the floor damp, the window left open from the night before. Victoria lay deep asleep, hidden by pillows and covers, only a few strands of long, dark hair escaping. Confused, he tried to recall the events of the night before, when a sorrowful feeling filled his gut. Lowering his gaze, he left the room.

Monday was a full day of church business and Daniel liked to start early. By six-thirty he was ready to go, but he felt sluggish, hesitant. The anger and jealousy he felt the night before seemed to belong to someone else and again, he wondered, why? Why the sudden strong feelings, so quick to rise, so foolish later? Why their torment? Why his torment? She deserved better. He knew better. And yet, at the moment, he felt so justified. The sin of self-righteousness, pride, jealousy. Lowering his head and closing his eyes, he gripped the kitchen counter and prayed. He could hear the coffee pot percolating like his tumbling thoughts and feelings of regret, sorrow, and hope. Grabbing a scrap of paper, he scribbled a few lines. "So sorry Vic, all my fault, will always love you." Looking around the kitchen, he considered where to leave his note, when his eyes fell on the kitchen sink. Knowing Victoria never left dirty dishes, he grabbed a piece of tape and placed the note on the window pane above the sink. Closing the door behind him, he was met with the sun, peeking out above the tall pines. Sunlight filled the wet and cool shadows, burning, releasing, freeing the night's hold. Let there be light, Daniel thought. Genesis and the story of creation filled his mind, his love for morning and the feeling of new, fresh beginnings. Awash with the waters of forgiveness, please, he prayed, the dampness and dew rising, higher and higher, enveloping his body, mind, and soul. How much we need the dark to appreciate light, the cold to love warmth, sin to be bathed in the love of forgiveness. Suddenly, overhead there was a cry. He looked up as a hawk screeched across the treetops, its cry for attention making him think of Victoria. Oh Vic, I am so stupid, he thought. Exhaling slowly, he lowered his head. Knowing he must talk to her soon, he looked at his watch, a full day ahead of him. Tonight, he promised. One more day, just one more day.

Victoria woke to bright sunshine, Daniel's absence and an alarming time on the bedside clock, twenty after eight. She would have to drive Steady to school and even then, he would be late. Rushing around, she threw a dress over her head, ran a brush through her hair, plastered on some pink lipstick and hollered across the hall for Steady to get up. Covers on the bed were in a heap and leaving it unmade, Victoria glanced at the bed, gritted her teeth and hurried down the hall to wake Steady.

"Wake up," she said blowing out her breath as she came to his open door.

His bed was made, clothes put away, and even the shades were up. Surprised she headed downstairs.

There, sitting at the kitchen table, his little legs swinging back and forth, was her son. He was dressed in his favorite two-piece leisure suit, bright red with an equally bright Hawaiian shirt underneath. Victoria suppressed a smile, his chubby cheeks and little boy behavior so funny in this tiny, trendy replica of a grown-up outfit. It was supposed to be for special occasions only. She was about to send him back upstairs to change, when she considered his self-reliance this morning and held her tongue. His hair combed, his school books ready to go, he was eating a bowl of cereal. An apple sat on the table, along with a glass of chocolate milk. He even set a place for her too.

"Hi Mom," he mumbled with a mouth full of milk and cereal. "You look sleepy."

Victoria tilted her head to the side and smiled. "How long have you been up?" she asked.

"7-0-0," he said, holding up his hands and miming the numbers. With the last zero he brought his thumb and index finger to his right eye and growled, "Morning, Mattie."

Victoria felt herself relax and she laughed out loud. "Okay, little pirate. Last bite. We need to get you to school." Reaching for his dish, she was halted.

"It's okay, Mom. I can do it." Steady jumped down from his seat and began cleaning up.

Grabbing her keys and purse, Victoria realized she forgot the letter to Maria. Out of sorts and preoccupied, she walked out of the kitchen and didn't see Daniel's note taped to the window above the sink.

Just outside the living room door, she paused, remembering the other night, Matthew's strange behavior and Daniel, catching her for the second time watching Matthew. He was so angry. Her hands began to shake and she dropped her keys. Hitting the floor, the impact rung out and echoed throughout the house. The back door slammed and she looked up, the trunk another reminder. Suddenly, it hit her, keys. That's it, the key, she thought. Matthew must be after the key, the one worth millions. Her eyes widened and a small smile tugged at the corners of her mouth. How preposterous. Really? And yet, considering Matthew's shrewdness, she suddenly frowned. What could he possibly know? she wondered.

Glancing at her watch, she lifted the lid to the trunk and ran her hands along the lining, just as Matthew did the night before. Nothing. Just about to walk away, something caught her eye. In the back corner, where the lining met the edge of the trunk, the stitching was slightly different. Yesterday, the sunlight so bright, it would have been hard to notice. Last night with the moonlight casting shadows, it would have been impossible. Once again, she ran her hand across the lining and there it was, a small thickening. Quickly, she grabbed a pair of scissors and snipped the stitches. There, wrapped in a small piece of pink fabric, was a small key, a frayed and worn pink ribbon tied to the top. About two inches long, it was made of gold and at the head of the key was the most beautiful design of diamonds and emeralds.

The drop-leaf desk, she thought. Steadying her hands, she tried the key in the desk, a perfect fit. Locking and then unlocking the desk, she marveled at the beauty and elegance of such a delicate little key. Iris, she whispered, what now? Looking around the room for a sign, she stood there, key in hand, when Steady came barging through the front door.

255

"Mom. Time to go," he cried. "Mrs. Washington will be so mad."

Victoria jumped. Catching her breath, she rewrapped the key and placed it in the desk drawer. Hurrying from the room, she grabbed the letter to Maria and wedged it under her arm, distracted by her thoughts of Matthew, the bank and the key. An idea was forming, a way to get rid of Matthew. She needed those bank reports. In her haste, she didn't notice the letter fall from her arm. She didn't see it land on the desk, get caught in the drawer as she closed it. As she stepped onto the porch, the heat of the day greeted her. Stepping over yesterday's newspaper, the front page lying face up, she pulled the front door hard to close, the front windows shook and the letter wedged in between the drawer and side of the desk. At that moment, the faintest hint of lilac swept through the room and filled the house.

Chapter 15

Matthew sat in the corner booth by the front window. Mid-morning on a Monday, Clarkston Diner was a busy place, the front door opening and closing every few minutes, a rush of people and warm morning air mixing with the smell of coffee, grease, and cigarette smoke. All seats were full, including the counter. A rush to clear dirty ashtrays, dishes, and lipstick stained coffee cups kept the busboys busy. Every few minutes Charlie, the cook, hollered "Order up," the sound of metal spatulas and cast iron ringing in the air. Lounging in his seat, Matthew held an air of ease and ownership about him. His large frame filled one side of the booth, his hand wrapped around the coffee mug, as if a child's toy, his long legs stretched well into the other side of the booth. A regular for breakfast, there wasn't anything unusual about Matthew other than he sat alone and did not smoke. Familiar faces raised a hand or said hello as they entered the diner, accustomed to his presence and his place. Cars drove up and down the street, stores began opening, and customers slowly went about their business. He was lost in thought, staring out the window, when Leona leaned over and filled his coffee cup, a cigarette dangling from her lips.

"Morning, Baby," she cheered, her perky, little feet bouncing.

"I hate it when you smoke," he said, not looking up, his voice hard, even.

Taking a step back, her eyes filled with tears. Leona didn't really like to smoke, she thought it looked sexy. A little over five feet, she was a pint-sized dynamo at the cafe, a good solid waitress, popular with the ladies, children, and men alike. She knew how to get the most out of people, sweet with the old ladies, cute with the old men, serious with the dads and moms, and playful with the children. Not particularly pretty, her complexion was a roadmap of teenage woe, her brown eyes just a little to close set, and her chin, well, one wasn't sure if she had a chin. Layering on a heavy amount of foundation and eye makeup, she made the most of her few attributes, thick, deep red hair, almost to her hips, a pair of strong, lean legs, and a big enough bosom to make most men dream about how much hair would cover how much.

Making a fist and releasing, Leona pressed her lips together and exhaled. "Well, you don't have to be such a brute about it," she whined.

Matthew continued to stare straight ahead. Leona followed Matthew's stare out the window and saw a woman enter the bank. The preacher's wife, Leona silently observed. Shrugging her shoulders just a tad, she tossed her hair over her shoulder, blew a mouthful of smoke in Matthew's direction, and turning on her little feet, swished her way back to the kitchen.

Matthew was oblivious to Leona's performance, her tears, pouting, and mouthful of smoke. Engrossed in the scene before him, his fingers played with the handle of his coffee cup. Five minutes later, his coffee untouched and cold, he watched as Victoria left the bank, her long black hair almost blue in the bright sun, dark sunglasses and long black sundress a picture of elegance and ease as she walked away. Matthew continued to lounge in his booth and stare out the window.

"Charlie wants to know if you're hungry," Leona snapped, her cigarette gone, instead gum, a slow bubble forming at her lips. Looking away, she jutted out her hip, tapped her toes and waited.

"Sure," Matthew replied, his voice bored.

Just about to turn and look at Leona, the first time that morning, he halted. Sitting straight up in his seat, he looked hard out the window. Across the street, Daniel entered the bank. He was in a hurry. Only seconds later, he was back out the door, a rolled-up piece of paper firmly in hand. Leona, refusing to look in Matthew's direction, felt the heat of his disregard and blowing out her breath, pirouetted for the second time that morning and walked away, the force of her wake unfelt, ignored.

Matthew reached into his wallet and threw a few bucks on the table. Unfolding his large frame, he waved over at Charlie and left. Leona watched from behind the counter. Gum snapping, toes tapping, pen rapping, she glared as he walked out of the diner without a word. Lighting another cigarette, she inhaled deeply, looked around the room, her eyes settling on a young man, alone at the end of the counter. With a quick shake of her limbs, she eased a sweet smile, as well as a few top buttons on her blouse, and pulling back her shoulders, threw out her two best assets and approached, "Hello, darling," she began, "what ya' in the mood for this morning?"

Across the street, Matthew entered the bank, and giving time for his eyes to adjust, he focused on his surroundings. At the far side of the room was a long counter with windows. Small trays under each window allowed for pass through of materials from customer to teller. To the right, the last teller, a cute little blonde with an affinity for late evenings, appetizers, and pricey drinks, caught his eye. Batting her eyelashes, she waved him over with a quick and furious flick of her hand.

"Someone is looking for you," she chimed, her cute little chin danced up and down as she spoke. Bright red lipstick and too much blue eyeshadow stood in stark contrast to her chin length, curly, baby blonde hair.

Matthew leaned his arms on the counter, reached through the window tray, and lowered his voice a few registers. "Hmmm," he said. "Should I be interested?"

"Oh yes, and that's not all you should be interested in." Placing her hands under the window, she reached for his fingers playfully.

Matthew pulled his hands away, stepped back and shoved them in his pockets. He knew the drill. Too eager and she'd play with him for days. Unlike Leona, always ready to go, Kelly was playing her cards close, giving up nothing in the deal for a husband. Raising his eyebrows, he turned to go, when she called out, "Probably doesn't want her husband to know, being he's a preacher and all. Otherwise, why would she ask me to give you the message?" her voice light and lifting teased his ears.

Matthew turned, "What else?"

"Dinner? Eight o'clock?" she enticed, her smile bright.

"What. Else. Did. She. Want?" forcing a smile, he kept his voice soft, his neck muscles tense.

Dropping her gaze, blonde curls covering her face, she crumbled. "Reports. She was in with Mr. Warthington. Asked for detailed reports going back to last year. Church accounts."

Matthew stared across the room, the thin scar above his collar burned red and his breathing deepened.

"And she wants to see me?" he asked.

Kelly felt her grip loosening, his interest waning. Daddy's favorite, a spoilt and pampered young lady, she felt the sting of his rejection.

"Yes," she hissed, her eyes burning. "It's her, isn't it?" she asked, her voice trembling. "That's why the black wig. I thought you wanted something different, but all along, you want her." Covering her mouth, she realized she wasn't whispering and looked around. The lobby was empty.

Matthew relaxed and stepped closer. The scar above his collar, swollen now and angry. Reaching for her hands, he looked into her eyes and whispered, "Eight o'clock."

Kelly felt the hard sting of his eyes, the hot pinch of his hands and her heart raced. "I, I, I can't," she stammered.

Matthew dropped her hands, turned on his heel and left, paying no notice to the flood of tears that followed.

Earlier that morning, Daniel had been cleaning up after a few hours of paperwork at the church. Looking at his watch, he noted the time and with ten minutes' left before his meeting with Mrs. Thompson, he packed up his things and grabbed his keys. The phone rang. It was Mr. Warthington at the bank. "Victoria picked up the reports this morning," he apologized, "a page was left out. Should someone run it over to him or would he like to pick it up?" Daniel said he would pick it up.

On his way over to the bank, Daniel wondered about the reports. What reports? I didn't order any reports, he thought. What is she doing? The old angst burned in his gut. No, he thought. I will not do this. I will not be weak. Releasing his grip on the steering wheel, he tried to relax. Get the report. Go see Mrs. Thompson. Go home. Ask Victoria. Until then, no more. Must be a reasonable explanation. There must.

Rushing into the bank, he picked up the report and seconds later ran back out. Rolled up like a baton in his hand, he had held the missing page, wishing for all his life he could pass off this burden, pass off the uncertainty, this torment, but knowing he was the last leg of the relay, he had held tight, lowered his head and pushed on.

Chapter 16

On her way home from the bank, Victoria stopped at the end of the driveway to retrieve the mail. In a pile of bills and correspondence, there was the letter from Vanderbilt. Torn at the edges and stamped multiple times, it must have been lost. The letter inside, addressed to Mr. Jackson, was dated almost four weeks ago. Victoria read and reread the letter several times.

"Dear Mr. Jackson," It began. Victoria cringed. It was she who made the request.

"In response to your request, we have searched our records and below is a list of students from the class in question with the initials T.E.M. In addition, we have no student record of a Matthew O'Leary." The letter closed with a number for questions and additional information.

There were three names, their birth city, current address and telephone number. The first name on the list was a Theresa Elizabeth Milner, birth city Fayetteville, WV, current address Columbus, Ohio. Victoria moved down to the second name, Senator Theodore Eugene Monohan, birth city Miami, Florida, current address, Office of the Senate, Florida State Senate, Tallahassee, Florida. Shaking her head, she came to the last name, Thomas Edward Mooney, birth city Boston, Massachusetts, no current address on file. There was, however, a phone number.

It was the last name on the list that she called that left her speechless, sitting at the kitchen table. Dialing the number, it rang almost ten times before a small voiced, elderly lady answered,

"Hello."

"Yes, hello," Victoria began slowly. "My name is Victoria. May I speak to Thomas? That is your son, right?" she questioned.

"Yes, Tommy, our son," she said, her voice barely audible. A few moments passed and she continued, her voice cracking, "No, he is not available."

"Well, did he, perhaps, go to Vanderbilt and um, loose his class ring?" Victoria asked.

"I don't know," she cried softly. "Tommy came home, we buried, he's,"

In the background, Victoria could hear a male voice, stern, interrogating, "Who's that, Betty?" The voice became louder and louder and finally, demanding the phone, the receiver banged a few times and the man was on the line.

"Who the hell is this? You think this is funny?" he hollered.

"No, no, no," Victoria stammered. "I was just asking, because I may have your son's,"

Cutting her off, the man attacked, "What are you, some kind of peace freak? Yeah, Tommy went to Vanderbilt, but dropped out. Wanted to serve his country, just like his old man. We 'aint no yellow belly draft dodgers and Tommy wasn't no baby killer. You and your Hanoi Jane can go straight to hell. Tommy was a hero. Killed a slew of commie bastards before they got him. We've had enough of your kind calling here all hours of the day and night. If you call here again, I'll,"

Victoria quietly placed the receiver back in the cradle, shutting off the spigot of grief. It slowly dawned on her that Matthew either found or stole the ring. Either way, he never attended Vanderbilt. Victoria wondered if Matthew was even his real name. Then there was the watch, who did that belong to? And his back, those horrible scars, what happened to him? Too many questions and not enough answers. Placing her fingers to her temples, she made small circles.

The ticking of the kitchen clock broke her concentration. She looked at the Vanderbilt letter in her hand and her purse, and remembered her letter to Maria. Dumping out the contents of her purse, she was dumbfounded. What did I do with the letter? she wondered. Suddenly, Steady walked in the back door, hot and sweaty, his face red, eyes teary.

"Mom, where were you?" he cried. "You didn't come." Dropping his books to the floor, he stared.

"Oh Steady, I forgot," she cried and her heart surged. Dropping to her knees, she hugged him hard and kissed the top of his head. The heat of his body rose up to meet her and pulling away, she noticed the little red suit made a perfect match for his ruddy cheeks.

So preoccupied, she forgot about Steady's class sing-a-long. She forgot it was a half day dismissal. Taking in the suit, she realized today was a special occasion. Suddenly, her face fell and she looked away.

Pushing back his hair from his eyes, she said, "How about a nice glass of Kool-Aid? I have strawberry," she tempted. Met with an instant smile, she sat him down in a chair and filled his glass.

She picked up the Vanderbilt letter and the bank reports. It took Victoria less than an hour to confirm her suspicions. As far back as last October, Matthew was providing false reports, skimming money off church accounts in the form of false invoices and self-endorsed payments.

Looking over at Steady, the burn of bile rose in her throat. How could I forget my own son? she moaned. These papers, she thought, I should burn them, burry the whole mess. Give him the key and he'll leave, she thought. The sound of tires in the driveway, a car approaching fast, made her rush to the living room, look out the window. It was Matthew. Stepping out of the car, he slammed the door and in just a few strides he was on the front porch. His eyes were wild and vacant. Victoria panicked and threw the lock on the front door. Matthew rattled the knob and banged on the door. Stepping into the shadows, she watched as he walked the length of the porch, peering in the windows. He stepped off the porch and her heart sank. Shoving the papers in the desk drawer, she spotted the pink folded fabric with the key. Grabbing the key, she quickly closed the drop-leaf, locked the desk and shoved the key into her pocket. Running as fast as she could, she almost knocked over Steady in the hallway.

"Mom, Mr. Matthew's here," he said, a bright red stain around his mouth, his breath berry red.

"Yes. He. Is," she agreed, her breath short. "Here," she said placing the key in Steady's hand. Squeezing his palm tight she begged, "Steady, I need you to do me a big favor and hold onto this for me." She told him to go sit on the front porch swing and wait for her.

Steady went to open his palm and Victoria squeezed his hand shut again. "Don't look now. Hurry, Steady, hurry," she pleaded. "Wait for me."

Victoria heard the kitchen door close as the front door opened and Steady stepped out onto the porch. Placing her hands against her heart, she took a few deep breaths and closed her eyes. I can do this, she whispered. Get him to return the church money. Promise him the key. I can do this.

Matthew was standing on the other side of the counter, a glass of red Kool-aide in his hand. Gone were the wild eyes and the vacant look. Watching her, a knowing smile broke out across his face. Victoria held her breath and slowly, she smiled back.

Chapter 17

A few minutes passed. Neither moved. The clock's ticking filled the silence. Matthew, just moments before out of control and on edge, was the picture of composure and ease. He stared at Victoria and felt his pulse quicken, a small twitch beside his right eye, the only indication of the raging turmoil within.

Years of practice. He was good, very good at controlling his demons, at least on the surface. How many nights, his father, mean with liquor, had he hid under his bed while his mother had cried and pleaded, his hands pressed to his ears, eyes squeezed shut. Her only escape, her only vengeance, she set fire one night after his father passed out. As the fiery sun appeared above the Boston Harbor, Matthew's home burned out of control. He doesn't remember the fire, nor his mother's frantic search, calling his name. He doesn't remember the fireman carrying him down the ladder or his mother's body at the foot of his bed, her hand within inches of him. He only knows what others told him, his case worker, foster parents. Almost a year in the hospital, he was lucky to be alive. With no other family, Matthew had become a ward of the state, a victim of the system, its slow grinding cogs absent and oblivious to the wounds of a child that would never heal.

It was moments like this, when the fire raged within, that he felt his greatest control. Looking at Victoria, drinking her in, he felt the cusp of exploding energy, a need to restrain, savor, and the soft sweetness of impending cruelty.

With only the kitchen counter between them, Matthew reached out and touched her hair. Soft and smooth, he closed his eyes, his smile fading.

"I have what you want," Victoria said, her voice small.

"We," he corrected, his eyes still closed.

Ignoring him, Victoria pushed on, "I know about the money."

Matthew opened his eyes and stared at her. "I know. Your eyes. They tell me everything."

In a rush, he was on her side of the counter, his large hands cradling her face, tremors running up and down his arms.

Victoria felt the strength of his hands, the power of his restraint, as if holding back a floodgate of terrible passion. A hot stab of fear pierced her gut as she realized his obsession. It was her he was after, waiting for. Swallowing hard, her mind raced, her plan worthless. Praying that Steady would remain on the porch, she heard the front door open and footsteps.

Matthew froze. Victoria froze. Inches apart, their eyes locked as they stood still and listened. Someone was coming.

No Steady, no, she prayed.

Matthew held his breath. Yes, Victoria, yes, he prayed.

Moments earlier, Daniel pulled in the driveway, his thoughts a mess, anxious. Seeing Matthew's car, his jaw tightened, shoulders tensed. Slowly, softly, he approached the house. A sense of dread filled him. He could see Steady on the porch swing, fast asleep. Curled up in a ball, he was on his side, one hand under his cheek, the other arm extended, a tight fist. Daniel opened the front door and stepped into the hall. The living room was a mess. The old trunk was open, its contents all over the couch and floor. In the corner, papers stuck out of the drop-leaf desk, a few on the floor. The house was quiet, only the sounds of outside, a bird's call, leaves rustling. Daniel picked up a piece of paper from the floor. It was from the bank, November 1976, another February 1977. The report he picked up today, May 1977, this month. How long has she been doing this? he wondered. What else is going on? The room was hot and Daniel felt his collar too tight, his shirt a blanket upon his back. Pulling free a paper stuck in the desk, he was shocked, Vanderbilt University, a letter addressed to him, dated weeks ago. Daniel read the letter and froze.

No, Victoria, no, he prayed.

The kitchen clock ticked, the refrigerator hummed, faucet dripped. Pinned up against the kitchen sink, Victoria stood still, arms at her sides, limp. His hands, now around her waist were rough and hard and she winced. His eyes, intense and penetrating, were too much. Matthew buried his face in her hair.

Closing her eyes, she whispered, "No, Matthew, no." Pushing him gently away, she felt his grip tighten, saw his face turn angry. The counter dug into her ribs and something hard pressed against her stomach. Her thoughts on Steady, in a panic, she darted her eyes and caught sight of Daniel's note, his apology, taped to the window over the sink. Oh no. No, Daniel, no, she thought, where are you?

Matthew followed Victoria's gaze to Daniel's note, saw her features fall and felt the floor open up below him. Reaching into his pocket, he wrapped his hand around the cold hard surface of a gun. He didn't want to use it. It was all her fault. Just like his mother, she was weak and useless. Just like his mother, she would die begging him. Blinded by rage, he pressed the barrel up against her stomach and watched with satisfaction as her eyes widened, her face pleading. To his fury, she turned at the last moment.

There, standing in the doorway, was Daniel.

Out on the front porch, Steady lie on his side on the swing. Moving with the wind, back and forth, he felt the beginnings of waking and the pull of sleep. His body felt heavy, so heavy. His eyes just barely open, he felt the weight of his outstretched arm and in his tightly closed fist, the small and delicate key. In his dream, he was swinging. A woman, illuminated in sunlight approached. Walking slowly up the porch steps, she paused, picking up a newspaper off the porch floor. Placing a hand to her forehead, she dropped the newspaper and turned towards him. Floorboards creaked and he stirred. Slowly opening his eyes, he smiled. In the dying wind, the swing came to a stop, his little red pant legs revealing two different socks. He liked the woman. She was pretty, but sad. She was crying. Her hair was a mess and deep, dark circles made half-moons under her eyes. Hanging almost to her knees, her t-shirt was torn, the ragged edge laying silent against her leg like an upside-down half-masted sail of a ship too long at sea. He wanted to give her something. His fist uncurled. She extended her arm. He felt a warmth fill him, the touch of her hand, and a tingling sensation run up his fingers, converging at his wrist.

268

A moment passed, their eyes locked, hands clasped. In his dream-like state he felt a deep need, a piercing ache for his mother.

Suddenly, his eyes widened at the sound of gunshots. A heavy wave of fear washed over him, his grip loosened, sounds muted, and vision blurred. Overhead, clouds billowed, blocking the sun and like the deep and rapid descent of sleep, they carried him away, far away, far away.

BOOK IV

MOVING ON
Year 2017

Chapter 1

Monica closed the file and placed her hands in her lap. The room was silent, cold and sterile. White walls and windows into closed spaces and doors with alarms gave the place a forbidding feeling. Katie felt the heat of his stare. Lowering her eyes, she picked at her fingernails.

"Why?" he asked, his voice soft, stare fixed on Katie. Daniel couldn't take his eyes off her, this stranger, this woman, who, out of nowhere ten years ago, took an interest in his case and stuck by him. Being kept under high security, their meeting was never allowed. His new attorney, Monica, knew a few people, pulled a few strings and here they were.

"Mr. Jackson, please look at me," Monica directed. "Judge Carson agreed to retry your case."

With effort, Daniel slowly turned to look at Monica. Bones jutted out of thin, blueish skin stretched across his cheekbones. His eyes, deeply sunken, looked too large and vibrant. His wrists, fragile, cuffed and chained, lay on the table, fingertip to fingertip as if in prayer. She was the fifth lawyer in how many years? he wondered, almost forty. Tall and willowy, he marveled at her ease and confidence. Harvard grad, a pro bono case, probably needed a challenge.

"You do understand? The prosecutor is determined. It's a long shot." Monica's eyes were serious, her voice calm.

Daniel reached the tips of his fingers towards Katie, his eyes soft, mouth turned down. Thank you, he mouthed. An officer behind him stepped forward and stayed his hands.

"You know the rules, Pastor. No contact."

Daniel bowed his head and let his chin rest on his chest. No one said another word. At the ring of a buzzer, the officer laid his hand on Daniel's arm and helped him rise. Daniel didn't raise his head or look back. His unsteady gate, a shackled shuffle, rang out as he left the room, escorted beyond a maze of doors and locks.

Monica looked at Katie. "Coffee?"

272

Thirty minutes later, far away from walls that caged and gates that locked, Katie and Monica settled into a booth. The bitter aroma of coffee and the sweet smell cream filled the little cafe, a warm and inviting respite after their gloomy visit at the prison.

"He's dying, isn't he?" Katie asked.

"Cancer. Pancreatic. Stage IV." Monica sipped her coffee and took in the cute little coffee house, her eyes roaming.

"Why now? What's different now? Why did Carson agree to retry the case now?"

Still looking around the room, Monica replied, "Just buried his wife, three months ago."

Katie eyes grew wide.

Turning to face Katie, she added, "Yep, you guessed it, pancreatic cancer." A small smile played at the corners of Monica's perfectly lined lips.

Katie swallowed hard. What kind of person takes gain of such loss?

"Oh, don't look at me that way," Monica said leaning in closer to Katie. "Daniel got the shaft and we both know it. Everyone knows it. 'All the evidence points to motive', they said. Well, maybe with blinders on."

"Why did you take this case, Monica?" Katie asked.

"Lots of reasons. Publicity. Career. Blah. blah. blah. Official law firm line. Bottom line? Pro bono work helps their reputation. Representing crooks requires creative advertising. No more than three months, max."

"It's been over six."

"True." Monica sat back in her chair and fiddled with her coffee cup. "You should have seen him three months ago." Wiping lipstick off her cup, she looked at Katie. "He doesn't have long."

"You have your work cut out for you," Katie said.

"You have your work cut out for you, Katie." She handed her a thick file. "Keep it."

Katie looked up in surprise.

"Steadman, his son," Monica said. "Daniel needs a reason to live."

Chapter 2

The next morning, Katie woke early. Michigan in May always a served up surprises and surprisingly enough warm was on the menu. She parted the bedroom curtains and flurry of nature's activity welcomed her with song and dance. Down in the kitchen, a hot cup of coffee in hand, Katie opened the file from Monica. Attached with a clasp was a small manila envelope with the word "photos." On the other side was a thick stack of legal-sized paper, documents, and various other papers. The top sheet was stamped "confidential." Katie leafed through the documents quickly. Testimony, crime scene notes, correspondence, and contact information for police, legal, judicial, etc., almost forty years' worth.

Katie opened the envelope with the photos and spread them out on the kitchen table. A head shot of Daniel dated January 1977, a few Polaroids from church functions, crime scene photos, black and white, two bodies lying on a kitchen floor, a woman, her long hair covering her face, and a man, dark liquid pooled around the woman, and a stack of other photos, including a young boy around five or six years old, marked "Steadman," and a good looking young man, rugged and large, smiling at the camera, marked "M. O'Leary?" Katie looked at the photo closely and a shiver ran up her spine. She knew the face. Although he was smiling, his eyes were hard. It was the same face, that old polaroid at the Jackson farmhouse, she remembered, the cruel eyes, that shocking red hair. Turning the picture upside down, she turned to the right side of the folder, a few pages down was a photocopy of an obituary. Katie's eyes grew large. Dated June first, 1977, a Dr. Maria Thelen, Chair of Ancient Greek Studies at Vanderbilt University, died of complications due to breast cancer. The obituary stated, "after a brief illness." Katie blew out her breath, thought about the randomness of life, turned the page and continued to read.

The next time Katie looked up, Sarah was pouring herself a cup of coffee.

"Morning Mom."

Looking at her watch, Katie gasped. "Wow," she said. "Lost track of time. I forgot to wake you."

Sarah turned. "Mom, I am fifteen, you know."

"Yes, I know," Katie replied, her eyes soft as she took in her graceful and beautiful daughter. The resemblance to John was uncanny.

"Four o'clock, right?" Sarah asked. Raising her eyebrows, the tiny childhood scar on her forehead almost disappeared.

"Four o'clock," Katie answered. It was the anniversary of John's death, his official death. Five years. Ten since his disappearance. They were to meet at the cemetery and plant flowers.

A horn honked in the driveway and Sarah waved goodbye. Bus stop days were over and instead Sarah caught a ride with friends down the street. Katie watched her go, her long, dark, hair, a mess of wet curls covering her shoulders. White shorts and a pink tank top showed off her long, lean legs and strong arms, already tan from hours of hiking.

After John's disappearance, Katie had thrown herself into the Jackson affair. With so little information about her husband, she needed to do something, to save someone. Following her instincts, Katie went back to the old Jackson farmhouse. What she found was incredible. A letter. Yet, was it credible? If so, an innocent man went to jail, a little boy grew up believing his father killed his mother, and a murderer went free.

Katie dove headlong into saving Daniel, refusing to face her own nightmare. They never did find John's body. It took five years for the United States government to officially declare his death, the letter hand delivered by two officers, their chests covered with medals, their eyes sad, their salute firm. Katie knew he wasn't coming back, long before the doorbell rang and John went from missing to deceased.

Ever since that day in the driveway, when Jim had stepped out of his car to deliver the terrible news of John's disappearance, a slow awareness seeped through Katie's body and soul. Like waking from a hundred-year sleep, people, places, and things from the past and present began to clarify. They began to make sense and Katie finally understood what her mother told her that day at Say Jay's in Lapeer. That she had an ability to understand people at a deeper level, if only she let herself see, let herself free, to see the beauty of digging deep.

And now, Sarah, her tall strong athletic frame and quick smile a constant reminder of John, Katie understood, Sarah knew things too. Thinking back, her strange un-childlike behavior, her sensitivity and acuity to the feelings of others, the way she would talk to the old painting at Barbara's house, made perfect sense. It was just three years ago, their first hiking trip, that Katie had opened the door for Sarah to feel comfortable with her understanding. At the same time, Katie thought back to her own childhood and the parallels they formed.

For over three years, Katie kept at the Jackson case, fighting with the legal system, fighting for Daniel's innocence. Although she turned over Victoria's letter to the police, she never mentioned the strange woman at the bus or the small gold key. Trusting her instincts, a new experience for her, she held a few things back. Weeks turned into months and nothing happened. The police did follow up on the letter. The officer in charge, his smile a little too smug, his manner a little too carefree, told Katie it led to a dead end, a literal dead end, the woman Victoria wrote the letter to was deceased. In her frustration, obsessed, Katie isolated herself from friends and family, making enemies and creating distance between her and the ones she loved, even Sarah. It was her mother, Barbara, who had thrown up the shade, shedding light on the error of Katie's ways.

"Sarah needs you," Barbara stated, her arms crossed upon her chest, blocking Katie's way out the door.

Glaring, the intensity of her stare faltered, a dim, sad, and tired attempt.

"She rode her bike to the mall. All. By. Herself. Only twelve years old." Barbara's lips formed a thin line.

Katie's eyes grew large and she began to shake. Two highways and miles of no shoulder separated their house and the mall.

Dropping her keys, she leaned over to retrieve them, when her mother hugged her fiercely.

"A flat tire and her cell phone, thank God. Who knows what could have happened." Barbara breathed deeply. Katie let out a moan.

Breaking free of her hold, she looked at her mother. "Why didn't she call me?"

"That's the question, Katie, you need to answer."

In an attempt to reconnect with a tween daughter, Katie had packed their car, their old camping gear stale and earthy smelling, forced a belligerent twelve-year-old Sarah into the car and drove eight hours north into the Upper Peninsula for a week of hiking, bonding, and redemption. Baring her soul, she connected with Sarah, sharing their deeper understanding, their grief over John, and their love for each other. Since then, trips to the mall were replaced with trips outdoors, hours of hiking, followed by many more of peace and harmony.

Katie continued with the Jackson cause, but it did not consume her as before. No longer an escape from the pain of John's loss, she dealt with the raw edges of suffering head on. The bed was still way too big, the house too empty, the memories too hard, but Katie felt the hope of new beginnings in Sarah and surprisingly, her mother and Jim.

John's real estate partner, Jim, the showman, the life of the party, man of many outfits, the lover of a string of older women, bore the pain of John's disappearance and death with a heavy heart. He lost a business partner, a friend, the brother he never had. Left for the first time speechless, he became quiet and withdrawn. It was Barbara who heard his cry for help and reached out. What began as a friend helping a friend, grew into love, deep and lasting. Two years later, they married on the shores of Lake Michigan, an invisible John the best man, and Katie the matron of honor. Cold, even by Michigan standards, they had braved the wind and sand at the Sleeping Bear Dune's National Lakeshore, said their vows, and celebrated.

Now, watching Sarah leave, her bright pink tank top disappearing into the distance, Katie closed the Jackson file from

Monica, carefully placing the photos back into the envelope. Her coffee, long cold, made her gag as she thought about the crime scene photos, the wealth of new information she just learned that morning.

Yes, they believed Daniel suspected Victoria of having an affair with Matthew, intercepting his mail, and going behind his back with church financial business. Yes, they are confident he found bank reports and an unknown weeks old letter from Vanderbilt addressed to him. Yes, the crime scene indicated, Daniel found Matthew and Victoria in the kitchen, entangled in each other's arms.

Yes, the police found a little boy asleep on the porch swing, Victoria dead from a gunshot wound near the kitchen sink, and Daniel unconscious from a non-fatal bullet wound, a note in his hand, "Sorry Victoria, I will always love you," a gun nearby. And yes, evidence pointed to Matthew fleeing the scene, crossing the border into Canada and disappearing. A neighbor's eye-witness testimony placed Matthew's car at the scene, as well as a toll booth collector's recollection of his frantic crossing into Canada. All evidence pointed to murder-attempted suicide, the gun in Daniel's hand, the apology note, bank records and the Vanderbilt letter. Further investigation revealed that funds were skimmed from the church accounts, several thousand dollars, in the form of phony invoices and falsely endorsed payments. Testimony from a quick witted young teller, happy to bounce her blonde curls and point her finger, placed both Matthew and Victoria in on the bank scheme. Members from church, a Mrs. Thompson and Mr. Wilder, often offended by the quiet and aloof Victoria, were all too quick to step forward and express their views on her involvement with Mr. O'Leary.

Wrapping up the case in record time, Daniel was placed in custody, Steady with his only living relative, his paternal great-grandfather, Charles. Although over eighty years old, this crafty and shrewd billionaire still sat at the helm of one of the largest timber firms in the world. Steady's last sight of his father was in court. The gavel slammed down, murder one with intent, Daniel, two bailiffs pulling at his arms, cried for his son, dragging his feet and sobbing. It was cruel to bring the young boy to court, but Charles knew the child needed to see to blame. The script was written, the actors played their parts and Steady, the true victim in the case, knew the end before it was over. The next day, leaving behind forever a mother he loved and father he despised, he began a new life, steeped in hatred for his father, the man he was led to believe killed his mother.

But, as with most things in life, it was what you didn't know that mattered. For almost thirty years the truth was hidden, caught in the very thing that represented Jackson wealth and success. Victoria's letter to Maria Thelen, written, sealed and stamped, lost, waiting to be mailed, a time capsule of truth, was wedged in between the drawer and the desk. Handcrafted with Jackson timber, this ornate and beautiful piece of craftsmanship along with the key, encrusted with Jackson Irish diamonds and McGough emeralds, was handed down for generations, a passing on of Jackson pride, Jackson bride to Jackson bride. It wasn't until almost thirty years later that a distraught and lost Katie, running from a truth she knew and didn't want to face, had followed her instincts, answered Victoria's pleas, and found the letter.

And now, ten years later, after countless delays and denials, all because a judge lost his wife to the cancer that now ravaged Daniel, there was going to be a new trial. Finally, the letter could be introduced as new evidence, evidence that may provide a, "shadow of doubt." Monica said it was the first of many miracles.

After that day on the Jackson porch, the day she ran from Jim and the news she knew would break her heart, the day she trusted her abilities and perceptions, the very day she reached out to a little boy, and across time accepted a key, accepted fate, Katie believed in miracles. Yes, she believed in miracles, many, many miracles.

Chapter 3

Katie doesn't remember much about that fateful day she pushed Jim away in her driveway, stepped upon the Jackson farmhouse porch, and answered Victoria's urgent pleas. She doesn't remember getting there, grasping hands with a young Steadman, putting the small and delicate key in her pants pocket, or losing consciousness. She doesn't remember Jim picking her up off the worn and weathered floor, placing her gently in the car and driving her home, the old, abandoned farmhouse receding in the distance.

What she does remember comes in snapshots, slightly out of focus, fleeting images of a beautifully landscaped, nostalgic, freshly painted farmhouse, a recently printed newspaper, unbelievably dated over thirty years before, a young boy in a funny little bright red polyester suit on a porch swing, the glittering of diamonds and emeralds in the blinding sunlight.

It wasn't until weeks later, the news of John's disappearance known, close family and friends out of things to say and reasons to visit, that Katie had gone back to the farmhouse. She decided to walk.

At first, Sarah refused to go to school. Too young to understand her father's absence, she often forgot, only to break into tantrums and tears. Katie understood she wanted to be there if her father came home, only Katie knew waiting was futile. In the middle of the night, Sarah would wake with a cry, sobbing for Daddy. It took a week of fighting and forcing her up the bus steps for her to go peacefully.

A little too quiet and sad Sarah got on the bus and gave a half-hearted wave goodbye to Katie. The bus doors closed and Katie stood, watching it pull away. Mrs. Cook, concentrating on turning her car around, smiled weakly and waved. Even Mrs. Cook ran out of things to say.

Katie watched Mrs. Cook drive away. The empty street matched her mood, along with the rolling, grey clouds and impending storm. She thought about the strange woman, her absence since Katie was given the tiny gold key, another missing piece in the puzzle. Looking down the street towards home, Katie knew what waited for her, emptiness, long hours, too many reminders. Turning abruptly, she walked up the hill towards the Jackson farmhouse.

Throughout the blur of the past few weeks, Katie kept the tiny gold key on a chain around her neck. Going through the laundry, she found it in her pants pocket, remnants of an old pink ribbon crumbled in her hand. Immediately, a tingling sensation ran up her arm and she felt a funny, familiar dream-like feeling, and remembered the little boy on the swing. At the time, too distraught with the news of John, she threaded it through a chain around her neck. It seemed like the right thing to do and Katie felt deep down there was a reason she should hold onto the key.

Walking down the Jackson driveway, Katie paused at the clearing. Overgrown bushes took over most of the front yard, some well onto the second story. Worn boards and peeling paint begged for attention. A strong gust of wind came through and the screen door, hanging by one hinge, banged closed. Katie jumped at the sound, her heart pounding. Far to the left, a small cottage was almost completely covered with vines and overgrowth. It was hard to imagine it otherwise.

Taking a few deep breaths, Katie chastised herself for being a coward and walked up the porch steps. The steps were uneven and some of the floor boards rotten, others missing. A row of rockers, in all states of disrepair, ran down the side of the porch. On her right and old round table, two legs broken, leaned on its side, pendulating back and forth with the wind. Floor to ceiling cottage windows filled with cobwebs and dust looked dark and gloomy.

Stepping to avoid pitfalls, Katie lifted the screen door to the side and tried the key. She shook her head. The keyhole was three times the size of the key. Peering inside, she only saw darkness. Taking a deep breath in, she rattled the door knob and pushed. Slowly, the door opened. Standing in the hall, it took a few minutes for her eyes to adjust. Stale, musty particulates, undisturbed for years, swirled around her feet and resettled.

Wandering through the rooms, Katie scanned the study, taking in piles of paper, an old electric typewriter, opened desk drawers, contents spilled out and onto the floor. A small piece of wood, a round cross-section, deeply engraved with words, almost hidden in a thick layer of dust, sat upon the desk. Hundreds of books lined the walls like mausoleum residents, forgotten and forever silent. Something scurried across the floor and Katie hurried out of the room. Through the dining room, the table was set for six, a desiccated centerpiece of poppies and foxglove, a whisper of its former self, and out again, Katie walked towards the kitchen. Pausing at the threshold, she stopped. White sheets draped the room, crime scene tape curled upon the floor. A deep and painful wave ran through her gut and she turned away.

Back towards the foyer, she paused at the stairs leading to the second floor. The banister was leaning to the left and the bottom step was missing. Katie looked up and down the flight of stairs and turned away abruptly. A shaft of light coming from the living room landed at her feet. Dust particles swirled and danced, their eddies rising and falling with the illumination. Katie followed the shaft of light into the living room and felt a funny feeling, dream-like, fleeting and familiar. Suddenly, the light disappeared, reappearing a moment later. Katie looked around the room. The windows, tall and wide were almost completely covered with dust and dirt and yet, the light was blinding. The room was a mess. An old trunk stood open in the center, a gaping hole in the lining. Years of spiders and mites left white shelled casings, webs and carcasses on the lid and over the contents. A large oil painting hanging by a corner, warped and waving, gave real dimension to the ships at sea and the waves illustrated in oil. Katie felt her stomach lurch and she turned. Furniture, upside-down and destroyed, became homes to burrowing rodents, trails leading in and out of worn and repurposed upholstery by little four-legged creatures. Katie felt the room too warm and taking a step towards the window, stopped. A desk, ornate and heavy, lay on its side. Immediately, she was drawn. A deep cherry, just like her desk at home, it too had a drop-leaf. Yet, that was where the similarities ended. Katie's desk, smooth and simple paled in comparison to the intricate carvings on this beautiful and elegant piece of furniture. Trees, rivers, and pastures depicted a scene she was sure held meaning for the craftsman. A tiny keyhole caught her attention and she reached for the key. Her arms began to tingle and her heart race. Turning the key in the hole, it jammed. Katie jiggled the key, but it refused to give. Sitting back on her haunches, she wiped the sweat from her brow and frowned. Knitting eyebrows and pursing lips, she leaned forward and looked at the bottom of the desk. There in the back, where the back of the desk met the drawer was a piece of purple paper. A corner of what? An envelope? she wondered. Tugging, it refused to budge. Gently, Katie turned the desk upright and trying the key once more, it turned, the drop-leaf falling open, a cloud of dust filling the air. Pulling on the small drawer inside, a purple envelope slowly fell to the floor. Katie picked up the envelope and felt her head spin. The warmth of the room and smell of musk and decay were too much. Replacing the key around her neck she held the envelope gently and rising to go, she paused. A faint scent of lilac filled the room and then, it was gone.

Closing the front door behind her, Katie navigated the porch floor boards, walked onto the lawn, lay down on the grass and deeply inhaled the fresh air. Clouds and blue sky decorated the overhead pallet with baby blues and pure white. A formation of Canadian geese flew over, calling out in earnest to a straggler to catch up. She considered the old house. Strange, she thought, no family photos, not one. If only I could find a photo of Victoria, then I would know for sure. Katie thought about the strange woman, tall and elegant, her long dark hair. Slowly, the spinning abated, the tingling in her arms disappeared. Feeling better, she sat up, crossed her legs beneath her, and studied the envelope.

Addressed to a Dr. Maria Thelen, Vanderbilt University, the envelope was letter size and of lightweight. Victoria E. Jackson, 1222 Holcomb, Clarkston, MI 48346 was the return address. A thirteen-cent stamp, Bicentennial 1776-1976 with a bust of Benjamin Franklin and a map of the first thirteen colonies was in the upper right corner. There were no postal markings on the envelope. It was never mailed.

Turning the envelope over, she gently placed her fingernail under the seal. Little pressure and the flap was open. Pulling out the contents, unknowingly, a polaroid silently fell to the ground, face down. Opening the letter, she began to read,

"Dear Maria, I am afraid for our lives..."

Falling onto her back again, Katie closed her eyes and considered what she read. Victoria Jackson was terrified. Pouring out her heart, she documented the events leading up to her own murder, her suspicions about Matthew O'Leary and her cry for help. Yet, it was never mailed. Why? Katie considered the date, May 29, 1977. She remembered the date of the murder from her very first search of the Jackson family, the week John disappeared, late at night, surfing the internet. It was the thirtieth of May. The same date her father died. Victoria ran out of time, the letter jammed in the desk, and the truth remained a secret. A photo, she thought, what I need is a photo.

Standing up she placed the letter back in the envelope and stuck it in her jacket pocket. Stretching her arms overhead, she dropped at the waist to touch her toes and there on the ground, upside-down, was an old photo. Surprised, she turned it over. Katie's jaw dropped. A color Polaroid. Two of the three smiled, looking into the camera. Thick, curly, blonde hair and a handsome grin next to a rugged, large masculine redhead, his smile bright, eyes strangely intense, almost cruel, followed by a woman, Katie recognized right away, the high elegant cheekbones, long beautiful dark hair, the dark sunglasses, her expression serious. Staring closer, Katie noticed something else and her blood ran cold. The man in the middle, the redhead, his arms wrapped around Daniel and Victoria was off-balance. His arm around Daniel was easy, comfortable. The difference was Victoria. With Victoria, his grip was harder, the muscles in his forearm bulging, his fingers deep into her shoulder. Katie knew this must be Matthew. Katie had uncovered the key to the truth. Standing on the front lawn, she had the sudden urge to run. Now, Katie knew what Victoria knew. Fear.

Chapter 4

On her way to meet Sarah, Katie took the long way to the cemetery, bypassing freeways and meandering around the countless cottages that dotted the shores of Oakland County's numerous beautiful lakes. More lake than land, she thought. As she took in the sights, bright sunshine and spring colors, her mind began to wander, just like the roads, first right, then left, a little straight stretch, and then a sharp turn in the opposite direction. Yet, no matter how hard she tried, her thoughts kept coming back to her meeting with Daniel, his tired and worn face, kind eyes, sad smile. What could I possibly say to Steadman that I haven't already said? she wondered. How can I convince him to forgive his father? What does anyone need to forgive? Katie thought about her own life and what moved her to reach out to others when she was hurt, angry. Hope, she thought, wanting something better, the future. Gripping the steering wheel, she sighed. Knowing the answer didn't help. Katie knew hope must come from within.

In the months following the day Katie found Victoria's letter, she wrote numerous letters to Steadman, made many calls trying to set up a meeting. He was easy to find, his books selling in the millions. She thought, if only she could explain, face-to-face, what happened on the porch, maybe he would remember giving her the key, and possibly begin to see his mother's spirit at work, her unending efforts to prove Daniel's innocence, her wish to unite father and son. But Steadman never answered. Finally, after receiving a letter from his attorney threatening legal action if she did not, "cease and desist," Katie gave up. Katie knew well enough that when it came to matters of the heart, no amount of evidence could convince a person who refused to believe, until they were ready to believe.

Approaching the entrance to the cemetery, Katie pulled over to the side of the road. She was early and wanted to wait for Sarah. They would go in together. Putting the car in park, she pushed her seat back and closed her eyes. There has to be something I can do, she thought. Warm sunshine filled her car and leaning back, Katie placed her hands in her lap and exhaled. A car passed by and she opened her eyes to see if it was Sarah, when all before her a kaleidoscope of light, refractions and refractions of refractions filled her view. Leaning forward, the pattern shifted and instinctively Katie placed her hand upon her chest, covering the tiny key. The pattern disappeared. Removing her hand, it was there. Slowly, a thought began to form. How to convince Steadman. Wrapping her fingers around the tiny key, she wondered, but how? Just then, second car passed and pulled over in front of her. Sarah jumped out of the car, throwing her backpack over her shoulder, slammed the door and hollered goodbye. As the car pulled away, Sarah was surrounded by sunlight. Releasing her fingers, Katie freed the key once again. Sarah walked towards the car, as if on a sea of light diamonds. Sarah, the key, light, hope, Katie thought, and suddenly, she realized, what she was looking for, what she had to do, what they had to do, was right before them all the time. Sarah opened the car door and jumped in. With a bright smile and a torrent of words she kissed her mother and began chattering about friends, school, a year-end trip. Turning her hands this way and that, Sarah laughed at the light patterns decorating her hands, talking and laughing, her eyes bright, smile wide, all energy and life. Katie looked at her daughter and knew deep down that Sarah was her key, her key to living, her key of hope.

Placing her hand on top of Sarah's, she interrupted, "Sarah, I have something to tell you."

Removing the necklace, she gently placed it over Sarah's neck, the tiny key dangling among a sea of black curls. The light pattern shifted and took on a new array, a new dimension, the diffusion even greater, brighter. Katie marveled at the change and understood, Sarah was the true bearer of the key.

Taking a deep breath in, Katie began, "Next week, a very special person, Mr. Steadman Steinenbach, will be here, in Michigan, for a deposition. He needs our help."

Chapter 5

The court reporter stopped typing, the room went silent. Monica stood and walked to the windows, opening the blinds, a cascade of light filled the room.

"Well, that's a record," she said, her voice a tight clip.

The deposing attorney quietly tip-toed out of the room. Steadman, still in the same position, dark sunglasses hiding his expressions, remained still.

"Just how many times can you ask the same question?" she fumed to no one in particular. The door closed and realizing the court reporter left without saying good-bye, Monica looked at her hands and sighed. Reel in the bitch, she thought, chastising herself.

Taking a seat next to Steadman, she relaxed her shoulders and plastered on a do-gooder smile.

"Mr. Steinenbach, I apologize," she began. "I won't even pretend to know what you are going through."

Steadman looked straight ahead, his soft jowls against a crisp white collar. More than filling the chair, he was a large man, all hands and feet. What filled in-between did more than fill space, it owned space. Taking in the cut of his suit, pricey sunglasses, sharp shoes, Monica considered the man high-priced real estate. To Monica, choosing clients was like pricing real estate, you get what you pay for and although the client was the one paying, so to speak, Monica considered her time money and well, Monica had Tiffany taste on a mac and cheese budget. Never far enough away from her trailer park upbringing, memories of her dear old country dad, drunk and silly calling her his "little whipper," as in "w-h-i-p-p-e-r s-n-a-p-p-e-r," Monica felt the need of greed. And what Monica wanted, Monica won, literally, in the courtroom, every time. Only six years since passing the bar, barely free from law school debt, her double-digit record was all wins, no losses. Understanding this case could be a stepping stone to full-time representation, a well-endowed client, she considered this silent man and tred carefully.

"Mr. Steinenbach," she raised her voice just a notch and laid her hands on the table. "There is someone who wants to see you."

Monica opened the door. Steadman stared straight ahead as Sarah walked into the room and sat down across from him at the conference table. Looking at her reflection in his sunglasses, she saw what he saw, a young woman, a stranger. Sliding the back of her arm towards him, fist closed, she stared back. Slowly, she opened her fist. The tiny gold key, laying in the palm of her hand, covered with diamonds and emeralds, glittered in the filtered sunlight. A few seconds passed. Monica held her breath and watched. Slowly, Steadman reached out his hand and took the key. In his huge hands, it looked like a child's toy, so small, so fragile. He looked at the key for a long time and then began to cry, soft, gentle sobs. Monica stood still. She knew his reputation. Famous writer, career in the dump, reclusive, angry, difficult, more money than God. Flew in on his own goddamn plane, she grumbled to herself.

Sarah, a picture of youth and innocence, young beauty and grace, was across the room in a second.

Pressing her hands into his, she began, "My mother. You gave her this key a long time ago. She said to tell you it is time you take it back."

Steadman removed his sunglasses. His dark eyes, deep pools of black, dominant from his mother's American Indian lineage, looked back at Sarah and wept.

An hour later they were still talking. Monica paced the room. Will they ever shut up? she wondered. Looking at her watch for the millionth time, she finally stopped and cleared her throat. "Don't you have a plane to catch or something?"

Steadman and Sarah looked up at Monica as if seeing her for the first time.

Monica shook her head. "That's right, I'm still here, and oh by the way, you're getting a bill for this, Mr. Steinenbach."

Steadman smiled, reached into his pocket and placed a stack of cash on the table. "Save the stamp," he said. "Save the trees."

Sarah laughed, knowing full well his real fortune was in the forests and really, he didn't give a damn. Monica tried not to look at the money.

"How do you feel about old houses?" Steadman asked, looking at Sarah, his eyes kind.

"You know," her voice light, "there's this old farmhouse up the street from us."

"Splendid." Steadman replaced his sunglasses and taking her arm, they walked out.

Stopping suddenly, he turned to Monica, "Chill, baby, you're hired. That is, if you want the job?" His broad smile pushing up mammoth cheeks waited for her reply.

Opening her mouth and then closing it, Monica looked at Steadman and then at the cash on the table. Feeling as if she missed her plane, only to discover it was delayed and she would now board, she recovered quickly. Putting on her best, "Sure, if that's what you wish face," she smiled and exhaling, slowly chalked up another win for the, "Whipper."

Chapter 6

Katie placed her bags at her feet and waited. Early as usual, she was only one of the many that refused to be late. The early morning fog, only minutes before thick and wet at her feet, began to dissipate with the morning sun. A two-month ticket, anywhere in the continental US and Canada, "unlimited boarding," the website read. Katie knew she needed to get away, but where was the question. For the first time, she was without responsibility, without an agenda, things to do. Roaming sounded good. The train, a sleeping dragon, sat still on the tracks, remnants of the night's chill clinging to its windows and doors.

Just yesterday she put Sarah on a plane, first to La Guardia where she would meet Steadman at Sotheby's for the auction and then off to Paris. Meeting Steadman at the deposition and giving him the key was more than a good idea, it was fate. A friendship developed and Steadman encouraged Sarah to pursue her love of writing. Entering her short Story, "Crossing Lines that Divide," a story about a young girl from Ireland making her way in America, Sarah won a trip to Paris for the summer and a spot at the International Young Writers Conference.

As the crowds began to build, Katie picked up her backpack and slung it over her shoulder. A small carry-on case was between her feet. Katie traveled light. A few changes of clothes, an extra pair of shoes was all she packed. In her backpack was her laptop, Cannon T-3 Rebel camera, extra batteries, her passport and wallet, and her red notebook. No purse, no umbrella, no extras. On a, "as needed basis," she would buy what she needed, as it was needed.

A call from the conductor and the crowd began to mount the steps. As Katie took the first step, she felt a cleaving, the slight pull of gravity, a reminder, safe, secure, and then the gentle push at her back, anticipation of the unknown, the feeling of hope. Butterflies filled her stomach and a slight panic of forgetting, when the crowd moved and she was pushed up the stairs and down the aisle. Looking at the long row of seats, she decided a window seat, today. The prospect of simple choices, simple solutions was refreshing.

With Barbara and Jim beginning a new chapter in their lives, Sarah off to Europe, Steadman and Daniel on a somewhat meandering path of reconciliation, and John, his presence tucked deep inside her heart, Katie knew she was ready to roam.

Stowing her carry-on under the seat, she pulled out her backpack and the red notebook. Worn and faded. 70 sheets. 1 subject. Wide ruled. Dog eared, the cover falling off, the spiral bent and coming out at the bottom, it was more than a little worn out. The years faded John's little drawings. Running her hand over the cover, she thought about the last ten years, all they've been through, all she wrote. I will never forget, she thought, turning to the first page. Closing her eyes and placing her palm flat against the page, she saw herself all those years ago, sitting on the kitchen floor, wedged up against the corner cabinet, John's chipped Tigers cup beside her, lost in grief, she wrote for hours. She didn't need to read the page to remember. It was the week from hell, the emotional roller-coaster, and yes, my private awakening. As she turned the notebook at the spine to the back and a new page, the past folded away, tucked underneath, her shoulders eased, eyes brightened. Looking through her backpack for a pen, she sat back and let out a small laugh. Figures, no pen. Remember everything else. Forget a pen, she laughed to herself.

As the train began to pull away from the station, Katie watched as the landscape went from a slow picture show to fast forward to a Monet painting of green, grey, and white. Well, she thought, there goes the journal. Katie planned to write about her travels, as she always did with anything in life that was important. There was security in writing, a firm foundation, a silent supporter, always there if you needed to look back, to remember.

Letting out a sigh, Katie thought about simple choices and simple solutions. Of course, she could ask for a pen, but that wasn't the point. It wasn't *if* she had a pen, it was *should* she have a pen. Staring at the blank page, she thought of all her soul searching. I've done enough digging, she thought. Time to put the shovel down.

You know, she mused, I'm okay with the blank page. Sometimes, you needed to leave the page blank and just be. Be the Blank Page, she giggled inside. "Oh John, did you hear that one?" she whispered. Sometimes, you don't need a pen. Sometimes, you don't need a shovel. Folding her hands and placing them on the blank page, Katie looked out the window. The sun broke out from behind a blur of colors and filled her seat with a pallet of pastels. Closing her eyes, she let the warmth wash over her, she let the movement of the train take her, and for the first time, she let moments write the metaphors.

The End.

Made in the USA
Middletown, DE
20 November 2016